... Engl... ...on became ...cialised in Deaf education. She has been teaching in the Deaf community for 13 years in both England and Scotland, working with students who use British Sign Language. Nell began losing her hearing in her twenties, and now wears hearing aids. She lives in North Lincolnshire with her husband and son. Nell is the author of novels *The Silent House* and *Silent Night*, featuring BSL interpreter Paige Northwood.

By the same author:

The Silent House

SILENT NIGHT

NELL PATTISON

Published by AVON
A division of HarperCollins*Publishers* Ltd
1 London Bridge Street
London SE1 9GF

www.harpercollins.co.uk

A Paperback Original 2020

First published in Great Britain by HarperCollins*Publishers* 2020
1

A catalogue copy of this book is available from the British Library.

ISBN: 978-0-00-836178-5

Typeset in Sabon by Palimpsest Book Production Limited, Falkirk,
Stirlingshire
Printed and bound in UK by CPI Group (UK) Ltd, Croydon CR0 4YY

MIX
Paper from
responsible sources
FSC www.fsc.org   FSC C007454

For Stuart

Prologue

As he stared at the body on the ground, a snowflake fell on the back of his neck, making him flinch. A moment ago, anger had been boiling in his veins, but now it had frozen into fear. The knife in his hand looked dull in the half-light. It suddenly felt scalding in his palm, and he dropped it. He took a step back, feeling the snow crunch beneath his heel.

Out of the corner of his eye he saw a movement. Was there someone in the bushes? What if they'd seen him? He waited for a minute, his breath fogging in front of him, but he saw nothing moving amongst the snow-laden trees surrounding the clearing. Maybe he'd imagined it.

He bent down and felt for a pulse, his fingers trembling as they touched skin, slick with blood. A feeble flutter greeted his fingertips, and he stepped back in shock. The eyelids flickered and the mouth moved slightly, as if the person in front of him was trying to speak, but then the movement faded. Holding his breath, he felt for the pulse again. Nothing. They were gone.

1

As the realisation hit him that he had just watched someone die, he stood up and stumbled backwards, coming up against a tree trunk. His breath came in short gasps and he looked around feverishly. He couldn't shake the feeling he'd been seen. Why didn't they show themselves?

Should he go back to the cabin and pretend he'd never left; that he had been safely asleep with the others? That seemed to be the safest option.

As he turned to leave, he jumped, a hand flying to his mouth. Someone had been in the bushes all along, and now they stepped out onto the path, a look of horror on their face. He had to do something, explain himself, but he couldn't think through the pressure of the blood pounding in his head. They looked from him to the body, then back again.

What have you done? they signed.

He ran.

Chapter 1

Saturday 24th November

The boy had been missing for at least three hours before I arrived.

Snow had fallen heavily overnight, and it lent an eerie quality to the park surrounding Normanby Hall. I knew it well and I regularly came here in nicer weather; my sister and I would often bring a picnic and sit under the trees in the summer. It looked completely different in the snow. Tree branches sagged under the weight of it, and all sound was muffled as if everything had been covered in a layer of felt. The sun was weak, fighting through the sickly yellow sky. I was sure there would be more snow soon and I worried about getting home later – it had been a precarious drive up here.

Police officers greeted me on my way through the gates and directed me to a part of the car park that had been cleared of snow. It seemed no cars were being allowed in that morning other than those who were there on official business. Once I had found a spot, I pulled on my walking boots and trudged through the courtyard into the main part of the park, where a PC directed me towards the hall, from where the search was being coordinated.

'Stay close to the tape, please,' the PC said, indicating a line of blue and white police tape that had been strung up along the path. I didn't know if it was there to keep foot-prints to a confined area, or simply to stop anyone getting lost in the woods. With everything covered by a blanket of white it would be easy for me to lose my bearings.

As I approached the huddle of people ahead of me, one familiar figure stepped away from the group and walked towards me. There was no mistaking the broad shoulders and dark skin of Rav Singh, and I felt a little flutter of happiness that he was here too.

'Paige,' Singh said, the smile on his face brief in defer-ence to the seriousness of the situation. But there was warmth in his deep brown eyes and I couldn't help but smile in return.

'DC Singh,' I replied, pulling off one of my gloves to shake the hand that was offered. I hadn't seen him since February, when I had interpreted for the police who were investigating the murder of my sister's goddaughter, Lexi. It had been a harrowing case that left the Deaf community reeling, and my life had been in danger more than once. That experience had made me reluctant to work with the police ever again, especially after my sister had suffered a life-threatening brain injury when the murderer attacked her, but I'd told myself that this time would be different.

'It's DS now,' he said, turning and leading me back towards the group. 'I took my exam months ago, but a position only just became available. So, this is my first case since my promotion.'

'Congratulations,' I told him, feeling genuinely pleased

for him. In my experience he was an excellent detective, compassionate and dedicated.

'You remember DI Forest,' he said, nodding at the tall woman in front of us, her dark hair pulled into a severe knot at the nape of her neck, which was covered by a dark blue ski tube. I wondered if he was teasing me; DI Forest and I had locked horns several times when I'd first been asked to interpret for the police. She nodded at me, and I returned the gesture.

'I'm really pleased you're here,' Singh said with a smile, then blushed. 'I mean because we need you. To interpret. We've been working with a member of staff until now,' he continued, his words coming out in a rush, 'but he's not a qualified interpreter.'

'What happened?' I asked. Any information they could give me would help when I was interpreting, so I understood the context of the situation and who I would be interpreting for.

'There's a group here from Lincoln School for the Deaf,' Singh replied. 'Five students and three staff members. They're staying in one of the cabins in the woods, for the weekend. When they got up at seven thirty this morning, one of the students was missing. The head teacher went out to look for him around eight but hasn't come back. There's been no sign of either of them since.'

I checked my watch: 10:45. It seemed strange for the head teacher to be gone for so long without contact.

'Two people missing? I was only told about the boy,' I said.

'Technically we can't treat the teacher as a missing person yet,' Forest replied, 'because he's only been gone for a few hours, so right now we're focusing on finding the boy. The staff discovered he was missing when they woke up this morning, but nobody has seen him since half past ten last night.'

I nodded, understanding the seriousness of the situation. A missing deaf teenager would be considered to be at risk, whether he'd disappeared of his own accord or someone had taken him. The communication barrier might make it harder for him to get help in an emergency, and he could be confused and isolated.

'His name is Leon and he's fifteen,' Singh told me. 'According to the staff, he's a nice lad and nothing out of the ordinary has happened recently that might precipitate him running away.'

'What about his family? Are they deaf or hearing?' I asked, wondering if the police would need me to liaise with them.

Forest shook her head. 'He's in care. The five students on the trip are permanent residents at the school. Leon's mother died when he was eleven, then his father went to prison a year later, so he was taken into the care of the school, which is registered as a children's home.'

'As you can see, he's particularly vulnerable, which is why we've brought CID in straight away,' Singh told me, his face grave.

'Okay. What do you want me to do?'

'The staff and students are all waiting in the cabin. We've cleared it as a crime scene, so we thought it best to contain them there until you arrived to help us take statements,' Forest replied. 'The pastoral support assistant called the deputy head when he realised both Leon and the head were missing, and she told him to call us while she drove up here.'

'Who's searching for the boy at the moment?' I asked.

'There were some staff from the park, but we've asked them to team up with uniformed officers,' Singh explained. 'We don't want anyone getting lost in the woods, so we need people who know the grounds. And I've asked them for the CCTV from the gates, but there are several different ways in and out of the park that aren't covered by cameras.'

'There's an awful lot of land to cover,' Forest said with a frown. 'There are parts of the park we don't think have been searched yet, and we have no idea which direction Leon might have gone in. But now you're here, Paige, we'd better go and see if there's anything else the school group can tell us.'

The DI strode off through the snow, not waiting to see if we were following. Singh held out his hand to indicate I should go first, and the two of us set off down the path through the woods.

'No sign of the head teacher where you've been searching?'

He shook his head. 'No. It does seem very strange that he hasn't turned up yet, but we're keeping an open mind at the moment.'

We walked in silence through the trees for a few minutes, the sounds of our footsteps eerily muffled by the snow, then Singh stopped short and turned to face me.

'How are you doing? You know, after . . .' His voice tailed off. I knew he was referring to when we'd worked together in February, when my sister and I were both attacked by the person who'd murdered a little girl.

I shrugged. 'I'm okay. I had a couple of sessions with a counsellor but I wasn't comfortable talking to her. It's . . .' I shook my head. 'It doesn't matter.'

'No, tell me,' he said, and I could see genuine concern in his eyes. 'I've been worried about you, not having any sort of debrief afterwards. If you'd been a police officer there would have been support we could put in place. As it was, you were just left, really.'

I scuffed my toe and thought about what to say before I replied. 'The problem with counselling was that she didn't just want to go over what happened the night I was attacked, but everything that led up to Lexi dying, and before that. There's too much in my past that I don't want to be raking over again. So, I didn't go back after the second session.'

Singh moved as if about to put a hand on my shoulder, but then let his arm drop back to his side, and I realised how close we were standing to each other. 'Do you mean about the deaths of your parents?'

I had told him about that back in February. My parents and my younger sister, Anna, were all profoundly deaf, and I grew up as part of the Deaf community. Our dad died suddenly when I was in my first year of a textiles design degree at university, and I dropped out in order to support Mum and to try to get Anna through her exams. Then Mum developed cancer, and all the responsibility fell on me. I became an interpreter to help pay the bills, using the British Sign Language that had been my first language, and somehow never found my way into a different career. But that wasn't what the counsellor had been trying to delve into. I could have coped with that; I felt like I'd come to terms with the loss of my parents, still being so close to my sister.

'No. Other stuff,' I said, running my hand over the trunk of the tree I was standing next to, a dusting of frost clinging to my glove. I could sense that he wanted to ask more, but I wasn't prepared to talk about it, so we stood in an awkward silence for a moment.

'How's work at the moment?' he eventually asked. 'Getting plenty of jobs?'

I winced slightly. He'd managed to touch another nerve, but I didn't feel I could ignore this question.

'Not really. The agencies have a lot of influence, and it's difficult working as a freelance interpreter and building up a decent reputation.' I looked up at him, finally, and gave him a quick smile. 'Max has been really supportive, though.'

Singh nodded. 'Max?' His tone of voice was hard to decipher. 'Max Barron?'

'Yeah.'

'You're still in touch, then?' he asked, glancing at me then looking away again, towards the dense line of trees along the side of the path. Singh had met Max at the same time I did, during the investigation into Lexi's death, because Max was connected to her family.

'Yeah, we're . . .' I cleared my throat, suddenly feeling embarrassed. 'We're seeing each other.'

'Oh. Well, that's good,' Singh said, though his face didn't match his words.

'What?'

'Nothing. I mean . . . nothing.'

'Seriously, Rav. What's wrong?'

He shrugged. 'I don't know. I just didn't think he'd be your type, I suppose.'

'What's that supposed to mean?' I asked with a short laugh, but my stomach was starting to churn with annoyance at his tone.

'Nothing. I'm sorry. I shouldn't have said anything.'

'You and I don't exactly know each other very well outside of work,' I pointed out. 'I don't think you'd really know what my type is.'

'You're right. Forget I said it.'

He turned and continued walking away from me, and I paused for a moment before I followed him. When we'd worked together before, Rav Singh and I had got on well, and I thought we could have become friends, perhaps even closer than that, but then I didn't hear from him after the investigation was over. Then again, I hadn't got in touch either, so I couldn't really blame him.

We continued in silence for a moment, being careful where we stepped. There was a slushy line of footprints where several people had obviously walked before us, and we stuck to it.

'So, who are the staff members that were on the trip with these kids?'

'The head teacher, a support assistant as well as a social worker,' Singh replied, referring to a notebook he'd pulled out of his pocket. 'The social worker isn't technically school staff, but she joined them on the trip. They last saw Leon around half past ten last night, when the kids went to bed. He was sharing a room with two other boys, but they didn't notice him leaving the room at any point. When they woke up this morning and realised Leon wasn't in the cabin, they checked his belongings, but his bag had gone.'

He looked up at the branches above us, which were dipping ominously with the weight of the snow on them. 'It was still snowing when they got up, so any tracks away from the cabin had been covered and they couldn't tell which way Leon had gone. The head teacher, Steve Wilkinson, went out to look for Leon, but he hasn't been seen since either, and he's not answering his phone. The support assistant went out to try and see where he'd gone, but when he couldn't find them he called the deputy head, and she told him to call the police.'

'Were there any witnesses?' I asked, keeping my eyes on the path so I didn't fall over in the snow.

Singh shook his head. 'Nobody we've found yet, but there's already an appeal out on social media and there'll be something on the local news, so if Leon left the grounds, hopefully we'll find someone who saw him. If he's still in the park, though, I think it's unlikely anyone can help. Theirs was the only occupied cabin, and it's not exactly the sort of day for people to go for an early morning run through the park.'

'There's more snow forecast,' I said, throwing another glance at the heavy sky above us.

'All the more reason to search as much of the area as we can now,' Singh replied. 'If Leon's out there somewhere and the weather gets worse, it's going to make our job even harder.'

As we rounded a corner, I could see a wooden cabin ahead of us. I didn't often come into this part of the park, and looking around me I could see how easy it would be for anyone to lose their bearings without the paths as landmarks.

'For now, we'll interview the staff and discuss the best way to take statements from the pupils.'

'Do all of the students use BSL?' I asked. Just because they went to a school for the deaf didn't necessarily mean their first mode of communication was sign language.

Some deaf people sign, some speak, and many use a combination of both.

'As far as I know, yes. The staff member who was interpreting for us before you arrived certainly signed to all four of the students,' Singh replied. I was pleased he'd paid attention, but he'd probably learnt from last time not to make any assumptions about the deaf students, and that I would ask questions like that.

'Are the staff hearing or deaf?'

'The pastoral support assistant and the missing head teacher are both hearing. The social worker is deaf, and so is the deputy head, but we haven't had much chance to talk to her yet.'

Forest was standing in the doorway of the cabin, and she gestured at us to join her. We walked into a large communal area with some sofas and a log burner, the seats occupied by a couple of uniformed officers, four teenagers and three adults. One of the women was slim with dark hair, sitting very primly on the sofa, whilst the other was dressed in a brightly patterned jumper that looked hand-knitted, her mass of strawberry-blonde curls making her look a little wild. As I looked over at the third staff member, a churning sensation began to build in the pit of my stomach. I must be mistaken. I blinked a couple of times, but the man who was half turned away from me still looked the same. He had the build of someone who used to play rugby but had spent more time in the pub than on the field recently, with dark blond hair cut close to his head. I took a step backwards, out into the freezing air, and took a deep breath. How the hell could it be him?

'Paige, are you okay?' Singh appeared next to me and

I swallowed deeply. There was no way I could let my emotions show.

'I'm fine,' I replied, taking another deep breath and stepping over the threshold again. The man had his back to me, so I thought he probably hadn't seen me yet. One of the uniformed officers directed the staff members towards us. I clenched my hands into fists and pushed my shoulders back, preparing to come face to face with him. The three of them got up and crossed the room to speak to DI Forest and DS Singh.

Forest introduced the dark-haired woman as Liz Marcek, the deputy head, and the one with all the curls as Sasha Thomas, a social worker, before turning to the man. He needed no introduction, but the detectives didn't know that. Mike Lowther, my ex-boyfriend, who I had last seen over three years ago in my hospital room.

Chapter 2

'Hi Paige.'

I didn't trust myself to speak and just nodded in response. Singh looked between the two of us, confused, but I didn't fill him in.

'How are you?' Mike asked.

'Er, busy,' I replied as I turned to Singh. 'What do you need me to do?' I signed as I spoke for the benefit of the two women. Liz Marcek, the deputy head, signed a question to the detectives.

What's happening? They've told us to wait here but we haven't been given any other information. Have you found Leon? Is he okay? And where the hell is Steve?

I interpreted this for Singh and Forest, who glanced over at the students. Some of them were watching us, and I knew they'd be able to see anything I interpreted for the staff.

'Do you want to speak to everyone together?' I asked Singh, nodding at the teenagers who were watching our conversation eagerly, and he understood my meaning. Sign language can be easy to 'overhear' even from a distance, so he might as well include them in the conversation.

Singh explained that he'd talk to them all together, and the deputy head moved over to where the students were sitting. I could feel Mike's eyes on me, but I avoided his gaze. If I'd had time to prepare myself for seeing him, perhaps I could have kept my cool and looked at him with dignity, but as it was I didn't know how to react. He'd always had his own version of events, so his perception of our break-up might be very different from mine.

On the day I last saw him, I had been in hospital for two days, and then by the time I was discharged the following day he was gone from the flat, leaving me not only with scars but also a mountain of debt. Anna wouldn't let me sink into the pit of despair that lay in front of me, and dragged me back from the brink. She was also the one who helped me find a way to avoid selling the flat, though even now my finances were still in dire straits because of the mess he'd left me in. What was he doing here, working in a school for the deaf? The last job he'd had when I knew him was in a call centre, though he'd lived off my earnings for the last two years of our relationship. He hadn't been able to sign before we met, had never even met a deaf person until I introduced him to my sister, Anna, and Gemma, my best friend. I couldn't put my finger on why, but it rankled that he'd taken the skills I'd taught him and used them to get himself a better job when I was the one still struggling financially.

Shaking myself, I focused on the task in hand. I couldn't let Mike's presence affect the way I did my job. It would be humiliating if I screwed up just because he was there, watching me.

'I need you all to pay attention, please,' Singh said, addressing the group. He paused to give me time to interpret what he'd said, and I was pleased to see how easily we slipped back into a good working partnership.

'At the moment we don't know if Leon has left the grounds of the estate or not. We have police officers and park staff out searching, but there are three hundred acres to cover. There are also police officers going into the local area to see if anyone has any information; if anyone saw him walking outside the park or waiting for a bus. I need all of you to think carefully about anything Leon said or did yesterday that was unusual, or different. If any of you can think of where he might have gone, it's very important that you tell us. We need to make sure Leon is safe. He won't be in trouble when we find him.' He looked at Liz Marcek. 'We're still trying to get in contact with Steve Wilkinson. The number you've given us is going straight to voicemail.'

A couple of the teenagers turned to look at each other, one continued to stare straight at Singh and the other looked at the ground. It had been thirteen years since I'd left school, and it felt like a lot longer, but I tried to put myself in their position. The five of them were all in care, with the residential part of the school acting as a care home year-round for those students who needed it. Foster carers who could use BSL were rare, so the arrangement worked well and ensured consistency for the students. Anna had gone to Lincoln School for the Deaf, so I knew a little about it already, although I had only been to the school a couple of times when I was a teenager, to watch Anna starring in drama performances.

Just because they all lived together didn't necessarily mean they were friends, but I knew from Anna's stories it was likely the residents knew each other pretty well. Leon was fifteen, and there could be all sorts of reasons a fifteen-year-old would run away, but until the police discovered *why* he'd gone it might be harder to figure out *where* he'd gone. I cast my eyes over the group again, and realised one of the girls was looking at me, her head tilted slightly to one side, one hand fiddling with the pendant around her neck. She was dressed in very drab clothes, dark jeans and a grey jumper that was too big for her, and her mud-brown hair hung limply.

I decided to take the initiative. *Have you thought of something?* I signed to her.

The girl looked over at the staff members, then shook her head.

Cassie, it's okay. If you know something, you should tell them, Miss Marcek told her, but the girl shook her head again.

I don't know where he went, she signed, and I interpreted for the detectives. She looked at me again, something like defiance in her eyes. *He's been looking forward to this trip for weeks.*

Forest and Singh had a quick whispered conversation, then asked if they could take the staff aside to speak to them for a few minutes. We went through a doorway off the living area, which led to a small kitchen, leaving the students with the uniformed officers.

'We need to decide how to proceed from here,' Singh said. I began to sign his words, at the same time as Mike did.

I turned to him, but still did not look him in the eye. 'I'm here to interpret, please try not to confuse the situation.'

17

Singh must have noticed the tension between us because he gave me a look before he spoke. 'Paige is right. Whilst we appreciate your help earlier, Mr Lowther, we find it best if we use our own interpreter.'

Mike held up his hands. 'Sorry, it's just automatic, you know?' He flashed Singh an apologetic grin, and I felt heat rise up my neck. Swallowing hard, I nodded at Singh to continue.

Why the hell did Steve go on his own? Liz Marcek signed, shaking her head. *This is completely unprofessional, he knows the school policy for dealing with an incident like this. When Mike let me know what had happened I thought I'd better come up.*

Singh nodded. 'I understand. I'm sorry to keep you waiting around here, but at the moment I think it's safest if we keep the children all in one place.'

Can we help with the search? Sasha Thomas, the social worker, asked, her eyes bright with concern.

Forest seemed to consider this for a moment. 'There's no reason why you can't go with a uniformed officer and help,' she replied. 'We need all of the help we can get to cover this amount of land. I've only got half the number of PCs I'd like for an operation of this size, but they're all I was allowed.'

One of us will need to stay with the students, Liz Marcek told Sasha.

'I'll stay,' Mike said quickly. 'Paige and I can catch up while you're out there searching.' The smile he aimed at me looked charming, but I wasn't going to fall for it.

'No, we'll leave a PC with you,' Forest said brusquely. 'Paige will need to accompany Ms Thomas, if she's joining the search party.'

I breathed a sigh of relief. Forest had probably said that in order to stop me from putting my feet up while I was being paid to interpret, but I didn't care what her motives were as long as she didn't leave me alone with Mike.

Singh led Sasha and me back outside, where he introduced us to a PC.

'Ryan, I'm adding you to the search party, with Paige and Sasha here.' Singh pulled a map out of his pocket and handed it over, indicating which part of the estate hadn't been covered yet. 'If in doubt, follow your own footprints back here again.'

The uniformed officer nodded and set off away from the cabin, taking us further from the hall and deeper into the woods. Before we turned a corner and lost sight of the cabin I looked back; someone was watching us from the window, but I couldn't see who it was.

It's getting darker, I pointed out to Sasha. *I think it's going to snow again.*

She shook her head. *I told them we shouldn't have come, with this forecast. But Steve was determined not to cancel. A bit of snow will make it all the more exciting, he said.* She rolled her eyes. *This is more than just a bit of snow, but he wouldn't listen, and he's the head so has the final decision.*

Why did you come with them? I asked.

They needed a woman, she replied with a wry smile. *None of the female staff could come this weekend, or so they said, so Steve asked me.*

PC Ryan was walking slightly ahead of us and glanced back at us occasionally, but as he couldn't follow the conversation he carried on trudging through the snow in silence. Sasha and I stopped signing for some time, as we looked around us, searching for any sign of Leon or Steve as we went. The trees along the side of the path were thinning out, and the expanse of virgin snow ahead of us was widening.

'We'll go as far as that stand of trees, there,' PC Ryan told me, 'then loop back around. According to the map we're getting closer to where the southern end of the estate meets the road, so we'll go that way to check for potential entrances or exits.'

I signed this for Sasha and she nodded. *How do we know he's even in the park?*

'We don't,' the PC replied with a shrug. 'But we still have to look.'

As we walked, I wondered why this particular part of the park was so open. The area in front of us was completely clear of trees, and it was an almost perfect square. It was only when I spotted a low, snow-covered building on the far side that I realised where we were.

'Is this the cricket club?' I asked Ryan, and he frowned, pulling out the map.

'Er, yes. Yes, it must be,' he said, his tone of voice not filling me with confidence. I hoped we were going to be able to find our way back to the cabin.

'In which case, we're closer to the road than you thought,' I pointed out, but he didn't say anything.

'We should check the pavilion,' he said. 'It would be an ideal place to shelter.'

I signed our conversation for Sasha, and she nodded.

That's a good idea. If he's still in the park it'd be a good place to hide. Nobody is going to be playing on this pitch for a little while.

The three of us crossed the pitch and approached the small building.

'Look,' I said, pointing to where a pane of glass had been broken.

PC Ryan put out an arm. 'Don't come any closer,' he said. 'There might be evidence and we don't want to compromise it.'

'There's less snow around the door, as if it was pushed open from the inside,' I pointed out, and Ryan nodded, already on his radio. He explained where we were and what we'd found, so we then had to wait for the detectives to come and find us. Sasha kept shifting from foot to foot and trying to peer through the window, anxious to see if Leon was inside.

After a few minutes had passed, I felt something soft brush my cheek and looked up.

'It's snowing again,' I said, as more fat flakes drifted down.

'Just what we need,' Ryan muttered.

Come on, let's check round the back, I signed to Sasha, who had been pacing restlessly. She nodded her agreement and followed me. Leaving Ryan waiting for Forest, we stomped through the snow and looped round behind the pavilion.

I feel responsible, she told me. *I should have realised something was wrong.*

Don't say that, I replied, trying to reassure her. *Nobody knows what happened, yet.*

I know, but . . . She stopped and paused. *What's that? What?*

That, over there?

I followed where she was pointing and squinted into

21

the trees. As I moved closer I spotted what looked like a pile of material at the base of one of the trees, half covered in snow.

I don't know. Stay here, I'll have a look, I said, pushing my way through the frozen undergrowth. Sasha shook her head and followed me, and we approached together. As we got closer, we saw it wasn't a pile of material, but a person.

Oh God, is he okay? I asked as we got closer to the man on the ground. He was lying on one side with his back to us. I could see a head of well-styled grey hair, some high-quality outdoors clothing and an expensive pair of walking shoes, one of which had come off and was lying about a metre away. A thin layer of snow covered him, setting off alarm bells in my head.

Sasha reached out to shake him, and the man's head lolled in a sickening way. As his head tipped to the side I saw a huge gash on the side of his neck, and a vibrant splash of red on the snow to the side of him, spilling out from the wound. It was clear he was dead.

I retched and took a step back. My head was spinning.

Who is it? I asked, though I was sure I already knew the answer.

Steve Wilkinson, Sasha replied, her face pale. *The head teacher.*

Chapter 3

It took nearly an hour for the forensics team to arrive from Scunthorpe, with the snow coming down thick and fast by the time they arrived. Sasha and I were back in the cabin with the rest of the school group when Singh came in looking like he'd just returned from an expedition to the North Pole. Forest had informed Mike and Liz that Steve was dead and it didn't look like an accident, but they hadn't told the students yet. They knew something was wrong and kept asking questions, so the tension in the atmosphere was almost unbearable.

Singh beckoned to the staff and we all gathered in the kitchen once again.

'There's no sign of Leon, but it looks like someone has been in the pavilion today. The forensics officers are collecting evidence at the moment.'

What happened to Steve? Liz asked. *I can't believe this is happening.*

'I can't answer that question right now,' Singh replied. 'We'll need to wait for a post-mortem.'

Do you think Leon is dead as well? Did someone attack them both?

'I'm sorry,' he said, shaking his head gently. 'I really don't know, but you need to trust us to do our jobs. I promise you we'll do our best to find out what happened.'

He looked back into the room where the four students were huddled together on a sofa, signing to each other.

'I see no point in you and the students staying here now,' he told Liz. 'The roads have been gritted, and were cleared this morning, but I don't want you to be here any longer than necessary and risk getting stuck. We'll need to speak to each of the students tomorrow to see if they have any idea what might have happened, and when they last saw Leon and Steve. I think it's best if we come to you at the school rather than asking you to bring them to a police station.'

Liz Marcek nodded. *I think that's a good idea. I can sit in on the interviews as an appropriate adult.*

Sasha frowned and turned to her. *As the children's social worker, I think it would be more suitable for me to be with them.*

For a moment I thought the deputy head was going to argue, but she inclined her head.

Of course, she signed.

'I'd appreciate that, thank you. Now, could you ask the students to collect their belongings and we'll escort you all back through the park to your minibus.'

What about Steve's belongings? Sasha asked. *His bag and everything are still here.*

'I can pack them up,' Mike said. There was an eagerness

24

in his eyes that I remembered well, and I wondered if Steve had any valuables that might somehow end up in Mike's possession, but Singh shook his head.

'No, thank you, the forensics team will want to take those. That's another reason it's a good idea to get the students out of the cabin as soon as possible.'

Of course. I'm reluctant to leave without all of the students we brought, though. Liz looked at Mike and Sasha. *Could one of you stay here in case Leon turns up, then get a taxi back to school? You can put it on the school account. I'll drive the minibus, and come back for my car tomorrow. I would feel more comfortable knowing one of us was still here.*

'Sure, I can do that,' Mike replied, jumping in before Sasha could respond. He kept his hands behind his back as he spoke, flashing me a triumphant smile, as if he expected praise for not signing his response. I ignored him, interpreted what he'd said and waited for Singh to agree to their proposal. Once he had, we went back through to the main room. The four teenagers were signing to each other but stopped the moment we approached.

Miss Marcek explained to them that they were going back to the school but refused to answer any of their questions, and they all looked dismayed.

Can't we stay here and help? one of the boys asked.

No, the police have it all under control. I need to make sure I keep the rest of you safe and get you back home.

But what if something's happened to Leon? What if he's been kidnapped?

Mike walked over to the group and signed something to the boy, but he had his back to me so I couldn't see what had been said. Whatever it was, it must have allayed

25

some of the boy's fears, because a moment later they were all collecting their bags. We led them out of the cabin, where a group of uniformed officers took over, to guide them back to the car park. I turned to Singh as Mike started walking back towards us.

'What about me? Do you still want me here?'

'For now, yes please. If Leon does come back, or we find him, we'll need an interpreter.'

'I can do that,' Mike replied as he approached us. 'You don't need Paige here. I'm sure she's got better things to be doing with her Saturday.'

I ignored the comment and continued to look at Singh, who was clearly trying to work out what the issue was between the two of us.

'I'm afraid that wouldn't be appropriate, Mr Lowther.'

'Why not? I can communicate well with Leon. I'm a familiar adult, he'll respond well to me if he comes back.'

'Because you're one of the last people to have seen a murder victim alive, and it would be a conflict of interests,' Singh replied, his voice terse. Mike held up his hands in defeat, his charm having failed for once. I was stunned: Mike was a suspect in Steve's murder.

'I believe you were sharing a room with Mr Wilkinson. While we're waiting, can you identify which items in the room belong to him?' Singh asked. 'Then you can pack your own belongings.'

Part of me wanted to speak up, to tell Singh not to trust Mike with anyone else's possessions, but I knew I couldn't say anything, not without good reason. My stomach was churning with the stress of being physically close to Mike, my mind flooded with negative memories, and I suddenly felt like I couldn't breathe.

'I'm going outside,' I told Singh, holding up my phone. 'Call me if you need me back.'

Before he had a chance to protest, I turned on my heel and walked away in the direction of the woods.

For about ten minutes I kept my head down, paying attention to nothing around me, only focusing on my own breathing. I watched my feet as they made fresh imprints in the newly fallen snow. The snow was already finding its way in through a gap between my hat and scarf, and I wasn't following one of the paths the police had marked, but I didn't care; I wasn't thinking about anything other than the situation I'd suddenly found myself in.

I'd been pleased to receive another call from the police – not pleased that a teenager had gone missing, of course, but pleased to be working with them again. Back in February, I'd hoped I could get some more regular work for the emergency services, but the Deaf community is a small one and so my work had gone back to being sporadic. In the last few weeks I'd even been toying with the idea of signing on with an agency again; they controlled so many contracts and, being freelance, it was hard to get a look in. If it hadn't been for my debts, I would have been financially stable with the work I was getting, but as it was, I was only just scraping by. And the one person I could safely lay the blame on for it was suddenly back in my life.

Now I had a dilemma. I could quite easily pass this job on to another interpreter, in order to avoid seeing Mike again. But I wasn't in a position to give up work, and by walking away I felt like I would be proving Mike right about some of the things he used to say to me, some of the things that still haunted me in weak moments. My involvement with the school would last as long as the investigation into the head teacher's death and until Leon was found. I'd just have to put up with him until then, and avoid him whenever possible.

I'd carried on walking as I thought, and when I looked up I couldn't place where I was in the park. Walking away from the cabin, further away from the mansion house, I'd wandered into part of the park I was unfamiliar with. I knew I should turn around and follow my own footsteps back to the cabin, but I didn't want to face Mike again until it was absolutely necessary.

Ahead of me was a stand of trees, so I continued in that direction for a few minutes, trying to focus on the job ahead of me rather than think about my ex. There was a crunch of footsteps behind me, however, and I looked round to see Mike approaching. He'd put on a bulky coat and thick gloves before leaving the cabin, and I wondered how long he'd been on my tail.

'Do they need me back?' I asked.

'No,' he said, stopping before he got too close. 'I just thought we could talk.'

I looked around me at the snow-covered fields and the woods surrounding them. There was nobody else around, and our voices sounded eerily flat. Part of me was instinctively on edge, being alone with Mike, even in such a wide-open space.

'What about?' I replied.

He spread his hands wide. 'Anything. Everything. We didn't exactly get any closure, did we?'

I folded my arms and didn't reply. What did he expect me to say? Anna and Gem had removed all of his stuff from the flat while I was in hospital, and had the locks changed just in case. He'd never tried to talk his way back into my life, although I'd had a few calls from him to begin with that stopped when I continued to ignore them.

'How have you been?' he asked, taking a step forward and giving me the smile that used to make me melt. I reminded myself that it had probably worked on dozens of women before and after our relationship, and during as well. I knew I had to stay strong in the face of his charm, though.

'I'm not interested in catching up, Mike. Let's just both do our jobs and leave it at that.'

He came closer again, but I turned and took a few steps towards the stand of trees.

'Paige, I think there are things we need to talk about, to work through.'

I was about to reply when I heard a shout.

'Where did that come from?' I asked.

'Does it matter? I'm talking to you, Paige.' I detected a tone in his voice that set off alarm bells in my head. Even after three years I recognised when his emotions were on the edge; the difference was this time I didn't care.

Pushing past him, I set off back in the direction of the cabin, wondering what had happened. Suddenly I felt a tug on the back of my coat, one of my feet slipped and I sprawled face first into the snow. The fall knocked the wind out of me, and I lay there for a couple of seconds before rolling onto my side.

Mike loomed over me, and I instinctively pushed my body away from him along the ground. He reached down and took my arm but I shook him off.

29

'Don't touch me,' I snapped.

'Oh for God's sake, Paige, don't be so pathetic. I'm just trying to help.'

I ignored him and struggled to my feet. My trousers were soaked through from the snow, but at least it had been a soft landing. Keeping my back to Mike, I set off towards the cabin again, trembling slightly. I told myself it was from the cold, but I couldn't shake off the memory of the tug I'd felt before I fell.

Chapter 4

The forensics team arrived at the cabin at the same time Mike and I did, so Singh led us back to the hall and out of their way.

'What happened?' he asked, looking at my snow-covered clothes.

'I slipped,' I muttered.

Singh cast a glance at Mike, but didn't ask any more questions. He led us into a room in which a few uniformed officers were drinking cups of tea; Mike took it upon himself to join them, but I sat as far away from him as I could. Singh fetched me a drink then disappeared, reappearing a few minutes later with a shiny silver emergency blanket for me.

'What's that for?' I asked, feeling my face flush.

'You're soaked, and I don't really want you freezing to death,' Singh replied, concern in his eyes. He started carefully tucking the blanket around my legs then stopped, looking embarrassed. I couldn't help but smile at him.

Even when he was busy and stressed he found the time for little moments of kindness, and it was one of his most endearing qualities. I told myself he would have behaved that way with anyone, though I secretly hoped I was getting special treatment.

'We heard a shout,' I said, remembering what had sent me hurrying back in the first place. 'Has something happened?'

'No, nothing like that. A branch snapped, narrowly missed one of the groups who were searching.' Pulling up a chair and lowering his voice, he continued. 'Paige, what's going on here? With you and Mike Lowther?' He nodded towards where Mike was sitting alone, now the PCs had left.

I shook my head. 'Not now.'

He looked at me for a moment and I wondered what he was thinking, but then he sat back in his chair and ran a hand through his hair.

'My first case as DS and this is what I get: a missing child and a murder all rolled into one investigation.' He let out a long breath. 'I'm already worried we're not going to find this kid. The weather's against us, and we don't even know if he's still in the park.'

I reached forward and squeezed his hand. 'It's only been a few hours. If he's run away he'll have headed for some-where to shelter.'

'We have to assume there's some connection to the murder. It looks like Leon was in the cricket pavilion,' he told me, keeping his voice low. I glanced over his shoulder to where Mike was getting a cup of tea and talking to a couple of PCs.

'No sign of where he went after that?'

Singh shook his head. 'We think there are two possible scenarios here – either Leon saw who killed Steve Wilkinson and ran away, or . . .'

'You think he might have killed his teacher?' I said, trying to keep my voice down.

'We have to consider the possibility,' he said, rubbing one of his temples. 'There's evidence he was in the pavilion, very close to where Steve Wilkinson was killed.'

'Was he alone?'

He gave me a calculating look before shaking his head. 'We don't know. But we're also considering the possibility that he's been abducted, maybe by the murderer.'

I suddenly felt a lot colder and pulled the blanket tighter around myself.

'I don't know how long we can carry on searching in this snow,' he said, looking out of the window. 'I'm worried we're already too late.'

He spoke the last sentence so quietly I almost didn't hear him. When I had worked with him before it was clear that Rav Singh cared about the victims he came into contact with, but this was the first time I'd seen him this vulnerable. I almost reached out to hug him, but as I moved he stood up and rubbed his hands together. As he turned, he noticed Mike hovering nearby.

'Mr Lowther, can you come with me please?' he said, professional once again. 'This seems like a good opportunity for me to take your statement. Then perhaps you can assist with the search, as you're dressed for the weather.'

I sat around for what felt like hours, but was only around ninety minutes, drinking tea to keep warm and chatting with the various PCs who drifted through. As the day went on and the snow continued, the search was looking more and more like a lost cause. It felt quite frustrating to be waiting around, but Singh wanted all bases covered and if Leon turned up they'd want to be able to communicate with him immediately. Once I'd dried off sufficiently I stood outside the front door to look across the park. The snow had almost stopped, but the light was already fading, giving the blanket of white a bluish tinge. The two-hundred-year-old Regency mansion looked impressive with its coating of snow, and I leant back against one of the columns while I waited.

Eventually, I saw a group of people trudging through the drifts on their way back to the house. Singh peeled off from the group and came over to me, Mike trailing after him.

'We're calling it a day,' Singh said, his face drawn. 'The weather is making it impossible and I don't want to put anyone's safety at risk. It's going to be a difficult drive out of here as it is.'

'Okay, what happens next?' I asked.

'Now that this is a murder investigation, DI Forest and I will be conducting interviews at the school, in case any of the students remember anything, while we wait for the report from forensics. We'll try to get access to Leon's phone and social media, too. Given the circumstances, we're going to be treating Leon's disappearance and Steve Wilkinson's murder as connected.'

'Where do I fit in?'

'For now, you'll mostly be working with us to take statements from the students, those who were here today and any others who are friends with Leon and might be able to give us some information. We'll also be speaking to staff to try and establish why someone might have killed the head teacher. But can you come to the station first thing tomorrow for the briefing? Then we'll see if there have been any developments and prioritise from there.'

'Sure. Can I go home now?'

Singh nodded. 'I'm sorry for keeping you here in this weather. I'll come with you and make sure you can get out of the car park.'

Mike had been standing nearby, listening in. When he heard that everyone was leaving, he sidled over and addressed Singh.

'I'm supposed to be getting a taxi back to the school,' he said. 'But I don't think I'm going to be able to get one out here in this weather.'

'You're right,' Singh replied. 'I'll arrange for someone to give you a lift into Scunthorpe, then you should be able to get back to Lincoln from there.'

I thought Mike looked a bit disgruntled that he wasn't being offered a lift all the way home, but he didn't comment. That didn't surprise me. Mike didn't usually pick fights with men; he found them harder to intimidate.

When we got to the car park, the three of us walked to my car. Thankfully, a couple of the park staff had been doing their best to keep a clear route out of the gates. I paused, waiting for Mike to follow Singh, but he stopped as well.

'You can travel back to town with some of the PCs,' Singh told him, and I flashed a brief smile at him to thank him for picking up on the negative energy between me and Mike.

'It's okay, Paige can give me a lift, can't you? It'll give us a chance to catch up. You'll need to drive through

Scunthorpe to get home.' He gave me one of his most charming smiles, which I refused to return.

There was a brief pause and I watched my breath fog in the air in front of me. Making eye contact with Singh, I willed him to insist that Mike went with him.

After a moment that seemed to stretch on forever, Singh said, 'All the same, I think it would be better if you travelled with one of our vehicles. In this weather, I don't want to ask Paige to divert.'

For a moment I thought Mike was going to refuse, and then we would reach a stalemate because there was no way I would let him get in my car with me, but in the end he gave a nonchalant shrug and followed Singh to a police car.

'Hopefully we'll get a chance to talk soon, Paige,' he said over his shoulder as the two of them walked away from me.

Getting in my car, I leant my head on the steering wheel and took a few deep breaths. Now was not the moment to lose it. After all this time, I couldn't let him worm his way back into my head. Part of me wondered what he was so keen to say, but I knew it was probably only an excuse to get me in an enclosed environment with him.

Before I set off home I turned on the ignition to warm up the car, then I pulled out my phone to call my sister. I propped the phone up on the holder on my dashboard as it rang.

Hi, she said with a wave as her face popped up on my screen, blonde hair swept back out of the way. The heart shape of her face was similar to mine on my ID badge, an old photo that didn't reflect how my face had filled out in the intervening years. Apart from the difference in hair colour, mine much darker than hers, my sister and I seemed to look more alike as we grew older. She'd turned twenty-nine quite recently, and I knew she had a bee in her bonnet about her next birthday. Two years older than her, I could reassure her that it wasn't that bad.

Are you still out on that call?

Yeah, I replied. *I'm setting off home now but I have no idea how long it's going to take me in this weather.*

Are you still at Normanby Hall? What happened?

I'll explain later, I told her, though I wouldn't be able to give her much information. Still, social media would be full of Leon's picture by now, so it wouldn't take her long to figure out why I would be going to Lincoln tomorrow.

Something else has happened, she said, looking at me with a frown. Anna, like many BSL users, was sensitive to even minor changes in body language and facial expression, but I was still surprised she'd picked something up over a video call.

I ran a hand over my face. *Mike's here.*

What? she exclaimed. *What the hell?*

I know, it wasn't exactly a nice surprise.

What do you mean he's there?

I took a deep breath and exhaled slowly, willing my hands not to shake. *This job, it's connected to where he works.*

Is this the missing kid? Anna asked, cottoning on. She must have seen the appeal already. *Are you talking about my old school?*

I nodded.

What the hell is Mike doing working there?

I have no idea, I replied, shifting in my seat. I'd been

wondering the same thing since I'd first seen him. *I taught him to sign when we were together, so I assume he's used that to get himself a job.*

Anna shook her head, her face contorted into an expression of disgust. *I wouldn't want that man working with kids. He's not exactly a great role model, is he?*

I know. He tried to get me to give him a lift back into town.

Bastard. Hope you kicked him in the balls.

I laughed. *No, Singh rescued me.*

He can probably see through scum like Mike straight away, she replied.

He definitely picked up on something. I haven't told him anything, but I suppose I should. At least the basics, then he can make sure I don't have to be alone with him.

So, this kid went missing on a school trip? And Mike works there, and he was on this trip?

Yeah. Don't start getting ideas, I told her, not willing to admit I'd already wondered if Mike was involved. I was about to tell her about the murdered head teacher but stopped myself. I couldn't talk about it until it was released to the media.

Anna raised her eyebrows at me. *Don't assume anything, Paige. Make sure you tell Singh about him, then he can have a look into his background.*

I didn't have the energy to argue with her. Besides, perhaps it was a good idea to tell Singh at least some of what had gone on, so he understood why I wanted to avoid Mike as much as possible.

Have you told Max?

About Mike? God no. I don't want to open up that can of worms.

No, I mean have you told him you're still at work?

Shit. She was right, I should have told him earlier, but I'd lost track of time. We were supposed to be meeting up but I wouldn't make it there in time, especially not in the snow. Saying goodbye to Anna, I hung up and sent Max a quick text to tell him I'd have to postpone. I waited for a couple of minutes to see if he'd reply, and I was rewarded with the ping of an incoming message.

No problem. Maybe see you tomorrow instead?

Sure :)

Seeing his name pop up on my phone screen always made me smile. I had no idea what I'd be doing tomorrow, because it really depended on the weather and if I was able to get to Lincoln, but I really wanted to see him. We'd been dating for nearly nine months, and even though we were taking things slowly I had to admit it felt good to have someone who cared about me the way he did. At the beginning, I wasn't sure if I was ready for a relationship, though Anna and Gem had been encouraging me to get out and meet someone for a while. Things had been going well, Max had been so understanding whenever I'd been hesitant, and I was finally enjoying being part of a couple for the first time in a while. Now I'd stumbled across Mike again, and the reasons why I hadn't dated for three years all came rushing back, as well as the reasons why I'd fallen for Mike in the first place. Max was nothing like Mike, I knew that, but the way Mike had treated me still affected how I thought and behaved even now.

Shaking myself, I put the car into gear and pulled out of the gates, careful to avoid the huge snowdrift on the corner. There was a light covering on the road, but the grit that had been spread earlier seemed to have kept off the worst of it.

As I drove, I wondered what Singh and Mike had found to talk about while Mike was helping with the search. Had Mike told him about our relationship? And if he had, which version had he told?

Chapter 5

What was usually a twenty-five-minute drive took me nearly two hours. Some of the roads had been ploughed, but the village I lived in wasn't a priority, so only the main route had been cleared. After attempting to get near to the flat I'd given up and left my car three streets away and walked from there.

When I got home, I walked in to a scene that surprised me. Max was sitting on the sofa, telling Anna a story, and she was sitting on the floor laughing. The two of them looked so relaxed, I felt like I was intruding rather than entering my own flat. Max, like Anna, was profoundly deaf, and whilst he spoke when it suited him he preferred to use BSL. He worked in a school in Hull that had a specialist unit for supporting deaf children. I'd never seen him at work, but I could imagine he was great with the kids he supported.

Hi, I waved at both of them, dropping my bag on the floor and kicking my shoes off before flopping down onto the sofa next to Max. He gave my knee a squeeze and I smiled at him, leaning over to give him a kiss. His wiry copper hair was in need of a trim, but I quite liked him looking a little dishevelled. The grin he gave me still set butterflies fluttering in my belly, even now.

After nine months of dating, I was glad I'd reached a place where I wasn't bothered by him turning up unannounced. I never used to like surprises, because they took control away from me, and when I was with Mike I'd had so little control over anything that I had to hold on to what I could.

How was your day? he asked.

Terrible, I replied. *I didn't know you were coming over, but it's nice to see you,* I told him with a smile.

I thought you'd probably be exhausted once you'd finished work and battled your way home through the snow, so I brought wine and . . . he pulled out his phone, *the means to order takeaway.*

Anna and I both laughed at this – Max's awful cooking had become a running joke over the last few months.

If they can get here to deliver it, I pointed out.

He shrugged. *We'll find a way, I'm sure. So, what happened? Where have you been all day?*

I looked over at Anna, who gave a shrug to indicate it hadn't been her place to talk about it. Pulling out my own phone, I found one of the social media posts about Leon and showed it to Max. He scanned it and raised his eyebrows.

You were with the police? Oh, wow. But how did it happen?

They were staying in a cabin in the woods and when they got up this morning he'd gone.

So, he ran away? Max asked.

The police aren't ruling anything out, I told him, deliberately avoiding going into any further detail.

Could someone have lured him out of the park? Anna asked.

I have no idea, I replied, dropping my head back onto the sofa. *I'm going to the police station tomorrow morning, then they can brief me on what's happening next.*

Max put his arm around me and gave my shoulders a squeeze, and I felt myself sinking into him. I was tired and emotional; I just wanted to go to bed, but I felt like I needed to be alone tonight, at least until I made sense of this encounter with Mike. Now Max was here, though, I couldn't exactly throw him out, and I found his solid presence reassuring.

On the way home, I'd once again considered telling Anna about finding Steve Wilkinson's body, but then thought better of it. The police hadn't released details yet, so I had to remain professional and keep it to myself. It would be hard to keep my emotions buried, though.

Are you working next weekend? Max asked me.

I have no idea, it depends on how long this case takes. It's complicated, I added.

Okay. I wondered if you wanted to do something on Saturday.

Sure, if I'm not working.

Anna was still sitting on the floor, observing this conversation, then she shook her head, got up and walked out of the room.

Max frowned at me. *What's her problem?*

Shit, I said. *We've got plans next weekend, I'd completely forgotten.*

I followed Anna through to the kitchen, where she was sitting at the table with her phone in her hand. She ignored me when I sat down opposite her, until I took her phone and made her look at me.

I'm sorry. I forgot.

Since her injury in February, Anna's moods had sometimes been quite volatile, and I'd learnt that the best option to calm her down was to apologise, then talk it through afterwards. I sat there as she glared at me, until her shoulders sagged slightly and her face softened.

I've been looking forward to spending some time with you.

I know, and we will. I can see Max another time.

She gave me a small smile. *Fine. But I know it's only a matter of time before you ditch me for him. You're going to want to move in together, and then where will I go?*

Whoa, slow down. Remember how successful it was last time I moved in with a boyfriend? I'm in no hurry to do that again. It's not even that serious with Max.

You've been together for nearly a year. That's serious enough.

I shrugged, not in the mood for an in-depth conversation about my relationship with Max. He and I hadn't discussed the future, and I was perfectly happy with things the way they were, so I wasn't going to be the one to bring it up.

Is he staying over tonight? she asked, raising an eyebrow.

I rubbed my temples, hoping to dispel the headache I could feel forming. *No, I'll ask him not to. I'm too tired. It's been a horrible day.*

When are you going to tell him about Mike?

44

I'm not, I replied, giving her a warning look. *And you'd better not, either.*

I think it's something you two should talk about.

I shook my head. *Not now. I have too many other things going on in my head.*

Anna narrowed her eyes at me. *Like what? What else happened today?*

I can't talk about it, I said with a sigh. I was getting déjà vu, my mind flitting back to February. I hadn't tried hard enough to stop Anna getting involved. This time I had to protect her, because I hadn't protected her then.

That reminds me. I got a letter today, I told her. *About the brain injury support group.*

Anna rolled her eyes and leant back against the wall. *Not this again. I don't want to sit around in a room full of miserable people talking about how their lives were ruined.*

I frowned. *Do you feel like your life has been ruined?*

No, no, I don't. Honestly. She gave me a smile that looked more like a grimace as she battled to find the right words. *But I don't feel like the person I was before, if you see what I mean? Things have changed, the way I react to things and the way I function have changed. It's like I'm learning to be me all over again.* The earnest look on her face made me worry that I was forcing her to do something she wasn't ready for.

That's why I thought you should go to the support group, because there might be other people with similar experiences who'll understand what you're going through, I explained. *I can do my best to support you, but I don't know what it's like to be in the position you're in.*

She shrugged. *I don't know. What was the letter?*

I'd asked if they could provide an interpreter so you could attend.

And?

I shook my head. *No funding, of course. They suggested I go with you as your interpreter.*

Anna grimaced at this, but I didn't take offence. The whole point of a support group was that it should be a place where you can vent about your life and the people around you, as well as get support from people with similar experiences. Having her sister with her would skew that experience for Anna, because sometimes there might be things she wanted to say but didn't feel she could in front of me.

So, I can't go anyway? she said.

No way, we're not giving up that easily, I replied. *Groups like this should be accessible to all, and that includes providing an interpreter for a BSL user. I just need to work out who to take the fight to next.*

Anna rolled her eyes at me and stood up. *Come on, you've abandoned your boyfriend in the living room.*

He'll be fine, I replied, giving her a wry smile.

You need to keep him happy, he's buying us pizza, she reminded me, and I laughed.

When we went back into the living room, Max had his phone out. He showed us the takeaway app, already open and waiting for our orders. I explained about our plans to go to a Christmas market the following weekend.

Ah, well I won't intrude on that! he said. I'd talked to him a few times about my concerns about Anna, my worries about how her accident had affected her long-term, so I knew he understood that there were times when I had to prioritise her. I wished that I could let myself enjoy our relationship without worrying about repeating past mistakes, but there was no way I could put them out of my mind after today.

About half an hour later, the doorbell rang and I went down to the front door to collect our pizzas.

We'd ordered from the kebab shop in the village, and the young delivery guy appeared to have walked rather than try to drive in the snow. He handed over the pizzas without a word then trudged back up the road. As I watched him go, my phone rang in my pocket and I juggled the pizzas to pull it out.

It was a number I didn't recognise, but I stepped back into the hallway and answered it, checking the front door had shut behind me.

'Hi Paige.'

I breathed in sharply as I recognised Mike's voice.

'Don't hang up on me, please. I know you probably want to. I just wanted to make sure you got home okay. It's been a long day, the roads are really bad and I know you get tired doing lots of driving.'

'I'm fine, thanks,' I replied, my throat dry.

There was a sigh on the other end of the line. 'I wish we'd got to talk properly today.'

'We don't have anything to talk about.'

'Yes, we do,' he said. 'Paige, I never apologised for what I did, and I regret it. I want you to see that I'm not the man I was then. I made a lot of mistakes, and I'd like to try and put some of them right.'

I was so surprised by this, I leant back against the wall, the heat of the pizzas starting to burn my hand through the boxes.

'Paige?'

'I'm still here,' I said. 'I wasn't sure what to say.'

'That's okay, you don't have to say anything. I just wanted you to know I'm sorry, and I hope we can at least be civil to each other. I understand if you want nothing to do with me, but I couldn't sleep without knowing you'd at least heard my apology.'

'Okay. Well. Thank you for the apology,' I said. I didn't know what else to say in response, because I'd never imagined a scenario in which he actually took responsibility for the way he'd treated me.

'I'll see you soon, okay?'

'Okay.'

He hung up, and I stared at my phone for a moment before walking back up to the flat. I put the pizzas on the table, trying to figure out what had just happened.

You took your time, Max said with a grin. *Hope you haven't eaten half of mine.*

He thought he'd brought the wrong order, had to check, I lied. Anna narrowed her eyes at me, but I gave my head a slight shake. Now wasn't the time.

Just as I'd been getting to a place in my life where I'd put my past behind me, suddenly everything had been thrown into confusion again. Against my better judgement, I saved the unknown number on my phone as 'M', not putting his full name in case Anna saw it and had a go at me. I ignored the little voice telling me that if I was hiding it from my sister it was probably a bad idea.

Sixteen hours before the murder

I'm going to have such a shit weekend compared to you, Samira grumbled as she and Leon left their English lesson. He walked with her in the direction of the car park, where she'd be met by the taxi that took her home.

You'll be fine, you're going to spend the weekend watching what you want on Netflix, eating takeaway and ignoring your brother when he tries to make you tidy up. That sounds like a dream to me.

Samira laughed. *Okay, maybe, but I won't have you to chat to. You'll be too busy being all loved up.* She started making kissing faces, but Leon frowned at her.

Don't. I don't want everyone knowing about it.

Fine, fine, I'm sorry. She sighed dramatically. *Just make sure you text me and tell me what's going on, okay?*

I will.

Promise?

Promise.

Leon waved his friend off, then turned to go back into

the school. He'd left one of his books in the English room and he'd need it for his homework when they returned on Sunday. On his way back, he cut through the courtyard outside the management offices.

The sky was a gunmetal grey, and he wondered just how many outdoor activities they'd actually manage this weekend. There was snow forecast but Mr Wilkinson had said he wasn't bothered, they'd still be able to get outside even if there was a bit of snow on the ground.

Leon's eyes were drawn by the light from the head teacher's room as he walked past, and he paused for a moment. Mr Wilkinson was in there, pacing across the room, and Miss Marcek was sitting looking at something on the computer. As Leon watched, the head ran his hands through his hair, then signed something that Leon didn't catch.

Mr Wilkinson went over to the computer and pointed to the screen, then grabbed the mouse and brought something else up.

Don't worry about it, Miss Marcek signed. *It's obviously a mistake. I'll sort it out. You need to get ready for the trip.*

Yes, you're right. It's probably nothing.

The head turned back towards the window and Leon hurried away, not wanting to be caught snooping. He wondered what they'd been talking about – probably something boring like the school budget. His phone buzzed and he felt a frisson of excitement when he realised who it was – not long now, and they'd see each other face to face.

50

Chapter 6

Sunday 25th November

There was no more snow overnight, and by the time I walked back to my car in the morning the roads were much clearer. My route into Scunthorpe was quiet at this time on a Sunday morning. There were often a couple of walkers parked up at Twigmoor Woods early on, but the weather had kept them away for once. As I pulled out onto Mortal Ash there were some lorries pulling into the steelworks, but that route wouldn't be too busy until just before Morrisons opened. It was unusual for me to be up and out so early on a Sunday, but they wanted me at the police station by nine.

Singh passed me a coffee when I met him in the station lobby. He'd obviously stopped off for a proper one on his way in rather than offering me something murky from the station drinks machine.

'Marry me,' I mumbled.

He laughed. 'I think you should meet my family first.'

I laughed in return before taking a sip of the coffee, then the laugh turned into a yawn. Yesterday had been a long day, and I had lain awake until the early hours of the morning, thinking. Eventually I'd fallen asleep around three, but the four hours of sleep I'd managed to get weren't anywhere near enough.

'What's happening this morning?' I asked as he led me upstairs.

'First, we need to coordinate the team for the case.'

'You're treating it as one case, then?'

'Yes, one case with two branches. One murder, one missing teenager. Currently no solid evidence to say how they're linked, but the connection between them is too strong to ignore.'

We turned down a long corridor, passing a couple of offices and a conference room.

'How on earth did you talk Forest into having me at this meeting?' I asked. The DI was far from being my biggest fan, and back in February she'd been quite glad to see the back of me once the case was over.

'I reminded her that some of the officers would need advising on the most appropriate way to interview deaf people, and that you could provide that,' he said, not looking at me.

'Oh, I'm giving deaf awareness training? Couldn't you have asked me about that yesterday, rather than springing it on me now?' I complained, my frustration evident in my voice.

He gave me an apologetic look. 'I'm sorry. You're right, I should have asked you about it.'

I looked at him for a moment before nodding, accepting his apology. 'I don't mind doing things like that, but next time tell me in advance, okay?'

'Promise.'

He pushed open the door and we walked into a large room I'd never been in before. Several people were already seated, both detectives in plain clothes and uniformed officers. DI Forest was standing at the front of the room, and we headed towards her.

'Morning,' she said, with a nod in my direction. 'We're just waiting for a couple of other people then we'll get going.'

Singh pointed me to a chair at the end of the front row and I sat down, leaning on the wall and trying to shrink into it. I sat there for a few minutes, looking at my phone, until Forest called the room to order.

'Right, I want to make this a reasonably quick one. We have a complex case, with two very different aspects to it. A young man called Leon Ormerod went missing from a school trip to Normanby Hall, some time between ten thirty on Friday night, when he was last seen, and seven thirty on Saturday morning, when the staff found his bed empty. Leon is fifteen, and profoundly deaf. He wears hearing aids and attends Lincoln School for the Deaf, where he is in care.'

Forest indicated a board behind her, which had a photo of Leon along with the details she'd just given out. Leon looked so small, and I felt a stab of worry for him. Was he running from something? Or had he been taken? I couldn't bring myself to consider the possibility that he'd killed his teacher.

'At the moment we don't know if Leon left Normanby Park or not, and if he did whether he left of his own accord or was abducted. Someone had broken into the cricket pavilion towards the south end of the estate, where we found an item of clothing that a staff member

53

identified as Leon's. He must have sheltered in there for a short time, but there was no sign of him by the time we searched the building. We've been looking through the CCTV covering the park gates, but there are other routes in and out of the park.'

'We used to climb over the wall as kids.' A PC near the back had interrupted and Forest glared at him for a moment before nodding.

'Precisely: there are many points along the park boundary that aren't covered by CCTV, and Leon could have easily left without being caught on camera. The park is large, however, and with the snow we can't be certain he left until we've searched every part of the grounds. The search of the park was abandoned yesterday afternoon when the snowfall and light became too bad, but will continue today. Some of you will also be speaking to people in the local area to find out if anyone might have seen Leon.'

The DI glanced around the room to make sure she still had everyone's attention. 'Whilst searching for Leon, the body of Steve Wilkinson was found. Mr Wilkinson was the head teacher of Leon's school and was one of the staff supervising the trip. When it was discovered that Leon was missing, Mr Wilkinson went into the grounds to search for him at around eight yesterday morning, and nobody has reported seeing him since then until his body was found.

'There was no sign of a struggle in the cabin, which suggests that Leon packed his things and walked out of there, so we need to find out if he did this voluntarily or was lured out. The cricket pavilion where he had been hiding has a direct view of where the head teacher's body was found. At this point in time we do not know if Leon witnessed the murder and then ran, or if he was abducted by his teacher's killer. It's also possible that he murdered Steve Wilkinson himself. For now, we're going to work on the basis that these two incidents are connected.'

Forest looked around at the assembled officers. 'Due to the fact that Leon is extremely vulnerable, the search for him has to be our top priority. So far we haven't received any credible information as to where he might be. There are appeals going out on social media, and we're also going to be looking at CCTV footage from local transport companies. There are two different bus companies with routes that run near the park. No cars were permitted onto the estate yesterday, except for ours, so we'll also be looking for any CCTV footage of the surrounding roads, because if someone took Leon in a vehicle they won't have left by the main entrance.

'DS Singh will be liaising with the team involved in the search for Leon, and he and I will be conducting interviews at the school. Leon's classmates might be able to give us some insight into his state of mind, or indicate where he might go if he were scared or in trouble.'

A hand was raised at the back of the room, and Forest nodded at the man in question.

'What about his phone and social media?'

'We've put in a request to Leon's network provider for access to his text and video call history. Social media will take a little longer. We need to establish which apps and social networks he was using and then submit individual requests for access.

'I will be joining DS Singh at the school later today,' Forest continued, looking at the assembled officers. 'The rest of you will be divided up – some of you will be continuing the search, and others will be following up any reported sightings, anything that comes in from the social media appeal or by phone.

'The dead man, Steve Wilkinson, lived in Derbyshire. Derbyshire police have informed his next of kin, a sister, of his death, and we'll be putting out a statement later today. It's only a matter of time before the media jumps on this and starts spouting theories, so we need to try and keep a tight rein on the information that we're releasing. Is that clear?'

A chorus of yesses came from across the room. I dreaded to think what Forest would do to any officer she caught leaking information to the press, or even just being a bit lax with what they told their friends down the pub.

'Back to our murder victim.' Forest pointed to a board next to the one with Leon's information on. 'Steve Wilkinson had been head teacher of the Lincoln School for the Deaf since September. At first glance it appears he was stabbed in the neck, but the post-mortem will tell us more. There was a penknife lying nearby, covered in blood, so I think we can safely assume it was the murder weapon, but we'll wait for forensics to confirm. DS Singh and I will speak to the deputy head and find out more about Steve Wilkinson's professional and personal life. We'll also look into his work history and speak to his previous employer.'

A uniformed officer raised his hand, and Forest nodded at him.

'What about his friends and family? Will we be interviewing them?' he asked.

'He was new to the area, and as far as we can gather

didn't know anyone in North Lincolnshire,' Forest replied. 'As the murder occurred on a school trip, we're going to focus our investigations on the school for the time being. Of course, if any evidence turns up to point us elsewhere, we'll follow it.'

At this point Forest turned to me. 'Our British Sign Language interpreter will be Paige Northwood. DS Singh and I will be conducting interviews at the school to begin with, but there may be occasions during the course of this investigation when the rest of you will need to interview a deaf person. Whilst you've all received the general training on working with people with disabilities and speakers of other languages, I thought it best if Paige addressed all of you now to try and avoid any issues in the interview process.'

With that, she stepped aside and held out a hand, offering me the floor. I glared at Singh as I stood up, then plastered a professional smile onto my face.

'Morning. There are several deaf staff at the school, and of course the other students are deaf, so there are some points you need to be aware of. Firstly, not all deaf people communicate in the same way. Some speak, and don't use any sign language, making use of either hearing aids or cochlear implants. Some don't use any aids at all and rely completely on BSL. But many will use a combination of the two. Please don't make any assumptions – at the start of each interview, check how the deaf person would like to communicate. It might be that they're happy to speak their answers to you, but would prefer me to sign what you're saying to be certain they've understood. They might prefer to sign their answers, in which case I'll speak for them. Or they might not want an interpreter at all. Making assumptions can cause offence, which can then affect how the person concerned cooperates with you.'

I saw Forest nodding out of the corner of my eye, and felt my confidence increase slightly. 'When you work with spoken language interpreters, you'll often have to wait for them to interpret what you've said after you've finished a question, but with BSL I can interpret at the same time. However, I still require time to process what you've said and interpret it, so there might be times when I ask you to slow down, pause, or repeat something for clarity. As always, when working with an interpreter, please address the person you're interviewing, not me. I'm not the one answering the questions. The deaf person might only look at me when you're speaking, or they might choose to look between us, using your lip patterns, facial expression and body language to support their understanding.'

Someone at the back put their hand up, and I nodded at her, not expecting questions.

'While you're here, can you teach us some basic signs?'

Forest answered before I got a chance to. 'I'm happy to put in a request to those on high for some BSL classes, but while Paige is here we're paying her to facilitate our interviews, not teach you the alphabet.'

A snigger passed around the room, but everyone soon went silent again. I couldn't think of anything else relevant to say, so I stepped back and let Forest take over again.

'Right, if that's everything, we'd better get on and do our jobs. If you come across anything you believe to be relevant to the case, please pass it directly to DS Singh.'

There was a sudden noise as several chairs scraped back and everyone moved to get on with the tasks they'd been assigned. I waited until Singh had finished speaking to Forest, then he beckoned to me to join them.

'We're going to the school now,' he explained. 'We need to interview the staff who knew Steve and Leon, as well as all the students who were on the trip. One of them knows more than they're letting on about Leon's disappearance, and Steve's death.'

Chapter 7

It took me a little longer to get to the school than I'd hoped, not because of the snow, but because with thoughts of Mike and the bad memories he brought with him swirling around in my mind I missed the turning. By the time I pulled into the drive, I was annoyed and frustrated.

The main building of Lincoln School for the Deaf was an old house, with a couple of purpose-built annexes off to one side, and the residence building out the back. I couldn't see anyone in the car park, so I walked towards the main entrance, looking around me as I went. Someone had cleared a path to the front door and put grit down, though it looked as if the snow hadn't fallen as heavily here as it had in the park.

The main building had seen better days, although one of the newer blocks must have been built since Anna was a pupil. I wondered how many they had on roll – since the change in inclusion policies and the development of better assistive technologies, most deaf children now went to mainstream schools. Many schools for the deaf had closed, and those that had remained open often had to find ways to diversify in order to make them more attractive to a wider variety of students. Some opened up their doors to students with autism and communication difficulties, who benefited from the use of sign language to help them access the curriculum and express themselves. Others, like Lincoln, registered as children's homes, so deaf children in the care system could have a consistent supportive environment and social services didn't need to worry about finding foster carers who could sign. I had sometimes been involved in meetings when deaf families were looking at different school options for their children, and I knew that the schools for the deaf weren't above trying to tempt students away from their local authority schools.

I entered the house by the large, imposing front door, putting my shoulder to it when it stuck slightly. There was nobody in the entrance hall when I stepped inside, so I looked around to try and figure out where Singh and Forest might be. The door marked 'Head Teacher' was closed, and the sign conjured an image in my mind of Steve's body lying in the snow, making me shudder. Next to his office was an open door so I pushed it further open and poked my head around it. Inside were Singh, Forest and Liz Marcek; the DI and the deputy head were sitting on comfy chairs, which were pulled up to a small table by the window. On the adjacent wall was a desk, which Singh was leaning against.

When Singh saw me, he looked relieved, and I apologised for taking so long to arrive.

Can we start now? Liz Marcek asked impatiently. I noticed to my surprise that she was wearing a well-cut suit. I suppose I had expected a teacher at a residential school to dress down over the weekend, but perhaps she was putting on a professional face for the police. Her make-up was skilfully applied, but it didn't quite hide the fact that she hadn't slept well the previous night, if at all.

Is there any news about Leon? she asked as soon as I'd taken off my coat and sat down opposite her.

'Sorry, nothing yet,' Singh replied.

Liz shook her head slowly. *I was hoping he might have turned up overnight.*

'We'd like to speak to any of the staff who are in today,' Forest explained, mostly keeping her eyes on Liz but glancing around the room as well.

A few have come in, Liz said, *though not many. I'll make a list and you can decide who you want to see and when. I'll make the meeting room available for you.*

'Could you let us know who will require signing?' Singh asked. 'Then we can work out times with Paige.'

Of course. Liz crossed over to her desk, took a pen and paper and made a list.

'Thanks,' Singh said, taking it from her. 'We'd like to speak to you first, if that's okay?'

I assumed as much, she said, settling herself into one of the chairs. *I have a lot to do, parents to contact, but I'll tell you what I can.*

Pushing away from the desk, Singh took the chair next to me.

'Have you told the students about Steve Wilkinson's death?'

She grimaced. *Not yet. I didn't think it was appropriate last night, and I haven't managed to bring myself to tell them. I'll do it once we've finished here, though. They need* to know what's happened. *That's unless Mike has already told them*, she added, a sour look twisting her face.

'What is Mr Lowther's role here?' Singh asked.

He's one of our pastoral staff. They live in, and have responsibility for the students in residence overnight and at weekends. The other staff have the weekend off, as we weren't expecting to be here, so Sasha offered to stay with the students last night.

'So, Mike lives here?' I asked, out of curiosity.

Yes, he has a suite in the residence, as do the other residential staff. The students like him a lot.

I nodded, holding myself back from saying, *Of course, one thing Mike's always been good at is getting people to like him.*

'What can you tell us about Steve Wilkinson?' Singh asked.

What do you want to know?

'Start with the basics – how long has he worked here, is he generally well liked by staff and students, things like that.'

He's been here since September, Liz explained. *The previous head had been here for over thirty years, and she retired at the end of the summer term.*

'Where had Steve worked before, do you know?'

Liz glanced out of the window before she answered; there was a tension in her shoulders that suggested she was choosing her words carefully. The room we were in overlooked a small courtyard, where I presumed students would hang around at break and lunchtime. Steve's office next door would have a similar view, and I wondered if he would have preferred a view over the playing fields, something a little more picturesque.

He came from a special school in Birmingham, she replied eventually, her face impassive. *A school for children with profound learning difficulties. He hadn't worked in a residential school before, so that aspect was a bit of a learning curve.* She paused, though I had the sense there was something more she wanted to say.

After a moment, Singh spoke. 'What about deaf students? Had he worked with any before?'

Liz shook her head. *No. The governors felt his management experience was enough for this position, but he struggled a bit in his relations with the students.*

I wondered if this was the source of her tension. Someone with no experience of working with deaf students might not be well received in such an important position.

He knew some basic signs before he came here, Liz continued, *but not enough for a proper conversation.* She gave Singh an earnest look. *But he learnt as much as he could, he really threw himself into it. Whenever he had a spare five minutes he'd be practising, and he set up one-to-one lessons for himself with our deaf tutor a couple of times a week. He was coming on very well.*

'Was there anyone who had a problem with him?'

She shook her head. *Not that I know of. A change in management after such a long time is bound to be difficult, but Steve did his best to get everyone on side.*

'Was there anyone on the staff who was finding it difficult to adapt to working under a new head?'

She paused for a moment before replying. *No, I don't think so. Steve never mentioned anything that concerned him, and nobody has come to me with any complaints.*

Liz looked poised to sign something else, then thought better of it and sat back in her chair.

'We'll need access to Steve's office, as well as his pass-words so our tech team can have a look at his emails and online activity. At the moment, we're looking for anyone who might have a motive to kill him.'

Liz nodded. *I can lock his office until you're ready to go in. Saul is in today, he's our IT technician, so he can get you access to Steve's computer as well.*

'Thank you, but a member of our tech team should be here a little later. If your technician could give them access to the school computer network, that would be appreciated,' Singh replied. 'Now, we'd like to ask you a couple more questions about Leon.'

Liz nodded. *Sasha will be over soon and she'll be able to tell you a bit more, but I'll answer what I can. We both stayed last night, in the residence, but I don't think either of us slept, wondering what's happened to Leon.*

'I'll let you know as soon as we know anything. There were no signs of a struggle and he took his bag with him, which suggests he left the cabin of his own free will. I'm hopeful that he had a plan for where he was going and how he would get there, so we can hope he'll be found somewhere safe.'

I thought about the pavilion, and Leon breaking in. Had that been part of his plan? Was it just somewhere handy to shelter from the snow? Or somewhere to hide from a killer?

He's only fifteen, Liz said, shaking her head in desper-ation. *What was he thinking? If there was something wrong, he could have come to one of us and talked about it. We would have helped him, whatever the problem was.*

'Sometimes teenagers don't feel they can trust adults,' Singh replied gently.

She shook herself again, turning around to look out of the window. After a moment, she turned back to us. *Leon had been struggling with his lessons recently, but nothing that was a cause for concern. He just found the work challenging. Steve had spoken to him a couple of times, to ask if anything was bothering him, but nothing came of it as far as I know.*

Singh tilted his head to one side. 'Did Steve and Leon have a lot of contact? More than would be usual for a head teacher and a student?'

Well, Steve did tutor him a little, in science, because that was his specialism and he thought it might help, Liz replied.

'What about Sasha? What was Leon's relationship like with her?'

Sasha doesn't work for the school directly, though of course we have regular meetings about the students' welfare. There's a possibility Leon confided in her, but I'm sure she would have told us anything relevant.

'Was Leon a student here before he was taken into care?' Singh asked.

Yes, he's been attending here since he was eight. Before that, he was at his local mainstream school with support from a teacher of the deaf and a teaching assistant, but he was struggling socially. Being the only deaf child in a school full of hearing children can be very lonely, especially when there is a communication barrier.

'And he became a resident after his mother died, is that correct?'

No, it was around a year later, Liz replied. *Leon's parents had separated, and after his mother died he was in his father's custody full time. The man was abusive, but it was only discovered when Leon fought back and injured his father, and a neighbour called the police. In that situation no one was going to blame an abused twelve-year-old boy for defending himself, especially one who was going through the turmoil of having lost his mother.*

'Does he have any other family? Anyone he might go to for help?'

Liz frowned. *Not that I know of. His father is in prison, and I certainly don't think Leon would want anything to do with him.*

Singh made a note of this. 'We'll need his name so we can access the case file. Are you sure it's not possible Leon could have been trying to see his father?'

I can't imagine that he would want to see him, Liz replied, looking sceptical. *Besides, if Leon had wanted to see his father he could have spoken to Sasha and she could have arranged it, if she thought it was appropriate. There'd be no need for him to run away.*

'Still, it's an avenue we need to look into,' Singh replied. 'We'd also like you to make a list of who Leon is closest to at the school, which students are his friends and which staff know him well. Then we can prioritise our interviews.'

I've been thinking about that, Liz replied. *His closest friend is Samira. She's not a residential student so she won't be back until tomorrow, but I've emailed her family explaining the situation and asking for their permission for her to speak to you.*

'Thank you, that's very helpful,' Singh said with a reassuring smile.

There was a knock on the door, and a light flashed above it. In a school full of deaf students and several deaf staff, there would be a number of adaptations to make daily life accessible for all. Liz moved out of her chair to answer it, but Forest got there before her. Sasha stood in the doorway, wearing a long bohemian-style skirt and a bright red shirt, her curly blonde hair making her seem taller than she was.

Sorry, I've been busy with Cassie, she signed. She offered her hand to both of the detectives then sat down next to Liz Marcek. *Have you found Leon yet?*

I got the feeling that this was going to be the first question anyone asked us until the boy was found.

'I'm afraid not,' Singh replied, the frown on his face mirroring her concern. 'We're doing all we can to find out what happened and where he might have gone after he was in the pavilion. Miss Marcek has told us about his family history, and we want to rule out the idea that he might have wanted to visit his father.'

That's very unlikely, Sasha replied, confirming what the deputy head had told us. *I can get you his details if you want to make sure. Leon is such a lovely young man, but he went through a lot in a short space of time, with the death of his mother and then his father's abuse. The school had given him the option to become a residential student before, but when he'd just lost his mum the last thing he wanted was to end up living at his school.*

Sasha spread her palms wide. *After his father's arrest, it became the only option, and actually it ended up suiting him surprisingly well. As far as I'm aware, he's well liked, and he didn't tell me of any difficulties he was having.*

'Had there been any incidents of bullying, anything like that?'

We're very strict with our bullying policy, Liz interjected, before Sasha had a chance to reply. *We don't tolerate anything like that, whether it's in class or in the residence.*

Sasha waited for Liz to finish then turned back to us. *Not that I know of. There have been disagreements, but that's natural in this sort of environment. You have to remember these students are always together: they live in close quarters, and they only really socialise with each other. It can mean they're very close, sometimes so close that no outsider can really understand their group dynamics. At other times it can be like a dry bonfire and the smallest spark will set off an inferno. I try to maintain a strong relationship with the students here, and I visit once a week, but they don't tell me everything. They're teenagers*, she said with a shrug, as if that explained everything.

'Do you have any idea where Leon might go?'

I really don't know, she replied. *I don't know of any other family, and all of his friends are at the school.*

If he'd gone to a friend's house, their parents would have called the police by now, Liz replied.

I know, Sasha said, nodding sadly. *That's what I don't understand. Where could he have gone?*

Forest thanked the two women for their help and the two detectives had a quick conversation.

'We'd like to go to the residence and take statements from the students now,' Forest said, turning back to address the deputy head. 'I understand it's an upsetting time for them, but they're probably the people who knew Leon best, and maybe one of them has remembered something. We'd also like to see Leon's room.'

I'll come with you, Sasha signed, following us to the door.

Liz nodded. *Yes, please. I'd like Sasha to be present when you speak to the students, in place of a parent.*

The five of us walked out of the room and across the lobby to the front door. Before we reached it, Mike came in from outside.

Miss Marcek, can I speak to you please? he signed, throwing a nervous glance at the detectives.

Of course. Sasha, you can take the police over, can't you?

Before they disappeared back into her office, Mike smiled at me. I thought back to his phone call the previous night – had he really changed?

Chapter 8

The residence was a purpose-built block behind the main house. When Anna had been a student here, this hadn't yet been built, and her friends who were residential students had rooms in the main building, above the classrooms. She used to tell me stories of how her friends would creep down into the classrooms at night, although I always thought those tales were probably made up to make the non-residents jealous. Children have always had a fascination with schools after hours, and I was sure these kids were no exception.

As we entered the building, Sasha pointed out the security features. There was a camera above the entrance, as well as a key fob entry system. She let us in, and once we were inside there was another security door before we were in the main communal area. She told us the students' rooms all locked too, for privacy, although staff had spare keys in order to access them in emergencies.

'We'll have a look at Leon's room first, I think,' Forest said.

Sasha led us through a door to some stairs. At the top of the stairs we turned right down a short corridor, where the social worker pulled out some keys and let us into a room.

This room's his. He's not the tidiest, but then what fifteen-year-old is?

I looked around at the unmade bed and the clothes on the floor, and thought it could have been much worse.

'Does he have a tablet or a laptop?' Forest asked

No, Sasha replied, shaking her head. *The school has electronics they can use for homework, but they try to limit their screen time. All of them have phones, but I assume Leon had his with him.*

'We thought the same. Liz Marcek gave us his number yesterday, and we're set up to track the signal, but it's been turned off,' Singh told her.

If there's nothing else, I think I should get the other students together before Liz gets here to talk to them, Sasha signed. *I have no idea how they're going to take this news.*

She left us, and Singh started to look through drawers and shelves while Forest checked the wardrobe. I went out onto the landing, feeling awkward but not wanting to get in the way. While I waited, I had a look up the corridor. There were several rooms along here, and some more on the opposite corridor, and one was marked 'STAFF'. I wondered if that was Mike's room, then moved away quickly in case he came back and caught me prowling about out there.

The detectives didn't need me, so I went back down

the stairs, and looked through the glass panel in the door. To my surprise, Liz and Mike were in there with Sasha and the four students; they must have come in while we were upstairs. I would have thought the deputy head would want to wait for the detectives before she told the students about the death of their head teacher.

As the deputy signed, the four of them seemed to bunch together on the sofa. One of the girls started crying, but the older boy signed something I couldn't see and she blinked a few times, managing to stop herself. Liz and Mike shared a brief glance, and I found myself wondering what he'd needed to talk to her about so urgently.

Is there anything any of you want to ask me, or talk about? Liz signed to the students.

The four of them looked at each other, and something passed between them silently, because they shook their heads in unison. They all seemed shocked, but I still found myself wondering if they were hiding something.

Singh and Forest came back downstairs in silence, and I was curious whether they'd found anything useful in Leon's room. Together, we walked into the communal area, which had several sofas, a large television and a couple of games consoles. The four students stayed where they were, sitting in a line on one large sofa as if they'd been placed there. Sasha was standing behind the sofa, leaning against the wall, opposite Mike and Liz. When we entered, they all turned to look at the three of us.

I had better introduce you, the deputy head said. *Cassie here is the oldest of our students, she's seventeen.* She indicated the girl I'd spoken to yesterday when we were at Normanby Hall, the one I'd thought wanted to say something about Leon. *And this is Courtney, she's fifteen.*

73

The other girl looked at us with large eyes, expertly made-up. She was sitting with her slim legs stretched out in front of her as if to emphasise their length.

The other two students were Bradley and Kian, brothers who were fifteen and thirteen respectively. They sat close together, Bradley slightly further forward than his younger brother. I noticed that Bradley and Courtney were holding hands, but they pulled apart when Liz glared at them.

These two detectives are DI Forest and DS Singh, Liz told the students. *They're going to ask you some questions, and Paige is going to interpret for them.* She looked around, her gaze resting on each of them before she continued. *Remember what I told you. It's very important you answer their questions and tell the truth.*

'Thank you, Miss Marcek,' Forest replied. 'Where would be the best place for us to talk to Sasha for a moment?'

Liz showed the detectives into a small room next door to the communal area, which contained a couple of book-shelves and two computers. Mike hovered as if hoping to be invited in too, but Liz asked Sasha to join us before excusing herself and steering him away.

'Can you tell us a little about each of the students?' Forest asked Sasha, before they started on the interviews.

Sasha nodded and thought for a moment. *Kian suffers with anxiety, and when he's in a stressful situation he tends to run. The last time he got in trouble he ran off and we found him hiding under a table in the art room, his hands over his head. Bradley keeps him grounded most of the time, and we're doing a lot of work with him on how to control his emotions, but I think he'll struggle with it well into adulthood, even with the support we're putting in place.*

'What about Bradley?' Singh asked.

He will protect his younger brother to the ends of the earth and further if necessary, Sasha replied. *But he knows that this school is the safest place for him to be, and he trusts the staff to take care of him and Kian. This will have shaken him more than he'll let on.*

Courtney is obsessed with social media, documenting every moment of her free time, the social worker continued. *We've had to do a lot of work with her to stop her giving out her personal details, but she still doesn't really understand the dangers of talking to hundreds of strangers online. We monitor her social media, but she's old enough to have accounts so the school only take her phone away as a punishment if she's done something particularly risky.*

'And Cassie?'

Cassie can sometimes be a bit full-on. She has some learning difficulties, and she's very immature for her age. The most challenging aspect is the fact that she has no idea of her own limitations – she thinks she's very mature and very clever. I love the kids to have confidence in themselves, but if she had a better understanding of what she struggles with, she'd be able to work on strategies to counteract them and ways to get support. As it is, she insists she doesn't need any help, she'll manage perfectly well when she leaves school, she'll be able to get a well-paid job, live alone and be completely independent, when in reality she'll require a lot of support to guide her on the way to independent living. As for her social skills, sometimes she latches on to one of the other students, declares them to be her best friend and won't leave them alone. Some of them have been teasing her recently, saying she has an imaginary friend.

75

Singh and Forest listened carefully as I interpreted, then went back through to speak to the four students. While Sasha and the detectives had been talking, the students had closed in and formed a tight group, signing to each other but keeping their hands low so we couldn't see. I tried a subtle glance over through the doorway, but they were keeping their conversation well concealed. When the teenagers saw the detectives come back into the room they stopped their conversation and turned to look at them expectantly. Bradley shuffled further forwards beside his brother, almost shielding Kian from view. There was no sign of Liz or Mike.

Forest gave all the students a serious look. 'I understand this is very difficult for you, especially with the news you've just received, but there are some questions we need to ask you. I want all of you to think carefully and give us truthful answers. If you think something isn't important, tell us anyway, because it might be more important than you realise.'

Kian's eyes widened as I signed this speech; Courtney and Bradley looked at each other, worry lining their young faces, but Cassie didn't seem to react at all, sitting back with a little smile on her face. Was there something she knew, or did she not understand the seriousness of the situation?

Singh took over, sitting down opposite the four students, getting onto their level so as to not appear intimidating.

'First, we'd like to know when you all saw Leon last.'

'We don't know where he is,' Courtney spoke up quickly. Her voice was soft, with a nasal quality to it, but her speech was clear. The detectives knew from experience that not all deaf people were fully reliant on

BSL, but Forest still looked a little surprised to hear Courtney speak.

'Don't worry, we'll come to that later. Think back to when you last saw him,' Singh repeated, keeping his voice low and gentle.

A small line appeared between Courtney's eyes as she thought. 'Friday night, when we all went to bed. I didn't see him in the morning.'

Same, Cassie signed.

Bradley looked at his brother. *We went to bed about eleven, something like that. We didn't see him in the morning, did we?*

Kian shook his head, but didn't add anything. I wondered how often he let Bradley speak for him.

'Did any of you leave your rooms in the night?'

There was a pause before any of the students responded to this question, and I thought I could detect a slight flush on Cassie's face. A movement caught my eye: Bradley's hand snaking down to squeeze Courtney's. This time, however, none of them looked at each other, but each in turn claimed they'd been in their rooms all night.

Singh's next question established that they'd all been woken around seven-thirty on Saturday morning – Sasha had been in to wake the girls, and Steve the boys.

Mr Wilkinson asked us where Leon was, Kian told the detectives, his anxiety showing in the speed at which he signed. *But we didn't know, did we, Bradley? We said we didn't know. We didn't see him leave.*

'Okay, now let's talk about Mr Wilkinson. When did you last see him?' Singh asked.

'He and Mike were talking in the kitchen when we got up,' Courtney offered, Cassie nodding her agreement.

'They kept asking Bradley and Kian questions. We didn't know what was happening until Bradley told me Leon had gone.'

Bradley continued the story. *When we were all up, he went out to look for Leon.*

'He didn't come back to the cabin after that?'

All four students shook their heads.

'Did you see anyone else outside the cabin?' Forest asked.

There was a moment of hesitation as the four of them looked at each other again. *Well, Mike went out as well*, Cassie offered. *He said he was going to look for Leon and Mr Wilkinson. But he came back alone.*

I felt a sense of unease as a look passed between the two detectives. My head swam as a thought hit me – could Mike have done this?

Singh sat forward and looked at each of the students for a moment. 'I'd like you to think back before the trip. Had there been any problems between Leon and Mr Wilkinson?'

Oh, come on, you don't think Leon killed him? Bradley replied, immediately animated and ready to defend his friend. *He could never do something like that!*

'We're not assuming anything,' Singh replied, holding up a hand to try and calm Bradley. 'We need to cover everything, that's all.'

No, they got on really well, Bradley replied, then sat back and folded his arms, showing his refusal to engage with the question any further.

Kian looked nervous, but he nodded. *I don't know Leon as well as Bradley, but I don't think he ever said anything bad about Mr Wilkinson.*

The two girls nodded their agreement with Kian.

'Okay,' Singh said, changing tack. 'Did Leon give any sign that he was upset or worried about anything on Friday?'

Bradley seemed to think for a moment, then looked over at Courtney. *He seemed a bit preoccupied, like there was something on his mind, maybe. He was looking at his phone all the time on the bus and once we were in the cabin. Mr Wilkinson told him off a couple of times.*

Forest took over. 'Did he tell you why he was looking at his phone?'

Bradley shook his head. *No, and I think he definitely wanted to keep it private.*

'Thank you. We'll look into Leon's messages and see if that helps us work out what happened,' Forest assured the students. Far from relaxing them, however, I noticed a look of panic flit across the faces of Bradley and Courtney. Had the detectives noticed it too?

'What happened to Mr Wilkinson?' Courtney asked, a tremor in her voice.

'I'm sorry, but we don't know yet.'

'Leon wouldn't . . .' Courtney began, but then she stopped herself and shook her head.

'What were you going to say?' Singh asked.

'Leon wouldn't run away,' she replied, looking down at the table as she spoke. I didn't think that was what she'd been intending to say at first, but she didn't speak again.

The detectives stepped out of the room for a moment, had a quick discussion, then came back in and dismissed the students, with an appeal to speak to them if they thought of anything else. The four teenagers barely waited for me to finish signing this to them before they all got up and left the room together, arms folded or hands in pockets, as if they were deliberately avoiding communicating with each other until they were away from us.

I didn't know what to make of this group of kids. They were all in care, which suggested they all had difficult backgrounds, and who knows what sort of memories this situation might be bringing up for some of them. Still, there was something strange about the way they'd been behaving, as if they were only giving the detectives the answers they thought they wanted. Bradley and Courtney were clearly close, maybe not just friends, and Sasha had told us how protective he was of Kian, so where did that leave Cassie?

My thoughts were interrupted by a knock on the door. A tall black man stood there, his head ducked slightly as if he were trying to make himself look smaller.

Hi Saul, Sasha signed with a smile.

He nodded at her, then looked awkwardly at the two detectives, but didn't say anything.

This is Saul Achembe, the school's IT teacher, Sasha explained.

'I'm on speed dial for the residential kids in case the wifi goes down,' he joked, then suppressed his smile. 'I'm sorry, I shouldn't be making jokes under the circumstances. Liz said you needed some things from me, access to Leon and Steve's accounts.'

'Yes please,' Singh replied. 'We're looking at Leon's social media, but we'd like to see his internet history as well, see if there's anything he's been accessing through the school networks that could help our investigation.'

'I'll help in any way I can. Do you need me to access Leon's account for you?'

Forest stood up. 'I'll go and see if the tech guy has arrived. You can give him access and he can download what we need for now.' She turned to Singh. 'I'll meet you at the car.'

Saul nodded and stood back to let Forest leave the room first.

When we left the residence, Sasha said her goodbyes and crossed back over to the main building, along with Forest and Saul, whilst Singh and I went to the car park. A fresh dusting of snow had fallen while we'd been inside, and I could clearly see a trail of footprints leading up to my car, despite the scuff marks that showed some effort to conceal them. Had someone been trying to see inside? I looked around, my heart in my throat, but whoever it had been was long gone.

Fifteen hours before the murder

Cassie was bored. Leon and Bradley were having a conversation about the film they'd watched last night in the communal area, which she'd thought was crap. She didn't enjoy action films, especially not something set in space. She liked romance, the sort of film with a gorgeous lead actor she could fall in love with. Leaving the rest of them in the common room, she went back to her bedroom to get her bag. Mr Wilkinson said they needed to be ready to leave at half past four.

Closing the door behind her, she flung herself down on her bed, then rolled over when she felt something hard against her back. Picking up the object, she examined it excitedly. Another gift!

She tore off the purple paper and opened the little box. It was a necklace, with a small silver pendant dangling from it. At first she thought it was a dog, but on closer inspection she realised it was actually a wolf. Turning the paper over, she looked for the note. There was always a note.

In the end she found it at the foot of her bed. It read:

Dear Cassie,
You have been such a good friend to me, I wanted
to give you something special. The wolf represents
loyalty – you have been loyal, always helping me when
I needed it. Wear this and think of our friendship.

Beaming with pleasure, Cassie put the necklace on and
looked at herself in the mirror. The little wolf's head sat
in the perfect position at the base of her throat. Nobody
had ever given her jewellery before. She'd had other
presents, but nothing as special as this.

When had it been left? She hadn't been back to her
room since this morning, so they could have left it at any
time in the last few hours. Smiling to herself, she was sure
she knew who her secret gift-giver was, whatever Leon
said. He didn't know what he was talking about, and
she'd show him.

Cassie thought about going back out into the sitting
room wearing the necklace, just to see if any of the others
noticed. But she couldn't – it had to be a secret, her friend
had been very clear on that. If she started telling people
about the gifts they would stop, and that was the last
thing she wanted. She was special, and she would do
anything for her friend to keep it that way.

Chapter 9

Monday 26th November

Why won't they let us help?

There's a kid missing, we need to find him.

What are the police doing?

I waved my hands firmly at the group of deaf people who had turned up unannounced at Normanby Hall an hour earlier. A couple of PCs flanked them, giving the group sideways looks as we communicated.

Stop! I waved my hands high in the air to make sure I had their attention. *You know I can't interpret if you all sign at once.*

Some of them looked suitably chastised but a couple scowled at me, as if I was the one stopping them from helping. I didn't have any gloves on, because that would have made my signing really unclear, and my hands were aching from the cold. Rubbing them together, I wondered how much of my morning this was going to take up.

'What do you need to tell them?' I asked, turning to DS Singh next to me. He gazed past me towards the tree line for a moment, then looked back towards the crowd in front of us, huddled against the steps of Normanby Hall.

'I understand that you want to help,' Singh began, addressing them while I interpreted. 'A child is missing, a child from your community, and we appreciate all support that's offered to the police. But there is still quite a bit of snow on the ground in the park, and we don't know if there is still evidence buried underneath it. If we have too many people walking around, there's a chance it could make it harder for us to find Leon. Do you understand?'

A big man at the front rolled his eyes once Singh had finished speaking. *You don't care about the boy*, he signed, an accusing look aimed directly at the detective. *You should be encouraging people to help!*

'We doubt Leon is still in the park,' Singh replied, doing his best to reason with the man. 'It would be more helpful if you could share our posts on social media, and ask anyone you know in the local area if they've seen him.'

Most of the group were nodding in agreement with Singh, but the man at the front clearly wasn't satisfied. Seeing his friends were less than keen to start arguing with the police, however, he relented and stepped back, turning to sign something to a woman next to him. A moment later, they started to move towards the main gate, the two PCs trailing in their wake.

The officer who'd phoned me that morning had sounded very flustered when she explained that a group of deaf people had turned up at Normanby Hall. The police officers who were there had managed to establish that they wanted to help, but beyond that the communication barrier had been too great. I'd arrived about ten minutes after DS Singh, and it had taken us a good half hour to calm them down and convince them that their attempt to be helpful was anything but.

I understood why they wanted to do something. In a small community, you protected your own; even if they didn't know Leon, they identified with him in many ways, and they wanted to make sure he was safe. They'd just gone about it in the wrong way.

'Want me to wait around in case they come back?' I asked Singh, as he watched the group trudge away through the slush.

He nodded slowly, deep in thought. 'Probably a good idea. I'm off to look at the pavilion, if you want to come with me?'

It seemed a strange request, as I wasn't a police officer, but I knew from the last case that he liked to have someone to bounce his ideas off, and it looked like there was something on his mind.

We walked in silence for a few minutes, following the police tape through the churned-up snow. It was only once the cabins were in sight that I ventured to ask a question.

'What's on your mind?'

'I'm worried about Leon,' he replied.

I nodded. 'Do you think he's alive?'

Singh blew out a long breath. 'I hope so. If Steve's murderer also killed Leon, why haven't we found his body yet? No, I think he's on the run.'

'Do you think he killed his teacher?'

'Either that, or he knows who did it and he's trying to get away from them. Or they took him with them.'

I shivered. Leon was only fifteen, and whatever had happened I was sure he would be terrified.

We passed the cabins and carried on through the park,

until the cricket pavilion came into view. There was blue and white police tape around the building, but Singh lifted it up to allow me to slip underneath, then followed suit.

'What are you looking for?' I asked, allowing him to go first as we approached the door to the pavilion.

'I want to get a feel for the building,' he replied, glancing at the windows before pushing open the door. 'I want to try and work out what Leon could have been doing here, see what it's like inside, find out what he might have seen.' He gave me a brittle smile. 'Until we can work out what actually happened, it might help.'

I nodded. 'Whatever I can do.' I thought it didn't really matter who was there, he just needed a warm body to listen to his thoughts as he voiced them, but then he gave me a smile that made my insides glow. I realised he was genuinely pleased I was there with him, and felt flattered that he'd asked me.

Following him inside, I looked around at the bare wood of the floorboards and the panelled walls. The building was fairly basic, with one long main room, then two changing areas off to the right-hand side. Singh wandered through to check these areas, but I knew he wasn't looking for anything in particular. He'd be letting his brain process his ideas while he looked, then focus his attention on the areas that he felt mattered when he'd had that time to mull things over.

Not wanting to disturb his train of thought, I stayed by the door until he was back in the main room. Plastic chairs and folding tables with chipped veneer surfaces were stacked along the back wall, dust gathering on them. It was hardly the season for cricket, and I doubted this building was hired out for events in the way larger cricket clubs might be used.

'What am I missing?' Singh's voice startled me slightly; I hadn't realised he was standing right next to me.

'Why do you think there's something you're missing?' I asked, turning the question back round on him.

'We know Leon left the cabin at some point during the night or the early hours of the morning, because he wasn't there when the staff and students woke up at seven. We also know that Leon must have been in here, because the door had been opened and the snow outside was disturbed. No one else would have had that opportunity after the snow started other than Steve, and the few footprints we found were several sizes too small to be his. So, we need to know why Leon came here in the first place, and then why he left.'

'Maybe he just wanted a bit of time to himself, then realised it was freezing and this was the nearest place to shelter without going back with his tail between his legs?' I suggested.

Singh nodded slowly. 'That's possible. A fifteen-year-old boy would probably be too proud to go straight back if he was in a sulk about something. But if that was the case, why didn't he stay here?'

I turned to look at the window at the end of the long room, and nodded towards it. Singh and I both approached the window and looked out. From there, we had a clear view of the little clearing in the trees where Sasha Thomas and I had found Steve Wilkinson's body.

'He saw his head teacher being killed,' I murmured, taking a deep breath.

'Possibly,' Singh replied, tapping his fingers on the

windowsill. 'Or did he see Steve outside looking for him, then leave here in order to confront him?'

I couldn't imagine what might drive a teenager to kill one of his teachers, but I didn't contradict Singh. I knew the police had to consider all possible angles.

Singh turned back to the room and began to pace up and down. I ignored him and continued to look out of the window towards the clearing, almost as if the longer I looked, the closer I got to figuring it out. Why was I so desperate to come up with an answer? I realised it was because of Singh. Even though I wasn't a police officer, he trusted me with information about the case, and I wanted him to carry on putting that trust in me. On top of that, there was part of me that wanted to impress him. I felt my face flush slightly as I acknowledged that to myself, a slight churning feeling in the pit of my stomach, and I was glad I was still facing away from him.

I cleared my throat to bring myself back to the moment and shake these thoughts out of my head. Max was the one who had asked me out, the one I'd been enjoying dating for the past eight or nine months, and the last thing I wanted was part of my brain playing the 'grass is greener' game. Turning away from the window, I offered a suggestion.

'Could he have come here *after* Steve's murder?' I asked. 'He saw what happened, then ran and hid in here?'

Singh's eyes lit up. 'Of course, that's definitely an option. We'd assumed he was here before Steve died, but there's nothing to say he didn't arrive after. Though that still leaves the question of where he went next.'

I turned back to the window, but stopped myself mid-movement. Something had caught my attention, a slight glint in the corner of my eye. Bending down, I tried to locate whatever it was I'd just seen. Behind me, Singh watched.

'Here,' I said triumphantly, pointing at the tiny object I'd found. Singh pulled a pair of latex gloves out of his pocket and carefully picked it up, holding it up to the light from the window to see it more clearly.

'What is it?' he asked.

'It's a charm, I think. From a bracelet.'

'It's a letter C.'

We were both silent for a moment.

'C for Courtney, or C for Cassie?' I asked quietly as he continued to look at the charm.

'I don't know,' Singh replied, 'but I think at least one of these kids has been lying to us.'

Chapter 10

The sky was looking heavier when I arrived at the school later that afternoon, and I kicked myself for not putting some essentials in my car like water and blankets. If it snowed again there was the possibility I could get stuck on the way home and I didn't want to freeze to death.

There was a fancy black sports car in one of the reserved spots outside the main entrance. I briefly thought that it took a brave person to drive around in something like that in this weather; it didn't look like it was built for tackling icy roads. It was exactly the sort of car Mike had always talked about wanting when we were together – laughable really, because he earned very little and ate through my savings far quicker than I could replenish them. For a moment I wondered if he'd managed to get some horrendous loan and this was his car, but I shook the thought away. Even if it was, it was none of my concern any more. Still, the idea of him being able to afford something like that when I was desperately trying to keep my old car running bothered me a bit. When I'd thrown him out of my flat and my life, I'd had to accept that his debts were my debts now, and I was still paying them off.

Singh had driven down separately from Normanby Hall, and he and DI Forest joined me in the entrance hall. I was expecting to see a receptionist, but Liz Marcek was waiting for us, and she ushered us into her office.

Is there any news? she asked before we had a chance to sit down.

'Nothing yet,' Singh replied. 'We'll let you know as soon as we find out anything.'

She picked up a piece of paper from the desk behind her.

I've made a list of Leon's friends. Samira Hassan is his best friend, and we've received permission from her family for you to interview her. I should warn you, however, that she can be very flighty and prone to making up stories. She's forever coming out with tales about being left home alone when her parents go abroad, when we know full well she has a brother who is over eighteen who still lives in the family home. He spends more time with her than her parents do, I think.

'Thank you,' Singh said, taking the list from her. 'We'd also like to speak to some of your staff, those who know Leon best.'

Of course, there's his form tutor, Jess Farriday, Liz replied. *Mike of course, and the other residential staff, as they spend so much time with the residential students.*

'We'll need to know which of the staff are hearing and which are deaf,' Singh said, 'then we can make the best use of Paige's time with us.'

Of course. Jess will need an interpreter, Liz explained, *but Mike is hearing, as you know. If other staff wish to speak to you, maybe we could have a time set aside for when the interpreter is available?*

'That's fine,' Singh replied, 'but before we do anything I'd like to see Courtney and Cassie.'

A frown flickered across Liz Marcek's face. *Can I ask why?*

'There's a piece of evidence we need to show them,' Forest interjected. There was a pause; Liz was clearly hoping the DI would elaborate, but when Forest didn't give her any more information she nodded.

Okay. I'll bring them to you.

Liz set us up in a meeting room, then a few minutes later returned with both of the girls in tow. Cassie looked nervously between the two detectives while Courtney sat down primly on one of the chairs.

What's wrong? Courtney asked.

'We want you both to have a look at something we found at Normanby Hall,' Singh explained, pulling a small plastic evidence bag out of his pocket. I could see the shape of the charm, and wondered if either of the girls would claim it as theirs. Liz had stayed in the room and I could see her craning to see what it was.

Cassie took the bag from Singh and peered at it, then shook her head. *It's not mine.*

Courtney leant over and took it from Cassie's hand. *What is it?*

'It's a charm, from a bracelet. It's the letter C. So you can understand why we wanted to talk to you both.'

It's not mine either, Courtney replied, handing it back to Singh. *Is that it? Can we go now?* She stood, clearly impatient to leave. With nothing further to ask them, the detectives let them go back to class.

'It might not be connected to Steve's murder at all,' Forest pointed out. 'It could have been sitting there for weeks.'

'I thought it was worth checking, though,' Singh replied. 'Courtney was in a hurry to leave, so I'm not sure I believe her.'

When the two girls had been looking at the charm, I was sure that Cassie had looked at Liz before she replied. Maybe she had just been looking for reassurance, but there had been something in that glance that made me suspicious. I kept my thoughts to myself for now, though.

'We'll bear it in mind,' Forest said, then turned towards the door as it opened and Liz Marcek led in a curvy Asian girl. Samira Hassan looked older than fifteen, but that might just have been the attitude radiating from her the moment she saw the detectives. A man, presumably her brother, stood behind her, in a suit and bright white trainers.

'Is this going to take long?'

'We'll be as quick as we can, Mr Hassan, but it's important we speak to Samira.'

Why do I have to talk to you? I haven't done anything wrong. Samira folded her arms after signing this statement, and glared at Singh.

'Samira, thank you for coming to speak to us,' Singh replied, unfazed by the attitude. 'We don't think you've done anything, but you're the person who can tell us the most about Leon. Would you like to sit down?'

Did they send you because you're Asian too? They thought I'd be a good little Muslim girl and respect my male superiors? Samira replied, still standing.

Singh laughed. 'Well, I'm half Indian, half White Scottish.

My dad is a Sikh and my mum has no interest in religion, so I don't think that strategy would really work.'

The corner of Samira's mouth twitched but she fought off the smile and gave a big theatrical sigh instead. Throwing herself onto a chair, she shuffled her skirt down from where it had ridden up. Her brother sat down next to her and pulled out his phone, but then hurriedly put it away again when it earned him a frown from both the detectives.

Okay, what do you want to know? she asked, doing her best to look bored.

'Firstly, we really need to know if Leon has been in touch with you since Saturday.'

She shook her head. *Nope, not heard from him.*

I could see Singh watching her face carefully as she signed – even though he couldn't understand BSL, he could still observe her body language and facial expression for indications that she could be lying or hiding something.

'Has he ever talked to you about being unhappy at school?'

Everyone's unhappy at school, Samira replied, with an over-the-top roll of her eyes. *Why would anyone want to be here when they could be chilling out and doing whatever they want? But he wasn't depressed or anything, he put up with it same as everyone else.*

'Can you think of anywhere that's particularly special to Leon, where he might go if he was worried or scared?'

Samira appeared to think for a moment. *I don't think so. I mean, he lives at school. Where else has he got?*

Forest nodded, while Singh made notes.

'What about anything in Leon's personal life that might have affected his mood?'

Samira looked wary. *What sort of thing?*

'Anything that happened recently that could have upset

him, or made him behave out of character? Anything he might have been worried about?'

The girl inspected her nails for a moment, which were coated in a sparkly turquoise gel polish. I imagined she was breaking school rules by having them done like that, but I also suspected she didn't care.

There might have been something, she began, then shook her head.

'Samira, tell them,' her brother said, speaking and signing at the same time. 'Even if it's small, you need to tell them.' I got the feeling he was saying this to make her hurry up, rather than to emphasise the importance of her being open and honest.

Samira rolled her eyes again, but sat up a little straighter in her chair. *He was worried about how he felt about other people, if you see what I mean.*

The detectives both frowned, but I had interpreted her words as clearly as I could – she was trying to skirt around the issue, rather than her meaning being lost in translation.

I mean, like, who he liked. Like, boys, not girls.

'Leon's gay?' Singh asked.

Well, maybe, Samira said, tilting her head from side to side to show indecision. *That's the point. It's not as simple as straight or gay. I don't think he really knows. But he thought he might be, and he said he didn't really fancy anyone in particular, but he thought about boys rather than girls.*

'Had he talked to anyone else about this?'

Samira shrugged. *I didn't think so*, she signed. *Leon's my best friend, he tells me everything, but he holds himself back with other people so I don't think he'd come out to anyone else. This was a big thing for him, and he was only really starting to talk to me about it.*

'Could someone have found out, maybe bullied him?' Forest asked.

No, I'm sure he would have told me about that.

At that moment, Singh's mobile phone began to ring and he winced.

'Sorry about this,' he said, pulling it out of his pocket and checking the display. When he saw who was calling, he frowned and stood up. 'I need to take this, I'm sorry.' He walked out of the room and left Forest and me with Samira and her brother.

'Are we done, like?' he asked.

'Not just yet,' the DI replied, her voice icy. 'We have a couple of other questions.'

'It's just, I need to get to work, don't I?'

'I understand that,' Forest said, and I could see she was getting annoyed with his impatience. 'But it's very important we talk to Samira. A boy is missing, and he could be in danger.'

She turned back to the girl. 'Samira, are you worried about Leon?'

The question seemed to take Samira by surprise, because she hesitated before answering.

Of course I'm worried, because I don't know where he is. This isn't the sort of thing he'd do, just walk out and leave without saying anything. But I think he can look after himself.

The door opened and Singh walked back in, his phone still in his hand. He shot Forest a serious look, then sat down and immediately turned to Samira with more questions.

97

'Samira, did Leon ever mention anything to you about meeting someone this weekend? Anyone new?'

What do you mean? she asked, looking warily towards her brother.

'Did he tell you he was going to meet anyone while he was away on the trip?'

She shook her head, confusion the only emotion I could read on her face. I wondered what the phone call had been about, to make Singh change tack like that.

'Was he having any problems at school that he didn't want to talk to the teachers about?'

No, nothing like that. He actually likes school. Likes it more than I do, anyway, she added with another eye roll. It seemed like she was trying to keep up her attitude in order to mask real concern about her friend.

Singh rubbed a hand over his chin and looked thoughtful for a moment, then nodded at Samira and her brother.

'Thank you very much for talking to us, but I think that's all for now. We might want to speak to you again, if we find anything else out about Leon,' he told Samira. 'I'll leave you my mobile number, okay? And if there's anything you haven't told us, or anything you remember, you can text me.'

He handed over a slip of card with his phone number on, and Samira took it with a nod.

When they'd left the room, he turned to Forest. 'We've been able to access some of Leon's messages. It's possible he was talking to someone, arranging to meet them, but most of the messages have been sent through an app that's encrypted. They're working on it.'

'Meeting someone? So that could be where he was going on Saturday?' Forest suggested.

'Your guess is as good as mine,' Singh replied. He looked at me. 'We still need to speak to Mike Lowther. We didn't get a chance before Samira and her brother arrived. Are you okay waiting around for a bit, while we interview the hearing staff?'

I nodded. 'Sure. I'll find something to occupy myself.'

Leaving the room, I walked back to the entrance hall, turned a corner and stumbled headfirst into Mike.

'Paige! Hi. Where are you going?' His tone of voice was light, but I saw his eyes narrow slightly as he asked the question.

'Er, I don't know. I mean, I'm going for a walk. They don't need me for your interview. Obviously.' After his phone call the other night I'd found myself wondering if I should actually talk to him and let him have his say. Whatever happened, he was right: our relationship had ended very abruptly and neither of us had got a chance to express exactly how we felt about it.

'Everyone is really worked up about this, Leon being missing and Steve being murdered,' he said, shaking his head as if he still couldn't believe it. 'Do you know any more?'

'You'll have to ask the detectives about that,' I said. I knew I shouldn't be surprised at him trying to use me to get information, but I was still irritated. 'Shouldn't you be going there now?'

'Yeah, you're right. Sorry. I just wanted to stop and talk to you. It's really good seeing you again, you know. You look really good.' He reached out to touch my arm but I flinched before he could make contact and he dropped it again. 'I suppose I deserve that.' Giving me a sad smile, he walked past me towards the meeting room.

I went towards the front door, but I could see that it

was still snowing lightly outside. It brought me back to reality, and I spent the next ten minutes pacing up and down in the entrance hall, reminding myself why I shouldn't let Mike back into my life. Though that didn't mean I couldn't call a truce with him, did it?

I hadn't told Anna about Mike's phone call, or about his sudden desire to apologise. I knew exactly what she'd say if I asked for her opinion. She didn't understand the subtleties of it – all she knew about my relationship with Mike had been what she'd seen from the outside. She'd never seen the good stuff, and part of me wanted to be able to remember that fondly. Despite what had happened between us, I had some pleasant memories of the early part of our relationship, and I'd felt truly happy for a short time. Maybe by allowing him to say his piece, by accepting his apology, I could move on and enjoy my relationship with Max.

Thinking about Max gave me a pang of guilt. I'd never even told him about Mike. But then, really, when it came down to it, it was none of his or Anna's business. It was between me and Mike, and if I chose to hear him out when I had the opportunity, I was the only one whose opinion mattered.

A bell went, and soon a few students were milling around at the end of the corridor. I reflected on how the uniform had changed since Anna was here; the girls were mostly wearing trousers, which was unheard of fifteen years ago, and there were no ties any more. Anna had always complained about having to wear a tie, so I was sure she'd be glad to hear that the current students didn't have to suffer the same fate.

As I watched, Courtney and Bradley came past, signing furiously to each other, but I didn't watch too closely –

100

when you understand sign language, it's easy to find yourself eavesdropping on people's conversations without even realising it, and I didn't want to intrude on the teenagers' privacy. They passed Samira going in the opposite direction and didn't acknowledge her, but immediately stopped signing until they were past. Samira paused in the middle of the corridor and fished around in her bag for a moment until she found her phone. Frowning at the screen, she held it up as if making a video call, but it appeared the person she was calling didn't answer. After trying another couple of times, she shoved the phone back into her bag and carried on to her next lesson.

I garnered a few curious glances from students on their way past, but mostly they seemed preoccupied with their own thoughts, on edge due to recent events. Within a few minutes, the corridor was empty again, but I found myself curious to see more of the school. To my left was a cloakroom, and at the end of the corridor I could see the school hall. To my right, classrooms and what looked like the library. Wondering if I was even allowed to be down here, I set off towards the classrooms.

These appeared to be for the secondary students, and I passed an English room and one for the humanities. At the end was an open door, and I poked my head round it out of curiosity, only to be met by the sight of five students looking back at me over the tops of their PC monitors, including Bradley and Courtney.

'Can I help you?' I jumped at the voice, and stepped back again as Saul Achembe came into view around a computer. He was smiling at me, but I apologised anyway.

'Ah, don't worry, it's fine. This lot are working on personal projects, come in.'

I followed him into the classroom and perched where he indicated, on a stool next to his desk.

'Having a break? Or doing some snooping for the cops?' He asked the second question in a cheesy American accent and made me laugh.

'No, they don't need me at the moment, so I thought I'd have a wander. My sister came to this school, but I never really got to see it properly myself.'

'You have a deaf sister?'

'Whole family,' I replied. 'I'm the odd one out.'

'My big brother is deaf,' Saul told me. 'My parents learnt to sign when he was a baby, so when I was born three years later we all used it at home. He has hearing aids and he learnt to speak pretty well, so our parents gradually stopped the signing, but Isaac and I kept it up. We had a secret language that nobody else knew, it was amazing.' He grinned at me. 'I think it was only natural that I'd end up teaching deaf students.'

'Do you just teach IT?' I asked. 'Or do you have another subject as well?'

'No, just IT, but I also manage the network, handle all the hardware and software, and so on. When I'm not teaching, I'm checking the tablets are updated, or sorting out the projector for an interactive whiteboard, or more often than not resetting a password when someone's forgotten it.'

'Sounds busy.'

'I can't complain, really. I enjoy it. The only problem is the lack of money for new equipment, so I have to make sure we keep everything in good working order.'

As Saul and I chatted, I watched some of the students interacting. The three students I didn't know were all sitting together, with Bradley and Courtney next to each other on the opposite side of the room. Whenever I looked up, they were signing to each other under the table, but as soon as they saw me looking in their direction they stopped. Under the desk, I could see Courtney's foot hooked around Bradley's ankle.

'It's a bad business, this with Leon and Steve,' Saul muttered. 'I'm worried about how the kids are taking it.'

I was about to ask another question when the door opened and Liz Marcek walked in. All the students sat up a little straighter, but she was more interested in my presence.

Paige. Is there something wrong? Her lips were pursed in irritation, presumably that I'd been wandering around the school without her knowledge.

No, I was just talking to Saul about the school, I replied.

The police don't need her at the moment, so I said she could observe my class, get to know the school a bit better, Saul chipped in, and I flashed him a quick smile.

Well, if you're interested in a tour, I'm happy to oblige, Liz replied, holding open the door and giving me a wide smile that didn't quite reach her eyes. Recognising that I'd been dismissed, I walked out into the corridor and she followed me.

This was your sister's school, I believe. Have you never looked round?

No, I'd only been in the main hall before this week, I replied, wondering who had told her about Anna.

Then follow me. She marched off, her back ramrod straight and her nose in the air.

We spent the next twenty minutes looking around the school, from the nursery, which took hearing children from the local area as well as deaf children, right up to the secondary. I was given the spiel about their new science lab, as well as shown all of the assistive technology they had for the students.

All the students wear radio aids as well as their hearing aids or cochlear implants. This allows them to hear the teacher more clearly. All our students use BSL, but some of them also use spoken English, so the teachers use both.

Is it usually Sign-Supported English? I asked, referring to when someone would sign and speak at the same time, using BSL signs but in English word order. Liz looked mildly impressed that I knew what I was talking about, and I wanted to give her a gentle reminder that I'd spent my life in the Deaf community and my adulthood working with deaf clients.

That depends on the class. If a teacher has two students who prefer BSL, that's what they'll use. If the class prefers a mixture of communication modes, it's spoken English and SSE. All our teachers are highly experienced and use their own judgement.

We found ourselves walking down towards the hall as the bell went for lunchtime. Flashing lights were set up in each classroom and along the corridor to alert students to the change in lessons. Teenagers started to hurry past us to the hall, which was set up as a canteen. We stood back against the wall to let them past.

I need to supervise students at lunchtime, Liz told me, nodding at the corridor that led back to the meeting room and the entrance hall. *Can you find your own way back?*

I told her I could, then watched her stride down the corridor, stopping to tell a student off for not wearing his uniform correctly. After a few minutes, I followed her.

Having been to the local state school myself, it felt strange to be in such a small group of students. All twenty-three students could have lunch at the same time and they'd barely fill three of the tables that crowded the dining hall in my old school. I hovered in the doorway to the hall, watching Liz Marcek keeping the line in order. She chatted to every student as she stood there, asking some how their mornings had been, encouraging others to take a piece of fruit with their lunch. That was surely the value in having an environment like this, where the staff could get to know every single pupil and make them feel like an important part of the school community.

Glancing over to the other side of the room, I saw Cassie, Courtney and Bradley sitting at a table together. Kian joined them a moment later. Another boy tried to follow Kian, but the four residential students stared at him until he backed off and chose a seat elsewhere. A shiver ran down my spine at the way they coordinated their response to a perceived intruder into their little pack.

As I watched, Kian turned to Bradley.

Do you really think he did it?

Bradley shrugged. *I don't know.*

Shouldn't we have told the police?

No. Stop going on about it.

We need to try and get in touch with Joe, ask him what happened, Kian insisted, his eyes wide.

Why? We can't trust him. We can't trust anyone.

Courtney looked up and saw me watching, nudged Bradley and nodded in my direction. The four students turned to look at me, and I backed away. What had they been talking about? Who was Joe? And what were the four of them hiding?

Chapter 11

Who had the kids been talking about? Was this Joe involved in Steve's murder? I'd found myself getting distracted during the two interviews after lunch, wondering what the five of them were hiding. In the end, I didn't tell Singh about it, because really, what was there to tell? A group of students were talking about someone else. It wasn't evidence, and that was the only thing DI Forest would be interested in.

Before we left for the day, Singh turned to me and spoke quietly.

'I'll drop the DI back at the station, then do you want to meet for a coffee?'

My heart had a little flutter of excitement and I agreed, wondering why he didn't want Forest to hear his invitation. He named a coffee shop we'd been to before, then got in the car and left.

Approaching my car, I paused. The snow had stopped, leaving a smooth blanket around the other vehicles in the car park. Next to my car, however, there was a trail of footprints, leading from the path to the driver's door, then around to the passenger side. A shiver ran down my spine and I looked around me, suddenly feeling as if I were being watched. Was it the same person who'd been peering in my car earlier? All the windows that overlooked the car park were empty, however.

Before I got in, I checked the back seat and the boot, as well as my tyres, but there was nothing to indicate why someone had been looking at my car. I hadn't imagined it yesterday, and today it was even clearer. As I pulled out of the gates I checked around me again, just in case someone was watching me leave, but there was no one.

My drive home was dull but easy, a straight run up the A15, freshly gritted and clear of snow, so I could let my mind wander a bit. I wondered how the search party was getting on at Normanby Hall. Surely Leon would be a long way away from there by now? If he left the grounds with a purpose and hadn't been found yet, either it was because he'd been successful and made his way away from there without being recognised, or else something far more sinister had happened to him.

A forty-five-minute drive later I drove up Ashby High Street in Scunthorpe, looking for a parking space. In the end I turned down a side street and parked on the road, then walked back to the cafe Singh had chosen. I was the first to arrive, and I chose a table in the window. Only two other tables were occupied, one by a couple of young mums with pushchairs and another by an elderly man who had three different newspapers on the table in front of him.

I ordered two coffees and a scone, as I hadn't had the chance to have any lunch. Not knowing what Singh might want to eat, I figured I'd let him order his own. As I sat back at the window, I saw him standing outside with his phone to his ear, his other hand in his pocket and a look of concentration on his face.

A few minutes later, he pushed open the door to the cafe and sat down opposite me.

'What was that about?'

'The tech team have been going through Leon's school account. It looks like he'd been accessing a lot of chat rooms and a couple of dating sites after hours.'

'How could he get onto those on the school system?' I asked. I thought schools were supposed to have safety settings to prevent students accessing inappropriate material.

'That's one of the things I asked them. Apparently they can't figure that out without access to the system itself, so I've left a message for Saul Achembe to get back to me. Hopefully he can work that out. The other relevant thing, however, is that there are some messages that Leon saved. They're very flirtatious, and there are a couple of mentions of meeting up, but then nothing more after that. The techs say they're all from one account, but they think it's most likely that some have been deleted.'

'Who were they from?' I asked quietly, conscious that there were other people who could quite easily overhear us if they tried.

Singh glanced over his shoulder. 'They don't know. There's just a screen name. They tracked it back to a website, and the profile is claiming to be a sixteen-year-old boy, but that doesn't necessarily mean anything.'

'Is that why you asked Samira about Leon meeting someone?'

Singh nodded and took a big gulp of his coffee.

I shook my head slowly. 'You think this person might have persuaded him to run away?'

'That's a big leap right now, but it's certainly something we'll look into.'

We sat in silence for a moment, while Singh looked enviously at my scone. He went to order his own, and I waited until he had sat down and was settled before continuing.

'What about his social media?'

'Without his phone we can't track every network he was using. We know he was on Facebook and Snapchat, and we're trying to get access to his messages and WhatsApp.'

'Have you tried some of the video-based networks? OoVoo was a popular one with a lot of deaf people, but it shut down last year. There'll be others, though. Can you get his call records? He might be more likely to video chat with people rather than text them, depending on the situation.'

'We'll get all of that checked, thanks.'

Finally taking a swig of his coffee, Singh sat back and rubbed his face. 'I had really hoped for a slightly less complicated case for my first one as DS.'

I nodded sympathetically, but I couldn't help wondering why he'd asked me here for coffee, so I put the question to him.

'Why are we here, Rav? I know it's not just so you can tell me about what Leon's been doing online.'

He sighed. 'I wanted to ask you about Mike Lowther, and I got the feeling it wasn't something you'd want to talk about while we were still at the school.'

I felt like someone had poured a bucket of ice water over my head. Looking down at my lap, I examined my hands for a moment, before forcing a smile. 'Of course. What do you want to know?'

Singh spread his hands. 'Well, how do you know him? What's the source of this animosity I can sense between you?'

'Did you ask him?' I asked, looking down at my drink, scared of the answer.

'What? Of course not. It wasn't appropriate.'

I let out a sigh of relief. If I was going to have this conversation with Singh, I wanted to be the one to get my side in first, just to make sure he believed me. But I didn't really want to go into detail.

'He's my ex,' I replied. 'We were together for about five years, and we split up three years ago.'

Singh waited for me to continue but I resisted. 'I assume it wasn't a particularly amicable break-up?' he asked eventually.

I smiled ruefully. 'Not exactly. In fact, the whole relationship was pretty awful, to be honest. But it's all water under the bridge. I just wasn't expecting to see him on Saturday, and it wasn't a nice surprise.'

He gave me a long look, before his gaze dropped to my left arm, where I'd pulled my sleeve up in the warmth of the cafe. A jagged scar ran from the back of my wrist to my elbow.

'I've only seen your scar once before, when you were in hospital,' he said, too bloody clever for his own good. He wasn't changing the subject, he knew that. He was trying to tease information out of me like he would a witness, and I wasn't going to put up with that.

I folded my arms. 'I haven't seen you since February. I've always been wearing long sleeves.'

We sat like that for a moment, before he shrugged and

admitted defeat. 'Paige, you know if there's ever anything you want to talk to me about, anything you want to report, I'll be here for you.' He reached out to touch my arm protectively, but then seemed to think better of it and pulled away, looking embarrassed.

My face softened. 'I know that, thank you.'

'Okay.'

I looked at my watch. 'I'd better get going.' I needed to leave before I found myself getting too emotional.

He nodded, and stared into his coffee, brooding, as I put my coat on and left. Once I was outside I glanced at him through the window and he gave me a small smile before pulling out his phone.

Before I went home, however, I turned off towards Brigg, a small town near Scunthorpe, and, more importantly, where Max lived. I hadn't seen very much of him in the last couple of weeks, and it was about time I remedied that. My confusion over my feelings for Singh and the sudden appearance of Mike back into my life made me realise that I needed to look at what was right in front of me.

I pulled up outside his flat at the same time he did, and we met at the front door. When he pulled away from our kiss, he raised an eyebrow at me, his blue eyes glinting with mischief.

I don't know what I did, but it must have been good.

I grinned at him, flooded with warmth by the way he looked at me. *I just wanted to see you.*

Good, he replied, and I followed him into the flat.

How was your day? I asked him as he busied himself with the kettle.

He shrugged. *Same old, same old. Too much work, not enough people to do it. Yours?*

Busy, I replied, with a matching shrug. *Lots of people to interview in a school for the deaf.*

I hope you're being careful, he told me with a stern look. *Not like last time.*

Max and I had met when Lexi was killed. He knew full well how deeply I'd involved myself in that investigation, and he'd seen first-hand the level of danger I'd put myself in.

I promise, I signed, drawing a cross over my heart. *Still, it's a nasty situation. I hope they find the boy soon.*

There aren't too many places a teenager can hide in this sort of weather. Max nodded towards the window, through which I could see it had started to snow again. *If he's out there on his own, he'll be found soon.*

But what if he's not? What if someone has him? I asked.

Max frowned. *I don't know. I'm sorry.* He squeezed my shoulder. *I'm sure he'll be okay.*

Let's talk about something else, I told him. *I need something to take my mind off it, if I can't be doing anything useful.*

I stayed at Max's flat for a couple of hours, and by the time I left I felt more relaxed than I had in days. He was such easy company, and it always felt like he knew just what I needed him to say. I didn't know what the future held for the two of us – I was still wary about long-term commitment, given how my relationship with Mike had turned out – but the present was enjoyable and uncomplicated.

When I arrived home, I found Anna sitting in the living room watching a TV programme about bailiffs.

Want to go out and get something to eat? I asked her.

I'm watching this, she replied, nodding to the TV. I watched it for a moment, then stood between her and the screen.

No, you're not. Whatever that is, it's about as entertaining as a poke in the eye.

This brought a slight smile, and she looked down at the old T-shirt she was wearing. *I'll get changed.*

Ten minutes later, we wrapped ourselves up in coats and scarves and walked up the road into the village. Technically, we lived in a small town, but it was so small everyone who lived there referred to it as a village. We had a post office, a Co-op, a couple of pubs, a chippy and an excellent chocolatier, as well as an Indian restaurant, which was where Anna and I were headed. We didn't chat as we walked, which was unusual for Anna, but I realised that there were some things that were fast becoming the new normal, since her accident.

Any news about the missing boy? she asked me once we were seated.

I shook my head. *Nothing that I've been told. Hopefully he's safe somewhere, and just ran away.*

Anna gave a deep sigh. I waited expectantly for her to sign something but she carried on reading her menu, even though she always ordered the same thing. I had expected her to dig for details, especially seeing as I'd been at her old school, but she seemed disinterested, or perhaps preoccupied.

I saw the news about the head teacher, she told me. *I can't believe you didn't tell me yesterday.*

I shrugged apologetically. *You know the rules. It hadn't been released to the media, so I couldn't tell you.*

Has anyone told the police why Ms Villiers left? she asked, her eyes narrowing.

I frowned. *Who's that?*

The previous head, she was still at the school when I was a student.

No, why? Well, they were told she retired.

Anna shook her head, a smug smile spreading across her face when she realised she knew something I didn't.

What was it then? I asked, impatient for her to tell me and stop playing games.

Her smile dropped. *I can't remember exactly. There was some sort of scandal, I know that, but it was hushed up pretty well. All I know is that there were rumours flying around that Jane Villiers had been forced to leave by the governors, because of something she did.*

Can you find out what it was?

Anna chewed a mouthful thoughtfully before replying. *I think I know someone who might be able to tell me.*

I didn't push it any further, even though I wanted her to get her phone out and contact that person straight away. If something had happened at the school to force the previous head out, did that have any connection to the murder of her successor? And why had nobody at the school told the police about it?

Thirteen hours before the murder

You need to be careful, that's all we're saying. Don't do anything stupid, Bradley told Leon, but Leon wasn't interested. The boys were sitting in the room that was theirs for two nights, and Bradley had decided to confront Leon about his plans.

How the hell do you even know about it? he asked, anger bubbling up inside him.

Bradley looked at Kian, who hid his face behind the magazine he was holding.

Cassie told him, Bradley said, indicating his brother.

Shit. That little cow's been reading my texts. Leon was tempted to go and have it out with her, but Bradley held him back.

Don't. You know she's not worth getting into shit over.

Leon struggled against Bradley for a minute, then shoved him away and sank down onto his bed with his head in his hands. What if one of them told the teachers? That was the last thing he needed. It had taken him so much courage to get to this stage, he didn't want anything messing it up.

The door swung open and Cassie and Courtney wandered in. Courtney sat down on Bradley's bed, snuggling her body up against his, but Cassie stood awkwardly in the middle of the room.

You've been reading my messages, Leon said, standing and facing her.

No, I haven't.

Bollocks. How else would you know about . . . He broke off as the door swung open again. Mike stood there, his eyebrows raised when he realised all five of them were in the room.

Come on you lot, you know the rules. Girls in one room, boys in another. If you want to spend time together you do it in the communal room, not your bedrooms.

But what if one of us is gay? Cassie asked. The other four all glared at her, but she looked back with wide, innocent eyes. *What? It doesn't make sense if someone's gay.*

Mike sighed and held the door open, ushering all five of them out. Before leaving the room, Bradley grabbed Leon's arm and held him back for a moment.

Look, I know we haven't exactly been best mates, but I don't want anything to happen to you. You need to be careful.

Whatever, Leon replied, shrugging Bradley off. He didn't need advice from someone like him, especially after the things Bradley had got up to at school.

Chapter 12

Tuesday 27th November

There's something I need to tell you.

Sasha Thomas looked a little drawn, and I wondered if she'd been sleeping poorly since Leon disappeared. It had been over seventy-two hours, and the longer he was missing, the worse his chances of being found safe.

I didn't think it was relevant, which is why I didn't tell you yesterday, she began. *But last night I realised that I don't know what's relevant, and just because I don't see any significance in it doesn't mean it won't be important.*

'That's true,' Singh replied, encouraging her to continue.

She sighed. *Leon and Bradley fell out, a couple of weeks ago. It was pretty stressful for all of the residential kids in the days following.*

'Can you tell us what happened?'

I don't know exactly what happened. They were never best friends, but they always used to get on fine, until suddenly they couldn't stand the sight of each other. Bradley would scowl and leave the room whenever Leon walked in. It culminated in a fight.

One evening, a couple of weeks ago, Bradley just launched into Leon. He likes to come across as a tough kid, Bradley I mean, but it's all an act. Something like that was totally out of character. Leon's the one who's been known to get violent, but Bradley definitely started it.

Forest leant forward slightly, frowning. 'Other than defending himself against his father, this is the first we've heard about Leon being violent.'

He was in the past, but not any more, Sasha said hurriedly, clearly not wanting to portray Leon in a bad light. *After everything that happened with his dad, he found it hard to deal with his emotions. He would lash out, but we've done a lot of work over the last three years and he's like a different boy. I would have told you straight away if I'd thought Leon could have gone back to his old ways.*

'Did you find out what the fight was about?'

Sasha sighed. *They wouldn't talk about it. Once Mike got them separated he had a word with them both, but he said neither of them would say why they were fighting. But I have a feeling it had something to do with the fact that Leon is gay.*

'And you think Bradley had a problem with Leon's sexuality?' Singh asked.

I don't know for certain, but it was around the same time that Leon told me he was gay. It's possible he'd come out to his friends at the same time.

'And Mike Lowther spoke to both of the boys after the incident?'

Sasha nodded.

'We'll see if he remembers anything else about it and can tell us what he knows,' Singh said, making another note. 'You said this was about two weeks ago?'

Something like that, Sasha replied. *The issues between them rumbled on for a couple of weeks beforehand, then the fight was maybe ten days ago.*

'Did these problems continue?'

Things were a lot better in the couple of days before the trip, she explained, an earnest look on her face. *They weren't suddenly friends again, but they were at least being civil to each other, and sitting in the same room together. The other night, Leon and Kian were playing on the Xbox together, and I thought Bradley was going to start on Leon, but he just sat down and watched them. That was progress*, she added.

'And there was nothing that happened on Friday at the cabin, no reprise of the issues, no more fights?' Forest asked.

Sasha shook her head again. *No, they were getting on pretty well. The two of them were sharing a room, along with Kian, and they both seemed fine with the arrangement, so I assumed Bradley had got over whatever was bothering him.*

Forest cocked her head on one side, looking thoughtful. 'How has Bradley been behaving since Leon went missing?'

Sasha frowned. *What do you mean?*

The DI paused for a moment before elaborating. 'Does he seem to be worried about Leon? Upset at all?'

Sasha's frown deepened. *I know what you're suggesting. You think Bradley had something to do with Leon disappearing. I honestly can't see it.*

'We're not making assumptions at the moment,' Singh said smoothly. 'We need to know everything that might possibly be relevant, then we can decide what's important and what isn't.'

119

Well, Bradley has definitely seemed worried. He's been asking about what's happening, if Leon's been found yet. The look on her face suggested she wasn't convinced by Singh's reasoning.

I wondered if we'd be speaking to Bradley again today, given what Sasha had told us. If there was some stuff going on in Leon's personal life that upset him, that could have been the catalyst that led to him running away. And just because none of the adults who had been on the trip had witnessed another fight, it didn't mean it hadn't happened. Leon, Bradley and Kian were sharing a room, with no supervision overnight, so nobody really knew what had gone on in that room after everyone went to bed. The more people we spoke to, the more obvious it was that the police were wading into a minefield of conflicting information. I had no idea how they were going to figure out which details were important and which were irrelevant.

'Has Leon ever talked to you about any concerns he's had in school?' Singh asked.

Never, she replied, shaking her head emphatically. *He felt safe here, I'm sure of it.*

'What about any people he was close to outside school?'

No, I would have told you. He didn't have any family other than his parents. His mum is dead and there is no way he'd want to visit his dad.

'Can you tell us more about Leon's dad?' Forest asked, changing tack.

He's a violent man. That's why Leon's mum left him, but she never reported anything so social services weren't aware of his unsuitability as a parent. She looked down at her feet for a moment before continuing. *I feel partly responsible for what happened to him. I was one of the people who allowed Leon to go into his dad's custody. We weren't to know what he was like, without so much as a complaint filed against him.*

Leon hasn't told me all of it, but he said it started off small. The occasional cuff around the ear for not picking up after himself, or spending too long on the computer. But it escalated as time went on. His dad couldn't sign very well, and Leon's understanding of speech is limited, so the communication barrier caused a lot of problems. He didn't always know what his dad expected of him, which obviously caused frustration on both sides. By the time everything came to a head, I think Leon was being beaten on a regular basis.

Sasha's eyes filled with tears. *He hid it from everyone at school, because his dad told him he deserved it, that having to take care of Leon was the reason his mum became ill and died. I still wonder how none of us picked up on it. We thought the changes in his behaviour and attitude were because of grief, and he was at a transition point in his education as well. It got worse in the holidays, and that's when Leon snapped. His dad had cornered him in his bedroom, but he always carried a pocket knife and Leon managed to get hold of it. He gave his dad a nasty gash on the arm, then ran next door for help. The neighbour called the police and an ambulance.*

Forest and Singh both sat back when Sasha mentioned the knife and a chill ran through me. Hadn't Forest said that a penknife was found near Steve's body, and they presumed it was the murder weapon? Did this mean Leon could actually have killed his teacher?

After a moment, Singh asked another question.

121

'Was his father badly hurt?'

Not at all, Sasha said, her face suggesting she wished he had been. *It was only superficial. But Leon broke down when he spoke to the police, told them about the abuse, and the doctor's examination showed he'd sustained multiple broken ribs over the course of at least six months, as well as an awful lot of bruising. His father's lawyer tried to suggest that Leon had stolen the pocket knife earlier on in the week, making it a premeditated attack, but there was no evidence against Leon.*

The detectives and I sat in silence for a moment. I couldn't imagine what Leon had been through, losing his mum only to be handed over to a monster.

'Thank you, Sasha,' Forest said eventually. 'Is there anything else you can tell us about Leon and the state of mind he might be in at the moment?'

No, I'm sorry. Except, he had become a little more secretive of late, keeping his phone close to him all the time and never letting anyone go near it. I know you're trying to access his messages, so there might be something on there that can help you.

The DI thanked her again and asked her to fetch Bradley so they could talk to him. As Sasha left the room, she looked back at me for a split second, then closed the door behind her.

'Bloody hell,' Forest exploded, slamming her chair against the wall. 'How did we miss that? Surely someone should have looked into Leon's background and shown us that he attacked his dad with exactly the same weapon his head teacher was murdered with?'

Singh was as baffled as she was, and I turned away from them to look out of the window while they discussed what to do next. The sky was dark and soft white flakes were floating past the window with alarming frequency.

'It's snowing again,' I pointed out to the detectives. 'We'll need to keep an eye on it, so we don't get stuck.'

Forest frowned at my interruption, then turned to watch for a moment before replying. 'It's only light. Hopefully it'll stay that way.'

Her phone rang, and Singh and I waited as she had a brief conversation with whoever was on the other end.

'Finally, we're getting somewhere,' she said once she'd hung up, her eyes glinting with something that looked like triumph. 'They collected a number of blood samples from the snow at the scene. Most of it was Steve Wilkinson's, but there was another person's blood too, and they've identified the DNA. It's Leon's.'

Chapter 13

There was a delay before we could continue with the interviews, while Forest called the lab back to double check their results and ask for more information.

'Right, it seems they found Leon's blood on the penknife that was used to kill Steve Wilkinson. So, he was definitely there at the crime scene, and is now our main suspect.'

'We're assuming Leon killed Steve and cut himself in the process?' Singh asked with a frown.

'That seems the most obvious answer,' Forest replied. 'The knife belonged to Steve. According to Mike Lowther he had used it a couple of times on the Friday night, cutting branches for kindling so he could teach the kids how to build a fire. Lowther thought he was showing off, though that probably says more about his attitude than his boss's. I'm sure if Leon had cut himself with Steve's knife before Saturday morning, we would have heard about it.'

'Mmmm,' Singh replied, looking out of the window with his arms folded.

I turned to Forest. 'But what if Leon had come across someone attacking Steve? There could have been a struggle, and Leon could have been injured then.' I hadn't met the boy, but I still felt an urge to defend him.

Forest looked sceptical, and I thought she was going to snap at me for interfering, but she appeared to be thinking about my suggestion.

'If that happened, and that's a huge if, where is Leon?' she asked.

'The killer took him with them,' Singh replied, and I shot him a quick smile for backing me up.

'But why?' Forest stood up and paced across the room a couple of times. 'If you're going to kill one person, and there's a witness, why kidnap the witness? Why not just kill them too?'

'Because they only intended to kill Steve, and had no interest in killing an innocent child?' Singh suggested, trying hard to keep his frustration from his voice.

Forest shook her head. 'No, if you're willing to kill one person, you've stooped to a level where you'd kill anyone. Kidnapping Leon, if he's a witness, leads them to more problems. How can they ever let him go, if he's seen them?'

Singh's shoulders sagged. 'I don't know. But it's still possible.'

'And where did they put him? If one of the staff, or students, followed Steve Wilkinson out of that cabin and killed him, what did they do with Leon after he was injured?' Forest sat down firmly, crossing her legs and leaning back.

'Maybe they took him to the pavilion?' I offered, but she shook her head.

'There would have been signs of a struggle, and more

of Leon's blood if he was injured,' she replied, brushing off my suggestion.

'I think we should still consider it,' Singh began, but Forest cut him off.

'No, I'm sorry Rav. I know you want to think this boy is innocent, but we have to work on the likelihood that he killed his teacher.'

Neither of them spoke again until Sasha returned with Bradley trailing behind her. I was glad of something to break the heavy tension in the room.

'Hi Bradley,' Singh said, giving the boy a tight smile. 'We'd like to ask you a few more questions about Leon, if that's okay?'

Bradley shrugged and slouched into a seat. *Have you found him yet?*

'No, we haven't, and the longer he's missing the more worried we get. That's why it's really important that you answer our questions as fully as you can. Do you understand?'

Yes, I'm not stupid, he replied, rolling his eyes. I felt like his attitude had become more pronounced since Saturday, and I wondered what had caused the change in him. I gave Sasha a look and I realised she was wondering the same thing.

'We've heard that you and Leon hadn't been getting on well lately. Is that right?'

Bradley shrugged again. *We weren't best mates.*

'We heard it was a bit more serious than that.'

We had one fight, okay? Just one. That's all.

I could see straight through the bravado, and I knew Forest and Singh could too. I had no idea if they'd manage to bring Bradley round, though.

'What was the fight about?' Singh asked.

Don't know. Stupid shit. Doesn't matter now.

'Why doesn't it matter?'

'Because he's fucking missing, isn't he?' Bradley used his voice as he signed, and it broke on the last two words and suddenly tears were streaming down his face. He scrubbed at them angrily with the cuff of his jumper, as if they were to blame for all his problems. Sasha reached out a hand to lay it on Bradley's shoulder but he twitched out of her reach, so she didn't try again.

We sat there for a moment while the boy composed himself, then Singh sat back before asking his next question.

'Are you worried about Leon?'

Of course I'm worried. He's my friend and he's missing.

'A minute ago you told us you weren't really friends.'

Bradley exhaled sharply. *We weren't, for a while. But then we made up. It was okay again.*

'Can you tell us what the problem was?' Singh asked, pushing gently.

Bradley hesitated before replying. *I didn't like some of the shit he was looking at online. Kian was looking at it over his shoulder and started asking questions. It bothered me. But after a while I realised I was being a dick about it.*

'What sort of things was he looking at?'

His cheeks reddened. *Porn. Chat rooms. That sort of stuff.*

'And you didn't want your brother looking at it?'

No, he's too young for that crap. And besides . . . He stopped signing and looked at Sasha.

I'm not here to judge, Sasha said. *I'm just here to make sure the police respect your rights during the interview. Whatever you need to tell them, tell them.*

Bradley grimaced. *It was gay porn. Leon's gay.*

The detectives glanced at each other as Bradley confirmed what both Samira and Sasha had told them.

Wait, you already knew that, didn't you? the boy asked as he noted the lack of surprise on their faces. *Shit. Well now you know, I was the one being a dickhead. I wasn't comfortable with Leon being gay, but eventually Kian was the one who made me see that I was the one in the wrong. So, we made up. I have no idea what happened the other night.*

'Did other people know that Leon's gay?'

Depends if Cassie found out. If she knows, everyone will know. If she doesn't, it might still be a secret from most people.

'Do you think Cassie would have spread gossip about Leon?'

She spreads gossip about everyone, whether it's true or not. He looked up at Sasha. *I'm sorry, but it's true. I can't imagine her keeping something like that to herself. She's . . .* He paused for a moment and pulled a face, as if trying to find the best way to word something. *Cassie isn't very popular, which means she doesn't have much influence. If she was spreading something trying to get people to pile onto Leon, they'd probably be pretty sympathetic instead. This is a small school, and we kind of have to stick together.*

'If Leon was struggling with something, who do you think he would have gone to for support?' Singh asked, changing tack slightly.

Maybe Mr Wilkinson, Bradley replied. *I know he helped him with some of his science work when he was getting really stuck with it. He tutored Leon after school for a couple of weeks, maybe three, until he was really sure of the topics we were on at the time. But then Leon decided he didn't need the help any more and stopped the sessions. I think he gets on well with Miss Farriday too, so maybe he would have talked to her?*

I remembered Liz Marcek telling the detectives about Steve helping Leon with his homework, and I wondered if there was more to it. Why had Leon stopped his sessions? Was it just because he didn't need them any more, or had something else happened?

'Thanks Bradley,' Singh was saying. 'Is there anything else you've thought of that Leon said or did on Friday that might help us?'

The boy shook his head, and the detectives dismissed him.

'So, we still have no idea what might have happened to make Leon leave the cabin that night,' Singh said.

'Being gay makes him more of a target for bullying,' Forest pointed out. 'There could have been something more going on between Bradley and Leon. We only have his word for it that they'd put the animosity behind them.'

'He seemed pretty credible to me,' Singh replied, 'but you're right, it's still a possibility that Bradley or someone else made Leon feel so uncomfortable that he ran away. Though in such a close-knit group of students you would have thought that the staff would have noticed something that serious.'

I had been signing all of this for Sasha, as she was still in the room.

Teenagers can be very secretive, she told them, interrupting. *But Leon has been through a lot in his life and he's a resilient young man. For it to get bad enough for him to run away, I think that level of bullying would have been picked up.*

Forest nodded. 'We won't rule anything out just yet, but we need to be considering other motives as well. Right, we need to find Mike Lowther and speak to him. Paige, you can take a break.'

I followed Sasha out of the room, keen to be away from there when Mike appeared.

Do you want to come to the staffroom and have a coffee? Sasha asked me.

Sure, I replied, having nothing else to do.

We walked back towards the main entrance before turning down a corridor off the entrance hall, opposite the head and deputy head's offices. We passed the admin office, then went through a door on the left into a high-ceilinged room with several groups of low padded chairs.

The room was empty, so I chose a seat and sat down while Sasha made us drinks. I had never been in a school staffroom before. When I was a child, it was the sort of place that was always mysterious and out of bounds. Now that I saw the room, I was disappointed for my seven-year-old self. The walls were painted cream, and peeling in several places. There were a few anti-bullying posters on the wall, as well as some outdated flyers from the local branch of the National Deaf Children's Society. A notice-board on the far wall contained pictures of students with severe allergies or other medical needs, and the other walls were bare. A sheet of A4 was stuck on the back of the door, and on closer inspection it seemed to be a sign-up sheet for the staff Christmas night out.

Sasha brought our drinks over and sat opposite me, and I could tell there was something she wanted to talk about.

130

How long have you worked for the police?

I've been freelance for about a year now, and I circulated my details to the emergency services and hospitals when I stopped doing agency work, but I first worked a proper police investigation in February. I didn't go into the details of what had happened. It had all been too close to home and I'd spent the last few months trying to forget.

Sasha cocked her head on one side. *So, you're not with an agency?*

No.

But you don't work for the police full time either?

I shook my head. *No. I went freelance to try and work short-notice jobs, but it does mean I'm never sure what work is coming from one week to the next.*

I could see she was wondering why I would leave the protection of an agency, and I tried to explain.

When my dad died, my mum and sister were stuck in the hospital without any way of understanding what was happening. The staff tried to get an interpreter, but the earliest they could get someone was in four days' time. Until I arrived at the hospital, they weren't even sure what was happening. A nurse called me and told me my dad had died from a massive heart attack, but when I got there I was the one who had to tell my mum and sister. Nobody had wanted to try and communicate it to them, even by writing it down. Then I had to speak to the doctor and find out what had happened, and interpret it for Mum, while I was coping with the shock and grief myself. A relative shouldn't have to be the one to do that.

Then my mum got cancer, I continued. *I went to all her appointments with her, and I was happy to do it, but*

131

that meant I was the one who had to tell her the treatments weren't working. I had to tell my own mum she was dying. It hurt so much to have to be the one who did that, while still trying to process the idea myself. Does that make sense?

Sasha nodded. *It does.*

How often are you here? I asked, moving the focus of the conversation away from myself. Sasha was a relative stranger and I didn't know why I'd felt the need to share that much personal information.

Normally once a week, she replied, *but while Leon is missing I'm going to try and prioritise the school. The full-time residential kids have all had a rough start in life, for one reason or another, and now they're faced with a missing friend and a murdered teacher. That's a lot to deal with.*

Do you have any theories about Leon?

Sasha's mouth twisted into a grimace and she shook her head. *I'm really worried about him. Things have changed, recently. He's never been the sort of kid who bottles things up, you know? He's always been open with me, happy to discuss how he's feeling, things that are bothering him. I've never known him be afraid of going to an adult for help. But lately he's been quite secretive, and I can't help but wonder if that's related to what happened at the weekend. I'd put it down to normal teenage behaviour, but now I'm really worried that something might have happened to him. Do we even know for certain that he ran away? I know his stuff was missing, but what if there's something more sinister going on?*

I could see the fear on her face was genuine, and I was suddenly glad that someone cared so much for these kids. Living in a children's home must be a difficult way to grow up, especially when it was also your school, so you never had a break from either. For Leon, having been through such a traumatic event with the death of his mum, I imagined it was vitally important for him to know that there were people here who cared deeply about what happened to him. But how well did Sasha really know him?

I wanted to ask her more about her work, but the door opened and DS Singh stuck his head around it.

'Paige, would you mind coming back, please? We've just received some new information.'

Wondering what it could be, I told Sasha what was happening and she nodded. *Nice to chat with you.*

As I left the room I glanced back, to see Sasha watching me with a thoughtful look on her face.

Chapter 14

'This is our BSL interpreter, Paige Northwood,' Singh told the woman sitting in front of us. We hadn't interviewed Jessica Farriday so far, because she hadn't been in school until today. I smiled and interpreted Singh's introduction.

Northwood? she asked. *Are you related to Anna Northwood?*

She's my sister, I replied with a nod.

We went to school together. How sad is that? I trained as a teacher then came back to the same school. She gave a half-hearted laugh, then her eyes filled with tears. Her face was already red and puffy, so I assumed these weren't the first tears of the day. Her black hair was pulled back into a high ponytail, and she wore a dark blue tracksuit with the school's crest on it.

'Thank you for coming to speak to us, Miss Farriday,' Singh said. 'We'd like to ask you a few questions about Steve Wilkinson, if that's okay?'

Jessica nodded, picking at a nail that was already bitten down to the fingertip.

'You seem to be very distressed about his death,' Forest said, and I winced slightly at her harsh tone of voice. What was the new information they'd received?

The PE teacher smiled sadly. *I suppose there's no point in trying to keep it secret now. Steve and I had been seeing each other for a couple of months.*

Ah, I thought. That was what the detectives had found out.

We were keeping it quiet because Steve didn't want any of the other staff to think it was inappropriate, or that he was abusing his position, Jessica continued, swallowing hard. *And some of them would have been bound to accuse him of favouritism. It was easier to hide it. If things had got more serious, maybe it would have been different, but it was still early days.* She pulled a tissue out of her pocket and wiped her nose. *I said goodbye to him on Friday afternoon, just before they went on the trip. That was the last time I saw him. I went home after that, and he said he'd call me on Saturday if he got the chance.*

'Did he say anything to you about any concerns? Anything about the trip?' Forest pushed.

No, nothing. In fact, he told me he was looking forward to it.

'You hadn't made any plans to see him once they were back on Sunday?'

She shook her head. *I'd been to his a couple of times, but I was busy this weekend. It was my future sister-in-law's hen party on Saturday. We were out for most of the day and I stayed over at hers. I didn't hear the news from Liz until Sunday morning.*

DS Singh noted down the other woman's name and address, presumably to check Jessica's alibi.

'What about anyone who might want to harm Steve?' Forest asked. 'Can you think of anything he said that suggested he might have an enemy?'

She shook her head. *Never. I mean . . .* She bit her lip, then her gaze fell on the closed door to the corridor before she looked back at the detectives. *Mike is my ex. He's definitely the jealous type, and if he'd found out about me and Steve, maybe he might have said something to Steve. But I'm certain he didn't know.*

I caught my breath at the mention of Mike, then felt irritated at myself. What did it matter if he'd dated one of his colleagues? Had he treated her as badly as he'd treated me, or had he learnt his lesson?

'Why are you so certain?' Singh asked. I thought I heard a note of scepticism in his voice, but I had a feeling I knew what Jessica's answer would be.

Because he would have kicked off the moment he found out. He's not the sort of person to bide his time and let it stew. Unless Steve had some mad idea to cosy up to Mike in the middle of a trip and tell him about us, there's absolutely no way Mike had anything to do with it.

I knew exactly what she meant, and I could vouch for this side of Mike's personality. He found it hard to keep secrets, and he couldn't often bite his tongue when there was something he wanted to say. He usually reacted to anything that wound him up before he had the chance to think about it. There were times he could control himself, however, and I knew that those times were when he was most dangerous.

'And you're certain he didn't do that?' Forest said, even more sceptical than Singh had been.

Absolutely. He wouldn't have told Mike without consulting me first, and he certainly wouldn't have done it in the middle of a trip, while he was supervising students. Steve would never have been so unprofessional. More tears were running down Jessica's face now, and she looked desperate to defend Steve's reputation. *From what I've been told, they wouldn't have had time to talk about it on Saturday morning, so that only leaves Friday. And when I say Mike wouldn't have been able to keep his anger under control, I mean if he'd found out about it on Friday he would have killed Steve on Friday.*

There was a pause as the weight of this statement settled. 'So, you think Mike is capable of killing someone?' Singh asked softly.

Her eyes widened and she shook her head quickly. *No, no, that's not what I meant. I don't think he could. He's got a temper, but it would never go that far.*

I wanted to agree with her, but then I reminded myself that I'd never thought Mike would go as far as he did when we were together.

'Is he impulsive?'

Yes, but he can control himself.

'Has he ever been violent towards you? Abusive?'

I found myself holding my breath as I waited for her answer.

No, she signed, *but I didn't like his attitude towards me. He could be quite domineering. We were only together for a few months, and that's why I ended it. When I dumped him he smashed up a few tennis racquets in the PE stores, but I think he just needed to take his anger out on something. He broke equipment, turned his anger onto an object. He never lifted a finger to me.*

I let out the breath I'd been holding. That sounded more like the Mike I knew, in some ways. He had plenty of self-control when he wanted to. A small voice in the back of my mind told me Jess Farriday was obviously stronger and smarter than me, she could see the trouble coming a long way off and got out while she could, but I silenced it.

'What can you tell us about Steve's relationship with Leon?' Forest asked, giving Jess a searching look.

What do you mean? They were teacher and student, Jess replied with a shrug.

'We know that Steve tutored Leon in science for a short time. Did he ever talk to you about the boy, about any problems he might have had?'

No, he never mentioned it to me. I hadn't even realised he was doing it. We didn't really talk about work if we could avoid it.

'So you don't know what Steve thought of Leon, or if they'd had any disagreements in the past?' Forest persisted.

I'm sorry, no, Jess replied, more firmly this time.

Despite further questioning, she couldn't tell the detectives anything about what might have happened over the weekend, and they sent her back to her class. I'd been wondering if I should mention what I'd seen the previous day, with the students talking about someone called Joe, but I thought better of it. I wanted to make sure I was doing the right thing first, and that meant looking for Sasha and seeing what she knew before I spoke to Singh.

After reassuring the DI that I had my mobile on me, should they need me back, I walked out of the front door and round the side of the building, heading towards the residence where I expected Sasha would be. The building was locked, but I rang the bell and waited. After a couple of minutes I tried again, but still nobody appeared. The students would be in class, and it was possible that no staff were in there, but I thought I'd have a wander round the building just in case someone was around.

Turning the corner, I looked at the windows, but they were all covered with net curtains; thinking back to when I'd been inside, I realised the rooms on this side were all student bedrooms. Carrying on down the side of the building, I heard footsteps behind me and spun around, but couldn't see anyone. I paused, assuming they were about to come round the corner, but nobody appeared. I felt a creeping sense of dread as I remembered the footprints leading up to my car. Could there be someone trying to get me alone? You're imagining things, I told myself, shaking my head and approaching the large window to one of the communal rooms.

I cupped my hands around my eyes and pressed my face up to the glass to see if anyone was in the residence common room. Once my eyes had adjusted, I realised there were two adults in there, standing close together with their backs to me and signing. I didn't stop to try to see what was being said, but knocked gently on the window. Mike turned round and looked at me, a mixture of surprise and guilt on his face. Sasha followed Mike's gaze and raised a hand in greeting when she saw where he was looking.

Can you let me in? I signed through the glass, and Mike nodded. By the time I walked back round to the front door, he was holding it open for me.

'Sorry,' he said. 'I heard the bell but I thought it was

one of the students. They're not meant to come back here during lesson time.'

'It's okay. I was looking for Sasha, actually.' It felt strange to be talking so civilly to Mike, and I was surprised to find it wasn't as difficult as I would have expected.

'Sure, she's in there,' he said, with a nod towards the common room.

When I walked through, the three of us stood there awkwardly for a moment. Sasha and Mike had obviously been in the middle of a conversation that they didn't want to continue in front of me, but also I didn't really want to involve Mike in my questions about Joe, whoever he was. Sasha must have realised this, because she gave Mike a pointed look and he made his excuses and shuffled off up the stairs with a swift backward glance.

How can I help you? Sasha asked with a taut smile. I noticed the set of her jaw and shoulders looked very tense, and my curiosity was piqued. Had she and Mike been arguing? And if so, what about?

I wanted to ask you if there's a student called Joe? Either current or past.

Joe? Sasha's eyes widened for a moment, before her expression settled into a frown. *Why do you ask?*

Yesterday, the four students who were on the trip were talking about someone called Joe, about whether or not they could trust him, and if he had anything to do with what happened on Saturday. I wondered if it was someone they knew from school.

Sasha seemed to be taking in what I'd told her, before she shook her head slowly. *No, I don't know of a student called Joe. But I haven't been working with the school for as long as someone like Liz, so perhaps you should*

140

ask her. I was just on my way over to see her actually. Why don't you come with me?

She glanced over her shoulder in the direction of the stairs, before guiding me towards the door.

Do you need to finish your conversation with Mike? I asked, picking up on the tension in her body language.

Sasha laughed but there wasn't much amusement in her tone, and I wondered what they'd been discussing. She was probably wondering how long I'd been there when they noticed me, but I hadn't seen what they'd been signing to each other.

No, it's fine, she replied, and as we walked back round to the main building she stayed one step ahead of me, preventing me from asking her anything else. Once we were inside, Sasha walked straight into Liz's office without knocking, which surprised me. I hesitated for a moment before following her in.

The deputy head didn't appear to be busy for once, sitting in the chair behind her desk and staring out of the window. She smiled when she saw Sasha, but the smile became more rigid when she noticed that I was there too.

Paige, Sasha and I have a meeting arranged. I'm afraid it's confidential, discussing students. You understand.

I was about to reply when Sasha got in there before me. *It won't take long. Paige wanted to ask you something about past students*, she told Liz.

Well, not exactly, I signed, wondering if this was a good idea. I didn't want to get the kids into any trouble, and it was probably something completely harmless.

Yes, what is it? Liz asked, doing nothing to hide her impatience.

141

I looked over at Sasha, who was leaning by the window, then looked back to Liz.

I was wondering, are there any students called Joe? Or who might use that as a nickname?

I thought I saw a flicker of recognition in Liz's eyes, but then it was gone and she shook her head. *No, not currently. Why?*

What about past students? Anyone who left in the last couple of years?

No, nobody that I can think of. What is this about?

It's nothing, really, I replied, turning to leave, but Liz stood up and came around her desk to stop me.

Paige, if a representative of the police is asking me questions about my students, I'd appreciate knowing why. Her words were polite, but her face was stony.

I don't work for the police, I'm just the interpreter, I replied. *I saw some of the students chatting about someone called Joe yesterday, and I wondered who he was, that's all.*

Liz looked confused. *What made you assume it was a student? It might not have been anyone they knew at all. Maybe it was a footballer or some other celebrity.*

You're right, I replied with a nod, knowing full well she wasn't but desperately wanting to end the conversation. *I just wondered, that was all.*

I left her office, feeling as if I'd been shoved out of the door.

When I got home that afternoon, Anna was more animated than I'd seen her in a while.

I've asked around a bit, about the school, she told me before I'd even had a chance to take off my shoes. *Nobody knows exactly why Ms Villiers left, but someone told me it was to do with a major safeguarding incident.*

Safeguarding? That's serious. I'm surprised they kept that out of the papers. I was also surprised the police didn't seem to have any knowledge of it. *So, what actually happened?*

Anna pulled a face. *I don't know. I haven't found anyone who knows the details. But I've been thinking.*

I groaned. I got the feeling I wasn't going to like what she told me next.

I managed to get hold of an email address for Jane Villiers, and told her I wanted to catch up.

What did she say? I asked.

She said she's always happy to see ex-pupils, and invited me to meet her tomorrow.

I sighed. *Are you really going to go and grill her about why she left? If it's true and she really was shoved out a year early, she's hardly going to want to talk about it, is she?*

No, *I'm not going to grill her,* Anna replied with a triumphant smile. *You are.*

Twelve hours before the murder

Jess hovered in the entrance hall, wondering if she could get in and out without being seen. She hadn't counted on anyone else being in school this late, so had been irritated to see Liz's car outside in the staff car park. The minibus had gone hours ago; Steve would be safely in Scunthorpe, giving her ample time to do what she needed to do.

The door to Liz's office was open, and Jess could see the deputy head moving about inside. What was she still doing here anyway? Approaching Steve's office, she tried the door as gently as she could, not wanting to attract any attention from Liz in the neighbouring room. Locked. Time for plan B.

Jess opened the door to the admin office, knowing spare keys were kept in there. It took a few minutes of hunting, but she eventually discovered the key for the head teacher's office, still marked with Jane Villiers' name. Slipping it into her pocket, she went back into the entrance hall, noting that Liz's door was now closed. Maybe she'd gone, but Jess knew she still had to be vigilant.

Stepping into Steve's office, she closed the door carefully behind her. It had taken only a couple of attempts to see his password, by coming to see him in his office at lunchtime and after school and constantly hanging off his neck. He was trusting, which was an excellent quality that she valued in the men she dated.

Jess logged on to Steve's computer and started looking through files until she found what she was looking for. A movement from the courtyard outside made her jump, but it was just her reflection in the big bay window. Ignoring it, she went back to work.

She was so engrossed in what she was doing that she didn't notice the door opening until it was too late. Liz Marcek stood over her, and Jess quickly minimised the windows she had open. Had she been fast enough, or had Liz seen what she was up to?

What do you think you're doing? Liz's face was pinched with anger as she glared at Jess, demanding an explanation.

Steve asked me to check something for him, she replied, her mind moving quickly to come up with a plausible explanation.

Really? Liz asked, disbelieving. *And why would he ask you, instead of me?*

Jess laughed, a short, nasty bark. *What use have you ever been to him? You don't even notice what's going on right under your nose. Steve told me you're lucky you kept your job after what happened with Jane.*

Liz's face turned scarlet. *Get out of the head teacher's office. I'll be letting him know what you've been up to.*

Jess tried to close down the computer, but Liz smacked her hand away. She had no choice but to step back, leaving the room with a final glance at the deputy head.

Chapter 15

Wednesday 28th November

A feeling of guilt gnawed away at me as I thought about my day ahead.

Anna and I were visiting Jane Villiers that afternoon, and I hadn't told Singh about it. I knew I should have, but I didn't want to be accused of interfering again. There was a part of me that felt that accusation would be justified; who was I to be digging around into someone else's past? Would it actually help Leon, or was it an unnecessary distraction?

Walking into the main school building, I bumped into Saul, the IT teacher.

'Sorry,' I said, helping him to pick up the heavy textbooks and files I'd knocked out of his hands.

'It's fine, one more inconvenience won't make a difference,' he grumbled.

'Have you been thrown out of your room by the tech team?'

'Yeah. I mean, I could have helped. I know these systems better than anyone. If they let me help I bet they'd be finished quicker.'

I patted his arm sympathetically. 'It's probably a policy they have to follow, just to make sure any evidence they find is recorded properly. Don't take it personally.'

He nodded.

'Where are you taking all these, anyway?'

'Staffroom. I've got assignments to mark.'

'Want a hand?'

'Sure,' he said with a shrug.

I followed him down the corridor to the staffroom, which was empty once again. I assumed when teachers had any free time during the day they spent it at their desks. Max was a teaching assistant and often regaled me with tales of how many hours the teachers at his school worked.

I put the files down next to Saul as he sat, and he looked around the room.

'You know, we asked Steve if we could do up the staffroom, but he told us he couldn't possibly justify using some of the budget for our comfort when he could use it for something for the students instead. I get that funds are always tight, but that man had never heard of the concept of employee wellbeing.'

I cast a critical eye over the sink and the stack of mugs. 'You could do with a cupboard, at least.'

'Exactly, we weren't asking for a sauna and a two-thousand-pound coffee machine. We just wanted to feel comfortable in here. But according to Steve Wilkinson, it wasn't our job to feel comfortable. He'd even talked about taking away the comfy chairs and lining the room with work desks, so this could be "productive space",' he said, his voice dripping with sarcasm on the last two words. 'He expected everyone to be here by seven thirty every morning, even those who have young kids themselves, and he once told one of the primary teachers that if she was leaving at four every day he'd have to work her a bit harder. He made a joke out of it, but you could tell he honestly thought people should spend their every waking hour at work.'

I sank into a chair as Saul ranted on, about how Steve had organised a motivational speaker to come in and spur them on to work harder.

'Essentially, the woman told us that if we were stressed it was our own fault, and we needed to change the way we reacted to situations if we wanted to prevent stress. I'd never heard such a load of bollocks in my entire life, but half of the staff lapped it up. Some of them even printed out some little pithy quotes to stick above their desks, to remind themselves that stress is a choice, or some other nonsense. That was the thing about Steve. He got people to work harder by convincing them it was what they wanted to do, and when they were stressed to shit and burnt-out he told them it was their own fault. And most of them believed that too.' Saul shook his head as he paused in his tirade. 'You know the strangest thing?'

'What?'

'I still liked him, in a way. He had that sort of charisma that means you can't help but like someone, even when you can't stand them at the same time.'

I nodded, having some idea what he meant. In the interviews I'd interpreted, the staff had been very positive about Steve, about his desire to improve the school's results and create a wider range of opportunities for the students, but this was the first I'd heard of this other side to him. Maybe, as Saul suggested, many of the staff had been taken in by him. Or maybe they didn't see his demanding nature as relevant to his death. But how could so many of them be singing his praises?

'Has anyone asked you to speak positively about Steve, to the police?' I asked casually.

There was a heavy pause. 'No, nothing like that,' he replied eventually, but I noticed that he didn't make eye contact with me as he spoke. I decided not to push it, however, and maybe mention to Singh all that Saul had told me.

A moment later the bell rang and Saul left to teach a class. I hung around in the staffroom for a little while, but nobody else appeared so I went back outside.

The snow from the previous day had mostly melted, leaving piles of slush at the edges of the path. As I turned the corner towards the residence I heard footsteps and saw a movement out of the corner of my eye – a flash of a red coat disappearing around the side of the building, where I'd ventured yesterday to peer through the window. I followed whoever it was and rounded a corner to be faced with Samira, Leon's best friend.

She made a half-hearted attempt to hide the cigarette she was holding behind her back, but I raised an eyebrow at her when a plume of smoke escaped from the corner of her mouth. With a shrug, she took another drag then looked me up and down.

You going to tell on me? she signed, the orange glow at the tip of her cigarette tracing a pattern in the air as she did.

I'm not a teacher, it's not my job to tell you off, I replied. *Besides, you already know it's bad for you and it'll make you stink. Me telling you that won't make you quit.*

She stifled a laugh. *What do you want?*

I saw you coming down here, thought I'd see who it was, I replied honestly.

And now you know, she replied with a combative stare.

You always smoke round here?

She nodded.

I thought about the footsteps I'd heard yesterday. *Have you ever seen anything you shouldn't?*

A sly smile crept across her face. *Maybe. Why?*

Because your best friend is missing, I reminded her. *And your head teacher is dead. The police need to know anything you've seen.*

Her face fell. *Oh, nothing like that*, she replied, waving a hand dismissively. *I know who's sleeping with who, who's fighting, shit like that. I know what's going on with staff and students, because I stand quietly and watch. Cassie seems to think she knows shit about everyone, but she spends more time telling everyone how clever she is than she does actually observing anything.*

She blew out a cloud of smoke. *Leon will be fine, I know he will. He's been through some terrible shit, and he came out okay.* The hand holding the cigarette shook slightly as she took another drag.

You don't seem very worried about where he is.

She shrugged. *He'll have found somewhere to stay. He's resourceful.*

As she signed, I watched her body language. Her leg was jiggling constantly, and she kept looking up and blinking. Were her eyes watering because of the cold, or was her body betraying signs of something that she refused to admit to?

150

I smiled at her. *Well, if you think of anything, please tell the detectives. They just want him back safe.*

Samira let out a sarcastic little huff, but she nodded anyway. Grinding out her cigarette on the brick wall behind her, she kept hold of the butt rather than tossing it onto the floor. She gave me a nod, then walked away, back towards the school.

As I walked through the main entrance I heard my phone start to ring in my pocket. Before I could answer it, Forest looked up from her spot in a doorway and beckoned to me.

'We have a development. Come with me.'

I followed her into Liz Marcek's office, which was almost full already: Liz was sitting at her desk, Sasha was leaning by the window, a frown etched on her face, and Singh had a chair opposite the deputy head's desk. I joined him there, and Sasha moved around behind Liz so they could both see me as I signed.

What is it? Sasha asked, her face showing how worried she was that the worst had happened.

'There's still no sign of Leon,' Forest began, and both the women seemed to sag slightly. 'However, we've had full access to Leon's messages from his mobile provider, and it's not good.'

Sasha didn't take her eyes off me, but Liz's gaze flicked back and forth between me and the detectives.

Well? she asked. *What have you found out?*

'For the last six weeks, Leon has been communicating with someone who claims to be a sixteen-year-old boy called Joe. Leon and Joe started out messaging on a chat forum, where Joe told Leon he was a survivor of abuse.

The two continued messaging each other regularly, and gradually the messages moved from being friendly to more intimate. Some of the messages are of a sexual nature.'

I felt a churning sensation in the pit of my stomach. That's who Joe was, and the other students were talking about him. Singh had told me Leon had been talking to someone online – I should have made the connection. I glanced at Sasha and she grimaced at me; neither of us had realised the significance of the conversation we'd had the previous day.

'We're doing our best to find out who Joe is. There's a chance he really is who he says he is, but in this situation we have to assume the worst. The messages stopped abruptly on Saturday morning.'

So? Sasha signed, interrupting. *That doesn't mean that it had anything to do with Leon disappearing.*

'If you'd let me finish,' Forest said icily, 'you'll see there is a connection. Leon arranged to meet Joe when he was on the trip at Normanby Hall.'

Liz and Sasha looked at each other, the social worker closing her eyes and shaking her head, but neither of them interrupted again.

'According to what he's told Leon, Joe lives in Scunthorpe, and when he found out Leon was going on this trip he suggested getting a bus up to the park and meeting him on Friday evening. The messages show that Joe didn't turn up when Leon was expecting him to, but he apologised and said he'd meet him in the cricket pavilion at nine o'clock on Saturday morning instead. Leon replied to say he would leave the cabin before the teachers woke up, because it would be easier to get away then, and he'd be there waiting for Joe.'

152

Both Sasha and Liz looked at Forest expectantly but the DI shook her head.

'What happened after that is anyone's guess, because the messages end there. But we have to assume that whoever Joe is, they deliberately lured Leon out of the cabin and into the park, even when the snow was coming down heavily. Whoever it is certainly doesn't have Leon's safety in mind, and we're now going to work on the assumption that Leon has been abducted. We also have to consider that Steve Wilkinson discovered what was going on, tried to bring Leon back, and was killed as a result.'

A chill settled on the room that had nothing to do with the weather outside. I waited for one of the detectives to speak, but they were silent, letting the full impact of what they had discovered sink in.

This is ridiculous, Liz told the detectives, bristling. *We do a lot of work with the students on internet safety, there's no way Leon would have done something so dangerous and foolish.*

'I'm sorry, but we have the messages,' Forest replied bluntly. 'Leon did arrange to meet Joe, whoever Joe is.'

Liz Marcek stared at the detectives for a moment, then shook her head. *How can he have been so stupid? Oh Leon.*

'Is it possible Steve knew about this?' Singh asked. 'Could he have found out Leon was planning to meet a stranger while they were on the trip, and tried to stop him?'

Liz seemed to think about this for a moment, then shrugged. *I suppose so. If he thought that Leon was in danger.*

'Is there any reason he wouldn't want to involve you, let you know his concerns?'

She sighed. *I don't know. Steve liked to do things his own way, and that sometimes meant doing things himself rather than delegating or even discussing it with the rest of the staff. Maybe he didn't trust us?*

She looked sad for a moment, then turned to look at me. *You already knew about this. Why didn't you tell me the truth?*

I was so taken aback by this that I forgot to interpret her words for the detectives until Singh prompted me.

'I didn't know about it,' I said, as the four of them stared at me. I turned to Singh. 'A couple of days ago I saw Cassie, Courtney, Bradley and Kian talking about someone called Joe, asking if they could trust him. I thought maybe he was another student, so I asked Sasha and Liz about him.'

Singh nodded, accepting my explanation, though Forest's eyes remained narrowed. Even after I'd proven myself to be good at my job she continued to look for any sign I could be a problem to her, but I knew I hadn't done anything wrong this time.

Turning back to the deputy head, the DI stood up. 'In which case, I think we need to talk to your students again, and find out what it is they've been hiding from us.'

Chapter 16

Forest left Singh to interview the students, taking the opportunity to liaise with the tech team to see if they'd been able to trace Joe. Sasha took us over to the residence, where we waited for a very long ten minutes until the students shuffled in, dropping their bags on the floor. I was surprised to see Samira, because she wasn't one of the students who had been discussing Joe, but if Leon confided in her a lot then it was possible she also knew what was going on.

Kian sat on one of the sofas while his brother stood behind him, Courtney leant on Bradley, her phone out and her thumb moving quickly across the touchscreen, and Cassie and Samira sat on another sofa.

What's going on? Bradley asked. *Have you found Leon?*

'Not yet, but we need to ask you all some questions. We've found out that Leon was planning to meet someone at Normanby Hall on Saturday. A few of you have mentioned that he was on his phone a lot, so that was probably who he was messaging. Now, if any of you can think of anything he might have said to suggest who he was meeting, or where they were from, we need you to tell us.' Singh paused and looked around at each of the students. 'We need to make sure Leon is safe, and the longer he's away from home, the more risk there is for him.'

There was no response from any of the students. Singh looked at each of them again, his hard stare making a couple of them squirm. 'He was talking to someone called Joe. I know that name means something to at least some of you.'

Kian looked up at Bradley, who shook his head slightly, but the younger brother ignored him. *Leon told me a bit about him. The boy he was talking to*, he explained.

'Thank you, Kian,' Singh said, then looked at Sasha. 'Do you think we can talk to Kian in private?'

She nodded and looked at the others. *Put the TV on for a bit. Kian, can you come into the library and tell us a bit more?*

Kian looked up at his brother again then back at the detectives. *Can Bradley come too?*

'Yes, if you want.' Singh probably realised Kian would feel safer with his brother present, and would therefore be more likely to open up to him.

All five of us moved next door, and once we were all seated Singh looked at Kian.

'What did Leon tell you about the person he was talking to online?'

His hands shaking slightly, Kian signed, *He told me he was at school in Scunthorpe, he was sixteen, and he hadn't told anyone else he was gay. He liked Leon's pictures, and he sent him some too.*

'Did you see any of these pictures?'

Kian shook his head. *Leon said it wasn't fair on Joe, showing me his pictures without permission.*

'Did Leon tell you his name?'

Yes, I knew he was called Joe.

Singh nodded, conveying to Kian that he was pleased the boy had told the truth. 'What about any other details, like what school Joe went to?' he asked.

Kian shook his head. *I don't know. Leon said Joe could sign because there were deaf kids at his school.*

Sasha looked concerned, and I could tell she was trying hard not to ask some questions of her own. Singh tapped his fingers on his knee for a moment before he asked his next question.

'Did Leon tell you he was going to try and meet this boy on Saturday?'

Not on Saturday, no. He'd said he wanted to meet him in person, but Joe had said no because he was scared of coming out to his friends and family.

'Do you think Leon might have told Joe where you were all going on the trip?'

I knew Singh was wondering if 'Joe' was really someone else entirely, the sort of person who might want to entice a fifteen-year-old boy away from the safety of his teachers, but I hoped he was wrong.

I don't know. He said he and Joe talked about everything, though.

'Kian, is there anything else you haven't told us?'

The boy shook his head. Singh raised his eyebrows and fixed him with a stern look, but Kian shook his head again.

Stop badgering him, Bradley said. *It's not his fault, I told him not to tell you anything.*

'Why?'

To protect him. What's happened to Leon is shit, but I didn't want my brother getting involved with the police, being a witness.

Bradley's eyes were shining, and I wondered what the two brothers had been through together. I got the feeling that whatever it was, Bradley had been the one to report it and to speak to the authorities in order to save his brother some distress.

'I understand that Bradley, I really do, but every bit of information we get can help us. Leon might be in danger, he might be sleeping on the streets, or he might be with someone who wants to hurt him. Do you understand that?'

Bradley flinched as Singh spoke. *Of course I bloody understand that. I just want to keep my head down and protect my brother.*

Singh nodded. 'Okay. But please don't keep anything else from us.'

The boys both stood up and left, the older with his arm around the younger's shoulders. Before Singh had a chance to do or say anything else, the door opened with a bang, slamming back against the wall.

What the fuck is going on? What's happened? Samira stood in the doorway, her eyes blazing. *Has someone done something to Leon?*

Singh stood and faced her. 'Did you know Leon was talking to a boy named Joe online?'

Samira shrugged, but I could tell from her face that she had known.

'Did you know he arranged to meet Joe on Saturday?'

No, she replied quickly, but her face coloured slightly. She was lying, I was sure of it. But if she'd known, why wouldn't she have told the police, to help them find her best friend?

'I don't know why you're keeping information from us, when all we want is to find Leon,' Singh said, his tone firm but gentle. 'Why didn't you tell us about Joe?'

Samira shrugged again, the teenager's punctuation. *It was none of your business.*

'Did it never occur to you that Leon's disappearance could have something to do with Joe?'

The girl's eyes filled with tears. *I told him not to bother with online relationships, that nobody knows who anyone really is, and I thought he'd stopped. He told me he was going to stop chatting to Joe.*

'When did he tell you this?'

About a week ago. I thought he'd actually listened to me for once, but he obviously just lied to me so I'd stop nagging him. A tear rolled down Samira's cheek and she wiped it away aggressively. *Who is he?*

'Joe? We don't know, but we're doing our best to find out.'

She thumped the wall, then turned and stormed out. For a moment I thought Sasha was going to go after her, but then she sat down in her seat again and shook her head.

I hadn't realised they were all keeping such big secrets, she told Singh, and I could see that she was blaming herself.

'You said it yourself, teenagers keep secrets,' Singh replied. 'We can't force them to tell us what they know, especially when we don't know what it is they might be hiding. Perhaps I should speak to Miss Marcek about an assembly for all the students, about online safety. It's possible other students are behaving in the same way as Leon.'

I thought back to what Anna had told me about past safeguarding issues, and I wondered if they had been connected to the students' online behaviour. Should I ask Sasha what she knew? I considered it, but then decided not to. I didn't want to throw the cat among the pigeons and confuse the investigation with information that could be completely irrelevant. It'd have to wait until Anna and I had visited Jane Villiers this afternoon.

Singh spoke to Courtney next, but she completely denied having heard of Joe or knowing anything about what Leon had been planning. I knew she was lying, at least about the first part, but there was no way to prove it. Singh dismissed her with a rueful shake of his head, then ushered Cassie inside.

How would I know who Leon had been talking to? she asked, her eyes bright. *He never talked to me about anything.*

'We have reason to believe you knew about Joe, along with Courtney, Bradley and Kian.'

Did they tell you that? Why would they tell you that? I haven't been talking to anyone called Joe.

Singh frowned. 'I didn't say you'd been talking to him, just Leon.'

Cassie paused. *Whatever. I don't know who Joe is or why he's interested in Leon.*

'The other day you told us you knew things about Leon that nobody else knew. I want you to tell me what it is you know, Cassie.'

The girl shook her head. *I don't know anything. I was only joking.*

The flippancy of her comment didn't hide the tension in her shoulders; I didn't believe her. Singh asked a few more questions, but Cassie gave the same answers until Sasha suggested they stopped. The DS was frustrated, but he agreed, as he wasn't getting anywhere.

As we left the library, I caught sight of Bradley sitting on one of the sofas in the common room. He stood up and came towards us.

You were watching us the other day, in the dining hall. You're the one who told the police what we were saying. Is that what you're here for, to spy on us?

He was taller than me and was as close as he could be without hitting me as he signed, and I could see the anger bubbling below the surface.

Bradley, that's not what happened. Sasha came to my defence.

Do you really wonder why Leon ran away? he asked, rounding on Sasha. *We've all been let down by adults who were supposed to protect us, but we all thought we could trust the adults here.* As he became more agitated, his signing got faster until I could only just keep up. *But we can't trust anyone, can we?*

He shoved past me, knocking me sideways into Singh, who caught my arms to stop me falling. As Bradley thundered up the stairs, Sasha looked after him with anguish on her face.

'What was that supposed to mean?' Singh asked, still holding on to my shoulders. Bradley's anger had shaken me, but Singh's touch was reassuring.

I don't know, but I'm worried there's still more they haven't told us, Sasha replied.

Chapter 17

Jane Villiers' house was a gorgeous little stone cottage straight out of a fairy tale. The garden was a mass of green and white, with evergreen shrubs heavy with snow and bare trees fighting for space, and it looked well-tended in a haphazard sort of way. A path wound from the low stone wall surrounding the property up to the front door, and the red-tiled roof was a little crooked, adding extra charm. Someone had carefully cleared the snow from the path and sprinkled grit over it. Ivy climbed up and around the front door, spreading its tendrils along and under the upstairs windows.

It was situated down a quiet country lane, and I struggled to find somewhere to park that wouldn't be blocking the road. Once we'd parked some distance away, Anna and I walked back through the slushy snow to the front of the house. Now we knew about Leon and Joe I was anxious to find out the real reason the previous head teacher left the school. It seemed like too much of a coincidence for such a small school to have two major safeguarding incidents in less than a year – were they connected?

Looks like something from a Disney film, Anna commented, a look of disapproval on her face. I got the feeling she'd had visions of Ms Villiers living in a smart city flat rather than this ramshackle cottage in a sleepy Wolds village.

As we opened the gate and crunched our way up the gravel path, I caught myself admiring the garden. Even in the depths of winter it didn't feel dead, more like it was on pause. There was an archway that we had to walk underneath to reach the front door, and I could just imagine it covered in roses in the summer.

We approached the cottage and a dog started barking inside; before I had a chance to press the doorbell the door was opened, and Jane Villiers stood framed in the doorway. Tall and broad shouldered, with short grey hair, she was wearing a pair of walking trousers and a heavy woollen jumper. She held the collar of a black Labrador that was straining to get past her.

'Who are you?' she asked, looking directly at me and not noticing Anna.

'Paige Northwood,' I replied, speaking and signing at the same time. 'I'm Anna's sister.'

The frown fell from Ms Villiers' face as she saw Anna standing behind me.

Of course, of course, come in, she replied, switching to BSL. She backed away, giving the dog a gentle shove so we had space to get in. I hesitated for a moment, but after a nudge from my sister I stepped into the house.

The woman looked over the two of us before letting go of the dog's collar and ushering us inside. The dog

163

bounced around our legs, sniffing our knees and whacking every limb and surface with its thick tail. Anna shied back from it a little, but I got down and gave the dog some fuss before he bounded into the next room.

Anna Northwood, she said, coming up to Anna and giving her a hug, then holding her at arm's length.

You've changed more than I expected, she told my sister once she'd broken away. *Come into the front room. Tea?*

Jane Villiers ushered us through into her living room, which looked like nothing had changed in it in several decades. The furniture was good quality but well worn, with a faded floral pattern on the matching sofa and chairs. The carpet was thick and there was a Persian-style rug in the middle of the floor that looked like the dog had been chewing it. Anna and I settled ourselves on the threadbare sofa, the dog coming and lying by our feet. I leant down and scratched him behind the ears, earning a thump of his tail in response.

So, what brings you to my neck of the woods? Jane asked Anna.

Anna smiled. *Paige told me you'd retired, and I got to thinking about my time at school. I wanted to see you and find out how you're getting on.*

And this sudden nostalgia has nothing to do with the murder of my successor?

Anna shuffled awkwardly in her chair, but it was clear that Jane Villiers still had the skills required to get the truth out of people.

We wanted to talk to you about why you left, Anna told her, wincing slightly in case her statement was met with anger, but instead Jane looked sad.

I did wonder if someone might be coming to ask me

about that, but I'm surprised it's not the police. Her eyes darted between the two of us.

The police know you retired in the summer, that's all, I told her, and she frowned at me. *I'm interpreting for the investigation,* I clarified, in case she was wondering where I got my information from. *Nobody has told the detectives that you left early.*

Well. I don't know whether to be pleased or annoyed about that, she replied. *I expect the school has done an awful lot to try and hush it up. I can't see how it can relate to what happened to that man, or to poor Leon. Have they found him yet?*

I shook my head, and her frown deepened.

What actually happened, Jane? Anna probed. *A couple of people I know said it was something to do with safeguarding . . .* She trailed off, hoping to prompt Jane into filling in the gaps.

The older woman sat back in her chair and crossed her legs, fixing Anna with a steely gaze. *Do you think it has any relevance?*

Anna looked at me before she replied. *We don't know. But we thought the police should know about it, in case it did.*

Jane nodded. *Sensible, especially when there's a child missing.* She took a drink of tea, then looked at us. *I'm not proud of how things went, but I can't say I would do it differently if it happened again.*

Anna and I both nodded but didn't interrupt. Jane was clearly building up to the story and we didn't want to derail her train of thought.

Near to the end of term in the summer, one of the primary teachers came to me, with a video camera. It was a school camera, one we kept for all teachers and classes to use in lessons. They were stored in the IT classroom where anyone could access them when they needed to. The teacher had taken it to use with her upper primary pupils, but she'd checked to see if there was anything on the memory card before they used it. I'm very glad she did, because when she watched it she discovered footage of two of the older students having sex, late at night in one of the classrooms.

I felt myself inhale sharply. Whatever I had been expecting, it wasn't that.

Bradley and Courtney? I asked, on instinct, thinking of the secretive signs of affection I'd seen passing between the two of them. Jane nodded.

You've met them, I assume? They're both good kids who had a rough start to their lives. I watched the start of the video, and it was clear that someone set up the camera and left it running for a while before the two of them came in. Her signing was sharp, belying the anger she felt at the memory. *When I asked the two of them about it they were genuinely mortified. I pride myself on knowing when any of my students are lying to me, and these two knew nothing about this video. They each said that they'd received an email from the other, saying they should meet in that classroom, yet each denied sending a message. It was a set-up.*

Jane's face twisted. *I know I should have informed the governors immediately. Of course I should have. But here were two vulnerable teenagers, underage, who had been manipulated, and then the video left where any of the children could have watched it. I decided that before I took it to the governors I would investigate and see if I could find out who might have done this.*

She stood up and paced around behind her chair. *You have to understand, I had no way of knowing if it was a staff member or a student. If I went straight to the governors with it, the story would have been out within a day, and whoever was responsible would have known to keep their head down. I wanted the element of surprise, wanted whoever it was to think they could get away with doing things like this. Then, they might become overconfident, and I would be able to catch them at it.*

I enlisted Saul's help, she continued. *I had to trust someone, and he was far more able than me to see if there was any, what's it called . . .* She waved a hand around before fingerspelling the word she was looking for, *metadata, that's what it's called. Something to help us track down who had planted the camera, and who had emailed Bradley and Courtney to get them to meet there in the first place. I also asked Saul to check for any videos having been uploaded to the internet from any school accounts. I wanted to make sure there weren't any other copies.*

Did he find anything? I asked, tense with anticipation.

Jane shrugged. *I don't think he had a chance to get started before someone went to the governors and I was hauled in for covering up a major safeguarding issue.* She came back to her chair and sat down with a sigh. *Both the students were under sixteen, and that was their main concern, rather than the fact someone had filmed them on school equipment without their consent, and for who knows what purpose.* She flung her hands up as she finished speaking, as if to show the futility of what she had been trying to do.

I was naive, she continued. *I thought that I had dealt with the incident in the best way for the students concerned*

– they were stupid, and whilst they weren't sixteen they both knew damn well what they were doing, I can tell you. It was the person who filmed them that I was concerned about, but the governors insisted they must have done it themselves. Jane gave us an agonised look. *They thought I should have punished them, when they were doing what horny hormonal teenagers have been doing since time began. Really, what would that have achieved?*

I had to be honest, she had a point. The idea that someone was sneaking around a school and filming students in compromising positions was horrific, and I understood why she'd wanted to try and track down the culprit on the quiet rather than reprimand Bradley and Courtney.

My mind was whirring, and I could tell that Anna's was, too. Was there any connection between this and what happened to Leon? Could Leon have been the person who filmed Bradley and Courtney, and if he was, what would they have done if they found out? We hadn't got to the bottom of the animosity between Bradley and Leon, and this could have been the cause.

So, nobody has told the police about this? Jane asked.

No, this is the first I've heard of any of it, I told her, shaking my head.

Well, they've done a good job hushing it up. Liz Marcek was always very precious about the school's reputation. She was horrified at the idea of students having sex on school premises, kept bleating about how the school would be closed. She sighed again. *We were hardly the first residential school where something like that had happened. But I shouldn't be too hard on her, she was grieving for*

168

her brother at the time and her behaviour was erratic. She refused to take any time off and wouldn't talk about it, but rumours were that he'd overdosed.

Jane seemed to have another thought, cocked her head on one side and looked at me. *Do the police suspect Leon of having killed his teacher?* she asked, a frown on her face.

At the moment they don't know exactly what happened, I replied, *so they're keeping an open mind.* I didn't want her to start grilling me about the case.

Jane nodded thoughtfully. *Well, I can't imagine that the boy I knew would hurt someone. How was he killed?*

Anna and I looked at each other. This wasn't something I had even discussed with her. *He was stabbed,* I eventually replied.

Jane grimaced. *They'll think it could be him, because of his history with his father. But it can't have been Leon.*

Why do you say that?

Because I know that boy, and he's changed. He can control himself, and I know he wouldn't have done something like that. She slapped a hand down on the arm of her chair. *I know Leon. I know all of my students, and just because I was forced out early doesn't mean I don't still think about them and have concerns for them.*

Could Leon have seen what happened? Jane continued. *Could he have witnessed his teacher being killed?* she asked me.

I don't know, I replied, *but it is possible. They were in the park at the same time, in roughly the same area, so the police can't rule it out.*

That could explain why he ran away, she replied. *If he's a witness, he will be terrified.*

Wouldn't he want to go to the police and explain what happened? Anna asked.

Not if the person who killed Mr Wilkinson is someone he trusted, Jane reasoned. *The school is Leon's only safe place, and if someone there has shattered that safety, he'll be scared and won't know what to do. If he goes to the police, maybe they won't believe him, then he'll be sent back to school to spend time with the very person he knows is a murderer.*

The atmosphere in the room felt suddenly heavy as Anna and I took in her words. Stunned by this potential angle, I realised something that made my blood run cold – if Leon had seen Steve's killer, the police weren't the only ones desperately looking for him.

Chapter 18

As I drove home, my mind was whirring. Anna was almost quivering, and I could tell she desperately wanted to sit down and start going through theories and suspects, but I was dreading it. The last time that had happened, my sister had crossed paths with a murderer and was lucky to still be alive.

I was glad of the icy weather, because it gave me an excuse to drive slowly, and it took us nearly an hour to get home. As soon as we were inside, Anna pulled off her coat and went to get a notebook. I was reminded of the wall of sticky notes she'd gathered after Lexi was killed, the piles of information she'd got from me or other people in the Deaf community.

No, I told her. *We can't do this again.*

She rolled her eyes at me. *I'm not going to go haring off without you, not this time. I learnt my lesson, okay?*

I didn't believe her, but I knew this wasn't an argument I was going to win.

Do you think the video of Bradley and Courtney could be connected to Leon disappearing? she asked.

That depends, I replied. *If Leon was the one who filmed them, then we have to consider the possibility that Bradley and Courtney found out and were bent on getting revenge.* I thought about what I'd seen of the two students so far: they were practically inseparable, and if Bradley was highly protective of his brother it made sense that he'd behave the same way for his girlfriend. He wasn't fully in control of the aggression that bubbled away under the surface; I'd witnessed that for myself this week.

They couldn't have kidnapped him, though, Anna pointed out. *Where would they put him? If he was still somewhere in the park he would have been found by now, even with the snow.*

Unless they were working with someone else? I suggested, but I knew it was far-fetched even as I said it.

How are a couple of teenagers in a residential school going to find someone to help them kidnap another teenager and not leave a trace? Anna asked, rightly sceptical.

Okay, we'll rule that out, I conceded.

Could one of the teachers have accused Leon of making the video, so he ran away? she suggested.

I let out a long breath, knowing I couldn't give her too many details about the investigation. *It's possible. That's something Forest and Singh will be looking into, I'm sure.*

We didn't look at each other for a moment, both absorbing the enormity of this prospect. My phone buzzed, and I couldn't help smiling when I saw Max's name on the screen.

Fancy going out for something to eat tonight?

On a school night? I teased.

172

I just wanted to see you, he replied.

I thought about it before I answered. The last few months had been difficult, negotiating my relationship with Max whilst trying to be there for Anna. There were times when I'd turned him down because I didn't want to leave her, but she seemed to be doing so much better recently. The thought of seeing Max put me on edge slightly, though. I hadn't told him about Mike yet, and I knew we really needed to discuss my history, but I didn't feel ready.

Do you mind if I go out tonight? I asked Anna.

She rolled her eyes. *Paige, you're thirty-one. You don't need to ask my permission.*

I'm not asking permission, I'm asking if you'll be okay on your own.

I'll be fine, Anna replied. *I'm also an adult, if you hadn't noticed. Go out. See your boyfriend*, she told me. *I don't want to be the one who comes between you.*

I replied to Max and he told me he'd pick me up at six.

Why didn't anyone tell the police about Jane Villiers being thrown out? I asked Anna once I'd made my arrangements for later. *It doesn't make any sense. It's not the sort of thing you can keep covered up for long, and when they find out they're bound to think it's suspicious.*

The whole thing makes the school look pretty bad, though, doesn't it? she reasoned. *I don't blame them for wanting to push anything negative under the carpet and pretend it didn't happen, when they're faced with a disappearing student and a murdered teacher.*

I wasn't convinced. *But surely they'll look worse when the police find out they tried to hide it?*

Are you going to call Singh to tell him? she asked, but I shook my head.

I'll see him tomorrow. Maybe by then I will have been able to make some sense of it all.

Max was punctual, as usual. I often teased him about how accurate he was with timings, and he put it down to working in a school and living his life by a strict timetable.

I waited inside the flat until I saw his car pull up outside, but as I watched I noticed a fancy sports car sitting a few metres down the road. Was it the same one I'd seen outside the school? They were the same model and colour. When I left the building I pulled the door closed firmly behind me, then tried to look up the road to see if anyone was in the car, but it was already too dark.

So, where are we going? I asked Max as I got in, trying to put my worries about the other car to the back of my mind.

Fancy going down to Lincoln?

Sure, I replied, not telling him that I was already sick of the A15 and the drive to the School for the Deaf.

On the way, he told me about his day and a couple of the kids he was supporting. He was passionate about his job, and it always shone through in the way he talked about the pupils he worked with. They'd had a new child start in the school's nursery and he was obviously loving working with her.

'This little girl has barely signed three words all term,' he was saying. 'Her parents are hearing and they say they're learning to sign but the teacher of the deaf thinks they're only really doing it when she visits, not using it on a daily basis with the child. Anyway, suddenly she signed this story to me! I'd told her the story a few times, last week and this week, and she pointed to the book and signed the story! It was basic, but she used so many more signs than I've seen her use before.'

He was beaming with pride, and I couldn't help but smile at him. He doted on his little niece, Kasey, and I caught myself thinking he'd be a great dad. As soon as the thought passed through my mind I stared forward out of the windscreen and tried to hide my embarrassment, as if Max would somehow be able to read my thoughts. I liked him a lot, but there was no way I wanted to think about anything more serious than the level of dating we were currently at. Not yet, anyway.

We parked near the Bail in Lincoln and Max steered me towards a little Mexican restaurant tucked away around the back. I'd never been to it before, and it was nice to be exploring new places with him.

Why the mid-week meal? I asked once we had some nachos in front of us.

Am I not allowed to ask to see you during the week?

I laughed. *Of course you are, but I know you get up early for work.*

He shrugged. *You told me that you and Anna had plans at the weekend, so I thought I'd try and see you a bit more during the week, then you can spend Saturday and Sunday with her. I know the last few months have been difficult for her.*

I'd almost forgotten that Anna and I had planned to go up to York for the Christmas market at the weekend. If the case was solved by then it would be a great day out, but I got the feeling I might end up working every day until it was.

I told him about Anna's enthusiasm for her new job, and he agreed it was a positive sign, but then gave me a serious look.

I worry that you're not completely over what happened at the start of the year, though. It feels like you've thrown yourself into supporting Anna, without taking into account the trauma you suffered as well.

I shook my head. *I'm fine, honestly.*

Maybe, but is it really wise you getting involved in another police investigation?

I could see the concern in his eyes, but I found myself getting a bit annoyed.

It's my job, Max. I'm doing my job. I don't know anyone involved this time, I lied. Max had probed a little about my romantic history, but I'd offered him very little information and he'd stopped asking. I didn't want to tell him about Mike while we were in the middle of a nice evening out. Every time I considered bringing it up, I told myself it wasn't the right time, and I could find a better one.

He was looking at me sceptically. *I just want to make sure you're looking after yourself.*

By not wanting me to do my job? I asked, a little more sharply than I had intended.

Don't be like that, he replied, looking hurt. *Of course I want you to do your job. I don't want you working yourself into the ground and ending up in a dangerous situation, though.*

I'm sorry, I said, reaching over and squeezing his hand. *I promise, I'm fine.*

He nodded. *No sign of the missing kid yet then?*

Nothing, as far as I know. I sighed. *I really hope he's okay.*

One of my exes works at that school, he signed.

Really? Who? I asked, but I had a sixth sense that I knew what was about to come.

Her name's Jess, she's the PE teacher.

I've met her, I told him, wondering just how many people in my life Jessica Farriday had dated.

Yeah, we didn't go out for long. She did her teaching placement at the school I work in when she was training. To be honest I think she was using me so I could put in a good word for her with the teacher who was assessing her. He shrugged. *Not everyone is charmed by my rugged good looks.*

I laughed. *Well, that's her loss.*

My mind was whirring. If Jess was the sort of person who dated men she thought could be useful to her, maybe Singh needed to delve deeper into her relationship with Steve. I made a mental note to pass this information on to him, although I knew DI Forest wouldn't be interested in any gossip or hearsay.

Here was an opportunity – Max had told me about one of his exes; it would be easy for me to segue into telling him about Mike. Before I could sign anything, though, I thought better of it. I'd just told him I didn't know anyone connected to the case, and if he knew my shitty ex was a potential murder suspect Max wouldn't stop until I'd backed off from this case. I couldn't do it.

After we'd finished eating, we walked down towards the cathedral, which was floodlit at an angle that made it seem even more imposing than it did in daylight. There were still traces of snow on the roof, and the frost on one of the rose windows glistened in the artificial light. For a while we walked without chatting, hand in hand, enjoying the crisp cold of the evening, and it gave me hope that I really was ready for a serious relationship again. Looking sideways at Max, I told myself that I had to learn to relax around him. He was really thoughtful, he treated me well and made me laugh, plus I found him really attractive. I had to stop letting my past dictate how I behaved in the present.

I pulled out my phone and texted Anna.

Not coming home tonight.

We held hands as we walked back to the car, but then I stopped dead. The car park was almost empty, but at the opposite end sat the same sports car I'd seen earlier on my street. I hadn't checked the number plate, but it was the same make and model, so surely that was too much of a coincidence?

Is everything okay? Max asked, squeezing my shoulder.

I took a deep breath. *Fine*, I replied. Dozens of people must have those cars, I told myself, but the whole way home I kept checking behind us in case I saw it again.

Eleven hours before the murder

The kids and Sasha had picked a film to watch and they were all sprawled in front of the TV. Steve was sitting at the table in the corner, going over the itinerary for the weekend, which left Mike with nothing to do. He didn't really feel like watching whatever shit the teenagers had chosen, but he knew Steve would frown upon him sitting on his phone all evening. The bastard was always breathing down his neck, finding fault with him.

He sighed and chewed the edge of his index finger. He'd been really good, avoiding some of his most frequented sites, but the urge was pretty strong tonight. If he could get out of here for half an hour or so, get a couple of games in, then he could put up with it for the rest of the evening, he was sure.

'Just popping to the loo,' he told Steve, then slipped out of the room and down the corridor. He could kill a bit of time in the bathroom, though not too much. As he passed the boys' room, he caught sight of one of their bags lying open, a games console sitting on top. Mike ground his teeth as he stood there, looking at it. It was worth a few quid. Kian must have saved up for ages; the kids in care got a small allowance from social services, but it didn't stretch far. Knowing Bradley, he'd probably chipped in for it as well.

No, he told himself. You can't take anything from the kids again. The last time he'd been tempted by things students had left lying around he'd not known when to stop. He'd sold most of what he'd taken, but there'd still been a couple of items in his room when the shit really hit the fan, and he'd only just had time to dump them before bloody Liz Marcek had threatened to go to the police. Of course, she'd assumed it was a student stealing, but Mike knew if the police got involved they'd want to search every room, not just the kids'.

Carrying on down the corridor, Mike congratulated himself on not giving in to temptation. He didn't need the money that badly. His next big win was around the corner, bound to be. Yeah, he'd had a bad streak recently, but they said it was always darkest before the dawn.

A few minutes later, he was back, hand in Kian's bag. The console wasn't worth as much without the charger. Where the fuck was it? Mike became more agitated as he dug through the bag, not finding what he was looking for. He'd just pulled out a phone when he became aware of something blocking the light from the door.

'Mike? What are you doing?' Steve's body filled the doorframe.

'I thought it was a good opportunity to check the kids' bags for contraband.' Contraband? Mike swore silently at himself for being such a moron.

'You can't search students' bags without their permission,' Steve replied, his voice grave. 'And why did you suddenly feel that it was necessary?'

Mike didn't answer. Did he know about the thefts from last year? Steve hadn't been at the school then, so maybe nobody had told him about it.

'I saw Bradley and Leon talking about smoking,' Mike said, drawing himself up to his full height and pushing his shoulders back in a show of confidence. 'I was concerned that the boys were developing bad habits, and thought it best to nip it in the bud straight away. Especially with Kian being so young and impressionable.'

Steve watched Mike for a moment, studying him closely. 'Still, that doesn't give you the right to go through the students' belongings. If you thought they'd brought cigarettes with them, you should have told me, then I could have asked them and given them the chance to be open with me.'

Fat lot of good that would do, Mike thought, knowing that this group of kids was far from open with the adults around them, but he said nothing.

'I'm going to have to inform the rest of the senior management team about this,' Steve added, then stepped aside, gesturing for Mike to lead the way back to the main room of the cabin. All the way down the corridor, Mike could feel the head teacher's gaze on the back of his neck, and it made his palms itch. If he told Liz about this, she'd definitely make the link to the thefts. He couldn't let that happen. Balling his hands into fists, he focused on his breathing to keep himself calm as he rejoined the group.

Chapter 19

Thursday 29th November

Before I left Max's flat the following morning I called Singh and told him how Jane Villiers had come to leave her post as head teacher. I could tell from his voice that he was annoyed at me for keeping it from him, though I wouldn't have wanted to involve him if it had turned out to be completely unrelated. He wanted me back at the school so he could talk to Liz about it, and why the safeguarding issues had been deliberately kept from the police. I was secretly glad that I would be involved in that conversation, because it was something I was dying to know the answer to myself. He came to pick me up, because I didn't have my car at Max's, and as I was waiting I felt a bit weird about it. I was committed to Max, I really was, but my feelings for Singh often left me feeling confused.

Glancing up the street, I remembered the sports car I kept seeing the previous day. Should I tell Singh about it? I thought about it for a few minutes but decided against it; it was probably just my mind playing tricks on me.

'No DI Forest today?' I asked, getting into the passenger seat.

'No, she's gone to Steve's old school. There are a few questions she wanted to ask,' he said as we pulled away.

'What about?' I asked, my curiosity piqued.

He gave me a sideways look before replying. 'I shouldn't really be talking to you about this.'

'And when has that ever stopped you?' I teased.

'Forest would kill me if she knew how much I talk to you,' he said.

'Well she's never been my biggest fan.'

This brought a laugh, and I nudged him gently. 'What did you find out?'

'The staff at his previous school were happy to talk to us about Steve, and the accounts of him as a boss were quite different from some of the ones we've heard here.'

'That's no surprise,' I said. I had told him the previous day what Saul said to me about Steve working everyone too hard.

'Well it seems that this wasn't the first school where he'd done that. There were several complaints about the way he treated staff, and the expectations he had, to the extent where he was accused of bullying.'

'Wow. That's pretty serious.'

'He'd only been here for three months, so it's possible he'd only just started to get settled, which could explain why nobody was willing to speak negatively about him. By the sound of it, at his last school it was a gradual but sustained wearing down of people's spirits and goodwill. They had a high turnover of staff by the time he left, because a lot of people didn't stay there for long under his management. One of the senior members of staff told me that she suspected him of giving less than favourable references for those who spoke out against him, but there was no proof of that.'

Singh had been watching the road as he spoke, but now glanced at me. 'It gets worse, though. There was one man, a teacher, who was struggling with a lot of personal problems. He ended up taking drugs, but came clean to Steve and asked for his support in getting himself back on his feet.'

'What did Steve do?' I asked, with a feeling of foreboding.

'Sacked him instantly, reported him to the local authority saying he was unfit to work with children, and told the police he'd been driving under the influence of drugs.'

'What happened to him? The other teacher?'

'He killed himself,' Singh replied quietly.

I sat in stunned silence for a moment. Did anyone at Lincoln School for the Deaf know how cruel Steve could be? Could he have done something that terrible again, leading to his death?

We pulled into the school car park, and Singh turned off the engine but didn't get out for a moment.

'It wasn't entirely clear whether Steve left of his own accord, to explore a new role, or if he'd been pushed out eventually by the governors. If he'd been here much longer, I expect he would have ended up behaving in the same way, but the school was in need of a head teacher, so they might not have looked too closely at his history.'

Liz Marcek was waiting for us when we walked in.

I don't have a lot of time for you this morning, she told Singh. *Can it wait?*

'I'm afraid not,' he replied with a frown.

Fine, fine. She reluctantly led us into her office, where she sat down behind her desk rather than at the low table where we'd previously talked.

'Miss Marcek, can I ask why you didn't see fit to tell us the real reason behind Jane Villiers' retirement?'

For a moment Liz sat motionless, like a deer faced with a poacher's lamp. She clasped her hands together and looked down at her desk, and when she looked up her face was noticeably paler.

To be honest, I didn't want it to end up in the newspapers, she replied eventually, looking defeated. *When it happened, we managed to keep it quiet, and I thought we'd escaped with the school's reputation intact. Now suddenly there are reports about a missing student and a murdered teacher, and I'd thought the worst thing that could happen to this school would be some journalist finding out about underage students having sex in a classroom. As it is I'm already trying to calm parents' fears about their children's safety. Can you imagine the uproar if that got out as well?*

'While I understand your concerns, there's a big difference between telling a journalist and telling the police.'

How was I to know it wouldn't get out? she asked indignantly.

Singh folded his arms, tension showing in the rigidity of his jawline, and I could tell he was working hard to hold himself in check. 'We have procedures to follow in any investigation regarding which information is released to the public. Unless we felt it was in the public interest to know we wouldn't have shared it. It wasn't your place to decide whether or not we needed this information. There could be a connection to Leon's disappearance and

185

the video that was made of Bradley and Courtney, and we've wasted valuable time because you were more concerned about the school's reputation than you were with us finding a missing, vulnerable child.'

I'd never seen Singh this angry before, and I was taken aback, feeling the weight of his disapproval as I interpreted it for Liz. She sat, motionless, for several seconds after he'd finished, before her hands began to twitch slightly. I could tell she wanted to snap back at Singh for having the temerity to tell her off as if she were a child, but I thought she also knew that she deserved every word of it.

'Is there anything else you haven't told us, Miss Marcek?' Singh asked, his expression stern.

The deputy head took a deep breath, then shook her head.

'Were you aware that Steve Wilkinson had a reputation for bullying staff in his past school?' Singh snapped.

A strange expression flitted across her face, but was gone before I could identify it.

No, she replied, sitting forward in her chair and looking at Singh across her desk. *I wasn't involved in the hiring process when Steve was appointed. I didn't know anything about him until he arrived in September.*

I found this hard to believe, given that Liz was the most senior member of staff at the school after Jane left. But why would she lie about it? There was a pause as Singh and Liz eyeballed each other across the expanse of her desk, before Singh nodded and stood to leave. I followed him out without looking at Liz, glad to be away from the atmosphere in that room. Singh made an exasperated noise.

'I'm sick of people thinking they know my job better

than I do,' he growled. 'There's a kid out there who might have been kidnapped by a paedophile, or who might have frozen to death in the middle of a field, and she's more concerned with what people think about the school!'

I put a hand on his arm to try and calm him, then slid it around to his back. Gradually, the tension in his shoulders reduced.

'I need to call Forest and see if there's anything else she wants me to do while I'm here.'

He started to walk away, but I called after him. 'I think you're doing a good job.'

He gave me a small smile before putting his phone to his ear, and I sat down in the entrance hall to wait. Before I got a chance to settle myself on the bench seat under the window, I heard footsteps approaching and turned to see who it was. Jess Farriday had a frown on her face, and it was directed at me. I smiled at her in an attempt to defuse whatever was coming, but it was unsuccessful.

You need to stop playing games, she snapped at me.

I was taken aback, genuinely confused. *What are you talking about?*

You and Mike. She jabbed a finger at me and I took a step back. *I know you've got a history, and you should see him since you appeared. He's wandering around like a lovesick puppy.*

That's nothing to do with me, I assured her.

Of course it is, she replied with a scowl. *He's told me how you blow hot and cold, how he's tried to show you how he feels about you but you ignore him when it suits you.*

Hang on, I replied. *Where the hell has this come from? If Mike's told you this then you need to consider how reliable he is. I have absolutely no interest in Mike Lowther, which he knows. Our relationship was over a long time ago, and that's all there is to it.*

She made a sceptical noise and shook her head. *He told me you were a cold-hearted bitch.*

The insult stung, but it didn't surprise me. *There are two sides to every story, Jess. I don't think Mike would be too keen on you hearing my side of our relationship. It doesn't paint him in a very positive light. But if you want to keep believing everything he tells you, that's entirely up to you.*

She paused for a moment, and I could see her considering what I'd said, but then shook her head. *Of course you'd say that.*

You said yourself that you ended your relationship because he was too controlling, I pointed out. *Think about that. Anyway, why are you even bothered about this? He's your ex.*

Jess didn't answer my question, but looked away, a slight flush rising in her cheeks. As I looked at her, realisation dawned.

Are you sleeping with him? I asked, trying to keep my question casual.

And why is that any of your business? she retorted.

It's not, you're right. I held my hands up in defeat. *I just wondered if that was why you'd suddenly decided to have a go at me about him. It would make more sense if he wasn't your ex.*

It's not serious, she said with a shrug.

Why would you go back to someone like him after the way he treated you? I asked, genuinely confused. *I can tell you, he's done far worse in the past.*

She didn't reply, but folded her arms defiantly. I really wanted to ask how she could sleep with someone else only days after her boyfriend was murdered. Had those tears been just for show, to convince the detectives that she was grieving?

Fine, don't listen to my advice, I replied, throwing my hands up. *I can't force you.*

Jess looked me up and down, then turned to leave before pausing. A sour smile twisted her lips. *I should have known what you were like. I know your sister, after all*, she signed, then turned and stalked off.

Moments later, Singh was back, beckoning me in the direction of the deputy head teacher's office.

'Paige. Quickly, please. We need to speak to Liz Marcek again.'

Still seething from the comment about Anna I hurried into the room after him. Before she had a chance to ask what the problem was, Singh marched up to her desk.

'You can install a program on some phones to back up your messages, and then they can be downloaded to a computer. Our techs found some of these messages between Leon and Joe, downloaded and saved in a secret folder.'

Leon's messages were backed up to a school computer? Liz asked, confused.

'No, it wasn't Leon that saved them. It was Joe.'

Liz started to sign something, but Singh held up a hand to stop her.

'The messages were downloaded by Steve Wilkinson. Steve was Joe.'

Chapter 20

The staffroom was packed, and the mutters that were going round put me on edge. Singh had briefed Liz Marcek, and she was preparing to tell the rest of the staff about what had been found on Steve Wilkinson's account. Singh had insisted that I interpret – it wasn't appropriate to use another member of staff when they didn't know what had happened.

Liz waved her hands to attract attention, and as all the faces turned to her she began.

I'm sorry to interrupt your day like this, but we've had some very serious news. Leon still hasn't been found, she hastily added, as some of the staff put shocked hands to their mouths, obviously assuming the worst. *However, the police have discovered a possible link between Steve's death and Leon's disappearance.*

A few people started to mutter or sign to each other, but Liz stamped her foot to get their attention again. *Don't interrupt, please. I don't want to extend the lunch break.*

The offenders looked suitably chastised, so Liz continued.

On examination of Steve's computer, it seems he was sending messages to Leon, posing as a sixteen-year-old boy called Joe. The nature of these messages was romantic, and at points sexual.

Gasps went round the room.

Obviously, the police need to investigate a lot further to see if this was something Steve had been doing for a long time, and if any other children had been put at risk. I will be speaking to the governors about the best way to handle this discovery. For now, this information must not be shared with our students, under any circumstances. It is vital that we pay strict attention to even the slightest hint of a suggestion that Steve behaved inappropriately towards any of them, girls or boys. I know you are all familiar with the safeguarding policy, that any disclosure is reported immediately to the designated safeguarding lead, but if any of you took any concerns to Steve that you think were not dealt with, please come to me with them now. We'll need to review all our safeguarding records as well, to ensure no student has slipped through the cracks.

There is no doubt that this will get out to the media at some point, but until it is released by the police I do not expect to read anything about it beyond the walls of this school. If there is a leak from the staff, the person responsible will be suspended with immediate effect. I have made the decision to share this information with all of you in order that we can come together to ensure the safety of our students. The governors and I will contact Ofsted so they are aware of the situation before it becomes public knowledge, in order to try and limit the damage to the school's reputation.

She finished, and her shoulders dropped. I noticed how tired she looked, despite the well-applied make-up. It must

191

have been difficult, suddenly having the headship thrust upon her in tragic circumstances, and now having to deal with this shocking revelation. I felt for her in that moment, as I saw how strong she was forcing herself to appear on the surface.

Singh waited around for the rest of the lunch hour, in case anyone had anything they needed to tell him immediately, but the staff mainly looked stunned. After reminding Liz Marcek to pass anything she discovered on to the police as soon as possible, Singh and I left.

We walked through the car park in silence towards Singh's car. We didn't talk much on the drive back to Scunthorpe, both of us lost in our own thoughts. Had Leon arranged to meet Joe at Normanby Hall and then discovered his online boyfriend was actually his headteacher? Had he killed Steve and then run away to escape the consequences? Or had someone else discovered what Steve had been doing and killed him in order to protect Leon? If that was the case, Leon must have seen something and run away because he was scared. I shook my head. It was so tangled. And that poor kid, finding himself in that situation – whatever had happened, he must be terrified.

When we pulled up outside my flat I asked if Singh wanted to come in for a drink.

'I'd love to, but I need to get back to the station. We're going to be working all night on this, I expect.'

'I just don't get it,' I said. 'How can Steve have been Joe?'

Singh thumped the steering wheel. 'Men like that, they don't give a shit about the kids they target. He probably got off on seeing Leon round school, knowing the conversations they'd been having.' He shook his head in disgust.

'Some people would be glad he's dead, but I'd rather he'd lived to see the inside of a cell for the rest of his life.'

I wasn't sure how I felt about it but I knew Singh was right: he should have faced justice, not been murdered, regardless of his crimes. On the spur of the moment, I reached over and gave Singh a hug before I got out. He looked taken aback by my display of affection, but smiled at me before he drove off.

Inside, Anna got up as soon as I walked in.

What's happened? I know something's happened, she told me. *I can see it all over your face.*

I shook my head. *I really can't tell you about this one, I'm sorry. But it's serious. Very serious.*

Is Leon dead?

A shudder passed through me. I didn't know the answer to that question. Had Steve been able to hurt or abuse Leon before he had been stabbed? It didn't bear thinking about.

Not that I know of.

I needed a bit of time to myself, so I told Anna I was going to have a shower. I turned the water up as hot as I could bear and stood underneath the water until my skin felt bruised. Even then, it was an effort to turn it off and step out, back into the world where things like that could happen.

I wrapped a towel around my hair and went back into the living room, where Anna was scrolling through her phone. Another thought had occurred to me.

Do you remember Jessica Farriday?

Anna put her phone down and stared at me, her eyebrows raised in disbelief. *Do I remember Jessica Farriday? Is that what you asked?*

Yeah. She told me the other day that you were at school together, but I forgot to mention it.

Anna laughed but there was no humour in it. *Oh, I could never forget her. Do you remember when I was about fifteen, I had a week or two where everyone completely ignored me? Even some of the teachers ended up doing it.*

Yeah, that was awful, I said. I had been seventeen at the time, and fully prepared to come to Anna's school and sort out the bitches myself.

Well, that was Jess Farriday's doing. She was the queen bee, and she loved nothing more than playing people off against each other. When I wouldn't bow down and worship her, she did everything she could to make my life hell, until she got bored of me and went to work on someone else instead. What the hell were you doing talking to Jess Farriday? Anna tilted her head on one side. *Oh, wait. Is she working at our old school?*

Yeah, she's the PE teacher.

Anna gave a snort. *Of course she is. Any chance to prance around in her shorts, I bet. She made sure the lads all followed her around like puppies when we were at school, and I bet she tries that with the male staff now.*

I wouldn't know about that, I said, but it did seem to ring true given what we'd discovered. I couldn't share information about Jess's relationship with the dead head teacher, and I probably shouldn't tell Anna that she'd also dated both Mike and Max.

She was the sort of person that, if she found out two other students were together, she'd do her best to split them up, just for the hell of it, Anna said, her mouth twisted into a distasteful expression. *Maybe she'd want the lad for herself, but mostly she just didn't want any attention taken off her.*

Sounds like a nightmare, I said.

I mulled it all over as we sat watching something mindless on the TV. I wondered if any of this was relevant to the investigation. Maybe Jess still behaved the same way as she did when she was a teenager; was it possible she was only having a fling with Steve in order to advance her position in the school? What Max had told me about her certainly suggested it was possible. Unfortunately, the one other person I knew who had been in a relationship with her previously wasn't someone I wanted to talk to about it. Mike and I had been civil to each other and I hoped it would carry on that way, but if I started asking him questions about his ex that might lead into territory I didn't want to cover. And what was her motivation for taking up with him again, just as all of this was happening?

The doorbell went, and we frowned at each other. Neither of us was expecting anyone, so I went to the intercom to find out who it was.

'Hi Paige, it's Mike. Can I come up?'

I felt a chill run through me, as if he'd known I was just thinking about speaking to him.

Anna looked inquisitive and I pulled a face. *Mike*, I signed. Her face dropped into a scowl. *Don't let him in.*

I'm not going to. But I'll go down and talk to him at the door.

Without asking, she followed me out. When I opened the door to the building, Mike was leaning against the wall.

'Hi,' I said to him, giving Anna a sideways look, wondering how she'd react. 'Why are you here?'

'I need to talk to you,' he said, standing up and reaching for the door as if to push it open. I paused for a moment, unsure of what to say, but I stepped outside with Anna and pulled the door shut behind us so he couldn't get into the building. Anna was glaring at Mike and looking at me for an explanation.

'What about?' I asked.

'It's freezing out here,' he said. 'Can I come in?'

I looked over again at Anna.

'No, I'm sorry. It's not a good time.'

He frowned. 'I only want to talk to you. Is that not allowed now?'

'It's allowed, but not right now. Anna's got work to do and I promised I'd help her with it.' It wasn't strictly true, but it was a handy excuse.

'Paige, this is silly. Let me in.'

'No.'

He looked surprised, and I realised that I'd probably never said no to him before, or at least not for a very long time. Mike was probably expecting me to still be the same person I was when we were together, but I'd changed a hell of a lot in the last three years.

'As always, your sister comes first,' he replied with a roll of his eyes.

'Of course she does.' I folded my arms and stared at him defiantly. If he genuinely wanted to apologise for the way he'd treated me, so we could both move on, he wasn't being particularly successful.

'Paige, I'm sorry, okay?' He let out a long breath. 'I'm sorry, you just have this effect on me. Three years, and now suddenly you're here and I can't stop thinking about you. It makes me so mad, you know, that we threw away such a good thing. So, I forget myself sometimes.'

'We can talk about it, but not right now. You can't turn up at my front door and expect me to drop everything.' I turned to walk inside and he put his arm out. Anna moved as if to get in between us, but I shook my head at her.

'Wait, I've not said what I came here to say, yet,' Mike said, a note of impatience in his voice.

'And I've told you, now isn't the right time.'

Before he had a chance to respond, Anna pushed past me, hands flying as she ranted at my ex-boyfriend.

I reached over and put a hand on her arm, stopping her mid-sign.

Anna, what are you doing?

Telling this bastard exactly what I think of him, she signed back to me, her eyes blazing. *I can't believe he's allowed to supervise children. How do you know he wasn't the one who killed the head teacher?*

Mike was watching all this with a raised eyebrow, a smug expression on his face.

'Can't control your tempers, can you? You're both the same, a pair of hysterical bitches.'

I rounded on him. 'What the hell? A couple of days ago you were apologising to me and begging to talk to me, then you throw that insult at me?'

He looked genuinely embarrassed. 'Sorry,' he said. 'She got me so worked up.'

For a moment I was about to accept his apology, until my brain waved a little red flag at me. Whenever he got angry at me, his eventual apologies were empty, and usually involved blaming me. 'I'm sorry, you just make me so angry' was one of his most common phrases. Now he was just switching to gaslighting my sister instead of me.

'Piss off, Mike. And don't come back here.'

I saw his fists clench and I tensed, ready for flight, but with a curl of his lip he backed away.

'Okay. Well, hopefully we can get together soon and have a chat,' he said, his jaw tight with pent-up anger.

Mike walked towards the pavement, glancing back at me as he went. Anna and I went inside, but she didn't ask for an explanation until she'd locked the door behind us.

What did he really want?

I have no idea. You didn't give him the chance to tell me. I knew I couldn't tell her about his sudden desire for closure on our relationship. She would fly off the handle, accuse me of getting involved with him again. That wasn't what was happening, but I didn't think she'd understand.

She frowned. *I've just thought. What if he wanted to tell you something about the case or the missing kid?*

Then he can tell the police, which is what any normal person would do, I told her, surprised she'd even suggested it.

You're right, she signed, stepping forward to give me a hug. She peered out of the window. *He's still there.*

I looked where she was indicating. *It looks like he's on the phone. He'll probably go soon.*

Mike stood outside staring at my flat for another ten minutes before he walked away. I'd been hoping he'd parked right outside so I could see what kind of car he was driving. Had it been him in the sports car who had followed me last night when I went out with Max?

Part of me wondered if I should have just let him in and heard what he had to say, but I was scared of the outcome. If he really had changed, how would I feel about the new, improved version of Mike? And if he hadn't, would he go straight back to his old ways once I'd invited him over the threshold?

198

Chapter 21

My phone went off at two a.m. and I considered ignoring it. Singh's name flashed up, however, so I sat up in bed and answered.

'Hi, Paige. Did I wake you?'

'It's two in the morning,' I replied. 'Of course you woke me. What's up?'

'I've had a call from Lincolnshire police. An alarm has gone off at the school in the middle of the night. They sent a couple of uniforms out and it seems it could be related to our case. They've passed it on to us, and Forest has requested I go down there.'

'So that means I have to go too,' I said, my voice weary.

'If you don't mind?' I could tell from his voice that he didn't want to go either, but at least it'd be easier if I agreed to go. They'd never get another interpreter in the middle of the night.

'Okay. Want me to meet you there?'

'I'll pick you up.'

*　　*　　*

Fifteen minutes later, we were on the road to Lincoln. Anna had been fast asleep when I left, so I wrote her a note and stuck it to the fridge, in case she woke up and found me gone. It was a battle to stay awake, and Singh and I couldn't even play many car games because there were so few other vehicles on the road at that time.

'What happened, do we know?' I asked.

'There was a break-in of some sort,' he replied.

'Why do we need to go now, instead of just sorting it out in the morning?'

'That one I can't answer. Lincolnshire apparently insisted that they wanted someone as soon as possible.'

I yawned in response.

When we arrived at the school, there was a police car sitting outside the main entrance, and lights on in a couple of the offices, so we went inside. There we found Liz Marcek and Cassie sitting with two uniformed officers, whose eyes lit up when we walked in.

'DS Singh,' he said, introducing himself. 'What's the problem?'

'We haven't been able to get anyone to interpret, so we haven't really got to the bottom of it, sir,' one of the PCs replied.

'Where's Mike?' I asked, signing the question as well as speaking. 'He could have at least helped out until I arrived.'

It's Mike's evening off, Liz replied. *I'm not sure where he is. I've tried to reach him, but he hasn't responded to my message.*

Typical. Singh looked to the PCs to explain what they knew so far.

'We got an automatic message that the alarm had gone off, so we responded and found a student had broken into

200

the head teacher's office.' They glanced at Cassie as they said this. 'The staff hadn't been aware of the alarm.'

'Isn't the alarm linked up to the residence?' Singh asked.

It should be, Liz replied, *but it didn't go off. I assume it must be faulty. I'll get an engineer in to look at it as soon as possible.*

I immediately wondered if it was simply a malfunction, or if someone had disabled it.

'Why are you here, Miss Marcek?'

It's our policy here that teaching staff take occasional shifts in the residence, in order to foster stronger relationships with the students. Tonight was my turn.

Singh looked surprised that the deputy head had included herself on the rota. 'Did Steve Wilkinson take shifts in the residence too?'

She nodded. *Sometimes. Not regularly, though.*

A chill ran down my spine at the idea of the man who had been grooming Leon supervising vulnerable children overnight.

Throughout this conversation, Cassie had been sitting with her arms folded and her head down, a sullen expression on her face. She was dressed in purple pyjamas and had fluffy slippers on, so she had clearly crept back into the building after the staff thought she'd gone to bed.

'Thank you, I'll take it from here,' Singh told the two PCs, and they looked relieved to be dismissed.

Taking a chair, Singh sat down opposite Cassie. 'Now Cassie, what's been going on?'

It took a moment for me to get her attention to sign the question to her, but when I did she sighed deeply.

I was looking for something, that's all.

'What were you looking for?'

She chewed her lip for a moment before replying.

I lost my phone. I thought maybe Mr Wilkinson had taken it.

'Why would he have taken it, Cassie?'

She shrugged but didn't reply.

Liz shook her head. *Cassie, how did you even get in here?*

There was a pause, in which Cassie looked at all of us in turn. A slow smile spread across her face. *I've got a key*, she signed.

A key? How did you get a key?

But Cassie refused to say anything else and couldn't produce the key when she was asked about it, saying she must have dropped it.

Liz pulled Singh aside. *I honestly can't believe that she got hold of a key to the head teacher's office. I must have left it unlocked by accident, and then when she opened the door, the motion sensor set off the alarm.*

'I think we should escort her back to the residence now,' Singh replied. 'I'm assuming you don't want to press charges?'

No, don't be silly. If we pressed charges every time one of the students in the residence came up with a silly prank we'd need a police officer here all the time.

We walked back over to the residence, where the lights were on in the sitting room. Bradley and Courtney were waiting for us.

What happened? Bradley asked.

Is it something to do with Leon? We saw the police. Courtney pulled her dressing gown round her, obviously self-conscious at the sight of us.

No, nothing to do with Leon, Liz told them. *Go back*

to bed. She had a sour look on her face at the two of them sitting there in pyjamas, which made sense now I knew their relationship had nearly cost the school its reputation.

No, Bradley replied, standing his ground. *I want to know what happened.*

I was looking for my phone, what's the big deal? Cassie flung herself down onto the sofa. *You didn't have to call the bloody police!*

'Cassie, you set the alarm off,' Singh explained. 'The school is linked directly to the police station. They had to come. You're lucky we're not going to arrest you.'

What were you doing, you idiot? Bradley asked her.

I'm not an idiot, she replied, her jaw clenched.

To my surprise, Bradley leant over and gave her a hug. *You're right, you're not. I'm sorry. But what do you mean, you were looking for your phone?*

Liz interrupted. *Cassie seems to have got it into her head that Mr Wilkinson might have taken her phone. Did he confiscate it while you were on the trip?* She directed this question to Cassie.

No, but I thought . . . Cassie didn't finish and let her hands drop to her lap.

You had your phone on Saturday, on the trip, Bradley told her.

Cassie nodded.

Well, didn't you have it in the bus on the way back to school? You showed me the post about Leon going missing and that video of the dog. You know, the one that couldn't catch the ball?

Cassie stared at him for a moment, as if she was willing him to understand something. *Yeah, you're right. But* . . .

A look passed between the two of them, and Bradley's expression changed as Cassie's meaning dawned on him. He turned to Courtney, who frowned, but then she obviously understood too and her eyes widened.

Should we go back to bed now, Miss Marcek? Bradley asked.

The deputy head looked puzzled at this sudden change in attitude. *Yes, I suppose so.*

'No, wait a moment,' Singh said. 'What is it that you three aren't telling us?'

The teenagers all put on their most innocent expressions. *Nothing, sir*, Bradley replied, laying it on thick.

Singh looked at them. 'If I find out that any of you are hiding something that could help us find Leon, or find out who killed Mr Wilkinson, we'll be having a very serious conversation about wasting police time. Do you understand?'

The three of them nodded, but none of them volunteered any new information, so Liz allowed Bradley and Courtney to go back to bed.

Cassie, you wait a minute, the police want to speak to you.

Come on Miss Marcek, she knows what she did was wrong, Courtney said. *Can't it wait until tomorrow?*

Absolutely not. You've got Paige and DS Singh out of bed in the middle of the night, Cassie. The least you can do is sit here for ten more minutes.

She shooed the other two back to their rooms, watching as Bradley climbed the stairs. It looked like he was going to try and sign something to Cassie behind our backs, but then he noticed me watching him and he carried on up.

'Cassie, why did you think your phone might be in Mr

204

Wilkinson's office?' Singh asked once the other two students had gone.

The girl sat with her hands between her knees, watching us. She shrugged, but didn't offer any other response.

'Cassie, I'd like you to answer the question.'

Someone told me it would be there.

'Who told you that?'

She shook her head. *Just someone.*

'Was it another student?'

No response.

'Or an adult?'

Again, no response from Cassie.

Singh sat back in his chair and thought for a moment. 'Is there a reason you decided to go and look in the middle of the night?'

Cassie looked up at Singh, her eyes wide. *They said I had to go at midnight, then nobody would see me.*

Singh gave her a sympathetic smile. 'Do you think someone might be trying to get you into trouble, Cassie?'

The girl was taken aback at this question, and looked to Liz before she answered.

No, they wouldn't want that. They wouldn't want me to get into trouble.

'They told you to go and look in a locked room in the middle of the night. They probably knew the alarm was going to set off and the police would come. Maybe they thought it would be funny to get you into trouble. Did they give you the key?'

Cassie shook her head, but the hurt in her eyes showed she believed what Singh was saying was at least possible.

'That sort of person isn't worth protecting,' Singh said gently.

For a moment, I thought Cassie was going to tell him the truth, but she shook her head. *I can't remember who it was,* she signed, not making eye contact. *I must have misunderstood them. It's my fault.*

Singh tried a few different ways to persuade Cassie to talk, but all to no avail. Eventually, Liz sent her off to bed.

'Is it possible that Cassie is telling the truth about having a key?'

I suppose it's possible, although I don't know what she could have done with it between opening the door and her being caught. And where would she have got it from in the first place? Liz asked. *I've been keeping Steve's office locked, at least until the governors make a decision about who is going to take over the headship. There are only two keys that I know of – I've got one, and the other is in Karen's office. She's our school business manager.*

'Surely Steve must have had one?' Singh asked.

Well, of course he did, but his personal effects are with the police. He will have had his keys with him on the day he died, I assume.

Could Cassie have stolen Steve's key while they were on the trip? Leaving the mystery of Cassie's key unsolved, we set off home.

'What are those kids hiding?' Singh mused. 'Did you see the way Cassie looked at Bradley?'

'Yeah, I don't know what that was about. He changed his tune pretty quickly. It must be something to do with her phone being missing, but I don't know what.'

'Whatever it was, Courtney is obviously in on it too. They all know something and they're keeping it secret.' He scratched his chin, his stubble making a rasping noise as he did. 'Do you think they could be involved in Steve's murder?'

'I have no idea,' I replied, stifling a yawn. 'I can't quite see them all banding together to kill Steve, if that's what you're wondering. You'd think Mike and Sasha would have noticed the whole group trooping off into the woods on Saturday morning.'

'You're not very helpful when you're tired, are you?'

'I'm solar powered,' I replied.

Before Singh dropped me off I turned to him.

'Was Liz right? Did Steve have keys on him when he died?'

'That's what I'm going to check, first thing in the morning. Until then, though, I think we can both manage a couple of hours' sleep.'

'I doubt it,' I replied. 'Everything is going to be going round in my head, I don't think I'll get much rest now.'

He grimaced. 'I know what you mean. I can't figure out how everything links up. I mean, now that we've found out about the grooming, at least we have a motive for Leon killing Steve, and if he did, then it makes sense that we found his blood at the crime scene. Maybe Forest was right, Leon might have discovered who "Joe" really was, taken Steve's knife, and cut himself while he was killing his teacher. He must not have realised he was hurt, or he wouldn't have left the knife there. It feels like the most likely scenario right now. But what's going on with these kids? What do they know that they're not telling us?' He gave me a look of genuine confusion.

'And who did that charm belong to?' I added, reminding him of the small letter C that we'd found in the pavilion. 'Was someone else in there with Leon: Courtney or Cassie?

207

And was he hiding there before he killed Steve, lying in wait, or did he break in afterwards for somewhere to hide?'

Singh made a frustrated noise at the back of his throat. 'I don't know. Something still feels wrong to me. We're missing something, I can tell.'

We sat in silence for a moment before I got out of the car.

'You'll figure it out,' I told him.

'I hope so,' he replied with a sigh. 'I'm worried that if we don't find the answers soon, it'll be too late for Leon.'

Ten hours before the murder

Cassie glanced over at Leon sitting on the sofa next to her. Should she tell him the truth now? Bradley had said Leon was making a mistake, and she didn't know what to do. What would her special friend want her to do?

Come with me, she signed to him. *I need to tell you something.*

Without waiting to see if he was following her, she got up and went to the room she was sharing with Courtney. Inside, she sat on her bed and waited for Leon.

A few minutes later, the door opened. Leon didn't sit down, but stood, palms spread.

What? You going to explain why you've been reading my messages?

I haven't been reading your messages.

Bullshit! Leon kicked the corner of her bed and she shrank back.

I haven't, I promise, she insisted. *There's something I need to tell you. Something about Joe.*

For fuck's sake, not you as well? I've had enough of this from Bradley.

He turned to leave, but Cassie stood up and grabbed his arm. *You have to listen to me. Stop talking to me like I'm stupid. I know things that you don't know. I know who Joe is.*

Yeah, I get it, he signed, shaking her off. *You all know everything about Joe. Joe was your friend first. Whatever. I've heard it all, and I don't give a shit.*

No, I mean I know who Joe really is.

Leon stared at Cassie for a moment, and she grinned at him, hoping he realised she wanted to tell him her secret. A moment later, however, she realised she'd seriously misjudged the situation.

Stop trying to mess with other people's lives, Cassie, Leon snarled. *Or one day you're going to get hurt.*

He stormed out of the room, slamming the door behind him.

Chapter 22

Friday 30th November

'Good morning. My name is Ravjit Singh, and I am a detective sergeant with Humberside police. We're here to talk to you today about safety, specifically how you can stay safe online.'

I stood at the front of the school hall next to Singh, interpreting for him. Given what had come to light about Steve and Leon's online chats, it had been agreed that it was important for the students to have a reminder of basic online safety. Years Five and upwards were present in the assembly, Liz Marcek having deemed it to be inappropriate for the youngest pupils.

Some officers had been through all the recovered messages, and they had discovered that Leon had told 'Joe' an awful lot about himself, including what school he went to, and that he was a residential student. He'd also told him about a few of the activities and trips he'd been on recently, specifying places and times. Of course, Steve had already known this, but if Leon had been talking to a predator from outside the school, they could have used that information to find him.

Bradley, Kian, Courtney and Cassie all entered the hall together and sat down in a line. Bradley's leg jiggled nervously, and Kian had a groove in his forehead from frowning. Courtney was doing her best to look relaxed, but I noticed her chewing on the edge of her fingernail. Even Cassie was looking worried, but that could have had more to do with her breaking into Steve's office just a few hours earlier. Sasha came in after the four of them and stood at the side of the hall. She hadn't been in the school yesterday, but I wasn't surprised she'd made the effort to be there today.

Once the official presentation was over, DS Singh came back to the front of the stage and addressed all eighteen students.

'I know you all think you know how to keep yourselves safe, but recent events in the school suggest that not all of you are taking it to heart. It's so easy to think it won't be you, but children are targeted online every day by people pretending to be someone they're not. It's possible Leon was planning to meet someone he met online, a person he thought he could trust with his personal information.'

Suddenly, all the attention was on Singh. I thought it was most likely because they were desperate for information that felt forbidden, information their teachers had been keeping from them, but I hoped at least some of it was out of concern for their fellow pupil.

'We still don't know where Leon is. He might be in hiding, scared to let anyone know where he is. Or, someone might be keeping him away from his friends and the people who care about him. We've been looking at Leon's phone and his online messages. Remember, Leon has had exactly the same education as you. He's had all the talks about online safety, the same ones you have. He knows the advice and the rules you're told to follow. He met someone online, and he believed what they said to him, even though we now know they weren't who they said they were. And now Leon is missing.'

Singh paused for a moment to let these words sink in. I could see Samira on the back row, biting her lip, tears in her eyes, and she caught my eye briefly before looking away. She looked terrified – but was she scared because she knew what her friend had been doing, or because she didn't?

A girl put her hand up. I didn't recognise her; she looked a couple of years younger than Leon. Singh nodded to her.

Did Leon kill Mr Wilkinson?

I interpreted this question for Singh, and I also signed it again for the students who hadn't been able to see the girl. All eighteen of them stared at Singh, waiting for his answer.

'We're still trying to find out what happened. Remember, if any of you think you know anything, we're here and you can talk to us. If there's anything you're worried about, anything that scares you, please come and tell us about it. Our job is to help you and protect you. Even if there's someone in the school that you're worried about, please tell us.'

There was a pause as I saw this sinking in, some of the students realising the seriousness of the situation. Was there someone in the school that posed a risk to these students, or had that risk been eliminated now Steve Wilkinson was dead? A thought occurred to me, and I wondered if Singh had been looking into the idea of the murderer being some sort of vigilante, trying to keep the students safe from a predator.

There were no more questions, and Singh dismissed them. As the teachers led their students out of the hall, Liz Marcek came over.

I think that was a little unnecessary, suggesting there might be someone close to them who wants to hurt them. If you've scared any of my students, I will not be happy. Her jaw was set in a solid line as she glared at Singh.

'I'd rather scare them into taking extra precautions than let them think online safety isn't important, and I want them to realise they can come to us with anything they've witnessed or experienced in school that has made them uncomfortable. I'm sorry if that doesn't quite go along with your ideas, Miss Marcek, but my priority is the safety of these children.'

When Singh got angry, he didn't shout. He spoke clearly and calmly, and the only indicator that his emotions were high was the flashing of his eyes. Liz held his gaze for a moment, then nodded.

'I checked the list of Steve's personal effects after Cassie's claim about finding a key,' Singh continued. 'There were two bunches of keys found in his room in the cabin, one of which held his house and car keys. I assume the others are for the school.'

He showed Liz a photo of a set of keys and she pointed to one of them. *That's his office key, so it's definitely accounted for. I don't understand where Cassie got one from.*

She walked off, looking puzzled, and I knew how she felt. I had been sure that Cassie had taken Steve's key, but it was accounted for. Maybe this mysterious friend she had talked about had given it to her?

Singh looked at me and shook his head. 'I probably shouldn't have said that, about keeping the kids safe, but I didn't like her insinuation. I believe in protecting the children from the gory details of this crime, but these kids aren't going to respect us, and therefore talk to us, unless we're honest with them.'

He began to pack up the laptop that had displayed the presentation, and Sasha came over to speak to me.

I can't believe this is happening. Her face was drawn and there were dark circles under her eyes. *Liz called me yesterday to tell me what the police had discovered about Steve. How did I miss something like this?*

Both Steve and Leon hid it very well, for different reasons, I replied, trying to reassure her, but she didn't look convinced.

I know that's how men like him are successful, because they can blend into society and often nobody would suspect them. But still. I feel like I should have realised something was going on with Leon, and then followed it through.

Singh came back over to us and Sasha gave him a nod in greeting.

'I think there's a student waiting to talk to us,' he said, looking towards the doorway. I turned and saw Cassie, leaning on the doorframe. She beckoned to us.

'Hi Cassie. Is there something you wanted to talk to us about?' Singh asked as we approached her.

Cassie laughed, and shook her head. *You think people will tell you things about this school?*

'We're hoping that people will tell us anything that's worrying them,' Singh replied, choosing his words carefully. 'I'm sure there are stories and gossip that have nothing to do with Leon and Mr Wilkinson. But if anyone

215

knows something that might help us with our investigation, they really should talk to us about it.'

Cassie nodded slowly. *What if someone knows something, but they're not allowed to tell you?*

'They'll always be allowed to tell us, Cassie,' Singh said, looking her in the eyes. 'If someone has told them that they're not allowed, that other person hasn't got their best interests in mind.'

For a moment, I thought Cassie was going to tell us something, but then Jess Farriday appeared behind her.

Cassie, you need to get back to class, she told her. *Don't waste the detective's time.*

The girl hesitated, then backed away, watching us as she left.

'Miss Farriday, can we help you?' Singh asked, his voice curt. I could tell he was angry at her dismissal of Cassie.

I wanted to make sure Cassie got back to her lessons, she replied. *You've wasted enough of the students' time already this morning.*

She turned and stalked away. Somehow, I didn't believe her. I wondered if she'd come back to see if any of the students were hoping to speak to the police. Sasha frowned at Jess's retreating back, then excused herself and went off in the same direction.

What could be going through Jess's mind right now? The man she'd been seeing had been exposed as a paedophile, grooming one of his own students. Surely she should be more shocked and horrified? Unless her relationship with Steve hadn't been what it had seemed. Anna had told me that Jess used men to get what she wanted, so maybe the police should be looking at what she might have wanted from Steve.

'Right, I think we should wait for a while, in case a student does want to speak to us, or in case Cassie comes back,' Singh said. 'I can't quite read her. I don't know if there's actually anything useful she can tell us or not. I know Sasha said she had learning difficulties, but she comes across as quite astute to me. Could it all be an act?'

He looked at me as he asked this, suggesting it wasn't a rhetorical question, but I shook my head. 'I'm the wrong person to ask. Her BSL is a little bit below age appropriate, I'd say, but all that means is she might have some level of language delay, it doesn't always point to learning difficulties. However, looking at it the other way around, if a student had learning difficulties, I would probably expect them to have some language delay. But I think you'd need an educational psychologist to answer that for certain. Could you ask to look at her school records?' I suggested.

'On what grounds, though?' Singh asked. 'No, I don't think we can do that at the moment, we just need to keep an eye on her. A couple of the students mentioned her imaginary friend, but what if this is a real person? She's claiming her friend is telling her not to talk to the police, and at first I wondered if this was a voice in her head, or if it was all just made up for attention, but I'm starting to think it could be an actual person who's manipulating her.'

'If Cassie's "friend" told her to look for her phone in Steve's office, it would make sense for them to be real,' I said. 'Why else would she break in there in the middle of the night?'

We thought about this as we waited, but no students

appeared over break time, and when the next lesson started Singh wanted to get set up for some more interviews. I'd forgotten to charge my phone overnight, so while he was setting up I went back to my car for a portable charger I always kept in my glove compartment. As I shut the car door I saw a movement out of the corner of my eye. On the far side of the car park, I could see two people down the side of the residential block, an adult and a female student. A bolt of adrenaline shot through me and I headed towards them. Given what we'd learnt about safeguarding issues in the school, I wasn't going to just sit there. Even if it was perfectly innocent, I knew that the students should have been in lessons.

As I approached, I realised it was Mike, and the student was Cassie. They were signing frantically to one another, and I could see by the expression on her face that she was giving him some attitude.

'Is everything okay?' I asked when I got close enough for Mike to hear me.

He whirled around. 'Paige. What do you want?'

'I saw you talking and I wondered why Cassie was out of class.' I could see something flaring in his eyes as I spoke – was it fear or anger? Behind him, Cassie took a step back and leant against the wall. Her eyes were wide, but I thought it was with interest in our argument rather than fear.

'That's between me and my student.'

I didn't speak for a minute, wondering what to do. I had absolutely no authority in this place, and yet something felt wrong, wrong enough for me to want to do something about it.

'You can go now, thank you,' Mike said to me, his

voice a low warning rumble, but I ignored it and reached past him to Cassie. As I did, my arm brushed his and I felt a burning sensation in my scar.

Cassie, come with me, I signed. *Miss Marcek wants to speak to you.*

The girl's eyes lit up. She slipped past Mike and walked towards me, waving goodbye to him as she went. I walked back across the car park with Cassie, not knowing what I was going to say when we reached the deputy head's office. Had I done the right thing? Or had I just interfered where it wasn't my place, and made my ex angry unnecessarily?

Chapter 23

I took Cassie inside and looked around for someone to escort her back to class. Liz Marcek was standing in the lobby having a discussion with one of the teachers.

Cassie, why are you out of class? she asked the girl, ignoring me.

Sorry, Miss Marcek, I'm going now.

The deputy head signed something to the teacher, then turned back to Cassie. *Come on, I'll walk with you.*

They both walked away from me without her asking for any explanation as to why I had been with Cassie or where we'd been. I was glad I didn't have to explain, but I was concerned that the deputy head hadn't even asked.

As I walked back to the meeting room, I wondered if I'd done the right thing. I told myself I should tell Singh what I'd seen, but I hadn't witnessed anything illegal or untoward. Mike wasn't the one who had been messaging students, that was Steve, and he was dead.

The detectives wanted to interview Jess Farriday again,

to see if she had had any suspicion about what Steve was doing. She was visibly trembling when she came into the meeting room, though whether it was from anger following the run-in in the hall with Cassie, or distress at the revelation about Steve, I couldn't tell. Singh had decided to continue conducting any interviews at the school in order to minimise the disruption for staff and students. That, and it was about fifty minutes from the school to the police station in Scunthorpe, so it prevented any wasted time asking staff to travel. Lincoln didn't come under the jurisdiction of Humberside police, being in Lincolnshire rather than North Lincolnshire, but because the crime had taken place at Normanby Hall it was still under Humberside.

It felt strange to be sitting here opposite Jess, knowing she had dated both my current and ex-boyfriend, and was possibly seeing Mike again. We were so different, in looks and temperament, yet we'd both been attracted to the same men. In her teenage years she'd been a bully; was she still the same? She was slimmer than me, and prettier, and I found myself wondering if Max would prefer her to me if he had the opportunity to date her again. Shaking the thought off, I concentrated on the conversation.

There must be some mistake with your evidence against Steve, Jess told the detectives as soon as she sat down. *You're wasting your time with this when you should be trying to find Leon.*

'What sort of mistake?' Singh asked gently.

There's no way Steve could have been involved in anything like that. Maybe he was trying to show the kids the dangers of talking to strangers online? she suggested.

'The nature of the messages that passed between him

and Leon go far beyond what could be considered reasonable in that situation.'

There was desperation in Jess's eyes, and I felt a pang of sympathy for her. It must be awful to discover the man you had been dating was hiding such a terrible secret.

I still can't believe it, she repeated, shaking her head. *He would never do anything like that. I was dating him, I'd know if he was the sort of man who would do something like that!*

Singh leant forward slightly. 'Miss Farriday, I completely understand your position. Nobody ever wants to know that someone they care about is capable of committing a crime, but unfortunately it does happen. Men like that are skilled at hiding their actions, because they know how other people would view them.'

Could there have been a mix-up with accounts? she persisted. *Maybe the techs made a mistake.*

'One of our forensic IT officers is examining the school system as we speak,' he told her. 'If anything got mixed up, or if things were transferred from one account to another, we'll know about it.'

That must be what happened, she insisted. *This wasn't Steve. He definitely wasn't that sort of person.*

Tears shone in her eyes as she signed this, and I wondered if she was more concerned about posthumous damage to Steve's reputation or damage to her own if people found out she'd been dating a sex offender with a preference for teenage boys.

'Are you sure you weren't aware of this before yesterday?' Singh asked, a cold note in his voice. His eyes narrowed, and I knew that meant he was on to something.

What do you mean? Jess asked, blinking rapidly.

'When we were looking into Steve Wilkinson's computer account activity, we found that someone had used his log-in details on Friday evening, around eight o'clock. At that time, Steve was already at Normanby Hall.'

There was a long pause.

And you think that was me?

'Apart from the residential staff, yours was the only other computer account accessed that evening, so we know you were in school.'

Another long pause, then her shoulders sagged. *Okay, it was me. But I had no idea about these messages to Leon.*

'Why were you using his account, then?' Singh asked, his face impassive.

Jess chewed her lip for a moment before answering. *I was looking at some of the budget data. I wanted to take some of the students to a disability sports competition in Bristol, but it would have required an overnight stay. Steve said we couldn't afford it. I thought I could have a look at the data and find a way of saving some money in another area, so that we could go on the trip.*

It sounded like a plausible explanation, though a bit altruistic for the Jess Anna had described to me. Would she really want to risk getting in trouble just so that some kids could go on a school trip? What was in it for her?

Singh didn't seem completely convinced either. 'How did you get his log-in details?'

Jess paused before she replied. *He gave me his password.*

'Really? He was your boyfriend, but he was also your boss. Why would he risk compromising his own privacy?'

He trusted me. Jess did her best to outstare Singh, but after an uncomfortable few seconds she looked away.

Without any further questions, Singh let Jess go back

to her teaching. He sat back and sighed, folding his arms.

'I don't know if she's telling the truth, but we have no evidence to contradict her. We have to assume that Leon is our main suspect now,' he said, though I thought he was talking to himself rather than me. 'Finding his blood at the crime scene makes it look like he and Steve fought, Leon was injured in the process, but he killed Steve. If Leon arranged to meet Joe, then found out his sixteen-year-old online boyfriend was actually his middle-aged head teacher . . .' His voice tailed off and he stared out of the window for a moment. 'Hopefully we'll be able to get a full record of the messages between them, then we can see if they arranged to meet. And maybe we'll get an indication of where Leon's hiding now.'

'Even if he did kill Steve, he's still a victim,' I said. 'He was abused by his father, then found out another man was trying to take advantage of him. He won't feel like he can trust anyone now, so where would he go?'

Singh was about to reply when there was a knock on the door. Before either of us had a chance to open it, Liz Marcek flung it open and stormed in, a tablet clutched in her hands. She shoved it in Singh's face and he took it from her, his frown deepening as he scrolled. I glanced over and saw the browser was open to a news page, and what appeared to be a story about a staff member grooming students.

'Who did this?' Singh barked.

I don't know. One of the staff just brought it to my attention. This didn't come from anyone in the school, so I want to know what the hell you're thinking of, leaking a story like this to the media?

Singh was skimming the story. 'It says a source close to the investigation. That could quite easily be one of your staff.'

Liz let out a snort, then turned to me. *Or it could be your interpreter. I've heard she has a reputation for trying to draw attention to herself.*

I was so taken aback at her accusation that Singh had to prompt me to interpret it for him. I opened my mouth to reply, to defend myself, but he cut me off.

'Miss Marcek, I understand that you're angry, but I will not accept unfounded allegations being levelled at my colleagues. The only people who know who leaked this are the reporter, and the leak themselves. This story is just as damaging to our investigation as it is to your school.'

To hell with your investigation, she signed, a snarl on her face. *The man's dead now, what does it matter who killed him if he was a pervert preying on our students? They've done us a favour.*

'And what about Leon?' Singh asked, standing up so he could look Liz in the eye. 'Should we forget about trying to find him? A vulnerable runaway teenager?'

For a brief moment I thought Liz was going to snap back at him, but she didn't reply, her hands clenched into fists at her side, and a moment later she stormed back out of the room. Blowing out a long breath, Singh rubbed his head.

'Shit. This has made things a lot more difficult. We need to track down this leak as soon as possible.'

'It wasn't me, Rav,' I said, but he held up a hand to stop me.

'Of course it wasn't you, I know that. I expect it was a member of staff looking for a bit of extra cash. I told her it was a bad idea telling them all about it yesterday, but I understand why she did it. If any staff members referred students' disclosures on to Steve, we need to follow them up and see if he dealt with them accordingly. This leak could easily have come from a staff member who has lost faith in this school's ability to handle safeguarding concerns.'

I didn't say that I was sure I knew who had put the idea into Liz's head that it might have been me – Mike hadn't been happy with the way I'd spoken to him last night, so it stood to reason that he could have leaked the story then tried to lay the blame on me in a twisted sort of revenge. Besides, he always needed extra cash, and he'd see this as an easy payout.

Singh called Forest to discuss what to do next while I sat in the entrance and waited. Liz had left the tablet behind, so I scrolled through the story. It didn't give out too much detail, which suggested that the person leaking the information didn't actually know that much, or they were holding some information back for more money. If it was Mike, that was definitely something he would do.

Mike was a gambling addict. Maybe he had his addiction under control at the moment, but when we were together it had ruled his life. When he wasn't at work, he was playing online games or going to the casino in Lincoln. Each month, when his own wages ran out, he started on mine. At first it was small amounts here or there near to the end of the month, with promises to pay me back. Then the amounts got bigger and the length of time before he ran out of his own money got shorter. If he was still gambling, I knew he'd do pretty much anything for money, and throwing his own workplace under the bus wasn't outside the realms of possibility. Of course, if the school was closed down due to safeguarding concerns he would lose his job, but he'd never been very good at looking ahead to the consequences of his actions.

I wondered if I should tell the police this aspect of Mike's

226

history, but was it my place? There was no suggestion that money had been involved in the crime itself, and I didn't even know if he was still gambling. Maybe our break-up had been the catalyst he had needed to stop for good, and I would be maligning him by bringing it all up again.

I looked around the entrance hall and wondered what would happen to the school now. Such a major failure in safeguarding procedures could put the whole place at risk. It would be a huge blow if it closed, both for the past students who remembered it fondly and for those potential future students who wouldn't get the benefit of its existence. Schools for the deaf were becoming rarer, with most deaf children attending their local mainstream school, but I felt there should always be an option, an alternative choice for deaf children and their parents. Many children could thrive in their local schools, but others needed the tailored curriculum and environment a school like this could offer. Where would the current students go if it closed? Would they go to their local schools? Would the five students in care end up in a children's home, in an environment where others struggled to communicate with them?

I didn't want to shatter Anna's memories of the school by telling her about the safeguarding concerns, but I knew she would probably read it herself soon enough, so I decided to be proactive and sent her the link before I set off.

Almost immediately, I got a text back from her.

I've already seen it. I need to talk to you when you get home.

I was about to send a reply when Samira appeared in the doorway, her eyes wide with distress.

Please could you come over to the residence? she asked, looking at Singh. *Something's happened.*

227

Chapter 24

Singh and I hurried after Samira, wondering what had happened. Was one of the students hurt? Sasha was there and she let us in, then she and Samira led us upstairs to Leon's room. The door was ajar, and when we looked inside the room was in a state. Drawers had been opened and their contents strewn everywhere, the mattress was tipped on its side and the bed had been moved away from the wall.

Samira found Leon's room like this, Sasha explained.

'Who has access to the residence during the school day?' Singh asked.

All the staff, and the students who live here, though strictly speaking they shouldn't be here between nine and three.

'Is there any way of knowing who entered the building?'

Sasha frowned. *I think there are CCTV cameras. You'd better ask Liz about that.*

Singh nodded. 'I will.'

He went into Leon's room and started having a look around, leaving me out on the landing.

I haven't told Miss Marcek, Samira told me, looking flustered. *I was coming to tell her when I saw you, so obviously I told you first.*

I stuck my head in the door and asked Singh if Samira could go. He came back out and fixed her with a stern look.

'Why were you here, Samira? You don't board, so you shouldn't even be in the residence.'

The girl shrugged and wouldn't look at him. *I wanted to have a look in Leon's room, see if I could work out where he might have gone. I miss him.*

'How did you get in?' he asked.

Samira blinked at him then looked down at her feet. *The door was open. Whoever left last must not have closed it properly.*

Singh didn't look convinced, but he nodded anyway.

'You can go and tell Miss Marcek now. We'll find you if we need to speak to you again.'

Samira glanced at Sasha before she left, but the social worker was busy looking past me into Leon's room. While I waited for Singh, I wandered over to the window on the landing and looked outside. The back of the residence was next to the sports field, and as I watched I saw a group of students approaching. It must have been break time, unless Kian, Bradley, Courtney and Cassie had all decided to skip classes at the same time.

The four of them stopped a short distance away, but a little too far away for me to pick up everything they were signing.

. . . Joe? Courtney signed.

I only told them a little bit, Kian replied.

Don't have a go at him, how was he to know? Bradley interjected.

I couldn't see Courtney's reply, and Cassie was just standing and watching the rest of them before getting involved in the conversation.

. . . tomorrow, she signed. I kicked myself for not being able to catch what she'd said.

That's stupid, Bradley responded.

Cassie turned as she replied to him. *Don't call me stupid. I'm the least stupid person here.*

Yeah, whatever.

The older girl shook her head and turned back to Courtney and Kian.

Mr Wilkinson didn't . . .

Yes he did, Kian replied. *We all know he did. We need to tell someone.*

No, Courtney replied. *That's a bad idea. We'll all be in trouble.*

I was wrenched away from observing the rest of the conversation by the arrival of the deputy head. She looked past me, out of the window, and frowned when she saw the four students standing together.

Sasha, go and chase those four back to class, please. I don't know what they're doing there but it's probably nothing useful.

Sasha looked like she was about to protest, but then glanced out of the window to see who Liz was talking about. When she realised which four students it was she sighed then headed down the stairs, and Liz went into Leon's room to see DS Singh. I followed.

What on earth happened in here? she asked, her eyes roving over the disarray. *Did someone break in?*

'That's what we want to ask you,' Singh replied. 'We need to check the CCTV from outside the building. There are no obvious signs of a break-in, so we assume it was someone with authorised access to the building. Does the school keep a log of who has entered the building and when?'

No, we can probably see when someone used a fob, but they're not individually identifiable. The deputy head wore a concerned frown. *How do we know if anything has been taken?*

'I don't think we can, without asking Leon himself.'

Could it have been Leon? Miss Marcek asked. *Could he have crept back in here to get something from his room?*

'I doubt he would have left it in such a mess,' Singh replied. 'Even if he didn't know where he'd left whatever he was looking for, he probably wouldn't have wanted to leave any trace of himself. No, I think this is most likely someone else.' He looked around him, hands on his hips. 'Can we find out if any students were out of class today?'

I'm sure I would have been informed of any truancy, but I'll check, Liz replied.

I thought about Cassie and Mike talking earlier and wondered if it was connected. Could one of them be responsible for this? I remembered the look on Mike's face when I had interfered and decided I wouldn't mention it just yet; I didn't want to wind him up unnecessarily. I didn't trust him not to retaliate.

The three of us left Leon's room and I had a quick glance out of the window again before we went downstairs.

The four students were still there, but they'd moved, and Sasha was now with them. She was signing something to them, but they didn't seem to be taking much notice of her. I wished I'd been able to observe more of their conversation; I was sure there was something they were keeping from the police, something to do with Joe.

'Hi Paige.'

I turned to see Mike behind me as I was walking to my car.

'Hi. Sorry, I can't talk. I'm not needed any more so I'm going home.'

'You can't be earning very much if they waste your time like this,' he said, continuing to walk towards me. 'I was surprised when I heard you'd gone freelance. How are you managing, doing it all yourself?'

'Perfectly well.' I had to resist telling him I had months when I was scraping around for every penny, but I bit my tongue. My financial difficulties were his doing, and part of me wanted to throw that in his face, but my current situation was nothing to do with him, and I didn't want him to have any information that he could somehow twist to use against me if he wanted to.

'What's up, Paige? Why are you being so rude?'

'I'm sorry you interpret my attitude as rude,' I said, 'but I just told you, I'm leaving.'

'I thought if you'd finished work for the day we'd finally be able to talk. You owe me that at least.'

I turned to face him, arms folded. 'What do you mean, I owe you?'

'I know we didn't have the best break-up, but you have to admit that I came off worse. You made me homeless and left me with nothing, when I had no idea you were even unhappy. If we'd talked about it, maybe things could have been different. I'm sure you've moved on now, but I thought we could at least be friendly, show an interest in each other's lives.'

I couldn't stop myself from rolling my eyes, and the moment I did I knew I'd made a mistake, because he took a step closer to me, making me uncomfortable.

'Don't roll your eyes at me, Paige, it's rude. I've apologised and I'm trying to understand things from your perspective, but you're not helping.'

I refused to rise to the bait and didn't respond other than by raising my eyebrows. For a moment we stood there, almost nose to nose, until he laughed and turned away.

'Good to see you're even more spirited than you used to be. I've missed that about you,' he said, reaching out as if to touch my face. I deflected his hand before he could reach me, and he laughed again. It wasn't a pleasant sound.

'Don't touch me,' I said, hoping the tone of my voice was warning enough. I regretted it instantly; I should have realised someone like Mike would take that as a challenge.

He smirked. 'You're probably used to having men touch you, I'm sure.'

I didn't respond. I wasn't going to rise to it. Looking over his shoulder, I hoped Singh or even Liz Marcek would appear again soon and give me an excuse to get away from him.

Following my line of sight, Mike stepped back for a moment and leant on my car.

'So, what are you actually doing here?'

'What do you mean?'

'I'm sure the police are able to employ better qualified people to interpret for them. That's the thing about you CODAs, you all assume you're better than other hearing people who can sign.'

Before he met me, Mike wouldn't have known what a CODA was – a child of deaf adults, meaning a hearing child brought up in a deaf family, usually using BSL. The part of me that wasn't desperately thinking of a way to get away from him was interested that he'd now picked up on this as a way to insult and undermine me.

'I'm here because I'm on the contact list should Humberside police need a *qualified* interpreter.'

I couldn't resist the dig about being qualified, after what he'd said. He was the sort of person who always assumed he was better at everything than the next man or woman, even if that person had spent years training and gained far more experience than he had.

He nodded slowly. 'I see, I see. Fine, don't tell me what it's really about.'

I took a step to the side and looked round him again. For a moment I considered going inside to look for someone, anyone, but Mike would follow me in there and he knew the building far better than me. He was leaning on the driver's side door, so I couldn't just get in my car and drive away.

'How long have you been working here, then?' I asked him. Several years ago I had learnt that the best way to deflect Mike was to ask him to talk about himself.

'Three years,' he replied. As long as we'd been broken up, then. 'I thought I might as well put my skills to good use. I've always been good with kids, I'm the sort of person they look up to.' He beamed at me, and I could

234

see him puff his chest out a little. God he was self-centred. And he honestly believed every word he said about himself.

'I hadn't taken any BSL exams before I started, but the head at the time could see how good a candidate I was. I did them as a formality, really.'

No mention of who it was that taught him to sign in the first place, then. I was surprised that someone as astute as Jane Villiers hadn't seen through Mike's arrogance, but maybe she'd hoped there was buried potential.

'But enough about me,' he continued. 'What about you? Are you seeing anyone?'

The sudden switch of topic startled me. 'I'd rather not talk about my personal life,' I replied, not making eye contact with him.

'So, you are seeing someone. Otherwise you would have just said no.'

I did my best to keep my face neutral. I wasn't going to give him the satisfaction of reacting to his comments.

'Who is he?'

I ignored him and continued to look past him, but he moved so his face was right in front of mine.

'I said, who is he? You know I'll find out, so it's easier if you tell me now.'

For once, I looked him in the eyes, and tried to stare him down. The last three years had strengthened me far more than I had realised, and I held his gaze for a full five seconds before I couldn't stand it any more. Dropping my eyes, I shook my head, refusing to answer.

He made an exasperated noise, then turned to see Singh walking towards us.

'Good to catch up with you,' Mike said to me, flashing me his most charming smile, which he then turned on the

DS. Before he reached us, Mike turned round and sauntered away, shooting a look back at me over his shoulder that made me shiver.

'What was that all about?' Singh asked in a low voice, and I wondered how much he'd heard.

I shook my head. 'Nothing.'

'It didn't look like nothing.'

'It's fine. I can handle him.'

'Paige, if there's anything you want to talk about . . .' Singh didn't finish the sentence, but I knew what he was thinking.

I took a deep breath. 'It's fine,' I repeated, remembering Mike's apology. Was he genuinely trying to make amends, but lapsing back into old patterns of behaviour, or was it all a calculated plan to suck me back in? I wasn't sure any more.

Nine hours before the murder

Steve's phone vibrated on the table, and a smile spread across his face as he read the message from Jess. It went completely against his own better judgement to date a member of staff, but he couldn't help himself around her. Sometimes he felt like he'd been powerless to resist her, though she insisted he was the one who'd seduced her.

'Someone's popular,' Mike commented. He'd been hunched over on one of the sofas all evening, and now the students were in bed Steve had been hoping Mike would disappear as well. He didn't like the man, found his attitude disturbing at times, and was hoping he could find a way to reallocate his role. Though if he really had caught Mike stealing from the students earlier, that would give him the perfect excuse to fire him on the spot. He needed more proof.

Mike got up and came to stand next to Steve. 'Who keeps texting you then? Girlfriend?'

Steve made a non-committal noise and carried on with

the paperwork he'd brought with him. The phone buzzed again, and his hand shot out, but Mike was faster.

'What the fuck? Jess? Are you sleeping with Jess?'

'What I do on my own time is none of your business,' Steve replied, keeping his voice as mild as he could.

'It is when you're sleeping with my fucking girlfriend.'

'Please will you mind your language while we're on a school trip.'

'The kids are in bed, now answer my fucking question.' Mike was standing too close to him, arms folded, jaw clenched. This was the last thing Steve needed, but he wasn't going to let the man intimidate him.

Standing and facing up to Mike, he looked him straight in the eye. 'Your relationship with Jess was over some time ago. You have no right to know what she or I are doing.'

'So, you are sleeping with her. You bastard.'

Steve ducked as Mike swung for him, but grabbed his arm and knocked him off balance.

'Remember who you're speaking to,' Steve growled. 'Attempt to hit me again and I'll have you arrested. As it is, you'd better start looking for another job.'

Mike snarled at him but didn't reply, instead turning on his heel and walking out of the cabin's front door, into the night.

Chapter 25

Saturday 1st December

When I arrived home the previous afternoon, Anna had flown at me the moment I walked through the door.

Who was it? Which member of staff?

You know I can't talk to you about this, I told her, weary from the last few days. *Is that what you wanted to talk to me about?*

Was it Mike? she asked, her eyes gleaming.

What? No! He's not a paedophile. How can you even suggest that?

She shrugged. *As far as I'm concerned he's a complete and utter bastard, so I wouldn't put anything past him.*

I sat down and pulled my shoes off, taking a deep breath before I replied. I was reminded of how Jess had reacted to the suggestion that Steve had been grooming Leon. Was I doing the same thing?

It wasn't Mike, I told her. *Is that what you needed me to talk about?*

She shook her head. *I sent the story to Jane Villiers, and she asked if you would go and see her again tomorrow.*

Just me? I asked, puzzled.

That's what she said, Anna replied with a shrug. *Maybe she knows something and wants you to pass it on to the police.*

If she's got something to report to the police she should contact them herself, I replied. *I'm not a go-between.*

Anna frowned at me. *No, but I thought you'd want the opportunity to do a little digging.*

Actually no, I don't. I want them to find Leon and for all of this to be over. I sat back on the sofa and closed my eyes, and stayed there for about ten minutes. She didn't bring it up again.

We'd agreed to postpone our trip to the Christmas market until things were a little less stressful, so when Max texted on Saturday morning and asked if I wanted to go out I jumped at the offer.

Where are we going? I asked as I climbed in his car.

He turned to look at me, and bit his lip as if he was thinking about something.

You might not agree to this, he began, *but I've had an idea.*

I waited for him to continue, unsure of what he was going to suggest.

The park at Normanby Hall is open to the public again, he continued. *Do you want to go up there for a walk? It hasn't snowed for a couple of days now, so the paths will be clear.*

Oh. I really don't know about that, I replied, my stomach churning slightly at the thought of going back there. It had been creepy walking around the park with Singh the other day, and I didn't know if I'd ever be able to think of the place in the same way.

I know you'll probably say no, because of what happened. I mean, you found a body, I know it's awful, but I thought it would be nice to go and make another positive memory, to try and balance out the negative. Remember that picnic, in the summer? We had such a lovely day. That's what I want you to remember about Normanby Hall. Do you see what I mean?

I couldn't help but smile at him. *I do see what you mean, yes. It's very sweet.* I reached over and squeezed his hand. *Okay, let's go. But then you're buying me lunch after.*

He gave me a grin and started the car. As he drove I tried not to think about the case, but every time I forced my mind onto other topics it kept drifting back there again.

The car park was busier than I had expected, given that it was still bitterly cold with some snow on the ground, but we found a space and layered up with hats and coats. I deliberately guided Max away from the house and towards the opposite end of the park, steering clear of the cabins and where we had found Steve's body. I was happy enough to test his theory about making positive memories, but I didn't want to push it too far.

I slipped my hand into his and enjoyed the warmth of his skin on mine. He gripped my hand, not too tightly, but just enough for me to know I was safe with him. We walked like this for a few minutes, along a little path through the woods and round towards the pond, which was half-frozen. Stopping, he pulled me closer and kissed me.

Pulling away a few seconds later, he laid a hand on my cheek. *How am I doing? Got some positive feelings yet?*

I giggled – I couldn't help it – and kissed him again.

We carried on walking, following a circular route, and soon the mansion house loomed ahead of us.

Maybe we could go round to the deer park? I suggested. *Sometimes you can see them feeding the deer in the run-up to Christmas.*

Max agreed and we set off that way, but then I paused. A familiar figure was walking in our direction: Sasha Thomas.

Hi, I signed to her, waving to attract her attention. She'd been lost in her own thoughts, staring at the ground as she walked, and seemed taken aback when I stopped her.

Paige? What are you doing here?

I introduced her to Max and explained his theory about doing something positive. She nodded then looked back in the direction she'd come from.

I wasn't doing that, unfortunately, she told me. *I can't stop thinking about Leon, and Steve.*

Glancing at Max, I hoped he would take the hint and leave me to talk to Sasha for a minute. He understood and made an excuse about going to look at the house, leaving us alone on the path.

Do you want a coffee? I suggested, pointing towards the cafe.

She looked reluctant, but eventually nodded. It wasn't until we were sitting opposite each other, warming our hands on hot mugs, that she even looked at me.

I'm worried about the residential kids, she blurted out. *I don't know why I came back here, what I thought it would achieve, but it was better than doing nothing.*

What are you worried about? I asked her.

I think there's something going on. They're too close

to each other, if that's possible. I could feel her leg jiggling nervously against the table leg. *We've had a few incidents and they've all completely closed ranks, so we've not been able to find out what happened and who was involved.*

What sort of incidents? I asked, thinking about Bradley and Courtney and the videotape.

She bit her lip. *I can't tell you. They're children in care, and I'm their social worker, so some things have to be kept confidential. But I know something at that school isn't right.*

Since Leon ran away, you mean?

No, she said, looking out of the window next to her. *I've been worried about it for a while. Have you ever known anyone who's been in a relationship with someone really manipulative? They're besotted with this person, but you know they've actually been completely brainwashed, and they're just not interested in themselves any more?*

I looked down at my drink. I'd never had a friend in that situation; I'd never seen it from the outside.

I know what you mean, I replied, not trusting myself to say anything more.

Well they're like that, Sasha continued. *As if there's someone telling them what to do. I think one of the kids has managed to get the others wrapped round their little finger.*

Which one? I tried to keep my eagerness at bay as I asked the question, but I felt like Sasha knew something which she was keeping to herself.

She threw her arms up. *That's what's so bloody frustrating, I can't figure it out. Cassie is the oldest, but I don't think she's bright enough to do something like that.*

Courtney isn't interested enough in the others. Kian's the youngest, he doesn't have enough influence, and Bradley wouldn't be able to keep something like that a secret.

I thought about what she'd said. *So, you think it was Leon? You think he was controlling the others somehow?*

I don't know, she said, pushing her chair back and drumming her fingers on the edge of the table. *He's bright, he certainly could pull something off like that. I don't know why he'd do it though, unless he got a kick out of manipulating the others. I've always thought he was likeable, but maybe he's been able to manipulate me too?* Sasha ran her hands through her hair and leant forward again. *This is ridiculous. This is the first time I've told anyone about it, and it sounds completely crazy when I try to explain myself.*

I gave her an apologetic smile. *I don't know the kids or the school well enough to know what you mean. How long has this been going on?*

Since September, I think, she replied. *Well, that was when I first thought something was wrong, when I went to visit them at the start of the school year. It's always a strange time of year for kids in care – they don't have a family to go to over the summer, so the adults who care for them in those six weeks sacrifice the time with their own families in order to give them some positive experiences.*

September was when Steve took up the post as head teacher. Was his arrival connected to the students' strange behaviour?

Were all five of them there for the whole summer? I asked, my heart aching for these kids who had nowhere else to go. *They don't have any other extended family they can go to?*

Sasha shook her head. *Not this year. Courtney used to go to her grandparents for some of the holidays, but there was a falling-out a couple of years ago and they stopped inviting her. The others have nobody.*

My heart ached for these kids, growing up without the love of a family, however well they were cared for.

Could something have happened over the holidays? I asked.

This is what I'm wondering. I asked them all, but they all insisted it was nothing. Except for Leon, who told me I was asking the wrong questions. Nothing else, just that. She shook her head. *I'm wondering if he was manipulating me.*

Or he wanted to tell you, but someone else was holding something over him? I gently suggested.

She took a deep breath and I saw her shoulders sag. *You're right. When he's not here to defend himself, I shouldn't be assuming it's anything to do with him.*

I didn't understand what she thought she'd achieve by coming back to the crime scene, but maybe she didn't know what else to do to try and make sense of it all. It seemed like having someone to talk to had helped, though.

Have you told anyone at the school about this? I asked as we finished our drinks and prepared to leave.

No. Until I have concrete evidence that something's going on, I can't do anything about it, she insisted. *I could be completely wrong, and it could be that the dynamic between these five kids is completely normal for a children's home situation. They've all been through some difficult times in their lives, and they all bear the emotional scars.*

The question we need to ask is, where could Leon be? I said. *If you think he could be manipulating the other students, is it connected to Steve's murder? Or is this situation with Steve posing as Joe something completely different?*

I don't know what's connected any more, she replied. *It's possible Leon was up to something unpleasant, but that doesn't detract from what Steve did. But could the kids be hiding something that would help us find Leon?*

I thought about that for a while, and my mind kept coming back to the times I'd seen the kids discussing Joe. I was still sure there was more they hadn't told the police, but how could we get them to talk? We walked back towards the house, where Max was waiting for us, and I wondered if Sasha was right about this. In which case, if one of the residential kids had some information about where Leon was and hadn't shared it with the police, was it because they were looking for a way to use it to their own advantage?

Chapter 26

When Anna and I had cancelled our trip, I arranged a spontaneous night out with my best friend, Gem. I'd invited Anna out with us, but she said she felt like a gate-crasher. While she was living with me, she said she was going to make an effort to see her own friends, and didn't want to feel like she was muscling in on mine. She would have been welcome, all of my friends knew Anna pretty well, but she declined the invitation anyway. On another night I would have tried harder to persuade her, but I liked the idea of spending a night without anyone who knew anything about the case. I knew if anything could take my mind off the last week it was a few cocktails and some dancing. We were meeting in a bar on Oswald Road and I took my time getting my outfit and make-up just right. Ever since I'd met Max I'd started to take a bit more pleasure in getting dressed up again, even when I wasn't seeing him. He'd certainly helped me get some of my old confidence back, telling me how thinking about me always made him smile.

When I arrived, Gem was already there, and there was a pornstar martini on the table waiting for me. I preferred a bellini, but I wasn't about to say no when someone else had already got the round in.

Hi, I waved to her as I arrived. Gem and I had been friends since we were children – she was the only deaf person in her family, and I was the only hearing one in mine, and opposites seemed to attract. We were inseparable as kids, and we had supported each other through some of the worst times in adulthood as well.

We drank and chatted for a couple of hours before we had enough cocktails inside us for Gem to suggest we dance. I'm as coordinated as a newborn giraffe, but I joined her for a couple of tunes anyway. It felt good to shake off my cares for a few hours and not worry about clients or the police or how my sister was getting on.

After about fifteen minutes of dancing, I wound my way over to the bar for a glass of water. I was hot and sweaty, unaccustomed to this sort of environment. I downed the water then turned to see Gem standing behind me with her hands on her hips.

Water? Lightweight, she teased. *Come on, more cocktails*.

She didn't listen to my protests and gave me her order, pushing me forwards to the bar. Once I'd been served I saw she'd found a table and claimed it, so I wove through the crowd to join her.

It's good to see you out enjoying yourself, she said with a grin. *Was Max okay with you coming out?*

I raised an eyebrow at her. *Still checking up on me?*

You know I always will.

I sighed. *Yes, and I didn't ask his permission, I told*

him I was coming out with you tonight so I could see him another night. And he was perfectly fine with that. He's probably out with his own friends tonight.

She squeezed my hand briefly. *Sorry for nagging, but after Mike I worry about you. A few days before you met Max you were insisting you had no interest in a relationship, and then suddenly you were dating some bloke you met during a murder investigation. You can't blame me for keeping an eye on you and how you're doing.*

I understand, Gem, of course I do. And what sort of friend would you be if you didn't do things like that? God knows where I'd be if you hadn't seen Mike for what he really was. I might still be in that same situation. I'll always be grateful for the way you cleared the flat before I got out of hospital, and for the support you gave me to put the pieces of myself back together afterwards.

She shook her head. *No, you wouldn't still be there. You would have realised eventually, without us constantly pushing you to get out.*

I nodded, deep in thought.

What? she asked.

I've seen him again recently. Mike.

What? He's got back in touch?

No, I'm working with the police again, and . . . I paused, wondering how much I should say. *He's connected.*

He's a murder suspect? Doesn't surprise me, she signed, her mouth a grim line.

That's not what I said, I admonished her. *Forget about the circumstances. The important thing is that I've been forced to speak to him and spend time in the same room as him, and I'm worried I've not got over the whole thing as fully as I thought I had.*

249

Gem frowned. *You don't mean you're still attracted to him?*

What? Oh God no, I reassured her. *No, I meant that I don't feel as confident around him as I want to be. I'm angry at myself for not being able to put up these mental barriers against him.*

Nobody ever expected you to be superhuman, Paige, Gem reassured me. *What you went through with him was horrible; nobody would be able to put all of that completely behind them. You know you could probably talk to Singh about pressing charges now?*

I shook my head. *I don't want to dredge it all up again. Besides, he's actually apologised.*

Seriously?

I nodded. *It surprised me too. It doesn't change anything that happened, but it does feel better to have him acknowledge what he did to me.*

I suppose. Don't get sucked in by him though, she warned.

I won't, I told her. *There's something else, though.*

What?

I haven't told Max about Mike.

Why not?

I thought for a moment before answering, looking round at the people dancing and drinking, enjoying their night out.

I think because I didn't want his pity. I didn't want him to think I was weak. And I didn't want him worrying about his own behaviour, trying to go out of his way not to be like my ex, if you see what I mean? Max isn't anything like Mike, and I know that because he's being himself in our relationship. I don't want him to change how he behaves because of how he thinks I might react.

But what happens when he finds out? Gem asked. *Because he will find out, sooner or later. Someone will say something to him, or to you when he's there, and eventually the story will come out. The longer you keep it from him, the more hurt he's going to be when he finds out just how much you haven't told him.*

Passing my empty glass from hand to hand, I thought about Gem's warning. I felt like I'd be risking everything I'd built up with Max by telling him about my past, but she was right. He deserved to know what I'd been through. He'd asked a couple of times about the scar on my arm, and all I'd told him was that I'd cut it on some broken glass. I think he'd known by my face that I didn't want to tell him any more than that, but he was probably still curious. And now that Mike had apologised and more or less admitted he was at fault, hopefully Max wouldn't be as angry about it. But had Mike really taken responsibility for the way he treated me? A little voice in the back of my mind was still questioning the motive behind the apology, but I silenced it.

Okay, I'll tell him. I promise, I added, looking at the sceptical expression on her face. *But how on earth do I bring it into conversation?*

Just sit him down, and say to him, I saw my ex-boyfriend today. He's an absolute piece of shit and I need to tell you exactly why.

I laughed wryly. *Yeah, that just about covers it.*

Seriously though, are you okay with having to spend time with Mike?

I nodded. *He wants to show me he's changed. I don't really believe it, but I think I should give him the benefit of the doubt.*

People don't change, Paige. They want you to think they do, but deep down they don't. If Mike's still trying to manipulate you, I worry what he'd do to you if he got you alone.

I brushed off her concerns. *He wouldn't be that stupid. Even though I didn't press charges back then, I wouldn't hesitate if he did something to me now.*

Does DS Singh think it's appropriate that you're around him?

What has Singh got to do with it?

She laughed. *Come on Paige, you know he likes you. Anna told me all about it.*

I felt a blush slowly rising up my face. *I think she's wildly inflated it. He's a nice bloke, and we get on well in a professional capacity, but that's it.*

Fine, fine. Gem held up her hands in defeat. *Still, I think you should tell him about your past with Mike, cover your back in a professional sense if nothing else.*

You've got a point, I replied. *He knows the basics, but nothing about what really went on. Though I think he's guessed it wasn't exactly a positive experience.*

Just think about it, Paige. And tell Max, too.

I nodded. *You're right. I will.*

I sighed. Just when things seemed to be going well between me and Max, I had to open up this can of worms. Hopefully he'd understand why I'd kept it from him and wouldn't make it all about him, but I felt I didn't know how he'd react to something like that.

Did I tell you he's been looking up courses for me? I told Gem, hoping to move the subject away from my disastrous previous relationship.

What sort of courses?

Textiles ones. There are accredited courses I can do from home, in my own time. It's not as good as going back to uni, but it's a start.

Max found these for you? she asked.

I nodded. *I told him about starting my degree but then dropping out to take care of Mum and make sure Anna finished her A Levels, and he said it was time for me to start thinking about my own dreams again.*

Gem nodded slowly, a look of approval on her face. *He might pass the test after all, this new man of yours,* she told me. *It's about time the two of you came round to mine again. I'd say it was your turn to host, but I don't want to risk Max offering to cook, given what you've told me about his culinary skills.*

I laughed, and Gem gave me a wink as she went up to the bar. My head was swimming slightly; I wasn't used to drinking so much, but I took a glass from her anyway. It was about time I let loose for a bit, and I didn't have anywhere better to be. As we moved back towards the dancefloor, I wondered if I could use this encounter with Mike to finally shake off that part of my life and move on.

Chapter 27

I closed the taxi door quietly, aware that it was one in the morning and many people on my street would be fast asleep. Fumbling in my bag for my keys, I didn't notice the shadow next to the doorway until it was too late.

'Where have you been?' Mike asked, his eyes roving all over my body. 'Have you been out?'

I could tell from the slight slur in his voice that he was drunk.

'What are you doing here?'

'Who were you out with?' he replied, not answering my question. 'Do you have a new boyfriend? You do, don't you. Who is he?'

'Go home, Mike.'

He shook his head like a dog trying to get water out of its ears. 'Just tell me, Paige. Who is he? Do you love him? Are you living together? No, then he'd be here. Who is he?'

His pleas were becoming more insistent. Even though

I believed his original apology had been genuine, his behaviour since then had shown me I couldn't trust him, and I didn't know how much control he would have over his temper when he was drunk. I walked past him and opened the front door, turning to block him from coming in behind me.

'Can I come in? We need to talk.'

'No, Mike. Look, you keep saying you want to talk, and that's fine, but you can't just turn up at my flat in the middle of the night and expect me to let you in.'

'I'm sorry, Paige, you just have this effect on me,' he whined. 'I still care about you, you know. If you just said the word I'd come back, it doesn't have to be like this.' I ignored him, and he sagged back against the wall. 'I'm not good enough for you any more, is that it? Or is it because you've found yourself a new bloke?'

'I'm not having this conversation right now. I'm going inside. Either you can leave, or you can sit outside all night, it's your choice.'

Going inside, I shut the door firmly, then took a deep breath. I had only taken one step towards the stairs when he started banging on the door.

'Paige! Paige! Don't do this to me! Why do you have to be so fucking cold?'

There was an edge to his voice that hadn't been there before, and I resisted the urge to turn around and open the door. Ignoring the repeated thumps from behind me, I crossed the hallway and went upstairs to my flat.

When I got inside, the door buzzer went off, accompanied by the flashing light above it. Mike was leaning on the bell for my flat, but I didn't let him in. I gently pushed open the door to Anna's room to check she was asleep, but the light didn't seem to have disturbed her. Creeping back out again, I sat down behind my front door to think.

After a few minutes, the doorbell stopped buzzing, and in the eeriness of the sudden silence I wondered if he'd given up and gone away. If he'd woken one of my neighbours, maybe they'd call the police – if that happened, it was his own fault.

I got up off the floor and went into the living room to look out of the window. I couldn't see any sign of Mike in the road outside, and for a brief moment I thought he'd gone. Then there was a thump on the door to my flat.

My heart in my mouth, I quietly took off my shoes then crept back to look through the peephole. Mike was leaning against the wall opposite, and as I watched he aimed a kick at the lock. I stepped back just in time, as the whole door shook.

There was a movement beside me and I jumped; Anna had woken up, and she must have felt the vibrations from Mike's assault on the door.

What the hell's going on? she asked, rubbing her eyes.

Mike's outside, I told her.

In the street again? she asked.

No, *right outside the door. He was here when I got home, but I don't know how he got into the building*.

She moved past me, towards the door, and looked through the peephole.

What does he want?

God knows, I replied. *I don't know if he wants to try and talk me into going out with him again, or if he just wants to have a go at me. I doubt he knows, to be honest. He's drunk*, I added, not that it excused any of his behaviour.

From memory, I knew Mike was his most erratic when

256

drunk. You never knew from one moment to the next if he was going to shout at you or cuddle you, if he was going to come out with some great romantic gesture or tell you a long list of everything that was wrong with you, that you were lucky he put up with you because nobody else would ever want you.

'Please open the door, Paige.' Mike's sorrowful voice drifted through the letterbox. 'I'm sorry, okay? I'm sorry for not listening to you, and for not asking when I could come round, but I didn't think you'd want me here.'

'Why did you come, then?' I asked, sitting down next to the door so I could talk to him.

'I thought it'd be a nice surprise.'

I paused, wondering whether or not to believe him. Did he really think I'd be pleased to see him? Was he that deluded? Looking up at Anna, I interpreted what Mike had said, and she rolled her eyes in disgust. For a moment I almost defended him, then I stopped. What was I doing, making excuses for this man? Just because he'd given me one token apology that didn't excuse what he was doing.

'If you go home now, we can forget this ever happened,' I said.

'I don't want to go home. I want to talk to you. The least you can do is let me in. Don't make me sit out here.'

I took a deep breath. 'If you don't go home, I'm going to call the police.'

Now that I was in the flat with Anna, I felt safe enough to threaten him like this. The last time Mike had turned up, he'd gone away on his own, so I could assume he'd do the same this time. I turned round, however, to see Anna with my bag in one hand and my phone in the other. I'd dumped it on the floor when I came in.

What are you doing?

Finding Singh's number.

Don't, he'll be asleep. I don't want to bother him with this.

Call 999 then. She had a look of determination on her face that I didn't want to argue with, but I took my phone off her and shook my head.

Mike's not going to do anything. He's drunk and stupid, that's all. I'm not bothering the police with this.

'Paige, please. Just open the door, sweetheart. I only want to talk. We need to talk, we never had any closure. I can't stop thinking about you.'

When I didn't reply, his tone suddenly flipped.

'I can get you fired, you know. You think you're so smart now, working for the police, as if they wouldn't use a better interpreter than you if they could afford it. Cuts mean they only have the budget for someone mediocre, you do realise that? You're not special, Paige.'

A shiver ran through me at his words, which echoed some of my own thoughts that came creeping in at early hours of the morning when I couldn't sleep. Anna was standing against the wall, chewing her lip and watching me closely.

I stepped forward and hugged her. *I'm sorry*, I signed to her.

It's okay. I know what he's like. She paused and looked down at her feet. *I'm sorry, too.*

What for?

I already texted Singh. She held up her phone, where she'd obviously saved his number while I was messing about deciding what to do.

I squeezed my eyes shut. The last thing I wanted was

258

to have Singh come out here in the middle of the night, thinking that I needed saving.

Did he reply? I asked her, trying to keep calm and not have a go at her. After all, she'd only done what she thought she needed to do to keep both of us safe.

She shook her head. *Not yet.*

I sighed. *We don't need Singh. I can get rid of Mike myself.*

She shrugged. *If you say so.*

I quickly texted Singh to say it was a false alarm and we didn't need any help. I could explain when I next saw him, but I didn't want him here now. It was almost a point of pride – my friends had got Mike out of my life the first time, now I had to do it for myself.

'Paige, for God's sake. Open this bloody door. By rights half of this flat is mine anyway, you know.'

That comment made my blood boil and it was all I could do to stop myself from wrenching the door open and shouting in his face. I'd used the scant inheritance I received from my parents to put the deposit down on this flat, and I'd managed to scrape together the mortgage payments even when Mike was taking most of my money. Thankfully, I'd set up a direct debit that went out as soon as my pay hit my account, so he never got the chance to get his hands on it. The deeds were in my name, and only mine, and that he had the audacity to suggest he should own half of it simply because he'd lived here for a while enraged me.

The thumps stopped, and I risked looking out of the peephole again. I couldn't see him, which worried me – I knew better than to think he'd left.

The letterbox clattered open and I stepped back. He

was sitting on the floor in front of the door, and his fingers snaked through as he sat there.

'Paige, you need to listen to me.' His voice was stern. 'I know you've got some crazy idea in your head about me, but you have to remember you're not always right. Sometimes you make mistakes. And this time you have definitely made a mistake. All I want is to talk to you, and now you're making me sit outside like a complete idiot. Your neighbours are going to be really pissed off at you, Paige. You've made me shout, and I bet some of them have woken up and are wondering what the hell you think you're doing.'

His voice sounded so reasonable, so plausible, and I remembered just how easily those words could snake their way into my subconscious and implant themselves there, ready for any moment of weakness. He didn't have the same effect on me any more, however, and I just stood back from the door where he couldn't see me and waited for him to give up.

What's he saying? Anna asked.

I signed the basics and she shook her head in disgust. *Does he really think that shit will work?*

I squeezed my eyes shut for a moment, knowing I was about to share something with Anna that I'd never properly explained before. *When you're at rock bottom and your self-esteem is long gone, it does work. Men like him, they wear you down until you'll believe anything negative they say about you. When they hurt you or steal from you or treat you like shit, it's your fault because you didn't listen to them, or you didn't look at them the right way, or give them enough attention, or tell them what you were doing for every minute of the day. Men like Mike, they have a way of making you believe it's only what you deserve for being such a terrible human being.*

Anna looked shocked, and I realised I'd never really talked to her about the way Mike had ground me down over the years. When I first got out of the relationship, I couldn't speak about it, because I was too ashamed of myself for allowing it to get that bad, for not being stronger or smarter or whatever else I thought I hadn't been.

The next couple of minutes dragged, the silence from the hallway strangely ominous. A few moments later I heard the door to the staircase bang. Anna and I moved to the front window, where we saw Mike leave the building and stumble across the pavement. He stepped back and looked up at the window, obviously expecting us to be there, then gave us a sneer and a sarcastic wave and sauntered off up the road.

I need to tell Singh about him, don't I? I asked Anna. She nodded and I sighed, then sent Singh another text asking him to come round in the morning.

When we'd calmed down enough to go to bed, I checked several times that the door was locked, and took the heaviest object I could find, a glass vase, and put it on my bedside table. We'd changed the locks when Mike left three years ago, but I wasn't taking any chances.

Eight hours before the murder

Where are we? What is this place? Courtney asked, looking around at the small building.

It's the cricket pavilion, Bradley replied.

Courtney pulled a face. *Not exactly romantic, is it?*

Someone would notice if we'd broken into one of the other cabins, though, he pointed out. Rooting in his bag, he pulled out a blanket that he'd brought with him and laid it on the ground, stepping back to admire his handiwork. His girlfriend rolled her eyes.

What? It's the best I could do.

Ignoring him, Courtney walked to the window and looked outside, fiddling with her bracelet as she did. They weren't meant to have brought jewellery with them on the trip, but it had been a birthday present from Bradley and she wasn't going to leave it behind. *I think someone's out there.*

Bradley joined her, peering into the blackness. *There's nobody. You're imagining it.*

There is! What if someone followed us?

Nobody followed us. It's fine.

She shook her head. *I've got a bad feeling about this. What if we get into trouble?*

Bradley put his arm around her and kissed her temple. *Come on, it's not like it's the first time we've done this. What's wrong?*

I just feel strange, she replied. *Like someone's watching us. I don't like it.*

Kissing her again, Bradley reached up and stroked her hair. *It's okay, I'll protect you. You know I won't ever let anything happen to you.*

I know, she replied, letting her body sink into his. *I just . . . I can't explain it.*

Taking her hand, Bradley led her over to where he'd laid down the blanket. *Let's sit here for a while, okay? We don't have to do anything.*

She nodded, looking back at the window. The shadow of a tree moved in the wind, setting her heart racing, but she tried to ignore it. She was sure Bradley was right. There was nobody there.

Hey, Bradley. She nudged him and pointed towards the window again. *It's snowing.*

Chapter 28

Sunday 2nd December

I hadn't had much sleep when the door buzzer went off the next morning. My mind immediately jumped to the conclusion that Mike was back, but when I answered the intercom it was Singh. He smiled at me but there was a worried cast to his expression too.

Letting him in, I shook my head. 'I'm so sorry. Mike was drunk when he turned up last night and Anna thought we'd need help getting rid of him. He went away on his own in the end.'

He squeezed my shoulder, and I thought he was holding himself back from hugging me, trying to stay professional. 'Don't apologise for someone else's behaviour. He was the one who was in the wrong. And I wanted to come, because I think it's about time you told me the truth about you and Mike.'

He gave me a probing look and I nodded, knowing he was right.

'That's why I asked you to come round this morning. You deserve to know.'

I put the kettle on and offered him a cup of tea. As it was boiling, Anna came into the kitchen and smiled at Singh. They'd met several times during the investigation into Lexi's death, and I knew she'd be pleased he'd come round. The three of us sat down in the living room as I told Singh exactly what happened after I got home from my night out.

Once I'd finished, he looked me in the eyes. 'You told me that Mike Lowther is your ex-boyfriend, but I think there's a lot more to it than that. Is there anything specific you want to tell me about?'

'I'm not pressing any charges against him. I've moved on and I don't want to have to relive it.'

He made an exasperated noise. 'I'm not just talking about making an official complaint, I mean so you have someone else who can help you, support you when things like this happen. I meant I'm here for you as a friend.'

I sat back and looked at Singh. I knew he was right, and even though I knew it was going to be difficult, it was time to tell him.

'Mike and I met eight years ago. I was twenty-two, he was twenty-seven. We moved in together quite quickly because his rental contract was coming to an end and he didn't want to renew for another year.'

Singh nodded, perhaps wondering where this was going.

'Of course, a lot later I found out that was a lie. He was being evicted for non-payment of rent. But I'm getting ahead of myself.

'When he moved in, everything was good for the first eighteen months or so. He contributed towards the bills and we enjoyed living together. I saw less of my friends, but it was a new relationship and that often happens. The money issues started first. He would borrow money from me just before payday, then he'd pay it back. But gradually, month after month, the date he asked me for it would get earlier. And then he stopped paying it back, and the amounts gradually increased. But we were in love, we lived together. In my mind we shared everything. I knew he didn't get paid very much. He worked in a call centre and I could see that he hated it. But it got to the stage where we couldn't really afford to have nights out. While we were watching TV he would always have his phone out. It turned out he was gambling. A lot.'

I sighed and rubbed my face. 'I should have taken better care of my finances. One week, when I was really busy and stressed with work, he started talking about how he thought he could get our bills reduced. Things were starting to pinch with how much he was borrowing from me each month, so I gave him the log-in for my online banking. I was pretty lax then, and I never really looked at it, only checking my balance at cash machines, so it took me several months to realise he'd changed my passcode. When I asked him to tell me what it was, he agreed, but then "never got around to it". If I pushed it, he'd get cross, and start accusing me of not trusting him. I was such an idiot.'

'It sounds like you were being financially abused,' Singh said gently. 'It happens to more people than you'd think.'

I nodded. 'It reached a head when he took my bank card then claimed he'd lost it. I tried calling the bank to get a new one, but it never arrived. Of course, he intercepted my post. He lost his job when we'd been living together for just over two years, but managed to hide it from me for another two. Two whole years I didn't realise the man I was living with wasn't going out to work every day, but was spending his entire time gambling online. He took out loans in my name, using my bank details, and by the time we split up I had thousands of pounds of debt. This was three years ago and I still haven't paid even half of it off.'

Singh blew out slowly. 'I'm really sorry, Paige, I never realised. But there's more, isn't there?'

I nodded. 'How did you know?'

'You flinch when you look at him. He was physically abusive, I assume?'

I shook my head. 'No, actually. He was very clever, and he never laid a hand on me.'

Singh looked puzzled. 'I assumed the scar . . .'

'No, technically that was self-inflicted.' I took a gulp of tea, knowing I needed to continue. 'In amongst the financial trouble, I didn't even notice him stopping me from going out. Not at first anyway. He would talk me out of going to see Gem or visiting Anna, saying he really wanted to spend the time with me, he missed me too much, things like that. Then it tipped over into the manipulative behaviour – didn't I care about him? Wasn't he enough for me? Couldn't I see how my selfishness was affecting him? Whenever I did see my friends, I felt guilty that I was leaving him alone, and I always made excuses to leave early. They could all see what I was blind to, and they all told me he was manipulating me, but I was in love. It worked in Mike's favour, because I didn't want to see them if they were slagging off the man I loved.

'As time went on, I never knew what sort of mood he was going to be in. We had some wonderful romantic evenings, when he told me just how wonderful I was, though he often followed it up with an assurance that if

I ever left him he'd kill himself, or me, or both. We had some evenings where he would calmly list all of my faults and flaws, and tell me just how lucky I was that someone like him loved me despite them. The worst times were when he let his anger loose – he would shout and rail at me as if I'd caused everything bad that had ever happened to him. Anything could trigger his rage, from him deciding he didn't like the meal I'd cooked to me painting my nails. I learnt to avoid a lot of triggers, but they were like Medusa's heads, more kept popping up until I couldn't keep track.

'Towards the end, he got annoyed at me going to work. I couldn't stop working, because as soon as I earned anything the money was gone. I'd found out about the gambling by then, encouraged him to get help, and he promised he would, but there was always one big win just waiting around the corner. Then he'd stop. Then he'd get help. It never happened, because the house always wins, especially with online gambling, but he clung to that excuse. Anyway, he started trying to stop me from going to work. One week, he called the agency and told them I was ill so couldn't take any jobs for a week. I was furious with him and called them back, but they'd already given some of my jobs to other interpreters. I managed to get some other jobs that week, but he told me I couldn't go. That I wasn't allowed.' I noted the bitterness in my own voice as I said that. 'We had a row about it – don't think I didn't argue back, I often did. I stormed out, went to work and did my job. When I got back that night, he apologised, and I thought everything was fine.

'The next morning I woke up to find he'd gone out early. There was a note on the table telling me he'd gone

268

to Lincoln to the casino and he wasn't going to come home until he'd made enough so I never needed to work again. He always saw it as making money, rather than winning money. He knew there were professional gamblers, so he started seeing himself that way, even though all he ever did was lose.'

I rubbed my face with a hand. I'd never told anyone about this after it happened. Even Anna and Gem only knew the absolute basics.

'The door to the flat was locked, and I couldn't find my keys, or my phone. We hadn't had a landline in ages – we'd been cut off for not paying the bill. I didn't look too hard that day; I actually thought he'd locked me in by accident, and I assumed my phone was somewhere in the flat. When I couldn't find it, I wondered if he'd taken it to sell. He didn't come back that night. Or the night after. Or the night after that. There was food in the fridge, though not a lot, and I found myself rationing it in case he didn't come home for a week.

'I don't know what finally made me realise that I needed to get out. Not just out of the flat, but out of the relationship. I can't pinpoint the moment I thought, "What the hell are you doing? How can you be living like this?" But it happened eventually. I tried shouting out of the window for help when people passed by, but this is a quiet village and on the rare occasion when people do go past either they're in their own world or they have headphones in. So, nobody heard me, and in the end I dug out a hammer and broke the window. He took my phone and keys, but he didn't think to take any tools.'

'So, the scar is from where you cut yourself breaking the window?' Singh asked, his voice hushed.

'Climbing out of the broken window, really,' I said. 'I threw a blanket over the bottom of the window frame to try and prevent that, but I slipped as I was climbing out and caught my arm on the glass at the side. I knocked on one of my neighbours' doors and they called an ambulance.'

I hadn't been signing the story while I was speaking. It was enough effort just to tell the story without telling it in two languages at once. As I came to the end, I felt tears well up in my eyes, and Anna hugged me close.

'How long were you in hospital?'

'Three days. It probably would have been less, but Gem told the nurses that I was at high risk of domestic abuse if I was discharged any earlier. I didn't find that out until later. She and Anna had the locks changed and threw all of Mike's stuff into the corridor. When he came back, he found out I was in hospital and tried to visit me, but I knew by then the damage he'd done to me and I asked him to leave. When he wouldn't, the ward staff called security. That was the last time I saw him.'

'Until you saw him at Normanby Hall?'

'Until then.'

Chapter 29

Once I'd finished telling my story and managed to regain my composure I actually felt better. I had never believed the old adage that a problem shared is a problem halved, yet knowing there was someone else who knew the story and believed me gave me a confidence I hadn't felt before.

Singh asked about our plans for the day, and I had a quick signed conversation with Anna.

Should I ask him to come with me to visit Jane Villiers?

Anna pulled a face. *Do you think she'll still talk to you if he's there?*

I think so, I replied. *She doesn't strike me as the sort of woman who would be put off by the presence of a detective.*

Anna reluctantly agreed with me. I could tell from the sulky expression on her face that she wanted to come too, but Jane had asked for me, and she respected that. When I asked Singh if he wanted to join me, he was clearly exasperated at me for going behind his back. He accepted the invitation to join me, though I could tell he would have some questions for me about why I hadn't already told him about my planned visit.

The weather had improved since the beginning of the week, and I enjoyed the twenty-minute drive through the countryside. Jane Villiers lived on the edge of the Lincolnshire Wolds, the limestone ridge running roughly north to south through the northern half of the county.

Her house wasn't the only picture-perfect one in the village, and I admired several as we drove through. I could imagine there was a lot of pressure on residents to maintain the same standards as their neighbours when it came to their homes and gardens. One house we passed was next to a ford, and I could see the stream winding under the fence and through the garden, complete with a little ornamental bridge. I thought it would be nice to come back in the summer, when all the gardens would be a riot of colour.

Jane was waiting for us and had opened the front door before we reached it. She frowned at Singh, then looked faintly amused when I introduced him.

'I suppose I should have expected Paige to bring someone from the police with her,' she told him. 'You might have had a wasted trip, I'm afraid, Detective. I don't know if my concerns are really worth listening to.'

Singh gave her one of his winning smiles. 'I understand, but I might think of a couple of questions I'd like to ask you anyway.'

There was a pause, then Jane nodded, and led us into the front room again. I sat on the same worn sofa as before, while Singh stood and examined some of the pictures on the wall.

Jane came back in with tea and cake, and served us before sitting back and steepling her fingers, looking at us over the top of them.

'Now you're here, I feel almost foolish,' she said with a sigh, rubbing the bridge of her nose. 'I've been going over this in my mind repeatedly – could I have prevented this? Has this all stemmed from my failure to protect my students?'

Singh came and joined me on the sofa, resting his elbows on his knees as he looked at the ex-head teacher.

'Why do you think that?'

'In the three decades I worked at that school, we never had a single major issue until the incident that lost me my job. And now this, only a few months later. I feel there must be a connection of some sort.' Her eyes were flicking between the two of us, searching in earnest for a sign that we agreed with her. Or maybe she wanted us to disagree, then she was absolved of any connection between herself and the murder of the man who replaced her.

I looked around the room, and for the first time I noticed the photos on the end wall – they were the same as some of the ones I'd seen in the entrance hall of Lincoln School for the Deaf, whole school photos stretching back thirty years. I wondered if Jane had every photo from her time at the school.

'I think we've lost you,' she said, bringing me out of my reverie.

'Sorry,' I said, nodding at the wall in front of me. 'I just noticed all of the photos. How long did you work at the school?'

'For most of my career,' she replied. 'Thirty-two years, nineteen of those as head teacher.' The look on her face was a mixture of sadness and pride, and I wondered how deeply her swift exit from the school had hurt her.

'You must have seen a lot of people come and go,' I said.

'Yes, students and staff.' She turned to Singh. 'I don't think my replacement employed any new staff though, so if you want the gossip on any of the murder suspects, do let me know.'

I thought at first she was joking, and the curve of her lips suggested she was, yet there was a flintiness to her eyes that surprised me.

'Did you ever meet Steve Wilkinson?' Singh asked.

She sniffed. 'No. They didn't even give me a decent handover period, which would have been for the good of the school and everyone in it. As it was, I expect the first few weeks were a bit hectic for him. I can't say I had any interest in meeting him; I know it wasn't anything to do with him, me getting shunted off into retirement early, but I still felt bitter about it. And now the poor man's dead,' she said, shaking her head.

'Who do you think would murder him?' I asked. 'I mean, you should be a suspect, he took your job.'

Jane laughed at that. 'If only I had it in me to kill someone. No, I'm sure the police will cover all bases but they'll discover I wasn't anywhere near the poor man. If it could have been anyone at that school, I'd say Jess Farriday would be one to look at. The woman has naked ambition like I've never seen before.'

Singh and I shared a look.

'Ambition for what?' he asked.

Jane spread her palms wide. 'Influence. Control. She worked her way through a number of her male colleagues, to see what she could get out of them. Any piece of information she found out would be squirrelled away in her mind, in case it could be useful at a later date. And when I say useful, I mean be used to influence or manipulate someone into doing what she wanted.'

This matched up with Anna's account of Jess, and it made sense that she had been using Steve – if she wanted influence then who better to try and get her claws into than the head teacher. Was it possible she'd gone up to Normanby Hall to meet him and something had happened, something that had ultimately led to his death? I made a mental note to ask Singh later if he'd looked into Jess's alibi. Could she have slipped away from the hen party unnoticed for a while?

Jane was watching us carefully, and it was clear she knew she'd planted a seed of an idea in our minds.

'You don't think it could have been one of the students?' I asked, wanting to move the conversation on.

'What, Leon? Never. The boy wouldn't hurt a fly.'

'What about his father?' Singh countered.

Jane rolled her eyes. 'That was self-defence. The man was abusive, and Leon snapped. I don't blame him at all for what he did, especially as he only wounded his father and then went for help. This is completely different. He didn't do it.'

'You seem to be very confident of that, even without having the full facts of the case,' Singh told her, with a sideways glance at me. I shook my head to tell him I hadn't been passing on any information.

'The residential students are very close,' I said to her. 'They're secretive and don't mix with any other students, and there's a good chance they haven't told the police everything they know about this case. Have they always been like that?'

Jane frowned. 'They were always close, of course. That's natural, given their shared experience. But you're making it sound sinister. It was never like that. Are you suggesting something changed when that man took over?'

Singh frowned. 'Why would you say that?'

'I am not an idiot, Detective,' Jane replied, acid in her voice. 'Can I assume that the staff member who was discovered to be grooming students was the dead man? I saw the news online.'

Singh hesitated, then nodded. 'It was.'

'So, it is natural to assume someone killed him because of that.'

'That's certainly our main avenue of investigation at the moment.'

'But that doesn't mean it was Leon, regardless of his history. Did Paige tell you about the video?'

'She did. Our techs have been looking at the school network and we asked them to keep an eye out for anything similar. They haven't found anything untoward so far.'

She grunted. 'Well, I suppose it was too much to hope they hadn't covered their tracks. No, I believe these incidents are connected, and I think only an adult could have orchestrated all of this.'

'What about Mike Lowther?' I asked impulsively, and Jane's eyes flashed.

'He would seem to be an obvious culprit, wouldn't he? With his gambling problem, and his little habit of making off with other people's possessions. Oh yes, he was always busy trying to get money out of people he knew, particularly his girlfriends, and I was fairly sure he was responsible for a spate of thefts from the residence. If he found out what Steve Wilkinson was up to he might have blackmailed him. Mike wouldn't pass up a money-making opportunity. And I absolutely believe Mike would kill if he was backed into a corner and felt it was his only option.'

Neither of us responded to this for a moment. I felt as if a huge force had been aimed at my chest, and I put my head down onto my knees as a wave of dizziness overtook me. I'd trusted him. I'd believed him when he tried to apologise to me, even though last night's behaviour had proved he hadn't meant it. Could he really be a murderer? How could I have been so stupid to be taken in by him? I'd desperately wanted to believe he'd changed, because if he could change then maybe I could change too. I could forget about what he did to me and move on with my life.

I remembered Mike's posturing about how Jane had seen his potential and offered him extra training. It sounded like she hadn't thought that much of him after all. Of course he'd been lying, making empty boasts to try and impress . . . who? Me, or the police? Was he covering his tracks, trying to make himself look above suspicion?

'You think he'd blackmail someone who was grooming students, rather than going to the police?' Singh asked, unable to keep the incredulity from his voice.

I nodded in response to this question and Jane raised an eyebrow.

'I see you already know the levels of his scruples,' she said to me, and I felt my face flush.

'I agree with you,' I said quietly. 'If he saw a chance to get a large amount of money out of someone, that would be his priority.' My own words made me shudder, but it was true.

There was a long, heavy silence. Both Singh and Jane were watching me carefully.

'Thank you for your time, Ms Villiers,' Singh said after a moment or two, judging that it was time for us to leave, and reaching out to shake her hand. 'We're sorry to have disturbed your day.'

'Not at all,' she said, standing up and escorting us to the door. 'I hope you find Leon soon. I'm sure I'm right, you know – he knows what happened, but he doesn't think you'll believe him. He's hiding because he doesn't have a safe place to go. The school isn't safe for him any more because he knows someone there is a murderer.'

'You really think one of the staff members you employed could be capable of murder?' I asked as we were about to leave, my hand on the doorframe.

'Oh, of course. I'm sure all of us are capable of murder, given the right circumstances.'

Chapter 30

The drive home was a blur; I was on autopilot and I was surprised to find myself pulling into my usual parking spot. I barely noticed Singh saying goodbye and getting into his own car, so shaken was I by the possibility that Mike could be Steve's murderer.

By the evening I knew I needed to do something to drag myself out of my own thoughts, so I took Anna into Lincoln for dinner and a film. It was rare to find subtitled showings at the weekend, so I was thrilled there was one, hoping it made up for us missing the Christmas market. There was only one option with subtitles, so we didn't get to choose, but it had Bradley Cooper in it so that suited both of us just fine.

Popcorn or pick and mix? I asked her as we walked up Brayford Wharf towards the cinema.

Well, you need cheering up, she replied with a mischievous grin. *Both.*

I laughed. *Seriously? I'm still full of sushi.*

Popcorn is basically just air, she told me. *You can't be too full for popcorn.*

Okay. Sweet or salty?

My turn to choose, so salty.

We had the same argument every time we went to the cinema, and had done since we were teenagers. Anna liked salty popcorn, I liked sweet. Now we were adults, of course we knew we could buy our own, but it was still fun to repeat our childhood bickering and then in the end settle for a mixed tub to share. If I was honest, that was exactly the way I liked it now.

I'd bought our tickets online, so I went to the ticket machine while Anna browsed the sweets. While I was waiting for a machine, a group came in behind us and made a beeline for where she was standing, kids shoving each other in their effort to get to the pick and mix stand.

Sorry, sorry, one of them signed to himself as they bumped into her.

No problem, just be careful next time, my sister replied.

Wow, you sign! the boy replied, getting the attention of one of the others. *Hey, Courtney, this lady signs!*

My stomach dropped when I realised who the group were, and looked around me to see which adults were supervising them. Mike and Sasha were standing behind me waiting to collect tickets, and when he saw me his face went bright red.

'Paige. What are you doing here?'

I nodded to the machine. 'Seeing a film with my sister.'

'Yeah? Which film?'

I stared at him. 'The same one as you, obviously.'

Sasha was looking between us as if watching a tennis match, so I switched to BSL.

My sister is deaf, and we were really excited to see a subtitled film at the weekend, I told her.

I know, that never happens, Sasha replied with a smile. *We thought it would do these four some good to get out. It feels wrong, somehow, having fun while all of this is happening, but life has to go on, doesn't it?*

I agreed that it did.

And they're all going mad being stuck at the school, she continued. *They're still teenagers, at the end of the day, and they need to let off steam like any other kids.*

Sasha, do you mind if I talk to Paige for a moment? Mike asked, giving her a winning smile. I willed her to refuse, and point out that he was there to supervise the students rather than socialise, but she nodded and walked off. I collected our tickets and considered turning my back on Mike, but then I thought the quickest way to get rid of him would be to hear him out.

'I'm so sorry about last night,' he muttered once he'd collected their tickets. 'I honestly don't know what I was thinking.'

I nodded. 'Okay. Is that it?'

He frowned. 'What? I've apologised. What more do you want from me?'

'Nothing, Mike. That's the whole point. I don't want anything from you, and I haven't for the last three years. Your behaviour last night just showed me that you haven't changed at all.'

'That's not fair. I accepted responsibility for the way I treated you, and I hoped you'd accept some responsibility in return.'

281

'Responsibility for what? What is it that you think I've done to you?' I asked, trying my best not to raise my voice in a public place.

He let out a sharp laugh. 'Well, how about throwing me out of our home without ever explaining why?'

'You know full well why our relationship ended, Mike. You locked me in and left me for four days. Four fucking days, with no way of contacting the outside world other than shouting through the window.'

'I was coming back,' he said quietly. 'I wouldn't have left you there. I would never have done that to you.'

'But you did, Mike. You did do that to me.' I pulled off my jacket and showed him my scarred arm. 'I have to see this every day, and remember how scared I was that you were just going to leave me there, without food or a phone.'

He blinked, looking down at my arm. He reached out a hand, and for a moment I thought he was going to try and touch my scar, but then he pulled his hand away again.

Nodding, he turned away. 'I'm sorry, Paige.' Without saying anything else, he walked back to the group.

Anna had made her purchase, but hung back during this conversation, to her credit. She could probably tell from my body language that I didn't need any back-up, but she'd waited just far enough away that she could dash in to support me if necessary.

Should I ask? she signed as I rejoined her.

Same old shit, I replied.

She nodded, happy with this assessment. *Here, I got snacks*. She waved a huge bag of pick and mix. *You're queueing for popcorn, though. I need the loo.*

Keeping an eye on where Mike was, I joined the other queue and five minutes later brought her the tub of salty popcorn she'd requested.

I didn't think you were actually going to buy it, she said, looking at me askance. *What's going on? We always get half and half.*

I know. I shrugged. *But I figured you didn't get to choose the film, so at least you could choose the popcorn.*

She laughed, and we went in to find our seats. The screen was only a third full and we sat near the back. The group from Lincoln School for the Deaf were further forward, and we needed to pass them to get to our seats. I studiously ignored Mike, but I could feel Sasha's curious gaze on me as I climbed the steps.

About an hour in, I needed the loo, so I got up and went to the ladies'. While I was standing at the sink, washing my hands and wondering if I could ask Max to grow a beard like Bradley Cooper's, I heard a flush from a cubicle and Courtney came out. I moved over to dry my hands, watching her out of the corner of my eye. She hadn't realised it was me, and before she washed her hands she pulled her phone out of her pocket to send a message. Then she put it away and took out a second phone. The first had been in a sparkly silver case, but the second was all black. I blinked, and the second phone went away again. Why did a teenager need two phones?

Courtney smiled at me in recognition as I passed her, and as I made my way back to my seat I looked at the other kids. They were all watching the film, none with their phones out, and I cursed them for being so polite. Normally when I was in the cinema there was at least one teenager with their phone out the whole way through, if not a whole group of them. It was a wonder why they paid the extortionate ticket prices if they weren't going to bother watching the thing.

I managed to sit through the rest of the film trying to think of reasons why Courtney would have a second phone. As we walked out, I found myself steering through the crowd until we were behind the school group. I wasn't sure if Anna noticed, but I saw her raise an eyebrow at me as I moved nearer to them. With a slight shake of the head, I let her know to just follow my lead.

Out in the lobby, the kids were hanging around and waiting for Sasha. Mike was standing nearby, staring at the floor and brooding. I stood at the side of the room and took my phone out, pretending to scroll through it whilst watching the kids. My focus was on Courtney, wondering if she was going to pull out that second phone. Some of the things that had been happening at the school were perhaps making me more suspicious, but I had a feeling something wasn't right.

My patience paid off, but not in the way I expected. As I watched, Kian pulled a phone out of his pocket, shortly followed by a second phone. I thought I was mistaken for a moment, as his both had blue cases, but they were two different makes. Bradley spotted what Kian was doing and elbowed him, causing Kian to slip both phones back into his pocket. Did they all have second phones? Surely the school didn't have enough money for all the looked-after kids to have two phones each? Or was it a coincidence that Courtney and Kian both had two?

What are we doing, Paige? Anna asked, staring at the school group. *Is it something to do with Mike?*

I shook my head. *Why would a teenager have two phones?* I asked her.

She shrugged. *Maybe they thought they'd lost one, got a replacement, then found the old one.*

But then wouldn't they just keep using the better one? I asked. *Rather than carrying two around and using both.*

Yeah that sounds right, she replied. *Two phones would be confusing.*

Exactly. So, I don't understand it. I looked down at the floor with a frown, trying to work it out.

What are you talking about? Anna asked, confused.

Sasha hadn't come back from the toilet, so I ignored Anna's question and made an excuse, going back down the corridor. I managed to catch the social worker coming out of the ladies'.

Hi, Sasha, I waved to get her attention.

Hi Paige, are you okay? She stopped for a moment, so I seized the opportunity.

Why do the kids have two phones?

She frowned. *Two phones? What are you talking about?*

I saw Courtney with two mobile phones earlier, I told her, *and now I've just seen Kian has two as well.*

Why would they have two phones? she asked, looking puzzled.

That's what I'm asking you. I stared at her for a moment, but either she was a good actress or she didn't know what I was talking about.

Maybe that's not what you saw, she replied. *These kids are always messing about with each other's phones. Maybe Kian was using Bradley's, then you saw him take his own out?*

No, he put them both back in his pocket. I knew what

I'd seen. *And there weren't any other students around when I saw Courtney.*

Why are you watching the kids, Paige? she asked with a concerned frown. *Have the police asked you to do this?*

I was taken aback. *No, it's just coincidence that we're here at the same time as you.*

She nodded. *Okay. But this is feeling a bit weird now. Maybe you should go home.*

I took a step back. *Fine. I just thought it was odd, that's all.*

I watched as Sasha walked past me and back to the group, then waited until they'd left the lobby before joining Anna again.

I explained the full story when we were on the way back to the car.

That does sound suspicious, Anna signed. *But what do you think it means?*

I don't know, I replied. *And why was Sasha so quick to defend them? Was it just because she thought I was talking rubbish, or was it because she was trying to put me off?*

I was wrapped up in my own thoughts on the drive home. Did all of the kids have second phones? That would explain what Cassie had been trying to get Bradley to understand the other night, that the phone she was looking for was a secret. I had been sure the kids were hiding something, and maybe the phones were connected.

Sasha's attitude confused me. She was the one who knew the kids best, and she'd told me she was worried about something going on with them, yet she'd brushed off my concerns when I asked about the phones. Did she know more than she was telling me?

Five hours before the murder

The room was pitch black. Kian lay awake, clutching his sleeping bag tightly up to his neck. He didn't like the dark. He'd never liked it, and in his room at school he always slept with a light on. Bradley would have understood, but Kian didn't want to look like a baby in front of Leon, so he'd said he would be fine with the lights off. He hadn't considered that they were in a cabin in the middle of the woods, with no light coming from outside.

He reached into his bag and pulled out his phone to check the time, hiding it under the covers. 02:57. The torch function was quite bright, but he turned it on anyway, making his sleeping bag glow from the inside. Kian quickly shone his torch at the other two beds to check he hadn't woken Bradley or Leon, and his heart leapt into his throat. Their beds were empty.

Where had they gone? He lay still for a moment, wondering what might have happened. Knowing Bradley, he'd snuck off with Courtney again. But where was Leon?

All sorts of scenarios raced through Kian's mind, each one worse than the last, until he unzipped his sleeping bag, swung his legs out and went to the door.

Leon was probably just in the bathroom, he told himself. If he waited for a few minutes, he'd come back and ask why Kian was awake. He opened the door and saw a light at the end of the corridor, but it was coming from the living room, not the bathroom.

Without thinking, he padded softly up the corridor to where the light was spilling out from under the door, and pulled it open carefully. He poked his head around it.

Leon was standing in the kitchen, a mug on the table in front of him. As Kian craned his head round further, he saw that Mr Wilkinson was there too. Why were they up? Still, Leon was safe, so he should go back to bed.

As he backed away, letting the door close silently behind him, Kian wondered why the head teacher had put his arm around Leon.

Chapter 31

Monday 3rd December

The police hadn't booked me for anything that morning, but as I was eating my breakfast a text came through from Singh asking me to meet him at the school as soon as possible. I had a rushed shower and was dressed and out of the door within fifteen minutes.

'What was so urgent?' I asked, when I met him in the school car park. It was snowing lightly, the sky heavy and grey.

'I had a message from Sasha Thomas saying one of the students made a disclosure last night that she knew we needed to hear. I also need to talk to Saul Achembe; he emailed me to say there was some more information he'd found but would rather show me in person so he can talk me through the data.'

'Sounds serious,' I replied.

Singh nodded, and the two of us went inside. We waited for ten minutes for Liz Marcek to be free, and when she came out to greet us she looked grave.

I've prepared the conference room for you, she told us. *Sasha is already there, with Kian and the others.*

The surprise I felt was mirrored on Singh's face. Others?

The other looked-after students, to be precise, Liz Marcek continued. *Kian persuaded them to speak to you today.* She looked at Singh, concern etching deep lines on her forehead. *I'm very worried about how deep this is going to go. How many children did this man target?*

Singh held up his hands. 'Right now, I don't know what's happened or what any of these students wish to tell me. Hopefully everything will become clear soon, and we can get these children the support they need.'

We made our way to the conference room, where Sasha was sitting at one end of a table, the four students around it. Kian looked up when we came in, his face radiating worry. Bradley sat next to him and he put a reassuring arm around his brother. Courtney was playing with her phone, the one in the sparkly case, and Cassie was staring out of the window.

'Good morning,' Singh said to all of them. 'We understand you want to speak to us.'

Sasha looked relieved that we had arrived, and threw a look at me that was almost apologetic. *When Kian spoke to me yesterday, I knew it was something you needed to know about. Then this morning, the other three said they needed to come too.*

The three of us sat down and Singh looked across the table at Kian.

'Kian, please can you tell us exactly what you told Sasha yesterday? Try to remember as much as you can.'

The boy nodded and fidgeted for a moment before he began. *I've been messaging Joe too. We all have.*

My heart dropped into my stomach. Steve had been targeting all of them?

Singh looked around at all four of the students. 'All of

you have been in touch with Joe? The same Joe that Leon was talking to?'

One by one, they all nodded, but then they looked back to Kian. Bradley nodded at him, as if giving his brother permission to continue.

It started at the end of the summer holidays, Kian signed, his shoulders slumped. *We all got new phones; they were left in our rooms for us, with a note telling us not to tell anyone about the phone. Since then we've all had messages from someone called Joe.*

Part of me felt vindicated that I'd been right about the kids having two phones each, but I didn't enjoy the feeling. If only someone had spotted it sooner, maybe Steve's grooming of Leon could have been prevented.

Kian had paused for a moment and looked at Sasha.

It's okay, tell the detective the truth, she told him reassuringly.

With me, it started off friendly, Kian explained. *He was asking about football and what I like to do at the weekend. But then it got weird. He was asking me questions like if I like to touch myself and if I'd take photos of myself with no clothes on and send them.*

'Did it worry you, a stranger texting you?'

He said it was a wrong number, at first. Kian hung his head, clearly embarrassed that he'd fallen for a lie. *The first text was asking for someone called Matt. I replied and said he had the wrong number, he apologised, and then we started chatting.*

Singh nodded. 'Okay. Did you tell anyone about Joe?'

Kian shook his head vehemently. *Not at the time. It was only a couple of weeks ago when we realised we'd all been talking to Joe.*

'How did you all find out?'

When I saw Leon texting him, Kian replied. *I asked him about Joe, and he wouldn't tell me at first. But when I told him I used to get messages from someone called Joe too, we started talking. Then I told Bradley and he was really angry. He admitted he'd got a new phone too, then he asked the girls and we all talked about it. We asked a couple of the other residential kids, the ones who aren't in care and just board on a weekly basis, and they didn't know what we were talking about, so we knew it was just the five of us. It's stupid, I thought I was the only one. We all did.*

'Why were you angry?' Singh asked, turning to Bradley.

The older boy slouched in his chair and grimaced before replying. *I thought it was something to do with Leon. I've always told Kian not to give out his information, yet this Joe seemed to know all about him, what school he went to, what team he supported, shit like that. I knew he wouldn't have done it, so I thought maybe Leon had given our information to someone he knew.*

'Your information as well?'

Bradley nodded. *I'd been getting messages from Joe too, but there was nothing dodgy about them. I mean, he told me his dad was a violent alcoholic and he was thinking about running away with his little sister, to protect her from him. We talked about a lot of stuff, but the Joe I talked to was definitely into girls, from the things he said. But then when I realised he was messaging all of us, I wondered if Leon had told him things about us, so that he knew what to say. He knew how to make us open up, you know.*

Singh looked thoughtful for a moment. 'And what about

you two?' He looked at Courtney and Cassie. 'Do you have similar stories?'

I think it's a coincidence, Courtney signed. I noticed she was sticking to BSL this time rather than speaking, probably because the other students were using BSL too. *I don't think the person I was talking to is the same one as these three*, she told Singh, flicking her hair over her shoulder. *The person chatting to me was another girl, and she spelt her name Jo, without the e.*

This girl, she started off by talking about how much she liked school, and how many friends she had, Courtney continued. *It almost turned into a competition between us, you know? Who was more popular. Well, after a while she started talking about things she'd done to other kids. Mean things. She was saying how much fun she had making another girl cry, getting a boy into trouble for something he didn't do, even making fun of a teacher. I didn't think it sounded like fun, it was all a bit childish, and I told her that. So, she started daring me to do things.*

There was a long pause, and I noticed that Kian's leg was jiggling nervously again.

'And did you do any of those things?' Singh asked.

Courtney turned the colour of beetroot. *Maybe. A couple of things. I just wanted to see if she was right, that it would be fun, but I felt awful and I apologised afterwards.*

No, you didn't, Kian signed to her. *You never apologised to me for sticking my uniform in the sink after PE. How did you even get in the boys' changing rooms?*

You didn't apologise to me either, Cassie chimed in. *Those mints made me so poorly.* She turned to Singh. *She told me they were weight-loss mints but I had to eat two*

293

packets a day for them to work. But they have something in them that makes you go to the loo. It was horrible.

Courtney stifled a laugh. *Yeah, but I bet you lost weight, didn't you?*

'Okay, I get the picture,' Singh said, interrupting before it descended into an argument about Courtney's bullying of her fellow students. 'Why do you think this person is the same as the one who was talking to you, Kian?'

Bradley looked at the messages, Kian replied, looking to his brother. *He said the language was the same, like they used the same words and phrases. And they made the same mistakes too, spelling and grammar. Bradley's really good at English, better than me, so he could see the mistakes.*

'That's very clever,' Singh said, looking at Bradley. The older boy just shrugged, but Kian beamed at the praise of the brother he worshipped.

It's obvious, anyway, Bradley signed. *Five of us get a new phone, are told to keep it secret, and someone starts messaging us on it? Of course it's the same person.* He thumped the table. *I can't believe I was so stupid. I should have told a teacher straight away.*

'Don't blame yourself, Bradley,' Singh replied, with a shake of his head. 'You weren't to know what would happen.'

His reassurances didn't seem to have an impact on Bradley, who stayed slumped down in his seat.

'Cassie, what about you?'

It was Jo without an e for me too. But she didn't say any of the stuff she said to Courtney. She was the one being bullied, and she said nobody understood her except me. Cassie shrugged. *I thought she wanted to be my friend.*

'Were you all messaging Joe at the same time?'

No, Bradley replied. *Kian got messages first, at the start of September. Then it was you, wasn't it, Courtney?* The girl nodded, and Bradley continued. *Then Cassie, then me. Leon was the last person Joe started talking to.*

'Okay,' Singh replied. 'Can I go back to the beginning of your story for a moment? You said that you all got new phones. Do any of you know who they were from?'

The students all glanced at each other, but nobody volunteered an answer, so Singh looked to Sasha.

I don't know. You'd have to ask Liz if they came out of the school budget. She gave Singh a look that was easy to read – she knew they hadn't. If Steve had been the one grooming Leon, then he must have been the one to give them the phones, too.

The note with them said we shouldn't tell anyone we had new phones, in case they were jealous, and that we should only use them in private, Kian said. *We didn't find out about each other's phones, or about Joe, until a few days before Leon disappeared. When I realised we were both messaging him and told Bradley, he asked the girls, and we all agreed that we had to keep it a secret.*

Singh and Sasha looked at each other. 'I think I'm going to need to take those phones,' Singh said.

Courtney looked dismayed, but Kian and Bradley were already rooting in their bags for the phones.

I can't, Cassie said. *I told you. I lost mine.*

'That was the phone you lost? Have you seen it since the weekend you went to Normanby Hall?' Singh asked. I remembered that she had broken into Steve's office because she thought her phone would be in there, and if she was right maybe he'd been trying to cover his tracks.

Cassie shook her head. That explained what she, Bradley and Courtney had been keeping from him the other night – the other two realised Cassie was talking about her second phone, her secret phone, and they couldn't be the ones to share the secret.

'Okay, if it turns up please let us know. Do any of you still have the messages from Joe on your phones?'

They all shook their heads.

None of us have had any messages since Leon went missing. When we realised it might have something to do with Joe, we deleted everything, Bradley told the detectives. *I'm sorry, it was a stupid thing to do, but we were covering our own backs.*

'Don't worry. We can get in touch with the service provider and see if we can get a record of the messages. If we find out who was messaging you it might help us to find out where Leon is, and who killed Mr Wilkinson.'

Whilst we knew that Steve had been posing as Joe, the kids didn't, and Singh clearly wanted to keep it that way. I thought I couldn't be shocked any further, but this new revelation had succeeded. Had Steve been posing as Joe to all of them in an attempt to find the perfect candidate for grooming? I felt sick at the thought.

The students were sent back to class but Sasha stayed in the room with us.

I feel like I've failed them, she told us, shaking her head slowly. She looked devastated that she'd missed what was going on. *If I'd known sooner I would have come to you, but they're good at keeping secrets. Bradley has it in his head that he and Kian need to keep a low profile, in case they're split up or have to leave here and end up in some children's home. They were born in London, but they came up here for school when they were taken into care, because none of the London schools had places at the time when they needed an emergency placement. This is home now, but Bradley still holds a fear of London as a whole, because the person who abused him is there, albeit in prison now.*

'To me it seems likely that whoever was speaking to them knew them well enough to be able to build a rapport quite quickly,' Singh told her. 'The male version of Joe offered friendship to Kian and Bradley, and the same to Cassie but this time as a girl. Whereas to Courtney the female Jo offered competition, and egged her on to become the bully that all popular students have the potential to become. Popularity is power in a school environment, and they must have known just how to push Courtney's buttons. They worked their way round the students until they found one who responded in the way they wanted. Kian backed off when the talk became intimate, Bradley was never going to open up completely to a stranger. Courtney got bored of it eventually, and Cassie just wanted a friend, nothing more. Leon was the one who responded to Joe enough to be led into a relationship.'

'That's pretty scary,' I said. 'But surely it was Steve, wasn't it?' I was confused; I thought it had been obvious, but Singh didn't seem completely convinced.

A frown etched lines on his forehead. 'I still think there's something we're missing. It's highly unusual for a paedophile to target both boys and girls, so this doesn't quite add up.'

They got the phones only a couple of weeks after Steve started working here, Sasha pointed out. *That would explain why he gave phones to all of them – he didn't know the students well enough yet to know who best to target.*

'So, it's possible he delivered the phones, got to know the students over time and then gradually worked out which student would be the most receptive to his advances,' I suggested.

Singh looked thoughtful for a moment, a frown running deep furrows across his forehead. 'Something doesn't add up. We're missing something,' he repeated. He shook his head. 'I can't put my finger on it. I need to see Saul anyway, so I'll see if he can help with the students' phones. It'll be quicker than taking them back to the station and putting them in a queue for the IT techs. Paige, I don't think I'll need you again today, so you can go home if you like.'

Sasha and I walked out to the car park together while Singh went to look for the IT teacher. The sky was darker than before, the snow coming down heavier, and I was relieved that I could go home before the roads got too bad.

It looks like you were right about something going on, I told her.

She gave me a rueful smile. *I know, but I wish I'd been wrong. And you were the one who spotted the second phones. I'm really sorry about yesterday. I should have believed you.*

I shrugged. *I understand why you thought I was behaving oddly. I knew there was something strange about the phones, though. Hopefully this will help the police to get to the bottom of everything.*

She nodded, and we walked on for a moment, deep in our own thoughts.

You know, I need a new interpreter, she told me. *I was*

glad she'd changed the subject; I couldn't bear to keep thinking about all of the students being targeted.

What for? I asked.

I work here one day a week, but I'm a regular social worker and I have hearing clients, as well as plenty of meetings to attend. At the moment our office uses a revolving bank of interpreters, but I've convinced them to employ one for three days a week. I can use the other day for visits to deaf clients or paperwork, then.

When will it be advertised? I asked. The idea of a contract and a regular income was incredibly tempting, and working with someone like Sasha was bound to keep me on my toes.

If you give me your number, I'll let you know.

I gave her one of my cards, feeling like I had somehow proved myself to Sasha by pushing to find out what was going on with the students, and we parted. Before I got to my car, however, I was distracted by something on the ground outside the students' residence. Walking towards it, I felt my stomach churning as I realised what I was seeing, and I had to grab on to the wall to stop myself falling. Someone lay sprawled on the ground, lifeless eyes staring up at the leaden sky, blood staining the snow around his head.

It was Saul Achembe, and he was dead.

Chapter 32

Within half an hour, the building seemed to be full of police officers. DI Forest had turned up surprisingly quickly considering she'd travelled from Scunthorpe to Lincoln in heavy snow, and she was liaising with the detectives from Lincolnshire police who had also arrived on the scene.

I'd given my statement, then had been ushered back inside and wrapped in a blanket until I stopped shaking. Try as I might, I couldn't get the image of Saul's blood on the snow out of my head. Singh led me to the main hall, where all the staff and students were gathering.

There were a few uniformed officers dotted around the hall to make sure nobody left unless they were going to the toilet, and even then they had to be escorted by a police officer. Mike was prowling restlessly at the back of the room, occasionally stopping to talk to Sasha and throwing glances my way when he thought I wasn't looking.

'What do you think happened?' I whispered to Singh once all the staff and students were accounted for.

I could tell he was reluctant to answer, but I felt that I deserved to know, so pushed him for information.

'It looks like he had his throat cut,' he said eventually.

'Same as Steve?'

He nodded. 'Pretty much. It's the same MO, only a week after Steve's death, so the most likely conclusion is that they were probably killed by the same person.'

A shiver ran through me as I realised that everyone who had been in the building was in the hall with us, and that would include the murderer. If Leon had seen who killed Steve, and now they'd murdered Saul, then he was in danger: they might be coming for Leon next.

'I assume there's no CCTV or anything?'

'The one outside the residence still isn't working,' he said. 'But we're checking all the other external cameras in case someone came into the school this morning who we're not aware of.'

This put paid to the theory that Leon killed Steve and ran away in order to prevent himself being caught, unless he'd snuck back into the school to kill Saul. That seemed to be a particularly risky move, however, and there was no obvious motive for Leon to kill Saul. I thought the police would be forced to go back to looking at Leon as just a victim again and not a suspect.

'Did you find out what it was Saul wanted to show you?'

Singh shook his head again, looking annoyed at himself. 'No, I was looking for him when you found me and told me what had happened. We're going to get our techs searching all his files, but we have no idea what they need to be looking for. It could take weeks.'

I felt sick. Saul must have found out who killed Steve,

and possibly why they did it, but the murderer got to him before he could tell the police.

The snow continued to fall outside, building up against the window panes and obscuring the view. Singh and Forest had gone out of the room to form a plan of action, and I felt completely useless. A couple of the PCs organised drinks and fruit to be brought from the school kitchen and handed out – the last thing they needed was for any of the staff or students to get dehydrated.

After another half hour, Singh reappeared and came over to me.

'I need to speak to Liz Marcek, if you wouldn't mind asking her to join us outside.'

I crossed the hall and approached the deputy head, where she was standing with her arms folded, worry etched onto her face.

The police want to talk to you, I told her, and indicated where Singh had left the room and was waiting in the corridor outside the hall.

About time, she replied. *I don't know what on earth I'm supposed to do, keeping all the students cooped up like this.*

The entire school was there, from reception children up to Cassie, the eldest student. The youngest of them were already getting fractious, and one small girl was crying. I wondered if she could pick up on the tension in the room. The older students definitely knew something was wrong, and the theories would be getting out of hand by now, I was sure.

When we met Singh, he led us to the nearest classroom and we sat down.

'I think it would be best to send the students home,'

Singh began, but he didn't get a chance to continue because Liz interrupted him.

Absolutely not. These children have had enough disruption as it is, and if we send them home now there are some parents who will refuse to let them come back until you've solved this.

'I appreciate your concern, Miss Marcek, but do you really think this school is a safe place for any child right now? One of your staff was killed today. We don't know who did it, or why, but we know it must have been someone who was in the building and is now in that hall. On top of that, it's snowing heavily and we've been advised that the road to the school might be impassable in as little as forty-five minutes.' He paused for a moment to let his words sink in. 'I know the students are your top priority, and I am suggesting this in order to keep them safe.'

I can keep them safe, she signed, her face solid with determination.

Singh shook his head. 'I can't force you to do this, but I think you're making a terrible mistake. Some of those children are already scared, especially the youngest ones.'

But what if the school closes? she burst out. *What if this is too much for the parents, and they take their children to other schools? We won't be able to stay open with fewer students than we have now, and then what will happen to us?*

'Do you really think the parents will be happy with you if this has happened and you didn't call them straight away to let them know? To give them the option of collecting their child immediately?' Singh asked, his voice

303

calm despite the situation. 'If you keep this from them, they won't trust you again.'

Liz Marcek looked aghast, but this hit home and she nodded. *Okay. You're right. I'll get Karen from the office to start calling parents.*

She left the room, her shoulders slumped in defeat. The pressure that had been thrust upon her in the last week was immense, and I was surprised she'd held up as well as she had. I understood her desperate need to keep the school running, but Singh was right, the parents would be up in arms as soon as they found out that a member of staff had been murdered on the premises during the school day.

'Any idea what happened yet?' I asked him, and he shook his head.

'The CCTV doesn't show anyone entering the grounds who isn't already in the hall,' he said, loosening his tie a bit and running a hand over his face. 'In theory, we have our murderer trapped, but unless we can figure out who the hell might have done this we're going to have to let them go soon enough. We'll start interviewing staff soon, and we'll have to be vigilant when we're letting students leave in case anyone tries to slip away. The four students who are potential suspects will still be here, but I think we can rule out all of the other students.'

I chewed my lip as I thought about whether or not to ask my next question, but I had to do it.

'Rav, could it have been Mike?'

My fear must have shown in my eyes because he squeezed my hand. 'I can't lie to you, Paige. He's definitely a suspect. He followed Steve into the woods after he went to look for Leon.'

'When we were at Normanby Hall, he cornered me in

the woods after Sasha and I found Steve's body. I fell over, but it felt like someone pushed me. Could he have been worried I'd seen him kill Steve?'

Singh hesitated before he answered, which was all the response I needed.

'Shit,' I said. 'I never pressed charges for anything he did to me because I just wanted to close the door on that part of my life. But if it turns out he did this . . .' I let my voice tail off, because I didn't think I could bear the weight of that responsibility.

'This is not your fault,' he replied, his voice fierce. 'Victims of abuse always blame themselves for the abuser's actions, and this situation is no different. You have no responsibility for anything he may or may not have done.'

I nodded, but I couldn't stop my thoughts from straying that way.

'We need to interview the staff now,' he said. 'It might be a bit of a random order, so we'll need you to stick around. Is that okay?'

I agreed, and he went to find DI Forest to check she was ready.

The next hour and a half was a frustrating blur of interviews, which took place in a stuffy classroom. When parents arrived to collect their children, most of them were rushed straight out but a couple of parents wanted to speak to the police, which then delayed the interviews. One deaf parent kicked off because she wanted to speak to Liz Marcek, but the deputy head had gone off to escort one of the younger children to the car park. Forest managed to calm the parent down, with me to interpret, but that took at least twenty minutes.

Half of the staff couldn't remember when they last saw Saul, while several had seen him during the morning but couldn't say exactly what time. When all the children had gone, some of the PCs were dismissed while a couple of others went over to the residence with Bradley, Kian, Courtney and Cassie.

I was taking a break while they interviewed hearing staff when my phone beeped with a text from Max.

Can I pop over tonight?

I smiled. A night with Max would be a very welcome distraction. *Sure, but I don't know when I'll be home. I'll text you when I'm leaving Lincoln.*

Okay :) xx

I had a smile on my face when I got his reply, but it slipped when I heard a door open beside me and found Mike standing there.

'Used to be me who put that smile on your face,' he said with a grin that looked more like a leer. 'Who's the new man?'

I didn't answer, put my phone away in my bag and started walking away from him down the corridor.

'Don't just walk away from me, Paige.' I heard the anger in his voice but I didn't care. We were in a building full of police officers, even he wasn't stupid enough to do anything to me.

'Where the fuck do you think you're going?' Behind me, I heard his footsteps pick up pace as he chased after me, and he caught up to me right outside the door where the staff were being interviewed.

'I know it was you,' he hissed at me.

This caught me off guard, because I didn't have a clue what he was talking about.

'What was me?'

'You told Jess to keep away from me. Is that how it's going to be, Paige? Because you can't have me, nobody can?' He was shouting now, anger making a vein stand out on his neck. 'You're just a bitter, jealous bitch and you need to get your own life sorted out before you come messing with mine.'

'Messing with your life? You're the one who's been following me!' I snapped.

'What?' For a moment he looked genuinely confused. 'What are you talking about?'

'I've seen your car, Mike. Don't you have anything better to do than stalk me?'

His lip curled. 'I don't have a car, Paige. I always knew you were delusional but this is taking it a bit far, even for you.'

It took a moment for this to sink in. Was he telling the truth, or was he just trying to throw me off the scent? If it hadn't been him following me, who was it?

'You stupid cow,' he said, shaking his head. 'Are you trying to ruin my life again?'

I'd had enough. 'You really need to get help, you know that? You've brought all of this on yourself, with your ridiculous denial of what you did to me. You stole all my money and locked me in my flat for four days, Mike! And you wonder why I wouldn't want anything to do with you? I haven't said a word to Jess, she probably realised what a shit you are all on her own.'

The stunned look on Mike's face was still there when the door next to us was flung open. DI Forest stood there, her face thunderous as she looked between us both. I braced myself for the tirade, but she settled on Mike.

307

'Mr Lowther, you are disturbing our interview process. I would kindly ask you to control yourself.'

He hesitated, but she stared at him until he walked away.

'Thank you,' I said to her, and she nodded. Still surprised that she only railed at Mike for his behaviour, despite the fact I had been shouting too, I sat down to wait for the next time I'd be needed.

It took another hour before Singh came to find me, and I could see his exhaustion hanging beneath his eyes.

'It's as if a ghost came in and killed the man,' he said, shaking his head in disbelief. 'Nobody saw anything untoward, nobody thought Saul was behaving differently, and he didn't tell anyone what he'd found. We're getting absolutely nowhere. One of these people killed him, but I'm going to have to let them all go.'

He kicked the wall in frustration, and on impulse I gave him a hug. I felt the tension in his shoulders relax slightly as he returned it, then he pulled away and gave me an embarrassed smile.

'It's not your fault,' I said. 'Something will turn up. The tech people have his computer, don't they?'

Singh nodded.

'They'll find whatever it was, and you'll have them in the next day or two.'

'By which time they could be halfway across Europe.'

'Or they might still be here, hoping you haven't found anything.'

He nodded, but I knew he wasn't really listening to me. In his head, he was probably listing everything he could have done better.

'You should go home,' he told me.

I nodded. 'Okay. But ring me if you need me back, okay?'

On impulse, I gave him another hug before I walked to the door. I stepped outside and gasped at how bad the weather had become. The snow was over my ankles, and any tracks that had been made by parents' cars had already been buried. A figure came towards me and I backed away until I recognised Liz Marcek, bundled up in a huge coat.

It's no good, she told me. *The road is completely blocked.*

Looking past her I could see the tracks she'd made as she'd walked back to the school from the main gates. She must have been out to check if it was passable.

What are we going to do? I asked.

There's nothing we can do, she replied. *We'll have to wait here until it stops.*

I looked out at the snow and thought about Leon. I hoped he had shelter, wherever he was. He could be all alone, scared and hiding in the snow, and now whoever it was had killed Saul, Leon would surely be next on their list. I hoped the snow would stop soon, because I was convinced Leon was in grave danger.

Chapter 33

I didn't notice when the sun went down, because it was already so dark outside with the snow obscuring everything. A few of the staff had managed to get out before the roads became blocked, but many were stuck in the school. Forest, Singh and I were still there, along with a couple of Lincolnshire PCs. Forest had spent some time on the phone to the local council, insisting the route out of there was ploughed immediately, but it wasn't as simple as that. They had to prioritise hospitals first, then major routes; a handful of people stuck in a warm building with plenty of food in the kitchen certainly weren't near the top of their list.

We huddled in the staffroom, waiting for someone to tell us what to do. Liz Marcek looked like she wanted to take charge, but she reluctantly deferred to Forest.

There are some spare staff bedrooms in the residence, Liz said. *But not enough for all of us. Sasha is already using one, then there are three more spare rooms. And there's Mike's room, he has his own of course.*

310

I looked around the room and counted the number of staff left: seven, not including Mike, who was over in the residence with the students.

'And there are just the four students left?' Forest checked.

Yes, some of the weekly residential students didn't arrive this morning due to the snow, and the ones that did made it home.

Forest nodded. 'Okay. Given the circumstances I want at least two police officers in the residence at all times.' She looked at Singh. 'Rav, can you go over with one of the PCs, please. Make sure the students are reassured.'

We need to tell them what's happened, Liz interrupted, her face sombre. *They'll be wondering what's going on. I'll come over and speak to them.*

'Actually, I'd prefer it if you stayed here,' Forest told her. 'DS Singh and Paige can let the students know what's happening. Sasha can go with them.'

Liz looked like she was about to argue, but Forest was already beckoning to Sasha so I could interpret her request.

You can't make decisions like that and exclude me, the deputy head complained. *These are my students.*

'And it is my responsibility to keep them safe. Right now, I think a detective is the best person to reassure them that they are being protected, don't you?'

Liz twisted her mouth but she didn't reply, and Singh, Sasha and I went over to the residence. The forensics team had managed to get away before the weather worsened, and the area where Saul's body had lain was already covered with fresh snow. It was almost as if I'd imagined it.

When we walked in there was chaos: Bradley was on his feet, shouting and signing furiously at Mike, who was standing opposite him with his arms folded across his chest.

Kian was sitting in the corner with his hands over his face and Courtney had her arm round him, while Cassie was folded into a corner of the sofa, chewing her nails.

'What's going on?' Singh asked, stepping in between Mike and Bradley.

Nobody will tell us what the fuck is happening! Bradley fumed, breathing hard from between clenched teeth. *Someone else has been killed, haven't they? Haven't they?*

'Yes,' Singh replied, and Bradley was startled into taking a step back. He clearly hadn't been expecting an honest answer from the DS.

'Now, go and see to your brother,' he continued, with a nod to Kian in the corner, 'then come and sit down, so we can explain.'

Mike looked at Singh. 'I was handling it,' he said, his voice a low growl. A flicker of intense dislike passed across Singh's face, but it was gone again a moment later.

'We need to tell them what's happening,' Singh replied, then turned to the students. I stood next to him to interpret, and I noticed that Sasha deliberately sat on the opposite side of the room from Mike. Once or twice I caught her looking at him with a suspicious frown on her face.

'Earlier today, Mr Achembe was found dead. That's why there has been an increased police presence at the school, and why the other students were sent home. Until we discover who killed him, there will be police officers here to make sure you are safe.'

'To make sure we're safe?' Courtney asked, her soft voice quavering. 'Why wouldn't we be safe?'

'We have to take these precautions,' Singh replied.

'But you think someone is going to try to hurt us as well? Is someone going to try to kill us?' Courtney's voice rose as she became hysterical, then burst into tears. Bradley looked torn between keeping Kian calm and comforting his girlfriend, so Sasha stepped in and put an arm around Courtney.

That's not what they're saying, the social worker signed, holding Courtney's gaze to try and keep her calm. *They want you to know that you don't need to worry, because the police are here to protect you.*

But why do we need protecting? Kian asked.

I could see from Singh's face that this wasn't how he had envisioned this going. Mike had a smirk on his face that made me want to kick him, but I did my best to ignore him.

'Because you're children, and you shouldn't be involved in this sort of situation. If we could find somewhere else to send you, so you were far away from what's happening here, we would. For now, I'm going to stay here with you, as well as PC Brown,' he said, indicating the uniformed officer who was loitering by the door. 'If you're scared, please talk to us. And if you think you saw anything today, tell me. If there are any more secrets that any of you are keeping, it's very important that you share them now. Do you understand?'

The students all nodded, but none of them volunteered any information. Singh encouraged them to relax, and Bradley turned on the games console, but none of them seemed particularly interested. Around dinner time, Mike went over to the main school building to get some pizzas from the kitchen, which kept Bradley and Kian occupied for a while, but the girls just picked at their food.

As the evening wore on, I had to go back to the staffroom to interpret for Forest. Now the interviews were over, she'd stayed in the main building to keep an eye on the rest of the staff. The DI was happy for one of the teachers to stand in if she needed an interpreter for basic communication, but then she needed to speak to Liz to give her an update, which she thought was best kept confidential. Trudging through the snow back to the residence, I thought I saw a movement out of the corner of my eye. Spinning around, I held my breath as shadows loomed at me. Everything sounded strange, muffled by a thick blanket of snow.

'Is someone there?' I said, then felt embarrassed at my own idiocy. I turned around again and was about to ring the bell for the residence when I noticed a set of footprints leading around the side of the building. I followed them, and discovered they stopped outside one of the students' bedroom windows. Someone had been standing here not very long ago. As I turned to go inside, something else caught my eye – something glinting in the snow, reflecting light from one of the windows. I bent down to pick it up and saw that it was a charm bracelet.

My heart hammering, I slid back round to the front door and waited for someone to let me in.

'What's wrong?' Singh asked as soon as he saw my face.

I held up my hand to show him the bracelet but didn't speak, trying to work out which room the footprints stopped outside. Going through the communal area, I walked down the girls' corridor and stopped outside a door. Motioning to Singh to join me, I knocked on the door.

'What?' Courtney asked as she poked her head around her door.

'Courtney, did someone come to your window a little while ago?' I asked.

'My window?'

'Yes.'

Courtney shook her head, her eyes wide and innocent. 'No. I don't know what you're talking about.'

'Can we come in?'

The girl looked reluctant, but held her door open for us to squeeze past her. I pulled her curtains aside and checked outside; I was right. Beneath the window were the footprints I'd seen, with mine behind them.

'Someone was standing here,' I muttered to Singh, hoping Courtney couldn't hear me. 'I saw the footprints.'

'Did you see anyone outside?'

I shook my head, and Singh continued looking out of the window for a few moments. I still had the bracelet in my hand, and I showed it to Courtney.

'I've been looking for that,' she said, and moved to take it from me, but I pulled my hand away.

'Was that charm yours? The one with the C on it?' I asked.

She blushed scarlet, and nodded. 'Bradley and I went out that night, to the pavilion. We don't get time alone together normally. I didn't want to get into trouble.'

Singh took the bracelet from me. 'Why was it outside your window?'

Courtney shrugged. 'I don't know. I haven't been able to find it since we came back from the trip. I thought I'd lost it there.'

'When were you in the pavilion?' Singh asked her, his expression stern.

'Just after midnight. Bradley and I waited until the others were asleep, then we snuck out.'

Singh nodded, and thought for a moment. 'What about Leon? Was he still in bed when Bradley left?'

Courtney nodded. 'Bradley told me he and Kian were asleep, so he must have still been there.'

'What about when you went back?' he asked.

'Yeah, he must have been there then, too. Bradley was really confused at Leon being missing in the morning, because he'd been in bed the whole time we were out of the cabin.'

I didn't know if she was telling the truth, but Singh must have been satisfied, because he turned his attention back to the footprints outside Courtney's window. He'd finished speaking to her, so we both said goodnight and left her room.

'I'm going to go and speak to Forest over in the main building,' he told me. 'Will you be okay here?'

I thought of Mike, but what could he do with Sasha and a PC in the building? 'I'll be fine,' I told him.

When I went back into the communal area, there was no sign of my ex-boyfriend, and I felt myself relax. Sasha was watching TV, the PC sitting awkwardly on one of the sofas.

Have all the kids gone to bed? I asked her.

I expect Bradley is in Kian's room, but yes. Mike said he had to make a phone call or something, she told me. I looked at the expression on her face and thought this was a good time to ask her something that had been bothering me.

You know last week, when I came over here, you and Mike were having a conversation? I asked.

Yes?

What were you talking about?

Her face clouded, and I wondered if I shouldn't have asked, but then I realised her discomfort wasn't directed at me.

He's interested in the job I told you about, she explained. *I mentioned it to a few of the staff a couple of weeks ago, in case any of them knew an interpreter who might like to apply.*

Ah, I replied. *Mike isn't an interpreter.*

No, he's not, Sasha agreed.

But he thinks he's as good as a qualified interpreter, I signed, choosing my words carefully.

She nodded slowly. *He certainly was suggesting that, yes.*

We sat for a moment, looking at each other, then we both sniggered.

What did you think we'd been talking about? Sasha asked once her giggles subsided.

I have no idea, I replied. *You get paranoid, sometimes, doing this, and start thinking like a detective.*

Did you think we were plotting our next murder? Her face fell as soon as she signed this, and she shook her head. *I'm sorry, I shouldn't have said that.*

It's okay, I told her.

Sasha leant back in her seat and rubbed her eyes. *I'm going to go to bed. One of you come and wake me if anything happens.*

I agreed and she went off down the girls' corridor. For a few minutes I made awkward small talk with PC Brown, but then we both went back to watching the TV.

After about ten minutes, the door to the residence opened and four staff members came in. They'd decided to try and get some sleep in the staff bedrooms, as it didn't look like the road leading to the school was going to be cleared any time soon.

Singh was with them, and looked puzzled when they separated off to go to the spare rooms.

'What's wrong?'

'I thought there were only three spare rooms,' he said, before asking PC Brown to go back to the main building.

I nodded after Jess Farriday's retreating back. 'I believe she's planning on sharing with Mike.'

He raised his eyebrows. 'She's not wasting any time.'

I shrugged. 'People deal with grief in funny ways.'

'True,' he replied. 'But she lied to us about what she was accessing on Steve's PC the day before he died.'

'Really? What was she looking at?'

'Staff salary data, and the school accounts.'

I took a moment to absorb that information. 'Was anything missing from the school funds?'

'We can't find any evidence of that, but it certainly doesn't look like her relationship with Steve was purely founded on love.'

'That fits,' I replied, telling him what Anna knew about Jess, and reminding him of Jane Villiers' scathing assessment of her.

'It's possible she hasn't changed,' he said when I'd finished. He sat back and rubbed his eyes. 'You can go to sleep if you like. I don't think we're getting out of here until the morning.'

'I'm fine. Someone needs to keep you awake.'

He laughed. 'Okay then, tell me your life story.'

'You first.'

'Fine, fine,' he replied, launching into a detailed tale of his childhood. Despite what I'd said, I was exhausted, and the soothing tones of his deep voice soon lulled me, and I fell asleep with my head resting on his shoulder, feeling safe.

Forty-five minutes before the murder

'Have you seen Leon?' Steve asked.

Mike shook his head, not meeting the head teacher's gaze.

'He's not in his room.'

That made Mike look up. 'What do you mean? He's probably in the bathroom.'

'No, I checked there.'

Kian and Bradley came into the kitchen, rubbing their eyes.

Boys, where's Leon? Mike asked them, switching to BSL.

Bradley shrugged. Kian, wide-eyed, looked between Steve and Mike.

I don't know.

'He must be here somewhere,' Steve said, and disappeared back down the corridor again. A moment later he returned, beckoning to Mike.

'Go and get Sasha, and tell her to wake the girls. Leon's stuff has gone.'

'What?'

'You heard me. His bag, his clothes. They've gone. He's run away.'

Mike remained motionless, his mouth wide open, until Steve slapped him on the shoulder. 'Come on. Do it.'

'But look,' Mike replied, pointing out of the window. 'Have you seen the snow out there? He can't have done.'

'He's not here. His bag's not here. What else do you think could have happened? Go on, get Sasha, tell her what's happened.'

As Mike turned away from him, Steve's phone vibrated. He saw Mike's jaw clench at the sound of it, pulled it out of his pocket and frowned.

'Hang on. I need to go out.'

Mike looked outside. 'In that?'

'I'll look for Leon.' Steve already had his boots on, so grabbed a coat and stepped out into the swirling snow before Mike could argue.

Chapter 34

Tuesday 4th December

I woke around six in the morning and found myself curled up on the sofa with a blanket over me. Squinting blearily at Singh sitting on the opposite sofa, I yawned and sat up.

'The snow stopped a couple of hours ago, and the ploughs are out as we speak,' he told me. He must have woken up earlier and put the blanket over me before going to find out what was happening. 'I've told Liz I think it would be reckless to open the school today, but at least we can get home.'

I wandered into the kitchen and made coffees for the two of us and the PC who had returned at some point in the night. When I came back in, Singh was on his phone.

'Already?' he asked, then made a frustrated noise. 'Okay, I'll see what I can do.'

He hung up and turned to me. 'The road outside must be clear, because there are journalists and even a TV crew at the gate.'

'They were quick,' I said. The murder of a member of staff on school grounds during the school day was bound to be the news story of the week, but I was still surprised at how soon they'd appeared. Maybe they'd been contacted by the same person who had leaked the story about students being groomed.

I hung around for the next hour, waiting for instructions, then Singh and I went over to the main building to find Forest. Even though she didn't look like she'd been awake all night, I couldn't imagine she'd had so much as a quick power nap. The staff who'd been stuck overnight drifted over to gather in the staffroom to find out if they could go home or if the school would be open that day.

'Anyone not accounted for?' I asked Singh, after he'd had a long chat with Forest.

'We haven't checked yet. We're going to ask Liz Marcek to assemble all the staff and any students who come to school today in the hall at nine o'clock, then we can check.'

'Do you think any parents are going to let their kids come to school today, after what happened here? If it were me I wouldn't want to take that risk.'

'I doubt it, to be honest. Even if they're not put off by a murder and manage to make it through the snow, they'll have to fight through the journalists at the gate.'

At that moment, the deputy head appeared, so I interpreted Singh's request and she nodded.

I still don't believe any of my staff could be capable of this, you know, she told him with a haughty look. *There must be some other explanation.*

Singh didn't answer, and I couldn't really blame him.

As time went on, staff who had managed to get home the previous night began to drift in. When it got to nine, Singh went round the hall and checked every single name

322

against his list. Every staff member had come to work that day.

'I don't know if this is a good thing or a bad thing,' he muttered to Forest. 'If someone had done a runner at least we'd know who we were looking for. This just means they're cocky enough to believe nobody will work it out.'

'And when they're cocky, they'll make a mistake,' Forest said smoothly. She didn't seem to share Singh's frustration at the situation, and I wondered how she managed to stay so calm when there was a killer practically thumbing his or her nose at them.

As they had suspected, none of the students arrived for school that day, and Liz Marcek told the detectives she had been fielding emails all through the night and into the morning. Parents were demanding to know what was happening, if the school would be closing, and Liz didn't have any answers for them.

I don't know what I can tell them, she had told Singh angrily. *Until you tell me what's going on, I can't do anything.*

'I wish she understood that, right now, the reputation of this school is not our first priority,' he grumbled to me afterwards.

As we were walking out to the car park, a car pulled up and Jane Villiers got out. She was an imposing presence, and I could see why she had been the head teacher here for so long – it was almost as if the school suited her.

'I need to speak to you,' she said to Singh. 'Immediately.'

She was lucky she had caught us rather than another member of staff. Singh introduced her to Forest, then ushered her inside, where we were met with a startled Liz Marcek.

323

Jane. What are you doing here?

Reporting a motive for murder, Jane signed back. Liz took a step back, indicating that Jane and the detectives should go into her office. For a moment, the ex-head teacher hesitated, as if she wanted to use her old office, but then thought better of it. I hung back, but Forest ushered me inside with them, leaving Liz standing in the corridor, frowning.

'On Sunday night, I received an email from Saul Achembe. I've printed it off, but if you want access to the actual thing I'm happy to give you my password.' She slapped a printed sheet down on the table. 'I saw online this morning that he's been killed, and I can only assume that this is connected.'

Singh picked up the email and read it aloud.

'Dear Jane, I want to start by apologising to you. I'm sorry I didn't take you seriously last term when you thought something dodgy was going on. Once the governors removed you I didn't see the point in continuing the investigation you'd asked me to do, but given recent events I thought I should look into it again. The video itself hasn't been uploaded anywhere I can find, but when I was looking I found some emails between a student and a member of staff. I know the police have found messages backed up to Steve's account between him and Leon, when he was posing as someone called Joe, but these are between a different student and a different staff member. They'd been deleted and buried pretty well, but I managed to retrieve them all, and it's pretty unpleasant stuff. I've been having a dig around in Steve's account and he's got some hidden files with all of this in – he found out about it too, and I think that must be why someone killed him.

324

His files were dated the day of the trip, so he must have been preparing to confront them himself when he was murdered. I'm not going to mention any names right now, but I'll be speaking to the police tomorrow, and then hopefully this whole thing will be over. All the best, Saul.'

Forest took the email from Singh and read it over again. 'Well, it looks like Saul found our killer's motive. What the hell has been going on in this school? One teacher sending illicit messages to students is bad enough, but a second one?' She turned to Jane. 'Why do you think he wouldn't tell you the names of the student and the staff member?'

Jane threw her hands in the air. 'I have no idea! Maybe he was worried in case he was wrong, and he'd put it in writing? Maybe he was worried someone else might read it. He sent it from his school email account, after all.'

'Or maybe he wanted to give this person a chance to come clean, not realising they'd make him their next victim,' Forest muttered. 'Would someone else be able to access his emails?'

'I expect so, if they knew what they were doing. This system was never particularly secure. It would have cost money to tighten it up, and the governors controlled my purse strings far more than people realised.'

'Do you have any idea who he might be referring to?' Forest asked.

Jane gave her a withering look. 'Do you really think we'd be standing here talking about it if I did? I would have told you straight away! And if I'd had any idea who was behind the video I would have done something about it immediately, before I was shoved out and someone was brought in to take my place. At least it seems like he'd figured it out,' she added, grudgingly.

'And it's possible he was murdered for it,' Forest replied drily, 'so perhaps it's better for you that you didn't find out.'

'Thank you for this,' Singh added. 'It's definitely helpful. We'll give it to our tech team; it might give them a better idea of where to start, see where Saul was digging around in Steve's files and take it from there.'

The four of us left Liz Marcek's office to find the deputy head standing just outside the door, with Samira and her brother. When the girl saw her old head teacher she rushed forwards and threw herself at Jane, hugging her tightly. Jane looked taken aback, but automatically returned the hug, at which point Samira burst into tears.

'Whatever is wrong?' Jane asked, pulling Samira off her so she could sign the question.

Leon's gone! the girl wailed.

I know, he's been missing for days now. Is that what's upset you?

Samira shook her head. *You don't understand. He's gone.*

Gone from where?

Samira's brother shuffled uncomfortably. 'Leon's been hiding at our house.'

I was gobsmacked. Samira had done such a good job of pretending she was worried about Leon last week, getting worked up when she was asking if something had happened to him, that it had never occurred to me that she could be hiding him. She was clearly a very good actress. The detectives stared at Samira's brother, then both began to speak at once, but he held up his hands in defence.

'I didn't know! If I'd known she'd sneaked him in I

326

would've called the police, wouldn't I? I've not been home much the last couple of weeks,' he said, looking at the ground.

Jane Villiers drew herself up to her full height and glared at Samira's brother. 'Where are your parents?' she barked.

'Pakistan. They've been there for three weeks.'

'And you have been in sole charge of your teenage sister?'

He nodded.

'But you have neglected your care of her, by not even noticing that she had a friend staying with her for over a week? A friend that half of the country are looking for?'

The young man looked suitably cowed under Jane Villiers' onslaught, but Forest interrupted before it could continue.

'We can sort that issue out later, right now I need Samira to tell us everything that happened from last Saturday onwards.'

We trooped back into the deputy head's office, Liz and Jane both attempting to join us but being firmly refused by Forest.

Samira was trembling as she signed. *That Friday, Leon told me he was going to meet Joe. He texted me really early on Saturday morning, saying how excited he was, that he was going to meet him in the park. But then he went quiet, and the next thing I know he's outside my house. My brother was out, so I took Leon in and hid him in my room. Mo never goes in there, so I knew he wouldn't figure it out. Leon just made sure he only used the bathroom once Mo had gone out, and I brought him food when I was home.*

'What actually happened? Why did he run away?' Forest asked.

He told me he found Mr Wilkinson's body. There were tears in Samira's eyes as she finally told the secret she'd been hiding. *Someone saw him, and he thought they were going to blame it on him. So, he ran away, and he told me he had to hide until the police had proven it wasn't him.*

'Why didn't you tell us any of this?' Singh asked, trying to keep the anger and the frustration from his voice.

Leon told me not to. He said he wasn't safe.

'Who was it? Who saw him?'

Samira looked pained. *He wouldn't tell me. He said they were bound to tell the police he killed Mr Wilkinson, so he didn't want me knowing who it was and getting involved.*

'Nobody has told us about seeing Leon next to Mr Wilkinson's body, Samira,' Forest said. 'So that means the person who saw him is probably the real killer.' She paused for a moment to let the gravity of her statement sink in. 'Are you sure he never said anything that gave away who it might have been?'

Samira shook her head. *No, I promise. He was so scared.*

'When did you last see him?'

Yesterday morning, before I came to school. I don't know what happened, but when I got home he wasn't there.

Forest turned to Singh. 'We need to get a team out to the house to search for anything that might tell us where he's gone. Check for CCTV in the local area as well, see if there's any sign of him leaving on foot. He can't have gone too far, with the snow so bad.'

He was at home in the afternoon, when we were all in the hall, Samira offered. *I was texting him, telling him about what had happened to Mr Achembe. I told him he needed to go to the police, but he refused.*

'Are you sure he was at your house?'

She nodded. *We video chatted for a couple of minutes. I saw my room, he was definitely there. But I put my phone away because there was someone behind me and I didn't want him to be found out.*

'How were you communicating with him?' Singh asked. 'We've been monitoring his phone.'

Leon said you'd do that, Samira replied. *So I gave him an old one of my brother's.*

'Outsmarted by a couple of fifteen-year-olds,' Forest muttered. 'Okay. Thank you, Samira. We'll need the number of the phone you gave him. Is there anything else you can tell us? And I mean it. Lying to the police isn't a laughing matter, and you can get into trouble for it.'

That's all, I promise, she signed quickly, fear evident in her eyes. *Leon made me promise not to say anything. He was so scared. Where has he gone?*

'That's what we intend to find out.'

Chapter 35

The rest of the day dragged on for what felt like forever. Forest asked me to accompany Singh to Samira's house in case Leon came back again and they needed an interpreter.

Samira's family lived in a semi-detached house on a reasonably busy road on the outskirts of Lincoln. I sat in Singh's car for most of the time, huddled into my coat in an attempt to stay warm. The crime scene investigators turned up after half an hour, lugging various items of kit into the house with them. While I was waiting, I texted both Max and Anna to let them know what was happening. I'd kept them both updated the night before, and I didn't want either of them to worry.

I was starting to wonder if I could leave when Singh came outside and got into the car next to me.

'Not a sign of him,' he said. 'She was telling the truth, though. The lock on the front door has been forced, so someone broke in. There's a sleeping bag on her bedroom floor that's obviously been used, as well as various food wrappers under her bed. He didn't leave a note or anything saying why he'd gone, and Samira gave up her phone so we know he didn't text her to tell her.'

'So, he's been here all along,' I said, shaking my head in disbelief. 'If only she'd told you sooner.'

Singh groaned and rubbed a hand over his face. 'It was my own stupid fault for believing teenagers. But I honestly never would have thought a family could not notice there was a missing teenager staying in their house.'

'Will Samira get in trouble?'

'I don't know, at the moment. It really depends on what happens next.'

There was a parade of shops on the other side of the road, and I knew the police were hoping that one of them would have CCTV that might cover the front of Samira's house. They knew the reasonably narrow timeframe in which Leon had left the house, so that would help. Uniformed officers were knocking on the doors of houses nearby, in the hope that someone had seen something.

'Sir.' A PC approached the car and knocked on the door to get Singh's attention. The man held something up, and as Singh took it from him I could see it was a rucksack, matching Sasha's description of the one Leon had taken with him on the school trip.

'Where did you find this?'

'It was dumped in a bush next door,' the PC replied.

'Have you opened it?'

'No, sir.'

Singh called to one of the crime scene officers and asked them for a pair of latex gloves, which he snapped on before carefully opening the bag.

'It does look like it's probably Leon's,' he said, pulling

out a hoodie that Sasha had mentioned Leon had with him.

After a bit more rummaging, Singh pulled out a mobile. 'This is his original phone, the one we've been keeping an eye on in case he turned it on again. He's probably got the one Samira gave him with him. Forest has sent the details to the tech team to start tracking it.'

Singh put the rucksack and its contents into a large evidence bag, sealed and labelled it and handed it over to one of the crime scene officers. She looked at the list of contents and frowned.

'We just found another phone,' she told Singh, who looked puzzled.

'Where?'

'It had slipped under the table in the hallway. It was wedged quite far back, so I don't know if someone dropped it and kicked it under there by mistake, or maybe it fell down behind it.'

Singh went inside to find the evidence bag containing the other phone, and when he came back he looked grave.

'The phone they found inside matches the description of the phone Samira gave to Leon. It's locked, though, so we need to get it back to the station before we can have a look at the messages.'

'Why would he leave without his phone or his bag?' I asked. Maybe he'd heard about Saul's murder and had run because he thought he was in danger, but I couldn't see him doing that without his stuff.

'That's what I'm wondering,' Singh replied.

'Hang on. He had his original phone, his secret second phone, and also the one Samira gave him. Two of these phones are here, so does that mean he still has one?'

'You're right. We'll need to make sure the forensics

team keep an eye out for the third phone, though, in case he left that behind, too.'

I was about to ask another question when a PC waved Singh over to the house next door. As I wasn't police I couldn't really go with them, but I walked to the edge of the garden and loitered by the hedge separating Samira's house from the one Singh had walked over to. If I stood very still, I could hear the conversation.

'Please can you tell the detective what you told me,' the PC was saying.

An elderly lady spoke next, presumably the neighbour. 'I was letting the cat in, and I heard a noise coming from the house next door. I knew Samira should be at school, but I wondered if it was her brother. Sometimes he has people round and they play dreadful music, so loud. It's all thump thump and words that I can't understand.'

She paused, and Singh chimed in, trying to encourage her along. 'Could you see anything?'

'Yes, there was a black car outside, and as I looked there was a boy coming out the house. Someone else was with him, pushing him and grabbing his arm, but I didn't see their face. They had a big coat on, with the hood up.'

I shifted position slightly so I could see them through a gap in the hedge.

'Was it a man or a woman?' Singh asked.

'I couldn't tell, love. Anyway, they shoved the boy into the car, and they drove off.'

Singh asked the neighbour which direction the car had gone in, and she indicated up the road away from the city centre, and then he and the PC were walking back towards me.

'Did you get all that?' he asked me with a wry look, when he saw where I'd been standing.

I shrugged. 'Who was in the black car?'

'That's what we need to find out.'

I had travelled there with Singh, so I couldn't leave until he did. One of the PCs was dispatched to find out if there was any luck with CCTV from the shops opposite, and she came back with a gleam in her eye.

'We've got it,' she said. 'One of the shops has a camera that covers a good portion of the road. We can't see the people, but we can see the car stopped outside Samira's house. There might be enough detail to get a partial number plate.'

'That should help,' Singh said. 'Right, until then I'm going to go back to the school. We need to try and find out which other student Saul Achembe was referring to in his email to Jane Villiers.'

We didn't talk much on the journey back to the school. Singh was lost in his thoughts, and whenever I tried to engage him in conversation his replies were limp and distracted, so eventually I gave up. Shortly before we got there, an ambulance raced past us, lights flashing and siren wailing.

As we pulled up at the gates, we saw the ambulance parked outside the residence and my heart dropped into my stomach. Had something happened to one of the students?

'What's going on?' Singh asked the first person we could find, Jess Farriday. She had tears in her eyes as she turned to me and signed.

It's Mike. He's been attacked.

'Mike Lowther?' Singh checked. 'Attacked how?'

Someone stabbed him, she replied, sniffing as a tear rolled down her face. *I came to find him in the residence, and he was just lying there on the floor in the library.*

'But he's alive?' Singh asked.

She nodded. *I got Karen in the office to call 999.*

Singh went over to the ambulance to see what was going on, and a moment later two paramedics emerged from the residence with Mike on a trolley. They rushed him into the ambulance, one of them then getting into the driving seat while the other talked to Singh, before shutting the doors and leaving.

I stood next to Jess and watched the scene unfold, the irony not lost on me; both of us were Mike's ex-girlfriends, but I couldn't conjure the tears that Jess was still shedding. A treacherous thought in the back of my mind said maybe Mike had brought it on himself somehow, that he'd been attacked because he'd pissed off the wrong person. I felt a bit guilty for suspecting him of murdering Steve and Saul, but this attack surely meant he was innocent.

Singh came back to us and looked at Jess. 'Do you mind answering a couple of questions?'

She shook her head. *Was this the same person who killed Steve and Saul?*

'I don't know at the moment. Mr Lowther was conscious but confused, so I don't know if he'll be able to tell us who did this.'

A strange look flashed across Jess's face but I couldn't decipher it.

Why would someone attack Mike? she asked.

'That's something I wanted to ask you. Do you know of anyone who would want to?'

She shook her head, but she didn't look at Singh as she did. Instead she stared at me.

Mike went out with you, too. Didn't he? Her stare was

335

accusing. *He told me about it the other night, how he still loves you but you won't even talk to him.*

Not this again. 'What has that got to do with anything?' I asked, speaking and signing at the same time.

Maybe it was you, she signed, taking a step closer to me. *You look at him like he's shit on your shoe, maybe you wanted him out of your life for good.*

I rolled my eyes, shaking my head before I interpreted her rant for Singh.

'Miss Northwood has an alibi, because she was with the police when he was attacked, several miles from here,' he said drily. 'When you came over to the residence, did you see anyone else?'

Jess stared at me for a moment before answering. *No, nobody. Sasha and the students are over in the main building, having lunch.*

'Okay, thank you. I think perhaps you should go now.'

She walked away, throwing a glance back over her shoulder at me.

'What was that about?' I asked, genuinely confused as to why she'd decide to cast the blame on me.

'With Steve dead, maybe she was looking for another man to do her bidding, and she didn't like it when she found out Mike was pining for you, not her.' Singh watched me carefully as he spoke.

'Don't say it like that,' I replied. 'He doesn't miss me, he misses the way he was able to manipulate me. And that was an old version of me. He's not going to get back under my skin now.'

'Sorry,' he said, and he did look genuinely apologetic.

'You're forgiven,' I said with a wry smile. 'Is he going to be okay, though?'

I couldn't stand Mike for the way he'd treated me, but that didn't mean I wanted him to die. Even though I wasn't upset in the way Jess was, I didn't wish him ill. I just wished I'd never met him, or had seen through him much earlier in our relationship.

'The paramedics seemed to think it wasn't serious, but obviously they're taking him to hospital to have him checked over. He seemed very disorientated when I tried to speak to him.'

'Was it the same person?' I asked, echoing Jess's earlier question.

Singh sighed. 'I can't answer that, but it looks the same. Stabbing with a sharp implement. There was a kitchen knife lying on the floor next to where the paramedics found him, they said, which I assume was the weapon used. The murderer must have dropped it when they ran off.'

'You think they were interrupted?'

He nodded. 'Otherwise why didn't they finish the job? Jess might have saved Mike's life.'

Or maybe she was nearly caught in the act, I thought, but didn't voice it. Even though Singh knew my history with Mike, I didn't want to come across as the jealous ex blaming another ex.

'It's imperative we find Leon; he's in grave danger. This killer has been successful twice and it could have been three times if they hadn't been interrupted. I'd better go and speak to the deputy head while we wait for a crime scene crew,' he said, but when we walked over to the main building we discovered Liz Marcek was in a meeting with the governors.

'It's been going on for hours,' the receptionist, Karen,

told us, keeping her voice low. 'I took in tea and coffee a little while ago, but they didn't show any sign of wrapping it up.'

'You might as well go home,' Singh told me, and he walked me back to my car. 'Don't worry too much about Mike,' he said.

I didn't tell him that far from being worried about Mike, there was a part of me that wondered if I might be rid of him once and for all.

Chapter 36

I texted Max before I left, and he told me he'd meet me at my flat. I was looking forward to coming home and cuddling up with him. I needed a break from the case, from the atmosphere in the school, from everything to do with Mike, and I hoped an evening with Max would provide that.

I opened the door to the flat and immediately felt the tension in the air. Naively, I jumped to the conclusion that Max and Anna had had a falling-out and I would have to come in and smooth things over. When I walked into the living room, however, I could see that something had happened. Max was leaning against a wall with his arms folded and Anna was sitting on the sofa, her jumper pulled over her knees like she used to do when she was a teenager and she knew she was in trouble.

Hi, I signed to them both. *Everything okay?*

Why the hell did you never tell me about Mike? Max signed, the expression on his face a mixture of hurt and anger.

I shot a look at Anna, and she winced. *He started asking questions, and I wasn't going to lie to him. I'm sorry. I didn't realise you hadn't told him anything at all.*

When you said you didn't want to talk about your past relationships I assumed there'd been someone pretty crap, but I didn't expect this, Max signed, his face red. *And now you're working with him?*

I'm not working with him, I snapped. *He works at the school in Lincoln where I've been for a few interviews, that's all.*

And he's turned up outside your flat twice in the last week. Max glared at me. I glanced over at Anna but she avoided eye contact. *How could you keep something like that from me, Paige? I care about you but you have to trust me with this sort of stuff.*

Turning to face Anna, I stared at her for a moment until she shrugged and gave me a wide-eyed look.

What? she asked, trying her best to look innocent.

Would you leave us to have this conversation in private?

For a moment I thought she was going to dig her heels in, but she got up and slunk off to her bedroom. I recognised her body language – she knew she was in the wrong, but she would defend herself vehemently if she had to. I was too angry to bother with her at this point; I needed to sort things out with Max before we talked about what she'd done.

With Anna gone, I took off my shoes and sat down on the sofa, taking my time to try and stay calm. I was exhausted from broken sleep, and all I wanted to do was have a shower and try to forget about this case, but I wasn't going to get that chance just yet.

I understand why you're angry, but it's my past, my

history. That means it's my right to tell whoever I choose, or to keep it from them. Anna shouldn't have told you.

I'm glad she did, he replied, leaning against the wall opposite. *How am I supposed to help you, or protect you from a man like that, if I don't know about it?*

I made an exasperated noise in my throat. *I don't want you to protect me! Have I ever asked that of you? No. I can protect myself, or if I can't I'll call the police. Don't you see this is just like the problem I had with Mike, that he thought I was weak? He wanted to manipulate me; you want to protect me. Yes, there's a difference, but when do I get a say in it?*

Max looked at me with his mouth open, as if I'd just thrown my drink in his face.

How can you compare me to him? he asked slowly. *Do you seriously think we're alike?*

Of course not, but you have to admit that your reaction had the same sense of propriety over me, I replied, standing up to face him. *You see your role as my protector, which doesn't make us equal partners. Can't you see that?*

From the tightness of Max's jaw I could see that I wasn't explaining myself well. I put my head in my hands and thought for a moment.

Sit down, I told him. He resisted for a couple of seconds, but then did as I said.

How much did Anna tell you? I asked.

Everything.

Define 'everything'. I knew it was possible Anna had just given Max the bare bones, and when he related the story back to me I was right – she'd told him I had a manipulative ex who had now cropped up in one of my cases, and had turned up on the doorstep a couple of

341

times to bother me. For the second time in two days, I told the full story of what had happened between me and Mike. It was a story I hadn't ever intended sharing with anyone, and now I'd shared it with two people in a short space of time. I really hoped that Anna hadn't told Max that Singh knew about Mike before he did, though. The last thing I needed was extra jealousy piled on top of how he was feeling.

Once I'd finished, he sat back and shook his head. *I still can't believe you didn't tell me any of this, Paige. I mean, I understand now why you were so reluctant to get into a relationship in the first place. Maybe if you'd told me, I wouldn't have struggled to understand you so much.*

If I'd told you, you would have seen me as someone with too many issues, I replied, sitting forward as I attempted to explain it from my point of view. *Either you would have decided you didn't want to risk having those issues come back to bite you on the arse, or else you would have tried too hard to fix me. As it was, we went into our relationship with a clean slate, without any preconceptions of who the other person was and what they'd experienced. And it's been good, hasn't it?*

He nodded and gave me a small smile. *It has, but I feel like you've been closed off, as if you don't trust me.*

I felt tears prick my eyes and blinked rapidly. I really didn't want to let myself get emotional.

I do trust you, I told him. *I know that I have to trust you if this is going to work, and I've pushed myself not to close myself off from you since we've been together. I just didn't want to have to go into all of this about Mike, to rake it up and go over it again. I didn't want your sympathy, or your judgement.*

342

Why would I judge you? He looked irritated and I threw my hands up again.

Because people judge women who have been in abusive relationships! I stood up again and started pacing. *I know you're going to say you would never have judged me, but you wouldn't believe the number of people who I've heard talk about victims as if they were stupid, as if they could have easily got themselves out of the situation earlier, or not got into it in the first place. Not to mention those who say there must be another side to the story, what did she do to him, and so on. I didn't tell a lot of people what happened between me and Mike – even Anna and Gem don't know absolutely everything – because once it was over that was exactly how I wanted it. Over.*

Max shook his head and stood up again. Now that I was standing still again it was his turn to pace the room with his hands in his hair. I watched him for a moment, my stomach churning. Should I have told him sooner? Did I do the right thing? Or had I blown my chance to have a healthy relationship with a decent man?

Eventually Max stopped pacing and turned to look at me.

Anna said that Mike wants you back.

I felt a churning sensation in the pit of my stomach, a mixture of fear at where Max was going with this, and anger at Anna for throwing that revelation in the mix.

He's claimed he does, but I have no interest in him any more, I told him, stepping forward and putting my hands on his arms.

When she told me that, it made sense. Why you've been holding yourself back. I thought you might have been considering it, but then you realised he might be a murderer. The smile had gone, replaced with a stony expression.

What? I was aghast at his train of thought. *I was willing to hear Mike's apology, because that's what he claimed to be offering, but I don't think he actually has any remorse for what happened. Yes, I was stupid enough to think he'd changed, but that doesn't mean I'd ever consider dating him again, even if I were single.*

There was a long pause, and I had my heart in my mouth.

I'm sorry Paige, he signed, avoiding eye contact. *I can't think straight at the moment. I think I should go home.*

Fine. If that's what you want. I told myself I wasn't going to apologise for keeping something to myself when I didn't want to share it. If he chose to end things because of it, that was his problem. Still, as he walked out of the door I found myself bursting into tears.

It took a couple of hours for me to bring myself to look at my sister after Max had gone. She apologised again for telling him, and I decided I didn't have the energy to be angry about it. It had happened and neither of us could take it back, so I accepted it and tried to move on.

When I told Anna about Mike being attacked I could see conflicting emotions fighting on her face.

It's okay, I told her, *you don't have to be upset about it.*

Good. I don't really care what happens to that bastard.

I shook my head. *I wouldn't want him to die. I wouldn't wish it on anyone, however awful they'd been to me. But there were times before I threw him out that I fantasised about him being in an accident or something while he was out, about a police officer turning up at the door and*

344

telling me Mike was dead, then I could be free of him without actually having to break up with him. Does that make me a terrible person?

I'd been thinking about this the whole way home, worrying about my own reaction to finding out Mike had been attacked.

Of course it doesn't. It just means you knew you had to get out, but were too scared to confront him in case he went ballistic. Anna shrugged off my feelings as if they were completely normal, when I had expected her to be shocked by them, and that made me feel better.

This last week has been a nightmare, I told her. *Trying to deal with Mike, and now fighting with Max. This is why relationships aren't worth the hassle.* I tried for a wry grin, but it probably ended up looking a bit strangled.

I understand why you wanted him to have changed, Anna said. *You want to believe people are inherently decent, and that they care about what happens to the people around them. Unfortunately, not everyone does. Men like Mike are blind to other people's feelings. It's all about them.*

I nodded. *I think he only apologised to make himself feel good,* I told her. *If he hadn't seen me again, he never would have considered it. When we were together he only ever did something if he thought he could get something out of it, and this apology was no different.*

I'm really sorry about telling Max, she said, apologising for probably the seventh time. *I shouldn't have done it. I thought it was important for you to talk about it, but I shouldn't have interfered.*

I sighed. *It's okay. I'm hoping a bit of space will help him to understand why I didn't tell him. But I still don't know if Max is right for me, you know? It's fun, in a lot of ways, when I'm not stressing out about being in a relationship, but it doesn't feel like there's much fire there. Does that make sense? It's just . . . nice.*

Well there's always Singh, she replied with a wink, laughing when I rolled my eyes at her.

Don't start that again. That one's a dead end, I replied, trying not to remember how natural it had felt to fall asleep on his shoulder the previous night.

Okay, okay. What's going to happen now? she asked. *With the school, I mean. They can't keep it open if staff are being attacked.*

I don't know. I suppose I'll find out tomorrow. Whatever happened to Mike, though, it means the murderer is panicking, I told her.

What do you mean? she asked.

Two attacks in two days? They're trying to cover their tracks, and they're just making things worse. The longer it takes to find Leon, the greater the danger he's in.

Fifteen minutes before the murder

Sasha paced up and down in the living room. Mike had gone out about ten minutes after Steve to find out where the head teacher had got to, and the students were getting fractious.

What's going on? Where's Leon? Bradley kept asking her every few minutes.

I don't know where he is. Mike and Mr Wilkinson have gone to look for him. They'll be back soon.

You said that ten minutes ago.

And on it went. Kian looked like he was close to tears and kept wrapping his arms around himself. Bradley looked ready to punch someone, and Courtney was trying to keep him calm. Only Cassie seemed unruffled by the situation, curled up on the sofa, watching the others.

Can we go and help? Bradley asked.

No, Sasha replied with a firm look. *I don't want you getting lost out there in the snow. You might not find your way back here.*

We'd be careful, Bradley insisted. *We'd be able to follow our own footprints.*

No, you wouldn't, it's snowing too heavily. They'd be covered over in minutes, Sasha insisted.

Well we can't just sit here doing nothing! He turned to look at the others. *This is our fault. We could have stopped him.*

Why is it your fault? Sasha asked.

Bradley took a deep breath, then looked down at the floor. *We're his friends. We should have known. We should have stopped him.*

She shook her head. *It's not your fault. If Leon's run away, he kept his feelings hidden from everyone.*

Bradley nodded, but she could tell he didn't agree. A look passed between the students, and Sasha got the feeling they were keeping something from her.

They sat for another ten minutes before Bradley started pacing again. Sasha's phone buzzed with a video call from the lead social worker. She glanced at the students, wondering if she could leave them, but there was no way Nina would call her on a Saturday morning if it wasn't urgent. She slipped out of the room to take the call.

Ten minutes later, she came back into the room. All the students had gone. Fearing they'd left to search for Leon, Sasha grabbed a coat and raced out into the snow, looking for footprints. She didn't want to stray too far from the cabin, but she couldn't bear the idea of the other students getting lost – how would it look if Steve and Mike came back and she'd let them leave?

Panic was beginning to set in when she saw the four of them trooping around the edge of the cabin, Bradley with his arm around Kian, Courtney close behind them.

Cassie trailed at the back, dragging her feet through the deep snow.

Get back inside! she signed as soon as they were close enough to see. *Are you trying to give me a heart attack?*

We thought we could help, Courtney explained, her face a picture of misery. *But it's too snowy out here.*

That's what I told you. Come on, back in.

I didn't want to go, Cassie told her.

Shut up, Cassie, Bradley signed, but Sasha could see his heart wasn't in it.

They had just taken off their coats and boots when Mike stomped through the door. He went over to Sasha and turned his back on the four students so they couldn't see what he was signing.

I can't find either of them, Leon or Steve, he told her.

Sasha let out a long breath. *Okay. What do you think we should do?*

I think we need to call the police.

Chapter 37

Wednesday 5th December

I did my best to forgive Anna for telling Max. I ended up lying awake half the night, forcing myself not to text Max. This was his issue, I kept reminding myself, though there was a voice in the back of my head that continued to nag at me. If I wasn't ready to share that part of myself, it said, was I ready to commit to this relationship?

The next morning I got up late, so I was still in my pyjamas when Singh rang and asked me to meet him at the police station. I reminisced briefly about my days working for an agency when I knew in advance what jobs I was going to have each day, but on the other hand I genuinely loved working with the police. I felt like I was actually doing something worthwhile.

When I arrived, Singh met me in the lobby and took me through to an interview room, where Sasha Thomas was sitting next to Cassie. Sasha smiled at me and gave me a nod. A moment later, DI Forest walked in and we were ready to begin.

'Cassie, you and Sasha have come up here this morning

because there is something we need to talk to you about,'
Singh explained, his face grave.

The girl fidgeted in her seat as the DS continued. 'We
have had our computer experts looking at your school
systems, and they've found some messages between you
and a member of staff.'

Cassie's face drained of all colour and she stopped
moving, staring at Singh.

I don't know what you mean.

'There are lots of messages between your school computer
account and a staff account. They talk about the other
students, and Joe. They go right back to when Ms Villiers
left the school. The messages stopped in September, when
you and the others got your secret phones.'

Sasha's face was ashen as she watched Cassie for a
reaction. The pause before Cassie replied felt like it
stretched on for days.

I don't know what you mean, the girl repeated, looking
down at her feet.

Forest sat back and folded her arms. 'Lying to us won't
help you, Cassie. We've read the messages. You knew this
person was pretending to be Joe, and messaging all your
friends. They told you to pretend you got messages as well.'

Cassie looked around the room for a moment, then
looked at Sasha. *Am I going to get in trouble?*

Sasha shook her head slowly. *Just tell the truth. Right
now, that's the most important thing.*

I didn't want Mike to get hurt, Cassie said, anxiety
shining on her face. My heart sank at the idea that this
young girl was under his spell. I was sure he wouldn't get
involved with a child, however mature she looked, but that
didn't mean he wouldn't find other ways to manipulate her.

'Was Mike the person you were messaging?' Singh asked, and only then did I realise they didn't know who the staff member was.

What? No! It can't have been him, Cassie replied, sitting forward and giving the detectives an anxious look.

'Who was it, then?' Forest asked. 'We can't trace it back to a person. Whoever it was must have set up a new staff account under a fake name, because it doesn't tell us who you were sending messages to.'

But . . . she signed, then stopped.

'But what, Cassie?' Singh asked eventually.

Cassie looked at Sasha again. *I don't want to get into trouble. And I don't want anyone else to get into trouble.*

Tell them the truth, Cassie. Everything, Sasha told her.

Fine, the girl said with a sigh. *My friend told me I had to pretend I'd been texting someone called Joe or Jo. They said it was all part of the game.*

'Who is your friend?' Forest asked, her patience clearly wearing thin. I remembered the times before when Cassie had alluded to her friend, and comments from other students about this friend being imaginary. I also remembered Sasha's concerns, when she thought someone was manipulating the students – we had been sure it was Steve, but whoever Cassie had been getting messages from was at the school before Jane was fired, so Steve couldn't have been Joe after all. Who had been controlling her?

I can't tell you, Cassie signed, her eyes wide. *They told me never to tell anyone about them. I can't.*

The detectives looked at each other, then made an unspoken decision to try another tactic.

'You say this friend of yours was pretending to be Joe, sending messages to Leon. Is that right?' Singh asked.

352

Cassie nodded. *And the others. Not just Leon.*

'Well, some of the first messages that "Joe" sent to Leon were texts to his new phone. The messages were backed up to an email address at the school.'

Oh, I know. It was Mr Wilkinson's. My friend told me they could back up those messages, because then if they got caught we could pretend it was Mr Wilkinson. They said it wouldn't be a problem.

As Cassie signed this, her eyes darted around the room, and I wondered if she believed what she was saying.

'Is your friend a man or a woman, Cassie?'

I don't know, she said, but her face flushed and I thought she was lying. *They send me presents and leave me notes.*

'But you said you're not allowed to tell us who they are. So, you must know.'

She shook her head. *I thought I knew, but now I'm confused.* She bit her lip and looked down at the floor.

'Tell us a bit more about your friend then, and the things they've done,' Singh said.

Cassie looked puzzled. *I've told you everything: texting students, pretending to be other people. My friend told me all about it.*

'What about filming Bradley and Courtney?'

She swallowed, then nodded. *My friend knew they were sneaking around, so they got into their school email accounts, and sent them messages pretending to be from each other. They got them to meet in the art classroom, and set up the video camera to film them.* Her face fell. *But then Ms Villiers saw it, and she got into trouble for not telling the governors. I didn't want that to happen.*

'Why did your friend tell you about all this?'

They just said we were friends, and they cared about me. They needed me to pretend I got messages from Joe, so the others would trust me, and that I should keep secrets for them because they did stuff for me.

'What did they do for you?'

Got me things I wanted. Make-up, clothes, shoes. Sometimes I come back from lessons and I find new things in my bedroom. They even leave me cider sometimes, she signed with a mischievous grin. *The new phones were from my friend, but I wasn't allowed to tell the others. They said it was better to message that way than on the school computers.*

Forest sat back and folded her arms. 'Do you realise that your friend might be a murderer, Cassie? Do you realise they might be the person who killed Mr Wilkinson and Mr Achembe?'

The girl shook her head. *No, I don't think so. They wouldn't do that. They're kind. They're the only person who cares about me. All the others think I'm stupid, but they don't know. They don't know what I can do. I can make any of them do anything.* As she signed this last sentence, her eyes flashed dangerously, and it was obvious just how much she had enjoyed the power this secret knowledge had given her.

'Cassie, you say this person cares about you, but where are they?' Forest spread her arms wide. 'Are they here, confirming that you're telling the truth? Are they protecting you by confessing to what they've done, confessing to asking you to keep these secrets for you? No, Cassie. There's nobody here, only you.'

Tears sprang up in Cassie's eyes. *I'm scared.*

Singh leant forward and smiled at her. 'We understand

that, but it's our job to protect you and keep you safe. But we don't know who we need to keep you safe from.'

It started out with the presents, Cassie said. *They all had little notes, saying they were from a friend. Then I got text messages from my friend, just asking how I was. I felt like I could tell them anything and they'd understand. They didn't ask me to do anything for them for ages.*

'Why didn't you tell us any of this before, Cassie?'

Because I was told to keep it a secret, she insisted, her eyes shining. *I didn't want my friend to stop being nice to me. But then Mike was attacked.* She looked down at the table. *I'm worried it was my fault. I thought he might have been my friend, because he's always nice to me. Leon asked me about my new shoes and I told him I thought Mike had bought them for me. He thought it was really funny and told everyone I was making up stories about Mike buying me presents.*

The detectives looked at each other. 'We don't know if these things are connected, Cassie,' Forest said, 'but we need to look into them. Please will you let us have your phone, so we can see the messages you got from your friend?'

She shook her head. *I told you, I lost it.*

'Have you had any messages from your friend in the last week?' Forest asked.

No. They only text my new phone now, and I haven't had it since the weekend we went on the trip.

'What about the presents? Could you write us a list of what they gave you? And did you keep any of the notes that came with them?'

For a moment I thought Cassie was going to shake her head again, but then she sagged a little. *I kept some, yes.*

'Where are they?'

In a box in my room.

'Okay Cassie, when Sasha takes you back to school I'm going to come with you and collect those notes.'

Why? I want to keep them.

'They might help us to find out who your friend is.'

Can I have them back afterwards? There was an earnest look in her eyes, and I wondered how lonely she must have been for this 'friend' to get her so completely under their spell.

Cassie and Sasha left, and Singh was about to follow when Forest got a phone call. She held up a hand telling him to wait, and I hovered next to him.

'What?' she exploded. 'Are you absolutely certain?' There was a pause as the person on the other end spoke. 'Right,' Forest continued. 'I'll send a car and a couple of PCs to collect him. Don't let him leave. I don't care what you have to do, that man is about to be placed under arrest and if he discharges himself before my officers get there I will hold you personally responsible!'

She hung up with a snarl and looked over at Singh. 'I can't bloody believe it,' she began, then spotted me over Singh's shoulder.

'You, out,' she barked at me. 'You can't be here for this.'

I did as I was told, getting out of there before she had a chance to turn her anger on me any further, but I didn't leave the station. I wanted to know who was under arrest – had they found the murderer?

Chapter 38

Fifteen minutes later, Singh spotted me hanging about in the police station lobby.

'What are you doing?' he asked, keeping his voice quiet. 'Forest will throw a fit if she finds out you're still here.'

I shrugged. 'She told me to get out. I took that to mean get out of the room, not the building.'

He looked at me for a moment, then burst out laughing. 'You're sneaky, you know that?'

'I wouldn't have got where I am today without it,' I replied. 'Anyway, what's going on?'

Singh looked behind him, checking that Forest was nowhere to be seen, then took me back through the doors to a waiting room.

'Stay here. I'll come and get you in a while.'

'Do you need me to interpret?'

'No, but I think this is still an interview you deserve to hear.'

Puzzled, I opened my mouth to ask another question,

but he shook his head and left the room. I spent twenty minutes pacing in there, tensing every time I heard footsteps approaching, but each time they passed by.

My phone buzzed, and I felt a jolt of nerves when I saw that it was a text from Max.

Sorry for being a dick. xxx

It made me smile, and it lifted a weight from my heart that I hadn't even realised was there. After the bombshell of Cassie's announcement, I'd almost forgotten about our argument.

Come over tonight? he asked.

Sure :) xx

I kept expecting Forest to appear in the doorway, telling me to go home, but when the door finally opened it was Singh again.

'Come with me,' he said quietly, leading me through the corridor and directing me into a room. When I got in there I realised it was an observation room, and on the other side of the glass panel in front of me was an interview room. The walls were stark, breeze blocks painted a bland beige, and the only furniture was a single table and three chairs. Forest was sitting in one of them with her back to me. Mike was facing me, his expression neutral, but I could tell it was an act as his eyes were darting from side to side.

'What's going on?' I said quietly, unsure if sound would travel through the mirrored glass.

'You'll see,' he said, backing out and closing the door behind him, then reappearing a moment later in the room on the other side of the glass.

'Right, we're ready to begin,' Forest said, leaning forward and pinning Mike with a steely glare. 'Mr

Lowther, can you explain to us what happened to you yesterday afternoon?'

The expression on Mike's face was one I was familiar with, the face he used when he wanted people to trust him. I had learnt not to believe a word that came out of his mouth, but that facial expression worked on a lot of people; his charm was his greatest weapon. Could he have used that charm to manipulate Cassie?

'Well, I can't completely remember,' he said, running a hand over his short hair. 'It's a bit blurry.'

'Try your best,' Forest said, her tone sharp. Mike picked up on this and frowned.

'What's going on here? I thought you just wanted to take my statement.'

'And that's exactly what we're doing, if you'd stop avoiding the question.'

Mike hesitated, but then I saw his shoulders relax. 'I was in the residence, just checking some paperwork, and I heard the door open behind me. Before I had a chance to turn round and see who it was, I felt like I'd been punched in the arm. I fell over and hit my head.' He gave a little shrug and a smug smile. 'That's all I remember until I was being wheeled into the ambulance.'

'You didn't see your attacker at all?'

'No, they were behind me the whole time.'

Forest nodded, her lips pursed. 'Hmmm. Okay. And there was nothing else that could help you identify them? They didn't speak to you? You didn't catch a glimpse of their shoes as you passed out, anything like that?'

Mike wrinkled his brow as if he were thinking. 'Now you mention it, I think I saw their shoes. They were black, and quite small. And I felt their fingernails graze against

359

my neck. Maybe they were quite long?' His expression had now changed to one of earnest helpfulness, but once again I was convinced he was lying. I hoped the detectives could see it too.

'Let me check I've got this right,' Forest said smoothly. 'Just before you passed out, you saw that your attacker was wearing black shoes and had small feet. And you felt long fingernails scratch your neck. Is that correct?'

'Yes,' Mike said assertively.

'Why haven't you mentioned this before now?'

'I only just remembered. Your questions prompted me to remember.'

'Oh, I am glad,' Forest said, and the sheer force of the sarcasm made me realise that she had another agenda. Whatever it was, I didn't think it was going to reflect well on Mike.

'What about if I asked you if you'd smelled their perfume or aftershave, do you think you'd be able to remember that, too?'

Mike looked puzzled. 'I don't know. I haven't really thought about it.'

'Or if I asked you whether a specific person looked you in the eyes before trying to kill you, would you remember that too?'

This time, Mike didn't reply, but looked between the two detectives, trying to work out what was going on.

'You are lying,' Forest said, enunciating each word clearly and slowly for effect. 'The report from the doctor who examined you states that whoever tried to stab you did so from the front, not from behind you. They would have been standing right in front of you, looking you full in the face, in order to attack you. I don't understand how you couldn't identify your attacker in this situation.'

Mike shook his head vehemently. 'No, that's not how it happened. The doctor must be mistaken.' He paused, and I could almost hear the thoughts forming in his mind. 'Unless I've completely forgotten it. If I have concussion from hitting my head, I'm sure that could cause temporary amnesia. Then when I came round, I just assumed they attacked me from behind because I couldn't remember seeing them.'

'That's a lovely story,' Forest said, 'but I'm afraid that version isn't going to work either. The doctor has assured us that the person who attempted to stab you didn't do a particularly good job of it, and they only gave you a gash on your arm. The blow you suffered to your head was minor. In fact, he was surprised that you even lost consciousness.'

Mike looked sullen and stared at Forest. 'What are you accusing me of? I don't think I want to continue talking to you,' he said. 'I came here to give my statement, not to be badgered and accused of lying. I'll be putting in a formal complaint about my treatment here.' He stood up and made as if to leave the room, but Forest got to the door before him.

'Sit down, Mr Lowther. Or do I need to arrest you?'

'What for?' he demanded, calling Forest's bluff, or so I thought.

'Wasting police time with this absolutely appalling fabricated story,' she snarled.

For a moment they stood nose to nose, until Mike's shoulders dropped and he sat back down, putting his head in his hands.

'The inconsistencies in your story lead us to believe that

you weren't actually attacked,' Singh said, his voice icy. 'Instead, our current theory is that you faked this attack, stabbed yourself in the shoulder, knowing that someone would soon find and help you, and invented this story. Are we correct?'

I thought Mike wasn't going to answer, but he nodded.

'Out loud, please, Mr Lowther,' Forest barked.

'Yes, fine. You're right. Fuck's sake.' Mike thumped the table but didn't say any more.

'Our question now has to be, why? Why go to all of this trouble to try and convince us you were attacked?'

Silence. Mike rested his forehead on the table and looked down at the floor, ignoring Singh's question.

'I think I know this one,' Forest said, addressing her words to Singh. 'He did it because he wanted us to believe he was an innocent victim. He did it to take attention away from himself as the person who has been manipulating Cassie, killed both Steve Wilkinson and Saul Achembe, and then kidnapped Leon from Samira's house. Am I getting close, Mike?'

As she said this, Mike raised his head from the table and looked at them both, aghast.

'No! No, I had nothing to do with any of that!'

'Why should we believe you? You've been lying to us since you stepped into this room. How do we know you're not lying now? It would be the perfect way to throw suspicion off yourself, if you were also attacked by the killer.'

'What? Why the hell would I kill Steve and Saul?'

'That's what we'd like to know, Mike. Did Steve taunt you because he was seeing Jess after she left you? Did he make you angry? Or was it that he'd found out you were the one stealing from the school? We know you have a gambling problem.'

'That wasn't me, any of it! Yeah, I like to gamble, but I'd never steal!'

I snorted at this assertion, but I supposed he'd never thought of it as stealing when we were together. He'd seen everything of mine as being his.

'Really? What about the items that have gone missing from students in the residence in the last year? Including, most recently, a charm bracelet? It might not have had diamonds on it, but it still could have fetched you a bit of cash at a pawn shop.'

My mouth hung open for a moment after Singh mentioned the bracelet. Had that been Mike, too? From the look on his face, I thought Singh had got it completely right.

'The bracelet was . . . a mistake,' Mike said, his voice so quiet I could barely hear him.

'A mistake.' Forest's voice was dripping with sarcasm. 'You mean it was a mistake because there were police crawling all over school and you knew you could be risking more than a reprimand from your boss?'

'No! Anyway, I returned it.'

'Dumped it in the snow outside Courtney's window, you mean?'

'I was going to put it back inside. I went round to see if she was in her room, but then I heard someone coming, so I dropped it and ran.' He didn't look up once as he told this story, his shoulders slumped in defeat.

Singh sat forward, and Mike's gaze flicked upwards. The DS put on his best fake smile. 'Come on Mike. Tell us the truth. How are you mixed up in all this?'

'I'm not!' he yelled, pushing himself backwards so his chair wobbled precariously.

'Tell us why, then? Why the hell would you fake an attack on yourself, that so closely resembled the ways Steve and Saul were killed, if you're not the person who committed those crimes in the first place?'

To my horror, Mike began to cry. He put his head down on the desk and he sobbed, big ugly sobs that screwed up his face. The two detectives looked at each other, clearly surprised by the effect they'd had on him.

There was a long pause as Mike sniffled and tried to pull himself together, then he shook his head and thumped the table.

'It's all that bitch's fault. If she wasn't so cold to me, I would never have had to do something like this. She's messed up. She's messed ME up.' He took a big shuddering breath. 'You can't arrest me for this, I didn't know what I was doing. It's a mental health issue. I need to be assessed by a psychologist or something.'

My heart was hammering at this outburst. Was he talking about Jess? I hoped he was, but I wasn't confident.

'We'll certainly look into that,' Forest replied. 'You're claiming you did this for attention?'

He laughed coldly. 'Attention. You make me sound like the stupid little teenage girls I have to deal with every day. No, I did it to teach her a lesson. Paige fucking Northwood caused this. You should arrest her. She's cruel and manipulative, and I did this to show her just how much damage she's doing.' Mike stared wildly at Forest as he continued. 'You know she's dangerous. She manages to convince everyone that I treated her badly, but I would never do that. She's got

364

him wrapped around her little finger,' he said, stabbing a finger towards Singh.

Forest shook her head slowly. 'I can't believe this. You've wasted our time with this, when we could be out catching a murderer, and more importantly finding one of your vulnerable students. I'll be putting forward a case to have you charged with wasting police time, and anything else I can find that will stick. You'd better find yourself a decent lawyer.'

The detectives wrapped up the interview as my legs gave way and I sank to the floor in the observation room. How could Mike have done something like this? Faked an attack on himself, just to get a reaction out of me? Maybe the old me would have gone running to check he was okay, or let him back into my life out of guilt or duty, but there was no way in hell that was going to happen now.

I'd stopped shaking by the time Singh came back to get me.

'That's not what we were expecting,' he said. 'I'm sorry I let you listen to it now.'

'Don't be. I'm glad I heard it. He's poisonous, and I don't want anything to do with him, but I'm glad I know exactly what he said about me. I can't believe I ever thought he might have changed.'

'Come on,' Singh said, taking my hand to help me up off the floor. 'I need to go to the school to collect those notes from Cassie. Are you up to interpreting?'

I nodded and followed him. As we walked out to the car park, he hesitated. 'Do you mind driving? My car wouldn't start this morning so I got a taxi here.'

We got into my car and set off for Lincoln, not speaking,

both deep in our own thoughts. I was turning everything over in my mind when all of a sudden something struck me.

'How did you find out about the messages between Joe and Leon in the first place?' I asked Singh.

'What?' he said, coming out of a daze. 'Oh, we had his phone number so we got the network to give us access.'

'But how did you get that number? Who gave it to you?'

He paused. 'I can't remember. One of the staff. Why?'

'How did they know about that phone?'

Singh didn't reply, so I tried to explain my thinking.

'The phone Leon was using to message Joe was his second phone, his secret one. Nobody knew about those phones except for the students.'

'And the person who gave them the phones,' he said quietly. 'Shit. How did we not pick up on that?'

'Whoever gave you that phone number knew about Leon's secret phone,' I said. 'Which means they were the one who planned this whole thing, and they gave you that number instead of his usual number, because they wanted you to find those messages. They'd been setting Steve Wilkinson up, building up the evidence for months to destroy his life and his reputation, and now they're letting you finish it off for them.'

Singh pulled out his phone and made a call. 'I need to get someone to check the interview records and find out who gave us that number,' he told me as he dialled.

I tried to concentrate on the road, but I could feel the tension vibrating off him as he spoke to someone at the station.

'Okay, text me the home address.' He hung up, then a

moment later his phone beeped and my heart picked up its pace.

'Change of destination,' Singh said, then looked at me, remembering who was driving. 'Shit. You can't come with me.'

'Do you think Leon will be there?'

'Possibly.'

'Then tell me where to go. You can't waste time going back for another car,' I told him, and he gave in, telling me where to go.

'Where is this place?' I asked, looking at the address he'd typed into my satnav.

'Liz Marcek's house.'

After

Liz looked down at Steve's blood staining the snow and took a step back. The penknife he always carried around with him dropped from her gloved hand and landed near his body. She couldn't get any of the blood on her.

It had been so easy. After he found her messages to Cassie, she knew she had to act straight away. All it had taken was one text, telling him she knew who'd saved those messages, and telling him to meet her on the road. She'd parked there last night, before the snow started, then walked up to meet him in the clearing this morning. She'd brought a weapon with her, but when she saw his penknife sticking out of his pocket it seemed too good an opportunity to miss. Then it had just been a case of slipping up behind him when he wasn't looking. The knife was sharp enough to do the rest.

She didn't know how she was going to get her car out, but she'd worry about that later. Her heart racing, she looked up. Light was starting to creep into the sky between the heavy clouds but the snow was still falling. She needed to get out of there as soon as possible. Retracing her own footsteps, she got to the edge of the clearing and paused. Was there someone there? She ducked behind a bush and waited.

Her heart pounding, she realised there was someone approaching: it was Leon. She'd sent him a message as Joe, telling the boy to meet 'him' out here. That way, he could be found near Steve's body and she had the perfect person to blame.

When she had first started this, Liz had assumed that Kian would respond best to Joe's friendship, and had been surprised when Leon was the one who had opened up to 'him', but it had worked out well. With Leon's history, nobody would believe he wasn't responsible for Steve's murder.

As she watched, the boy bent down and picked up the knife, then pulled his hand away sharply. It was going even better than she'd hoped. He would leave his own DNA here, leading the police right to him. Along with the messages from Joe, the evidence was perfect.

But then Leon turned, and suddenly he was looking straight at her. She froze, her mind racing, but she realised she still had all the power. She was in a position of authority, and she knew she could terrify a fifteen-year-old boy into keeping his mouth shut.

What have you done?

The boy turned and ran. It didn't matter. She'd find him.

Chapter 39

We pulled up outside a large detached house in a smart area to the north of Lincoln.

'It was Liz?' I asked.

'She was the one who gave us Leon's number, so she must have known about his second phone. She's been planning this for months. But why? Why frame Steve?' Singh stared at the house as if something about it would give us the answer.

'There must be something we've missed, something in their shared past. This has been going on for months. Liz engineered the scandal that got Jane fired, and I bet she used her influence with the governors to make sure Steve was appointed as the new head teacher.'

'We haven't found anything that connects them before September,' Singh replied. 'If Liz has been holding a grudge against Steve, she's kept it pretty well hidden.'

'Had they ever worked together before? Did he bully her in a previous job?'

Singh shook his head. 'We would have found something like that. I think Liz has only ever worked at the school for the deaf.'

'If it wasn't related to work, it must be something more personal then. Family?'

'Nobody else lives here,' Singh replied, nodding at the house. 'They told me when I asked for the address. As far as we're aware she doesn't have any children.'

'It doesn't have to be a husband or kids,' I said, then a thought occurred to me. 'The first time Anna and I visited Jane, she told us that Liz had been grieving for her brother when the video of Bradley and Courtney turned up,' I told him.

Singh cocked his head on one side. 'You think Steve was connected to her brother's death? What happened to him?'

'Jane wasn't certain, but she thought he might have overdosed. When you went to Steve's old school, you told me you discovered that a member of staff was fired for taking drugs and Steve reported him for drug-driving. He ended up killing himself.'

A look of comprehension dawned on Singh's face. 'How did we miss that? I bet you're right. I bet . . .'

'He was Liz's brother.'

We sat for a moment, looking at the snow-covered garden.

'Is she at work today?' I asked.

'As far as I know. We need to see if Leon's here.'

I nodded. 'What do you want me to do?'

'Stay in the car. I mean it, Paige. Back-up are on the way, but I'm going to see if I can see anything through the windows in case he's inside.'

I knew I couldn't argue with him, especially after what had happened the last time we'd worked together in February, when I'd knowingly walked into a house to confront a murderer. I just hoped we weren't too late for Leon.

'Don't do anything dangerous, though,' I warned him as he got out of the car. He nodded at me, then crunched his way up the path to the front door.

I watched him ring the doorbell first, just in case there was someone in the house. He needed to do things the official way, of course, but I was anxious watching him. What if Leon was in the house? What if he was injured?

After a couple of minutes it was pretty clear nobody was going to come to the door. Singh walked around the side of the house, then disappeared from view.

I tried to wait patiently; I really did. But after a few minutes my curiosity got the better of me and I followed him.

I walked to the nearest window and peered through, seeing a well-furnished living room. There was no sign of Leon or Singh, so I carried on around the house until I came to patio doors leading into the kitchen. I tried the door gingerly, but it was locked. For a brief moment I considered breaking in, but remembered the police would be arriving soon.

As I turned round, I heard the crunch of someone walking over snow, and froze. Had Liz come home and seen my footprints leading round the side of the house? A sudden movement in front of me made me jump.

'Paige! I told you to stay in the car!' Singh gave me an exasperated look.

'I was worried something was going to happen to you,'

I told him, glancing over his shoulder towards the garden. 'Have you tried the summerhouse?'

I hadn't noticed the structure at first, tucked away in the corner of the huge garden, but from this angle it was obvious. It wasn't visible from the road, and I'd been concentrating on the house as I'd come round the back. The wood was painted a white that had weathered over time, and it blended in well with the snow.

'Not yet. You need to go back to the car.'

'I'm here now,' I replied, and I set off down the garden. He quickly followed, our feet sinking into a couple of drifts that came well past our ankles. A quick glance through the window of the summerhouse filled me with relief. Leon was curled up on a sofa, his hands and feet bound and a gag over his mouth, but he looked up when I appeared at the window, so I knew he was alive. I tried the door but it was locked, and when the boy saw me and Singh there was panic on his face.

It's okay, we're with the police, I signed to him through the door, but this didn't seem to calm him. Singh elbowed one of the panes of glass in the door until it broke, while I watched for the back-up he had assured me was on the way. Thankfully, it was only flimsy glass and didn't require much effort, but he was still careful when he reached inside to unlock the door. He didn't want a scar to match mine.

Once Singh had got us inside, I rushed over to Leon and untied him.

You don't understand, she'll kill us both, he signed to me as soon as his hands were free. He was shaking from the cold, his eyes wide with panic.

It's okay, he's a detective, and more police are coming,

I told him confidently, assuming they would have arrived by the time I got his feet untied and got him out of there.

Leon shook his head, but allowed me to guide him back through the garden to the front of the house, Singh letting me take the lead with Leon to keep him calm. The police cars I had expected were nowhere to be seen. It shouldn't be taking them so long to arrive, but we couldn't rely on them now.

'Come on, we'll get you to the station,' Singh told Leon with a reassuring smile.

No! We need to go to my school right now. The look in his eyes was one of pure panic.

'What?' Singh and I were both surprised by Leon's insistence.

She'll kill her. I told you! She's going to kill us both, he said, fear making him look younger than his fifteen years.

Singh and I looked at each other, confused.

'Kill who?' the DS asked. 'Who is she going after?'

I could see the concern in Leon's eyes as they darted between Singh and me, wondering if he could trust us.

She said she'd kill me like she killed Mr Wilkinson.

I remembered what Samira had told us. *The police know it wasn't you, you're not in trouble. They just want to take you home, okay?*

He nodded, tears in his eyes. *I've been so scared.*

I know, I know, I replied, giving him a hug. *But we need to make sure everyone else is safe too. Okay?*

He nodded again.

Who is she going after? I asked again.

Cassie.

Singh and I looked at each other, then I guided Leon

towards the car. I didn't want to take him back to the school, but we needed to prevent Liz from getting to Cassie.

Singh put a hand on my arm to stop me. 'Paige, stop. We'll send someone out to the school. We need to get Leon to a hospital.'

'You said you were getting back-up to meet us here but nobody's turned up,' I snapped, pulling my arm away and climbing into the driving seat. 'Ask them to meet us there, but we need to get to the school. If Liz sees we've found Leon maybe she'll give up and leave Cassie alone.'

He made a low growling sound in the back of his throat, but he could see I wasn't going to give in. As soon as he was in the car I tore off, yanking the steering wheel and taking the corner a bit too fast, the wheels skidding on the snow that was still lying on the road. For a heart-stopping moment I thought I was going to flip the car into a hedge, but I managed to control the skid and keep going.

Liz's house wasn't far from the school, and when we arrived I'd barely stopped the car before Leon leapt out.

That's her car, he told us, nodding at the sleek black sports car I'd been seeing everywhere, parked outside the main entrance. It was Liz who'd been following me, not Mike. I'd been so blinded by my past relationship with him that I hadn't stopped to think it might be something to do with the case.

'Paige, you and Leon stay here. I'm going to check her office first.'

I nodded, unwilling to do as Singh asked, but knowing I had to keep Leon safe. As he walked away, he glanced back over his shoulder at me, then went into the main building.

She won't be in her office, Leon told me, looking past the building towards the residence. *She'll be in there.*

I gritted my teeth. *We need to stay here and wait for more police. It's not safe.*

Why the hell did you bring me here, then? he asked, frustration making him animated when he signed. *We need to stop her!*

He was right, and it didn't take him long to convince me.

Fine. I'm going to check the residence, I told him. *But you need to stay here.*

No, I want to come with you, Leon insisted.

Absolutely not, I replied with a glare. *You told me Cassie's in danger. I'm not putting you in danger too. Stay here, and if DS Singh comes out again, show him where I've gone.*

He shot a furious look at me, but stood back against my car with his arms folded. Casting a glance at the main entrance, in case Singh was on his way back, I set off round the corner.

As I approached the residence my heart sank when I realised I wouldn't be able to get in. The door was locked, and I could hardly ring the bell and let Liz know I was there – if she really was inside.

Casting round for something I could use to break in, I hit on a plan. I balled up some snow and flung it at an upstairs window, hoping one of the boys was up there. The first and second snowballs brought no joy, but after the third one thumped against a pane of glass a small face appeared at the window. It was Kian.

Let me in, I signed to him. *But don't let anyone know I'm here.*

The boy frowned at me before he disappeared again,

376

and I wondered if he was going to trust me, but a moment later the door clicked and swung open.

Thanks, I signed, giving Kian a brief smile, then realising Bradley was standing behind him.

What's going on? Miss Marcek told us to stay in our rooms and not come out for anything. She said it wasn't safe. The older boy gave me a suspicious stare as he signed.

Where is she? I asked, my heart racing, trying to keep the urgency from showing in my expression. Bradley's eyes narrowed.

Why? What's happened?

Leon's safe, I told him, hoping to distract him with this information. *But I need to know, where is Liz Marcek?*

She went to talk to Cassie, he said, nodding in the direction of the girls' corridor.

Is she still there?

He shrugged. *I don't know. Why?*

Bradley, you have to trust me, I told him, looking him in the eye. *The police are coming, and DS Singh is on his way over. You need to look after Kian, and go and find some other adults to stay with and make sure you're safe. Is Sasha here?*

He shook his head, panic now visible in his eyes. *Miss Marcek sent her away, said she'd be here to keep an eye on us. Oh shit. It's her, isn't it? Oh shit.*

I heard a noise from the end of the girls' corridor; Cassie's room. Swallowing hard, I grabbed Bradley's arm and steered him towards the door.

Go, take Kian and go.

What about Courtney?

I'll try her door on the way past and send her after you, I promised, steering him towards the door.

For a moment Bradley looked torn between his brother and his girlfriend, but then he made up his mind and ushered Kian out of the building. Left alone in the hallway, I peered through to the communal area. It was empty. I didn't have anything on me that I could use to defend myself, so I ducked into the kitchen. Taking a bread knife from the side, I made my way up the girls' corridor.

I couldn't risk knocking on Courtney's door in case the vibrations carried through to Cassie's room, so I opened the door as gently as I could. The girl was sitting on her bed, watching something on YouTube, and she jumped when I caught her attention. Thankfully, she didn't question me when I told her to find the others, but slipped outside to join Bradley and Kian.

I paused outside Cassie's room. I could tell someone was inside, but I wouldn't know what was happening until I opened the door. Pushing it softly, I was greeted with the sight of Cassie sitting on her desk chair, her eyes open but unfocused, and my heart leapt into my throat. The girl blinked, and I breathed again. She wasn't dead, but by the look on her face she'd been drugged.

Looking up, I saw Liz Marcek standing by the side of the bed.

Oh, I'm glad you're here, Paige, Liz signed. She wore an expression of concern that I knew to be fake, but I thought it was safest to go along with her for now. *I think Cassie's taken something. She told me what happened, that she'd been messaging Steve and he told her about his messages to Leon.*

I nodded, unsure of what Liz thought was happening. *She and Leon must have killed Steve together when they realised what he was doing.* The deputy head shook her head slowly. *I wouldn't have thought she had it in her. But now she's taken something, I need to get her to a hospital.*

I'll call an ambulance, I replied, pulling out my phone.

No! she snapped, but regained her composure a split second later. *No, it'll be quicker if I take her in my car. By the time an ambulance gets here, in this weather, it might be too late.*

What has she taken? I asked.

I have no idea.

Yes you do, I replied, inching closer to her. *You gave it to her, didn't you? To keep her quiet about what she knew. She found out about your little plot to get rid of Jane, and you've been bribing her since with messages and little gifts. When she spoke to the detectives this morning she didn't give you up, you know.*

You don't know what you're talking about, Liz replied, a scowl darkening her face. She stepped forward, moving closer to Cassie.

The police are here, I told her, moving so I was blocking Cassie from her. I bent down to look at the girl, slapping her hand a few times. Cassie's head lolled as she tried to turn to look at me. Her hands waved vaguely, but she couldn't form a coherent sign.

Cassie was easy to manipulate, wasn't she? I signed, trying to distract Liz for long enough to allow the police to find us. *She was jealous of the other students, so you knew if you made her feel special, feel more important than them, that she would keep your secret.*

Liz sneered at me. *What would you know about it?*

I think I know a lot more than you realise. You blamed Steve for your brother's death, didn't you? I could see that this had hit home by the change in expression on her face, so I pushed on. *You wanted to make him pay, by ruining his reputation. You set up Bradley and Courtney, and engineered a safeguarding scandal to get Jane out of the way, then made sure Steve got the job in her place.*

That was easy, she replied with a harsh laugh. *I was on the interview panel, and I knew I could ask questions that made him look like the best candidate. The arrogant bastard thought he'd walked it because of his own skills, but I had never intended for the governors to choose anyone else.*

Once he was in the post, you started messaging the students, looking for one to groom, and saved the messages to Steve's school account. You had a problem, though, didn't you? I looked at Cassie, and Liz followed my gaze.

She saw me, with the video cameras, Liz told me, her face twisted with spite. *I didn't know if she'd realised exactly what she'd seen. She's not very bright. But I knew I needed to keep her on my side. She's been useful, though.*

I shook my head in disbelief. *Did you think she'd keep your secrets forever? Even after you killed Steve?*

I didn't always intend to kill him, she said nonchalantly. *I was just going to get him arrested for grooming, at first. But then he was here, in this school, my school, trying to change it, behaving like the arrogant bastard he has always been, and I couldn't stand it.* Liz's eyes burned with fury and I felt my heart rate increase with fear at what she might do next.

And you thought you could frame Leon for his murder?

Or Cassie, she replied with a callous shrug. *Either would do. Leon made it easier for me, though. He stumbled on Steve's body and picked up the knife. He cut himself. If he hadn't seen me it would have been easier.* She shook her head, as if she were just talking about a minor inconvenience in her life, not a serious crime.

While I had been trying to keep her distracted, I was planning. Could I grab Cassie and make it out of the room before Liz reached us? The room was small, and Cassie's chair was blocking Liz's path out of the room. Putting my hands on Cassie's shoulders, I applied enough pressure to slide the chair backwards slightly and wedge it in the gap. Noticing what I was doing, Liz lunged forwards, but I slipped my hands under Cassie's arms and hauled her towards the door, flinging it open and dragging the girl into the corridor.

I heard a clatter as Liz came after us, and a grunt as she gave up and climbed over the bed. I wasn't used to carrying heavy weights, and Cassie was nearly the same height as me. She was partly conscious and managed to bear some of her own weight, but I'd only got her as far as the communal area when Liz burst out of Cassie's room. Pushing Cassie towards a sofa, I grabbed the huge TV and launched it into Liz's path, slowing her down once more. Suddenly Singh was there, grabbing Cassie and trying to lift her. From outside, I heard sirens, and I got hold of Cassie's other arm, helping Singh to get her outside, where Sasha and Leon were waiting, the lights of two police cars racing down the drive behind them.

Chapter 40

Thursday 6th December

The atmosphere in the school was a sombre one when we entered the building the next day. There was a feeling of relief at the police having caught the culprit, but it was overlaid with the shock of finding out who had been responsible. I had insisted on being present when they interviewed Leon, despite Forest wanting to get another interpreter and grumbling about me getting myself involved again.

After all Leon had been through, it was agreed that it was best to take his statement in a familiar environment. Sasha met us at the door to the residence and let us in.

He's doing okay, considering, but I don't know how well he slept last night, she explained, ushering us all into the building. *I stayed over in one of the staff bedrooms, for a bit more reassurance, and he asked me if he could keep his door open. I'm going to arrange to get him some counselling.*

Sasha took us into the library, where Leon was already waiting. He smiled when he saw me.

Thank you for helping me, he said. *I don't even know your name.*

I'm Paige, I replied. *I'm the interpreter.*

You're not a police officer?

I shook my head. *No, I wasn't even supposed to be there yesterday*, I told him with a wry smile and a sideways look at DS Singh.

'I'm glad you were,' Singh told me. It had transpired that an argument had broken out between Lincolnshire and Humberside police forces over who should be attending, which meant they were delayed in getting to Liz's house. Apparently, DI Forest had gone ballistic, and for once I wished I'd been there to see it.

'Leon, we'd like to ask you some questions,' Forest began once we were all seated. 'We'd like you to think back to the day you went on the school trip and tell us what happened.'

Leon sighed and sat back in his seat. *I feel so stupid*, he signed. *I'd believed all along that Joe was real, that he cared about me. I should have realised it was too good to be true. He knew exactly what to say, you know? When I was down, or whatever, he could always say the right thing to cheer me up.*

I'd been messaging him that evening, but only had a couple of replies from him. We were supposed to meet up on Friday evening, but he cancelled on me and said he'd see me the next morning instead. I couldn't sleep, so I got up in the middle of the night and had a drink, but Mr Wilkinson found me in the kitchen and asked what was wrong. I made up something about falling out with Bradley and he was really nice about it.

The boy sighed again and shook his head. *First thing the next morning I snuck out and went to the cricket pavilion, then I got a message from him saying he'd be there soon. It was absolutely freezing, and my coat didn't really keep me warm, but I waited for a couple of hours. I texted him, but I didn't get a reply, then when I tried a video call it wouldn't connect. That's when I realised he wasn't coming. That maybe he'd been lying to me all along.*

Leon covered his face with his hands for a moment, then continued. *I was so fucking mad, you know? But I was embarrassed mostly. I know the others had been messaging Joe too, but I was the one who fell for him. I was the one who made the plan to meet up with him. He never wanted to video chat; I thought he was shy or something, but now I know the truth it seems so obvious. I didn't know what to do, because by then I knew people would have been looking for me. If I went back to the cabin they'd ask me where I'd been, but I didn't really have any other option. So, I picked up my bag and went back outside.*

'What happened when you left the pavilion?' Singh asked.

I wandered around in the snow for a while. It was coming down really heavily, and I couldn't work out which way it was back to the cabin. I was just beginning to panic when I saw Mr Wilkinson in the distance. He was walking towards a stand of trees, and he had his phone out.

'Did you see anyone else at that point?' Forest asked.

Not then, no. It took me a while to get to the spot where I'd seen him, because of the snow. And when I did, he was already dead.

'Tell us what you saw.'

He was lying on the ground with blood all around him.

384

I went up to him and I touched him, but I could tell he was dead. His eyes were open and he wasn't breathing. Leon shuddered at the memory. *I don't even know what I was thinking, but I picked up the knife and I cut myself. I was trying to stop the bleeding when I turned around, and Miss Marcek was standing there. She looked at Mr Wilkinson, then at me, and I knew it must have looked like I killed him. So, I ran.* He shrugged. *What else could I do? I didn't want her to blame it on me just because she'd seen me there.*

'Did you wonder why she was there? She hadn't come with you on the trip.'

I didn't even think about that straight away, he replied, shaking his head as if he was annoyed with himself. *Then when I did finally realise, I knew she must have been the one who killed him, but I still couldn't go to the police. I know what people think about kids who are in care, that we're all rough and just make trouble. And after what I did to my dad, who would you have believed – me or her?*

The detectives didn't answer, and I knew what they were thinking. They each liked to think they would have listened to Leon, but when faced with the plausible explanations the deputy head would have come up with, would they have believed him?

I went to Samira's house, because I knew she'd hide me without asking too many questions, he continued. *She was scared, but I told her it'd be okay. Her parents are away and her brother is never at home. It was actually pretty fun,* he said wistfully. *But I thought the police would solve it quickly and I could come home.*

'I'm sorry it took us so long,' Singh replied, and I could see from his face that he meant it.

I think Miss Marcek worked out where I was when she

saw Samira call me on the day Mr Achembe was killed.
Leon grimaced. *Samira was really scared, I don't think she noticed Miss Marcek was behind her when we were on video chat.*

I remembered Liz walking down the drive towards me. At the time, I'd assumed she'd been up to check the road, but really she must have been arriving back after kidnapping Leon from Samira's house. There had been plenty of time for her to slip away while the police were interviewing other staff members. The snow had been so bad by the time she returned, though, she wouldn't have been able to get her car all the way to the school. She must have abandoned it and walked the rest of the way.

I was in Samira's room when Miss Marcek turned up, grabbed me and shoved me into her car, Leon continued. *She threw my bag into a bush, but I'd dropped my phone in the hallway so she couldn't get it, and say anything pretending to be me. When we got to her house she locked me in the summerhouse. I asked her why she didn't just kill me, and she said she had to wait for the right time.*

Singh had told me earlier that Liz Marcek had confessed to planning to kill Leon and pin all the murders on Cassie by faking a suicide, making her leave a note about what she'd done.

Why did she do it? Leon asked, his eyes wide. *Why did she do all of this?*

The detectives looked at each other, obviously wondering how much they could tell him, but Sasha got there first.

She blamed Mr Wilkinson for her brother's death. Mr Achembe found some deleted messages she'd sent to Cassie and confronted her about it, so she killed him to stop him telling the police.

386

Leon nodded sadly, accepting this explanation. It would all be in the papers and online soon enough, so it made sense to at least tell him why he'd gone through such an ordeal.

We left the residence and went back over to the main building, where Jane Villiers was waiting for us in the head teacher's office.

'Now the case is solved I thought I could reclaim my old office,' she explained.

'Are you back for good?' I asked.

'The governors asked me to come in for now, as an interim head until the two management posts can be advertised. However, before that happens I think we'll have a battle to keep the school open. I know there have already been some parents indicating that they will be sending their children elsewhere, and Ofsted will be paying us a visit very soon.' She looked down at her old desk sadly. 'Many times in the last few months I've wished to be back here, but I never would have wanted it at the expense of someone else's life. Poor Saul. I was the one who got him involved. I feel responsible.'

'You're not responsible for anything Liz Marcek did,' Singh said firmly. 'She chose her own course of action, and nothing you did could have prevented it.'

'If I'd been included in the interview process for my replacement, perhaps I could have,' Jane countered.

'I don't think the death of Liz's brother would have been something Steve Wilkinson advertised. She didn't tell anyone else about it, so I doubt she would have told you either,' Forest replied.

'How did she do it?' Jane asked. 'Not the murders, but all the sneaking around? Getting Cassie involved, preying on the students like that.'

'Manipulating Cassie was easy,' Singh replied. 'All it took was some attention and a few gifts, and the girl would do anything for her. Liz wanted to find a way to get revenge on Steve, so she set up the messages. Over the course of a couple of months, she tried different angles with each student, until she found which one of them could be led down the path leading to a relationship. Cassie was roped in to help the others trust Joe. She never knew the idea was to get Steve fired, and most likely arrested. As it was, Steve found the files Liz had saved on his computer and showed them to Liz before she could reveal them – I expect her plan was to "discover" that he'd been grooming a pupil and have him removed. He decided his best course of action was to go to the governors on the Monday, showing them the messages and explaining that he wasn't responsible, never for one minute expecting that she would follow them up to Normanby Hall and kill him. When Mike called her to tell her about Leon disappearing she was already nearby. She just waited a while before coming back into the park and pretending she'd rushed up there.'

Jane Villiers shook her head. 'My job now is to try and save the school, for the sake of the students. I don't want to see any of those five go into a children's home. This is their home, and I am going to fight for them.'

I didn't doubt her determination, and I hoped the school would survive the fallout from what had gone on here. One woman's blind hatred, and desire for revenge, had led to so much damage.

Singh and I walked out together, leaving Forest to take a phone call.

'You solved your first case as DS, then,' I said to him.

He gave me a wry smile. 'Did I? I think you did, when you realised only the killer could have given us Leon's phone number. Without that, I think we'd still be clutching at straws.'

'Well, it doesn't matter how you got there. It's Leon we really need to thank. If he hadn't told us about Liz's plan to kill Cassie, we might not have got here in time. How is she?'

'She's recovering,' Singh replied. 'The hospital wanted to keep her in for a couple of days. Liz gave her a sedative, just enough to get her in the car and take her back to her house.'

'Good. I hope she gets some counselling. It can't have been good for her, having Liz mess with her head like that for months.'

He nodded then took my hand and squeezed it.

'Paige, I . . .' He stopped.

'What?'

'I was really worried, when I realised you'd gone in there alone. I don't know what I'd do if something happened to you.'

I looked at him, and remembered how relaxed I'd felt the other night when I fell asleep on him. Now we were facing each other in broad daylight, all I felt was confusion. I gently pulled my hand away from his.

My phone buzzed, breaking the awkward silence. It was a message from Max, asking if he could come over that night. I hesitated before replying, but then told him he could. I knew it was only a matter of time before I had to decide what I wanted, and I'd better make my mind up quickly. When I looked back up, Forest had come back out of the school and was gesturing to Singh.

'There's been some sort of incident at the football ground in Grimsby,' she told him. He gave me a fleeting smile then turned around and walked back to join her. I stood there in the car park and watched them drive away, picturing the two potential paths my life could go down from here, and not knowing which to take. I'd come close to danger more than once, and now I was starting to think I knew what I really wanted from my life.

Acknowledgements

Writing the second book in a series is far harder than writing the first one! Huge thanks are due to many people for the support, advice and encouragement I've received during this process. At the time of writing these acknowledgements, we're eleven weeks into the UK lockdown due to the Covid-19 pandemic, and life has been rather strange. I've been very lucky to be able to continue with my writing without too much difficulty, but I wouldn't have been able to do it without a lot of support.

My amazing agent, Juliet Mushens, who is eternally supportive and seems to understand exactly what I need and when I need it.

My wonderful editor, Tilda McDonald, who has taken my story and elevated it to something far more than I thought it could be, and who has given me confidence in my ideas. Also Beth Wickington, for joining Tilda in the editing process and complimenting me far more than I felt I deserved!

Sabah Khan and Ellie Pilcher, for publicity and marketing respectively – you do so much work behind the scenes, and even though I didn't get to do many events this year, I can't wait to see what we have in store in the future. Rebecca Fortuin for her stellar work on the audiobook, particularly for ensuring we had d/Deaf representation in this format. For production and sales: Catriona Beamish, Caroline Bovey, Kelly Webster, Jean Marie Kelly, Emily Gerbner, Charlotte Cross and Peter Borcsok.

Thank you to Sarah Whittaker for another stunning cover, and Rhian McKay for copyedits (it seems I have terrible aim when highlighting sections to be italicised!).

Friends and family have been invaluable, providing everything from cheerleading to childcare, and it certainly takes more than a village to get a book written! Thank you to: Hannah Bowman, Kate Davie, Kayleigh Christopher, Becky Page, Monica Warren, Jen Clapp, Mette Thobro, Vic Logan, David Bishop, Liz King, Kirsty Holmes, Shane Kilbee, Jo Binks, Debi Alper, Ruth Cheesley, Lizzie Monaghan, Becki Rothwell, Jillian Cranmer, Ange Robinson, Gemma Hall, Lynsey Lowry – so many people have supported me, believed in me, and recommended my books to others, and I am immensely grateful. If I've forgotten anyone, please forgive me!

Special mentions: Faye Robertson, for always answering my weird police-related questions – all errors and flights of fancy are always my own; Nick Quantrill and Nick Triplow, for their excellent work supporting writers around the Humber region; Nick and Mel Webb at The Rabbit Hole bookshop in Brigg, for being fantastic advocates for local writers; Philippa East, my Lincolnshire partner-in-crime; Clare-Louise English and Lara Steward for championing my writing from a d/Deaf perspective. To my interpreter friends, I'm sorry for taking liberties with your job.

Thank you, as ever, to my parents, Glynis and Mark; to Will, Michelle and Alice; and to Gary, Edna, Julia and Patrick. To Stuart, for always being there for me and believing in me when I need it most, and to Albert, for giving me a reason to keep writing.

Don't miss the next mystery featuring Paige Northwood

THE
SILENT
SUSPECT

Only he
knows the
truth.

Only I
can save
him.

NELL PATTISON

Coming Spring 2021